Praise for
THE RETRIEVAL ARTIST SERIES

The Retrieval Artist universe is rich and exciting, and Rusch's characters are real beings (Human and otherwise) struggling against overwhelming odds. The thrills are nonstop, and the tension keeps increasing with each successive book [in the Anniversary Day Saga]. If you're a nail-biter, you might want to wear gloves for these.

—*Analog*

[The Anniversary Day Saga is] one of the top science fiction sagas in recent years.

—*The Midwest Book Review*

Instant addiction. You hear about it—maybe you even laugh it off—but you never think it could happen to you. Well, you just haven't run into Miles Flint and the other Retrieval Artists looking for The Disappeared. ...I am hopelessly hooked....

—Lisa DuMond
MEviews.com on *The Disappeared*

An inventive plot and complex, conflicted characters increases the appeal of Kristine Kathryn Rusch's *Extremes*. This futuristic tale breaks new ground as a space police procedural and should appeal to science fiction and mystery fans.

—*RT Book Reveiws* on *Extremes*

Part science fiction, part mystery, and pure enjoyment are the words to describe Kristine Kathryn Rusch's latest Retrieval Artist novel.... This is a strong murder mystery in an outer space storyline.

—*The Best Reviews* on *Consequences*

An exciting, intricately plotted, fast-paced novel. You'll find it difficult to put down.

—*SFRevu* on *Buried Deep*

A science fiction murder mystery by one of the genre's best.... A book with complex characters, an interesting and unpredictable plot, and timeless and universal things to say about the human condition.

—*The Panama News* on *Paloma*

Rusch continues her provocative interplanetary detective series with healthy doses of planet-hopping intrigue, heady legal dilemmas and well-drawn characters.

—*Publishers Weekly* on *Recovery Man*

...the mystery is unpredictable and absorbing and the characters are interesting and sympathetic.

—*Blastr* on *Duplicate Effort*

Anniversary Day is an edge-of-the-seat thriller that will keep you turning pages late into the night and it's also really good science fiction. What's not to like?

—*Analog* on *Anniversary Day*

The latest Retrieval Artist science fiction thriller is an engaging investigative whodunit starring popular Miles Flint on a comeback mission. The suspenseful storyline is fast-paced and filled with twists as the hero comes out of retirement to confront his worst nightmare.

—*The Midwest Book Review* on *Blowback*

Fans of Rusch's Retrieval Artist universe will enjoy the expansion of the Anniversary Day story, with new characters providing more perspectives on its signature events, while newcomers will get a good introduction to the series.

—*Publishers Weekly* on *A Murder of Clones*

This new Retrieval Artist Universe novel is action-packed and continues where *A Murder of Clones* leaves off. These must be read in order to fully appreciate the suspense and mystery that is taking place.

—*RT Book Reviews* on *Search & Recovery*

The Anniversary Day Saga just keeps getting more interesting and more complicated. Each addition is eagerly anticipated and leaves the reader anxious to discover what will happen next, who the bad guys are and what it is they are hoping to achieve.

—*RT Book Reviews* on *The Peyti Crisis*

…the way Ms. Rusch structured the book was very much along the lines of a chess master arranging the pieces for a devastating endgame. … This is one of the best series out there.

—*Futures Past and Present* on *Vigilantes*

Starbase Human puts all the pieces in place for the big showdown/crisis in *Masterminds* [the final book in the saga]. I highly recommend the Anniversary Day Saga. It's one of the major events in science fiction this year.

—*Amazing Stories* on *Starbase Human*

THE RETRIEVAL ARTIST SERIES:

The Disappeared
Extremes
Consequences
Buried Deep
Paloma
Recovery Man
The Recovery Man's Bargain (Novella)
Duplicate Effort
The Possession of Paavo Deshin (Novella)

The Anniversary Day Saga:

Anniversary Day
Blowback
A Murder of Clones
Search & Recovery
The Peyti Crisis
Vigilantes
Starbase Human
Masterminds

Other Stories:

The Retrieval Artist (Novella)
The Impossibles (A Retrieval Artist Universe Short Story)

MASTERMINDS

A RETRIEVAL ARTIST NOVEL

KRISTINE KATHRYN RUSCH

WMG PUBLISHING

Masterminds

Book Eight of the Anniversary Day Saga

Copyright © 2015 by Kristine Kathryn Rusch

All rights reserved

Published 2015 by WMG Publishing
www.wmgpublishing.com
Cover and layout copyright © 2015 by WMG Publishing
Cover design by Allyson Longueira/WMG Publishing
Cover art copyright © Skypixel/Dreamstime
ISBN-13: 978-1-56146-625-2
ISBN-10: 1-56146-625-5

For the fans
Thanks for joining me on this journey

Acknowledgements

I owe so many thanks on this project. People who kept me honest, people who helped me get to work, people who made sure my details were correct. (The mistakes are all mine.) I owe special thanks to Paul B. Higginbotham for help with the court system, Dean Wesley Smith for help with dome structure, Annie Reed for finding all the things I missed, Colleen Kuehne for catching the important details, and Allyson Longueira for getting every last bit of this project through production.

Thanks also to Kevin J. Anderson, Stanley Schmidt of *Analog,* and Sheila Williams of *Asimov's* for buying the short stories I wrote to explain details to myself. You kept me focused on the series quality, which I needed as I got deeper into the project.

And finally, thanks to all you readers. Your enthusiasm has kept me chugging, even when the going got difficult.

Author's Note

Dear Readers,

Here we are! The final book in the Anniversary Day saga. I'm relieved to be here, and a bit disappointed as well. Writing this has been an adventure for me. I've never done anything this large this quickly.

Publishing used to demand that writers only publish one book per year. (Which is why I have so many pen names—leftover from those days. I write too fast to stick to one book per year.) Now, we can publish as many books as we want.

Or as many as we can write in a short period of time. Telling this story properly tested my writing speed and my attention span. I've never spent years on one story before, and I had to do so here. Parts of this saga were written as long ago as 2007, and other parts just last week.

I am relieved to turn to other projects, but, before you ask, I will return to the Retrieval Artist universe. I came up with too many new story ideas in that universe while writing this saga.

For those of you who picked up this book first—I'm sorry. It is the eighth book in an eight-book saga. For those of you who expect all of the Retrieval Artist books to stand alone, these eight books don't (although I suspect you can read A Murder of Clones *all by itself with no ill effects). You need to start the saga with* Anniversary Day *and move onto the remaining seven books.*

If you haven't read the Retrieval Artist series before, start either with Anniversary Day *or any book between* The Disappeared *and* Anniversary Day. *The list of Retrieval Artist novels is in the front of this book (or the back of the ebook).*

Again, thank you for coming with me on this journey and for reading the saga! I appreciate it, and hope you enjoyed reading it as much as I enjoyed writing it.

—Kristine Kathryn Rusch
Lincoln City, Oregon
September 27, 2014

MASTERMINDS

A RETRIEVAL ARTIST NOVEL

SEVENTY YEARS AGO

1

THUMP. THUMP. THUMP. SHUFFLE. DRAAAAAG.

Jhena Andre huddled in her bed, covers nested around her, her favorite doll cradled against her chest. She woke up, heart pounding, afraid someone was in her room—and someone was—but then she heard him mutter, and she realized—*Daddy!*

She wanted to go back to sleep, but she couldn't. Daddy sometimes came to her room to make sure she was okay. Sometimes he just held her. Sometimes he stared at her from the door.

Her room was the best room in the house. He painted the walls— Daddy wanted to be an artist Once Upon A Time, before It All Went Down, which Jhena knew meant the day that Mommy died and everything changed. Greens and golds and touches of sunlight, bits of color. The tall grasses waved and glistened. Sometimes the sky turned gray and rains fell, but not for long. Then the sun came out and the grasses gleamed. The air smelled fresh—Daddy said it smelled like fresh-cut grass—but Jhena thought it smelled like green.

Daddy's paints made everything come alive, except Mommy.

Jhena's brain skipped—that memory everybody wanted to know or not know, the memory everybody told her to forget or not forget, the memory of the day It All Went Down. All she had from that day was Daddy and her favorite doll. Her favorite doll didn't have a name because Mommy said they'd name it together, and smiled, and never smiled again.

Jhena pulled the doll close, and listened to the rustling. The air didn't smell green. It smelled like sour hot chocolate and the sharp sweaty smell Daddy got when he got scared. He hadn't taken her special cup from the room. He always did or the bots did or someone did, because in the morning her special cup always got clean, and ready for that night's chocolate, which she drank while Daddy read stories and she looked at the swaying grasses on the wall.

Thump. Draaaaag.

Daddy was taking stuff out of her closet. Her stomach started to ache.

Then Daddy swore, and Jhena sat up.

He turned around so fast she thought he was going to fall down. One hand out, catching the wall, disappearing in the grasses kinda—shadows of them always crossed skin but not really shadows. Echoes, sorta. The grasses couldn't be on skin unless they got painted there, and Daddy said that nothing should get painted on skin.

"Jhen," he said in a voice she'd never heard before. Like he wasn't ready and he was scared but he wasn't scared of her. "Baby."

Then he sighed, and she thought maybe she heard another bad word, but she wasn't sure.

He waved a hand, and dawn started in the grasses. The light in the wall was her nightlight. She thought maybe a minute ago there was a full moon—the night-time light—but Daddy changed it. That orange glow meant get up, even though her eyes felt sandy and the clock she hid under the edge of her night table had a 2 as the first number, not a 6. She knew the difference.

She was a big girl now.

"Oh, sweetie, I didn't want it to go this way." He looked scareder than he had before, like she was the daddy and he was the little girl and he'd been doing something wrong.

Jhena pulled her doll close, clutching the blankets. The light was just enough to see his familiar face, all twisted in something like a frown, his black hair mussed, and his brown eyes wet like they'd been the day It All Went Down.

"Daddy?" Her voice sounded tiny. She didn't want it too, but she wasn't sure she should be loud. The day It All Went Down, Daddy picked her up and held her and shushed her and she was afraid he'd shush her now.

"I'm so sorry, baby," Daddy said. "I didn't mean for this to happen. If I thought it could happen again, I would have stayed in Montana."

Then Daddy grabbed something from the floor. Her duffle. He tossed it on the bed.

"You gotta stay here, baby, and be really really quiet, okay? My friends will come for you. They'll take you to Aunt Leslie. You remember Aunt Leslie, right? She'll take care of you."

He leaned over, all sharp sweat and cologne. His arms went around her and he squeezed too hard.

She said, "Don't wanna go with Aunt Leslie. Wanna stay with you."

"You can't, baby. I screwed up. Again. I screwed up again. I'm so sorry." He ran his hand through her hair, kissed her crown (*My princess,* he usually said when he did that), squeezed even harder. "I love you. I love you more than life itself. Can you remember that much, at least? That I love you."

Her heart was pounding. "I love you too, Daddy. Take me with you."

"No, honey. I can't. You'll be okay. I promise. Aunt Leslie—she's a good woman. She'll raise you right."

Raise? Daddy was raising Jhena. Daddy was raising Jhena alone ever since It All Went Down.

"Daddy—"

He put a finger over her mouth, shushing her. Then she heard the door close, the house telling someone that Daddy and Jhena were in the bedroom.

He stood up. "You stay here, okay? They'll come back here, and they'll take you to Aunt Leslie."

"Wanna stay with you," Jhena said, tears falling now.

"I want to stay with you too," he said. "But we don't always get what we want, honey. God, I wish I wasn't the one to teach you that."

He ran a hand over her head, cupped her chin, said, "I love you," and then walked out of her bedroom, his back framed against the hall light, his shoulders square.

He didn't look back.

But she kept looking at the space where he had been.

Looking and seeing nothing.

At all.

SIXTY YEARS AGO

2

ALONSO STOTT PULLED OPEN THE DOOR TO THEIR SECRET HIDING PLACE. Claudio had never seen his brother look so scared. Alonso's black eyes were wide, his lips bleeding like he had bitten them.

They'd found this place in the back of the house, a totally non-networked room, like someone had built it just for them, and they had never told Mom and Dad.

The room was tiny and square, with some handmade blankets on the scuffed floor. The boys didn't want anything in here made with nanofibers or that had any digital signatures. The boys didn't even let the bots see them enter.

The room was secret, that's what Alonso said, and Claudio believed him.

"You gotta get out of here," Alonso said. Tears pooled in his eyes. "Hurry."

"Why?" Claudio asked.

"The Wygnin are coming, and Daddy says—" Alonso's voice broke, then he shook his head. "You gotta get out of here."

"Mommy said the lawyers took care of the Wygnin." Claudio knew about the Wygnin. The Wygnin were bad, bad, bad creatures, evil creatures, that didn't like human people. Daddy had visited them and made them mad, and the Wygnin wanted Alonso for payment. The *firstborn*.

Mommy said they'd never give up the firstborn, and Daddy said they shouldn't worry, but Alonso worried. He found the room.

"Why can't I stay here?" Claudio asked.

"I think Mom knows about it," Alonso said. "You only got five minutes. Daddy's getting guns."

"To shoot the Wygnin?" Claudio asked.

Alonso shook his head, and more tears fell. "You go to that building I showed you, okay? You tell them you're not the firstborn, and that you'll never be firstborn, no matter what. You tell them to fight for you, okay?"

"Alonso, what's going on?"

"You tell them," Alonso said, his voice fierce. "I'm going to talk to Daddy."

Claudio didn't understand this. He didn't understand any of it. There were four years between him and Alonso, and sometimes that four years was pretty big. Like now. Alonso wasn't saying something.

"What are you going to tell Daddy?" Claudio asked.

"I'm going to tell him I'll go with the Wygnin," Alonso said. "Maybe he'll change his mind."

"About what?" Claudio asked.

"Using the guns," Alonso said. "Now get out."

He held the door. Claudio knew better than to argue with his older brother, but he didn't get it. If Daddy was going to shoot the Wygnin, then why would Alonso try to go with them? Mommy said Wygnin broke children and never gave them back. Mommy said it was the perfect punishment, and Daddy had goofed up really bad, but not to worry. The lawyers would protect them.

"What about the lawyers?" Claudio asked.

"They lost," Alonso said. "If you don't go, I'll kick your stupid little butt from here to Valhalla Basin."

Alonso wouldn't say that if he didn't mean it. He always kicked Claudio's butt when Claudio got in his way.

"I want to stay," Claudio said, but he was crawling over the blankets toward the door.

"No, you don't," Alonso said. He looked over his shoulder.

Mommy was sobbing. She was saying, "No, don't, honey. There's got to be another way. There's got to—"

Her voice just broke off, followed by a big crash.

"Get the hell out of here," Alonso hissed. He kicked open the secret side door—the one that led directly outside.

"What happened?" Claudio asked.

Alonso looked over his shoulder again. "I'll…tell you later, okay? Get out now."

Then he pushed Claudio, and Claudio tumbled toward the door, the jamb scratching his palms. He landed on the grass Daddy had been so proud of—*Real Earth Grass!* Daddy had said with pride, after it started growing.

Alonso closed the door behind him, and Claudio couldn't even see its edges. That was the beauty of the room, but it meant that if Claudio went back in, he would have to go in through the front door, and there was something wrong in the house. Something wrong with that crash, something in Mommy's voice he'd never heard before.

Besides, Alonso said he'd kick Claudio's butt if Claudio didn't go to that building. Claudio would tell them he wasn't the firstborn, and maybe they'd understand, and then they'd come back with him to the house.

Claudio ran, crushing the grass Daddy was so proud of, into the trees that Daddy had special-grown as a barrier against the other houses in the neighborhood.

The building, old and dusty and built long before Claudio was born, didn't look like it fit in. It was two blocks away, but Alonso said it got built when the secret room got built, back when people thought the Earth Alliance was abandoning Earth.

Claudio didn't know what that meant, but Alonso did, and that was good enough right now.

Claudio thought he heard a scream, then thought that wasn't possible, thought nobody screamed except when they were playing.

Only this didn't sound like an in-fun scream. It sounded like a really scared scream.

It sounded like Alonso.

Claudio ran as fast as he could, and tried not to hear the wail that came from his house.

That was Daddy. Claudio knew it was Daddy.

And then the wail stopped.

But Claudio kept running.

Because Alonso told him to.

FIFTY-FOUR YEARS AGO

3

PEARL BROOKS SET DOWN HER SCHOOL-ISSUED TABLET, AND OPENED THE refrigerator. Nothing. No money until the end of the month. They were out of fresh food, unless Pearl gave up some of her stash.

Mom couldn't work at her real job any more, not when they were on the run like this. And Mom's corporation didn't have Disappearance services.

The corporation is a nonprofit, sweetheart, Mom would say, like that explained everything. *Disappearance services aren't ethical.*

Neither was running, and living in tiny crap-ass apartments that had low-level refrigerators that didn't even say when food was close to spoiling. Mom had cried when the expensive, local-grown eggs they'd been doling out spoiled before they could use the last of them.

Pearl hadn't even known that eggs could spoil.

The breakfast dishes were still crowded around the sink. Even if Mom could afford a bot, she wouldn't get one—*too risky*, she said. She believed bots collected information, and maybe she was right. It was tough enough to find an apartment whose super didn't care if the in-house network worked or not. And the place was a mess—one bedroom (for both of them), a living room that wasn't big enough for living, and a kitchen so small the table had to be moved out if anyone wanted to cook.

Not that they wanted to cook. But they had no choice. Take-out was too expensive.

The only good thing about the apartment was the roof access. A side door, a few stairs, an almost-room-sized landing, and then the door to the flat space that overlooked this part of Injar.

Pearl liked the view. It was unusual. She'd grown up in Valhalla Basin, where everything was the same. But here, at a crossroads at the edge of the Earth Alliance, the neighborhoods had no regulation at all. She wasn't even sure if the dome had sections.

She could tell, just from glancing at the other rooftops, which buildings were built when. Different heights, different materials making the colors change from roof to roof, sometimes from floor to floor. Some buildings had add-ons, so they went from the dark gray of ancient permaplastic to the light gray of nanowallboard to the pale white of the latest building materials. Of course, those added-on buildings always looked like they were about to tumble over.

Maybe she would go up to the roof and do her homework. The days when she could do half her work on her links were long gone, and the school-issued tablet she had only worked half the time. She spent most of her homework time trying to log onto the school's public network.

She hadn't realized how good she had it, back when Mom worked for that nonprofit, Humans United. Back then, Pearl thought the two of them had no money.

Now that Mom was fighting for jobs in wealthy neighborhoods where people paid a premium for human-served goods that could easily be distributed by bots, Pearl was learning what "no money" really meant.

She looked at the tablet, then decided against bringing it. The day had been particularly hard. She was smart—she *knew* she was smart—but the kids were mean. They made fun of her clothes and her lack of links and her hair, and the fact she couldn't network fast in class. Today, they'd been particularly nasty about the fact that she had worn the same black pants just two days before.

She sighed, and pulled open the door to the hallway. Since Mom wasn't in the apartment, and didn't have a shift, she was probably on the roof. Maybe they could talk a little. Maybe Pearl could convince her this time that Pearl needed a job too. Just part time.

Pearl pulled open the door to the roof, then blinked as a waft of foul-smelling air hit her. It smelled like someone had vomited in the stairwell. Vomited and lost control of their bowels.

Pearl had never smelled anything quite like that before.

There were a lot of poor people in this building, and she knew for a fact that some of them had life-threatening illnesses. Not catchable by her or Mom, since they both had had all kinds of preventative medical enhancements back in the good old days.

Which gave Pearl an obligation to check out anything bad—at least, that was what Mom would have said.

Better us than anyone else, Mom would say, *because we can't get sick from it and so many others can.*

Like the two of them had a responsibility to the entire universe or something.

Pearl put a hand over her mouth and nose, and ventured into the stairwell.

"Hey!" she yelled. "Everyone okay up there?"

She half expected to hear Mom's voice floating back down toward her, saying she had it handled, but no one answered her.

Pearl took another step inside, then froze. Mom's too-tight black shoe sat like a sentry on the first stair. Mom only had one pair of shoes left, the pair that never had links in the first place. Mom hated the shoes, but couldn't afford another pair, and she certainly wouldn't take them off here.

Pearl's heart started pounding. The stench made her stomach turn.

"Mom?" Pearl asked, her voice echoing in the stairwell.

She took another step up, then stopped when she saw black fluid dripping down the stairs.

And brown skin draped along a railing.

And one naked foot with calluses along the outside of the big toe—from too-tight shoes.

Pearl took one more step, saw the other foot, unattached to an ankle but with the shoe still on.

"Mom?" Pearl said, voice trembling, not because she was calling her mom anymore. No.

It was a realization, an understanding, a loss.

Pearl turned away, swallowing hard to keep her own lunch down.

She knew what she was seeing. She knew. Mom hadn't hid any of it, not ever, even showing her holos of Disty Vengeance Killings. Allowed by Earth Alliance law.

Allowed.

Pearl had been prepared for the mess, but not the smell.

And not Mom.

Pearl had somehow managed never to associate those images with what could happen to Mom.

What had happened to Mom.

While Pearl had been in school, thinking she'd had a bad day.

She had had no idea how bad it actually was.

Until now.

NOW

4

MILES FLINT ATE SOME OF THE JASMINE RICE AND CHICKEN THING THAT Talia had reheated. He sat at the table in the kitchen of the United Domes of the Moon Security Office, marveling at the cleanliness of the room. Apparently, Talia had cleaned it after her appointment with the idiot at the Armstrong Comfort Center, a man who was so bigoted against clones that Flint actually feared for Talia's safety when he realized what was going on.

Talia got a lime drink out of the refrigerator, and poured it into a cup with ice. Something had changed since that morning's meeting with the therapist. Even though the therapist had been alarmed at her responses to his questions on clones, he had apparently said something that snapped Talia back to her old self.

Flint had no doubt that she would still have issues. He had always been amazed that she was so level-headed, considering all that had happened to her. She had lost her mother, discovered she had a father, and found out she was a clone, all in the same few days.

Then she had come with him to the Moon, settled in, and lived through Anniversary Day and, almost two weeks ago, the Peyti Crisis. During the Peyti Crisis, she had actually watched people she knew die—including a boy that she had some kind of relationship with. Flint never understood what kind, or how they really felt about each other, and given what Talia had told him, he wasn't sure she knew either.

"Can I start helping with the investigation?" Talia asked as she sat down. "I'm better now."

He didn't want to discourage her by saying that no one got better in the space of a morning. He didn't want trivialize her breakthrough.

As he contemplated what his response should be, she added, "I can't go back to school. All the schools are closed. If I can't go to your office, then I'm going to have to stay here during the day, and everyone's running around trying to stop the next attack or figure out what happened or find the perpetrators, and I'm sitting alone in a room feeling sorry for myself. Noelle looks like someone hit her with a truck, and she's still working. Rudra lost her boyfriend and she's still working. I haven't lost anyone, and everyone thinks I'm a mess."

Flint looked at her. Her copper-colored skin darkened as she realized what she had said. She tugged at her curls, so like his, then bit her lower lip.

"I'm *better*," Talia said as if she heard what he thought rather than his silence. "I *am*, and I need to keep busy, because if I don't, then maybe I will fall apart. Again."

Flint was having trouble thinking of what to say. After all, he had tried to get her involved just a few days ago, and she couldn't hold a coherent thought. Right now, she had energy, but he wasn't sure how long that would last.

Still, she had a valid point. She needed something to exercise her mind.

"All right," he said. "There's a lot of information that we need to filter through, and some of it is buried in places so encrypted and difficult to access that it takes time to break in even for someone like me."

"I could—"

He held up a hand to silence her. "I'll get the information out of those sites, but I could use help filtering it."

"I can do that," she said.

He nodded, then frowned, trying to think about which piece of information he needed to research that he could risk with Talia. After all, she might start on the research and then lose hours or days to the emotions that had overwhelmed her since the Peyti Crisis.

"Give me a moment to figure out what's best for us both," Flint said, "and—"

Miles Flint, this is Detective Iniko Zagrando. I need your help.

The message came through a back-up link that Flint actually had forgotten he had. He blinked, thought about it, and remembered that he had given it to Detective Zagrando three and a half years ago, when the man had helped Flint get Talia out of Valhalla Basin.

But something bothered Flint about the contact.

"What's going on?" Talia asked.

"Message." Flint stood, opened another link, and searched for information on where Zagrando was now.

Zagrando, Iniko. Detective. Valhalla Basin Police Department. Killed in the line of duty.

A three-year-old date followed, along with links to more information and actual footage of the man's death. There was something about a court case within the VBPD because he'd had no back-up at the time of his murder, and something about jurisdiction, and several obituaries.

Flint leaned against the kitchen counter. From there, he could see the hallway into the Security Office. No one walked past. Talia was looking up at him, her blue eyes narrowed in concern.

This was weird. Only a handful of people knew that Flint had met Zagrando. Flint couldn't think of any reason they would contact him. And he certainly couldn't think of any reason they would pretend to be Iniko Zagrando.

The rice in Flint's stomach turned over. He hoped this had nothing to do with Talia.

That thought alone made it imperative for him to answer the query.

Flint didn't respond directly to the message. Instead, he sent a completely new one, through the same old private link that he had established with the real Detective Zagrando three and a half years ago.

My sources tell me Iniko Zagrando is dead.

Flint wished Talia wasn't in here. He felt uncomfortable having this conversation in front of her, even though she had no idea what was being said, or even who he might be talking to.

Iniko Zagrando had saved her life in a number of ways. He had found her right after her mother was kidnapped, kept her out of the hands of Aleyd Corporation which would have gotten custody of her because of her mother's job in Valhalla Basin, and protected the information of Talia's illegal status as an unregistered clone.

Zagrando had been the person Talia had turned to in those early days after her mother had died, and he had come through. Talia had spoken of him very fondly, and Flint didn't want to harm that memory in any way.

Detective Iniko Zagrando is dead, this man calling himself Zagrando sent. *But Iniko Zagrando isn't. I was working undercover for Earth Alliance Intelligence. You can check that with Celestine Gonzalez, but do so fast, because...*

Flint stopped paying attention to the message and instead, contacted Celestine Gonzalez on a private link. He had met Celestine Gonzalez in Valhalla Basin about the same time he had met Zagrando. Gonzalez was an attorney who worked for the firm Oberholst, Martinez, and Mlsnavek, whom his ex-wife Rhonda had hired to take care of her interests on the Moon.

It didn't surprise Flint to hear Gonzalez's name. In fact, it reassured him that this man might actually be who he claimed. Flint had had many contacts with Gonzalez over the years, but no one knew how they met except Talia, Zagrando, and Gonzalez herself.

Sorry to bother you, Celestine, Flint sent. *I need a piece of information immediately. It's urgent.*

He flagged the message as important, which he felt only vaguely guilty about doing. Gonzalez was one of the few lawyers still on the job in Armstrong. Most had taken time off because the Peyti Crisis had hit the legal community hardest.

Gonzalez seemed to be the kind of person who worked after a crisis instead of taking time off.

I'm heading into court, she sent back almost immediately. *Can you wait an hour?*

No, he sent. *Do you remember Valhalla Basin PD Detective Iniko Zagrando?*

Yes, she sent.

Was he working for anyone besides the Valhalla Basin PD?

Why do you ask? she sent.

Perfect legal evasion, and probably enough for confirmation. Still, he sent one more message. *Because, I have an urgent communication from someone identifying himself as Zagrando, but he no longer works for VBPD. Did he tell you he was undercover for Earth Alliance Intelligence?*

I don't know if he was undercover, per se, she sent. *But when I checked Detective Zagrando's badge, I got a notification that he had Earth Alliance Intelligence clearance, Earth Alliance high grade military clearance, and Earth Alliance security clearance. Does that help?*

It helps, Flint sent. *Thank you.*

"What's going on?" Talia asked.

Flint held up his hands. "Just give me a minute," he said. "I'm having three conversations at once."

He lowered his head, and again used the old links to contact the man who called himself Zagrando.

What do you need? Flint sent to Zagrando.

No one responded. Flint frowned at Talia. She frowned back. Maybe this was a hoax to get him to check with Gonzalez. But how and why? He had used an encrypted link with her. That, plus his location in the United Domes of the Moon Security Office, made tracking or listening to his communications difficult if not impossible.

Then the response came, and it seemed breathless: *Please get me clearance with Space Traffic Control. I have information you need.*

Flint pushed away from the counter. On a good day, he would talk to DeRicci, but there hadn't been a good day in over six months.

That won't be easy, Flint sent back. *We've had some serious—*

I'm coming in hot, Zagrando sent. *There are factions in the Earth Alliance who don't want me to talk to you people. Please, do what you can. Please.*

Flint let out a small breath. That last detail—factions within the Earth Alliance—made him more likely to trust this so-called Zagrando. Only a handful of people here on the Moon knew that some of the clues to the attacks led back to the Alliance itself.

If Zagrando were part of the Earth Alliance Intelligence Service, he would have been in a position to get information on the Alliance's involvement. If he had information, it was possible that someone was trying to shut him up.

But that was speculation.

Still, Flint could intercede. He could get the ship into the port. He didn't have to let this so-called Zagrando into Armstrong. And, if the ship looked at all suspicious, Space Traffic Control could deal with it.

It would have to land in Terminal 5, where suspicious ships usually landed.

Send me the relevant information about your ship, Flint sent. *I'll see what I can do.*

Thank you, Zagrando sent back immediately. *Thank you so very much.*

Information about a high-end space yacht followed. Some of it was incoherent, something about a split-off section, a second cockpit, and an incomplete registration.

Flint would go through it, but he didn't have the ability to do so in this kitchen.

"What's going on?" Talia asked.

"Something very strange," he said. "Something very strange indeed."

5

DONAL Ó BRÁDAIGH TOOK THE LAST FLIGHT OF STAIRS TO THE UNDERBELLY of the City of Armstrong's dome complex. Most dome engineers took the elevators for ease and convenience. Walking deep underground exhausted most of the engineers he worked with. He couldn't even contemplate what they would do if they ever had to walk up.

He liked to think he took the stairs for the exercise, but ever since his wife Laraba died in the Armstrong bombing four years ago, he took the stairs for self-preservation. He wanted to stay in shape so that he could run if he had to, escape a substructure like this one quickly if necessary, climb parts of the dome if he needed to.

Some days, he saw disaster everywhere, and that had been before the Anniversary Day bombings. Now, his stomach was tight all the time, and he hated being apart from his daughter Fiona for the entire work day.

He worried that he wouldn't be able to reach her if he needed to.

He was also starting to worry about Berhane Magalhães.

Some days he saw that as a good sign. He was healing enough to have a new relationship. Sometimes he worried. Berhane was the daughter of one of the richest men on the Moon. Every now and then, Ó Brádaigh wondered if she was slumming when she was with him, biding time until she had a new relationship.

Ó Brádaigh shuddered. Some days, he felt like he was just obsessing about everyone and anyone, planning for the crisis that was yet to come.

Ever since Laraba died, he knew—so clearly that it woke him up at night—that he would never be able to control the world around him.

But he tried.

Oh, boy, did he try.

That was the other reason he used the stairs—trying to control the world around him. When he went down all those flights, he could see parts of the substructure beneath Armstrong, and look for faults or cracks or Moon dust leakage.

Moon dust was particularly sneaky because it took advantage of the most hairline of hairline cracks, and got into the environmental system. The environmental system near the oldest part of the dome, the part that covered Armstrong's historic district, was the most vulnerable. The locals all believed the dust filtered in through the dome somehow, not realizing that if it had, it would cause a leakage of atmosphere as well.

Instead, the dust came in below, in the substructure built to hold the dome's weight and control its sections, as well as the entire environmental system. There was no need to worry about the atmosphere leaking out here—the substructure was deep underground, surrounded by rock. Most of those meters were just support beams, but in the upper levels, there was an entire housing for various dome operations, and that was where the Moon dust snuck in.

Ó Brádaigh always found the problem first on the stairs.

Since no one used them, the dusting was almost impossible to see—gray dust on gray stairs. But his feet would slide. He always checked his shoes to see if he had brought the dust with him, and as he lifted his foot, he would see very fine prints on the top of the stairs.

Also, as he descended, he checked the environmental readings. The oxygen mix had to be as good here as it was above. So many problems started below and worked their way up to the surface. He wanted to catch the problems before human residents started having asthma attacks or tiny, elderly Ritories started turning blue. Ritories were even more sensitive than humans to the wrong kind of oxygen mix.

If his supervisors ever asked him what he would change about the way dome engineers worked, Ó Brádaigh would recommend that every single one of them take the stairs, both up and down. He would also recommend that dome engineers not use muscular enhancements, instead relying on their own strength to pull themselves along the dome's structure. Too many cheap enhancements failed, leading to accidents that cost the city money—and more importantly, at least to Ó Brádaigh— cost the engineers time.

The thing they never had was enough time to check, repair, and build everything. And now that nineteen out of the twenty largest domes were damaged in one way or another, engineers from all the domes were stretched beyond their limits.

Ó Brádaigh had even spent two weeks consulting on Tycho Crater's dome. The residents in Tycho Crater had no idea how lucky they were. The very center of the dome had exploded outward, but the dome sections had come down immediately.

And Tycho Crater's dome wasn't so much a dome as a covering over the crater itself, like a lid on a jar. If Tycho Crater's dome had been an actual *dome*, it might have fallen in on itself, depending on whether or not the sections fell in a timely manner.

Most domes were vulnerable in their very center, and fortunately for the Moon and its inhabitants, the Anniversary Day bombers apparently didn't know that. They picked targets on the edges of the domes, or famous targets, like Tycho Crater's Top of the Dome resort. They didn't target the center of the dome—the weakest point in the dome's structure.

The fact that he believed things could have been orders of magnitude worse had the Anniversary Day bombers actually been educated was something he kept to himself.

He didn't even discuss it with his fellow dome engineers. No one else would have considered millions dead lucky. He really didn't either. He just knew how much worse the explosions could have been.

He also didn't mention his opinion because he didn't want to give anyone ideas. The entire Moon was braced for a third attack, and if it was still in the planning stages, he didn't want to give the new attackers a blueprint in successful dome destruction.

But, because he had been thinking of it, because he had lost Laraba to an earlier explosion, and because he had seen the damage at Tycho Crater (and transposed that damage, in his head, to Armstrong), he had become obsessive about checking Armstrong's dome.

He figured no one else was doing it, at least to the degree he was. He started his day early and inspected an area of the dome that he knew no one else would be looking at. He got around the main parts of the dome once every four days, and worried that it wasn't enough.

This morning's inspection had been where the domes of Old Armstrong met the newer domes of the expanded city. Even though the locals referred to Armstrong's dome as one structure, it was actually many domes that connected on one edge. The openings between domes were seamless—at least to the average resident of Armstrong.

Ó Brádaigh looked at the edges and seams all the time. The dome sections were built into the seams of these domes, so that any endangered area could be isolated. The other sections were attached to the top of the dome, and came down within seconds.

Whenever Ó Brádaigh traveled through a dome, he looked up and stared at the sections, stored like folded curtains inside their protective unit. As a younger engineer, he had been assigned section duty—checking the storage container for the section, and the way that the dome itself tolerated the extra weight.

These days, he looked at all parts of the dome, making certain there were no vulnerabilities that someone could easily exploit.

And that was what worried him the most: the exploitation of the dome. Day after day, he found himself getting more obsessive about it, not less.

Last week, he'd started inspecting parts of the dome on his way home as well as before he started work in the morning.

He knew he probably shouldn't focus on all that could go wrong, but he couldn't stop himself. So he tried to reassure himself by doing unscheduled spot checks.

Like coming down here.

This particular area of the substructure housed most of the controls for the entire dome system. Some of the controls were ancient, and not used—such as for the airlocks that had existed in Old Armstrong's original dome. But many of the controls were the most important part of the dome—including the controls for the sections.

The sections could be controlled with very little effort from above, if one had the right access code or was near an area where a dome breach was occurring. At that area, the dome controls would theoretically become visible, and a citizen could slam a hand or an appendage against them and start a section unfolding.

Most people didn't know that, nor did they know that in the crisis four-and-a-half years ago, those controls did not appear. Not that it mattered. On that day, the sections to that part of the dome sensed the threat and came down automatically.

The automatic controls were programmed here.

And so were the controls for overrides, and for any official who had access to section Armstrong's dome. Most of the officials who had access were dead now. No one had replaced Arek Soseki yet. The deputy mayor did not have access, and no one would until the mayoral election, whenever that was going to be.

The person with the most control was United Domes of the Moon Security Chief Noelle DeRicci. She had control of the sections in Armstrong's dome, and she had received control of many of the sectioning mechanisms in the other domes as well during the Peyti Crisis, when the local officials didn't want the responsibility of sectioning their domes in response to the most recent crisis.

Ó Brádaigh didn't like the fact that one woman had that much power, no matter how smart and brave the press made her out to be.

But he knew she was the least his problems. One bomb with a large payload, set against the controls, might send all the sections down or make them inoperable or do something else, something he hadn't thought of.

The controls were housed in a reinforced building on the lowest available level of the substructure and, in theory, that building would have survived any one of the blasts that hit the domes in the past four years—the original Armstrong bombing that killed Laraba, and the Anniversary Day bombings.

But Ó Brádaigh didn't always believe the theory. He would rather find the bomb before it went off than hope to hell the building held when it did go off.

All the way down the stairs, he had told himself that such bombings weren't likely. It was almost impossible for anyone to get down here. Anyone who took the stairs had to show identification on every floor. They also had to recite a series of passwords to get down, starting with that day's password at the top, and the password for the day before at the next floor, and so on, until they reached the bottom of the stairs.

Then they needed a security code to get into the substructure itself—a code that changed every hour. They also needed to show a different part of the body for each scan. On some levels it was the palm, on others it was the eye, and in the substructure, it was the palm, eye, and a DNA check.

Ó Brádaigh had been a dome engineer long enough that he could come down here on his own for no reason except to check. But anyone with less than ten years' experience as a dome engineer in Armstrong needed permission to come down here—and needed someone like Ó Brádaigh to enter them into the system before they descended.

The elevators had similar requirements, annoyingly stopping at every floor before reaching the substructure. It was easier on the legs to take the elevator down (and back up) but it was harder on the patience.

Ó Brádaigh let himself through the three doors with their varying level of security that led to this layer of the substructure. He glanced at the time in the lower part of his left eye.

He had about fifteen minutes before he had to climb the stairs. He had to pick up Fiona, and he wasn't about to be late.

All he had time for was a quick walk around, and to check the exterior of the control building before he had to leave.

He wished he had more time. He realized as he stepped onto the flat gray platform that extended as far as the eye could see that it might be worthwhile to investigate the walls and floor of this large space as well.

Someday soon, when he had a few extra hours or when Fiona was with his mother.

On this day, though, he could only walk to the building, which was almost unnoticeable to the untrained eye. The building's exterior was designed to look like the wall, and some trick of the design or maybe some nano feature made the building seem two-dimensional until you were standing right next to it.

He could see the building because there were little shadows in the upper corners that wouldn't actually be there if the wall were as flat as it seemed.

He turned on all of his enhancements—the visual ones that saw the building in UV, night vision, heat vision, and on a nano- and chemical level. He was looking for flaws that didn't get reported to the control room on the ground level of the dome engineering building. He figured if someone was clever enough to put a bomb down here, they would be clever enough to beat the security system that had been installed down here before Ó Brádaigh was born.

The door to the building opened, and Ó Brádaigh just about jumped out of his skin.

His immediate supervisor, Vato Petteway, stepped out, then started when he saw Ó Brádaigh.

"What the hell are you doing down here?" Petteway snapped. He was a thin man, with a hooked nose and a narrow chin. His dark eyes never seemed to miss anything. "I didn't assign you the substructure."

Ó Brádaigh swallowed. His heart was still pounding hard, and he felt the adrenalin course through him.

"No, sir, you didn't," Ó Brádaigh said. "I just felt the need to double-check the area down here."

"Because what, you had a vision of disaster?" Petteway was good at sarcasm. Ó Brádaigh was one of the few engineers who could handle the man. In fact, Ó Brádaigh had prevented dozens of them from quitting over the years, by taking on Petteway himself.

"It's not hard to have a vision of disaster these days," Ó Brádaigh said.

Petteway's eyes narrowed. "You're one of my best engineers, Ó Brádaigh. I'd hate to get rid of you because you're lurking in places where you don't belong. Most people would consider your presence down here suspicious."

Ó Brádaigh's cheeks warmed. He hadn't thought of it that way. But he knew that the best way to handle Petteway was to challenge the man.

"Most supervisors would be glad that their employees cared enough to check on things even when off the clock."

Petteway snorted, shook his head, and pushed the door to the building closed. "Maybe a year ago, your point would be a good one. But right now? Everything seems suspicious."

"Yeah," Ó Brádaigh said, knowing two could play this game. "What are you doing down here?"

Petteway's shoulders slumped, as if Ó Brádaigh's question forced the man to examine his own motivations.

"I don't sleep any more, Ó Brádaigh, unless I've checked every vulnerable area of the dome at some point during my day."

Petteway ran a hand through his thinning hair. No matter how many enhancements he got, the hair thinned after a few years. Ó Brádaigh had seen Petteway go through nearly five enhancements in the time they had worked together.

"I know," Ó Brádaigh said. "That's why I'm here. If I didn't check, I'd be moving my daughter somewhere safer in the Alliance."

"As if there is somewhere safer in the Alliance." Petteway sighed. "I think we're all on such high alert here on the Moon that this is probably the safest part of the Alliance—at least at the moment."

"I hope you're right," Ó Brádaigh said. Then he glanced at the door— or what he could see of the door. It always seemed to disappear in that flat nano-illusion. "I've always checked the exterior of this building. What do you think could happen in there?"

"I don't know," Petteway said softly. "I'm past imagining what could go wrong. I never expected clones to bomb the Moon on Anniversary Day. I certainly didn't expect Peyti lawyers to try to do the same thing thirteen days ago. I've given up trying to predict. Now I just follow my instincts. If I feel like checking an area, I check all of it—inside, outside, roof, ceiling, floor, subfloor."

He ran a hand through his hair again, and Ó Brádaigh thought maybe he saw some strands come loose. Maybe the problem wasn't the enhancements after all, but the fact that Petteway pulled out hairs when he was under stress.

"Sometimes," Petteway said even more quietly, "it feels like I'm going crazy."

Then he realized what he had said. His eyes widened and he added, "Don't read too much into that."

Ó Brádaigh made himself smile. "I think there would be something wrong with you if you didn't feel that way. I was just thinking as I let myself in here that I had become obsessive about security. Our entire lives are different than they were a year ago. We're in a place that we couldn't have imagined then. Of course we're going to have odd reactions."

"Of course." Petteway tugged at his hair again. "Do you think we should hire security to guard this place?"

"I think we should have done that a year ago or ten years ago," Ó Brádaigh said. "But these days, how do we know we can trust the people we hire?"

"Maybe someone from the Security Office..." Petteway's voice trailed off.

"And then we prevent them from being on the surface and seeing a real crime occurring."

Petteway frowned at him. "You've already thought of this."

"That and a million other scenarios," Ó Brádaigh said. "I figure it's just safer if I check."

Petteway nodded. "I figure the same thing."

Ó Brádaigh had never seen his supervisor so vulnerable before. It was disquieting. But then, everything was disquieting nowadays.

"Normally," Petteway said, "I'd order you to stop checking the vulnerabilities, but I think that's what's keeping us safe. People like you and me, double- and triple-checking everything."

"I hope you're right, sir," Ó Brádaigh said. "I really hope you're right."

6

FLINT RAN A HAND THROUGH HIS BLOND CURLS. HE FELT SLIGHTLY breathless, as if someone had just knocked him off his feet. He knew why: the name Zagrando had brought back those days when Flint discovered that Rhonda was dead and that Talia existed.

"What happened?" Talia asked yet again. She had stood up as if she were about to leave the kitchen of the Security Office. Only she still clutched a glass nearly full of that lime drink. "You look upset."

Flint shook his head. "Not upset, exactly. But I do need to talk to Noelle."

"Can I come with you?" Talia asked.

That was a question, wasn't it? Did Flint believe Talia strong enough to handle new changes or did he try to protect her?

He had to make the decision quickly.

He had to make a lot of decisions quickly.

"Yes," he said after a moment. "You can come with me to see Noelle, as long as you don't say anything."

"Why?"

He looked at her. "You'll understand in a minute."

Without looking at Talia, he headed into the corridor. All day he'd been concerned about Talia's status as a clone, especially since the two crises on the Moon had been caused by clones. The hatred of clones was at an all-time high, and that made him afraid for his daughter.

Not even the chief of Moon security, his former partner Noelle De-Ricci, whom he trusted, knew that Talia was a clone. Now, with everything so very different, he preferred to keep it that way.

Flint glanced over his shoulder. Talia was following him. She'd managed to set that sickly green drink down before she stepped into the corridor.

DeRicci's assistant, Rudra Popova, stood up as Flint approached. Her long black hair glistened in the light. She was clutching a crumpled bag that had probably held her lunch.

"A few minutes ago, you said I could see Noelle," Flint said. "Can I still?"

"No one's in there besides her," Popova said. "Let me find out if she wants to—"

Flint didn't wait for Popova's response. He shoved the doors to the office open, and as he did, he heard Popova finish softly in a tone that said she knew Flint was no longer paying attention,

"—see you...."

He waited for Talia to join him, then he closed the door.

DeRicci stood near the windows. They ran floor to ceiling. Once they'd been the focal point of her office. Now, the mess along one wall caught Flint's attention first.

Mostly the mess was a meter-high pile of food cartons. Fortunately, they had nanocleaners inside them, or the stench in the office would be unbearable. As it was, there was a bit of an unclean funk, like the dorm room of a poor college student who couldn't afford the university's cleaning bot services.

He probably should remind her to clean them. She would have to go around some of them to get to the weapons cabinet on the far wall.

He wondered if she ever thought about that or if she had forgotten the cabinet was even there.

"Miles?" DeRicci said as she turned around. "Rudra hadn't said you were here."

Talia had been right; DeRicci looked like she hadn't slept in months. Earlier, Flint had seen how tired and gaunt DeRicci was getting, but he hadn't *noticed* it until Talia had pointed it out.

At some point, DeRicci might snap in just the way that Talia had.

"Talia," DeRicci said, nodding to his daughter in greeting.

Talia raised a hand in a hello, but—true to her promise to Flint—didn't say a word.

"I assume this is important?" DeRicci asked Flint.

"Yes," he said. He walked deeper into the room. That funk—sweat, clothes that needed cleaning, blankets that probably hadn't been washed since this all began—was worse the closer he got to the room's center.

"This is going to be hard to explain," he said. "I just received word through an old link from a police detective from Valhalla Basin."

Talia's head turned toward Flint so fast that she almost lost her balance. She took a step to steady herself.

"He had helped us when Talia's mother was kidnapped," Flint said.

Talia said, "Detective Z—?"

Flint held up a finger, silencing her, and then sent along their links, *Talia, you're here because I asked you not to talk.*

"Let me, Talia," he said out loud. "I have a lot of questions about this communication, but I don't have time to deal with them."

He didn't wait for Talia to nod or acknowledge his correction. He kept his gaze on DeRicci. "This man says he's in this solar system, and he's coming in—his word, 'hot'—with information that we need here on the Moon. He wants to land in the port, but he doesn't have the proper identification."

"Why not?" DeRicci asked.

"Because," Flint said, "official records say he's dead."

Talia put a hand over her mouth. Her eyes teared up. He should have warned her. He mentally kicked himself.

Is he? she sent.

I have no idea, he sent back. *Let me deal with this now. Questions later.*

She nodded.

DeRicci, who, as usual, missed nothing, saw Talia's movement and clearly knew that Talia and Flint were communicating on their links.

"Do you have reason to believe this man is who he says he is?" DeRicci asked.

"I don't know what to believe," Flint said. "But we don't have time to do much research. I can contact Space Traffic and ask them to let him in, but I needed your permission first. This is a security issue. I don't know if he's going to cause problems, but if he's coming in hot, he'll need protection, which will drain resources."

"God," DeRicci said. "This could be anyone. Or anything."

"Yeah," Flint said. "I've thought of that. I considered ignoring him. But the contact makes no sense if it is someone else. I mean, why contact me?"

Talia raised her eyebrows. She was thinking about that.

DeRicci crossed her arms over her chest. Her shirt bagged. Her clothes were usually too tight. Talia was right: DeRicci really had let herself go.

Flint continued, "If someone was going to try to do something to the Moon, you'd think I'd be the last person to contact. They'd reach out to you before contacting someone like me."

"Or the police," DeRicci said quietly. That was when Flint knew she agreed with him.

Talia was still frowning. She no longer had her hand over her mouth. Instead, she chewed her thumbnail.

"We can do a complete quarantine on the vessel, right?" DeRicci asked.

Flint looked at her, surprised. She was head of security for the Moon. She should know that.

And then he remembered: although he had gotten his start with Space Traffic, she hadn't. She knew how the port worked in theory, but not in practice.

"Yes," Flint said.

"And," DeRicci said, in that musing tone she often used when thinking out loud, "Space Traffic can search it for explosives before it lands."

"*Known* explosives," Flint said. "There are two danger points. When it enters the port from space, and when the authorities let the ship's door open for the first time."

DeRicci's mouth became a thin line. "I think I understand you, but I don't want to assume anything here. What exactly do you think could happen at those danger points?"

"If the ship explodes as it enters the port, particularly if it does so as it's transitioning into the terminal, then that part of the dome will shatter. The port's designed for accidents—some ship hitting the dome or burning on entry—but it's not set for *powerful* explosions."

"What do you mean, 'powerful'?" Talia asked.

Flint looked at her. Her blue eyes were wide. He decided not to chastise her for speaking. He suspected DeRicci was wondering the same thing.

"When I started at Space Traffic, we were all trained to worry about massive explosions. They would damage the port's part of the dome. That was one reason Arek Soseki had argued for moving the port outside the dome, remember that?"

He directed the last part at DeRicci. Soseki had made moving the port outside of Armstrong a pillar of his second campaign—before DeRicci had been tapped to act as Chief of Security. Soseki's proposal had been great for a campaign that had a tinge of bigotry to it—he was implying that non-humans shouldn't come directly into the dome, but have two points of entry: the port, and the trains to the center of the city—but everyone said that moving the port was impractical.

It was. The port had been inside the dome for hundreds of years.

"Massive explosions," DeRicci repeated.

Flint couldn't tell if she was processing or asking him a question. He decided to treat her words as a comment, and move on. He felt the press of time here.

"I think any explosion right now will have a terrible effect on the Moon," he said, "even if it doesn't damage anything but the entry to Terminal Five."

"Yes," DeRicci said. "You're right. And we can't see if he's carrying explosives?"

"We can see," Flint said, "but we don't know all of the explosives out there. We can also shield against an explosive outside the port, and once he's inside we can contain it. But we're vulnerable for a short few seconds as the dome opens and the ship enters."

DeRicci stared at him, as if she could find the answers in Flint's expression. He didn't know the answer. All she was probably seeing was the conflict he was feeling.

"And when the ship's door opens?" DeRicci asked. "More explosions?"

Flint shook his head. "Toxins, poisons, the stuff we usually quarantine for. Everyone will be suited up, but it could get into the system. The terminal has its own environmental system and can be isolated, but if it's an unknown toxin—"

"Then we're screwed." Apparently DeRicci knew that one. She let out a breath. "It's a risk. Letting him in is a big risk, but not letting him in might be as well."

"He can't just tell you on links?" Talia asked. Her cheeks were flushed. She knew Flint had told her not to talk, but she was disobeying him.

Only she wasn't doing so with information about Zagrando, which Flint appreciated. And she asked a good question.

"He said he was coming in hot," Flint said. "That means he's being pursued, and there's a chance whoever is pursuing him is monitoring his communications."

"So they know he contacted you," Talia said, with a touch of fear in her voice.

"Possibly," Flint said.

DeRicci was still staring at Flint. As his gaze met hers, she inclined her head slightly.

"Do you want me to contact Space Traffic?" she asked.

"No," Flint said. "Let me do it. If you contact them, the contact becomes official, and they'll want to know why we're letting in some unidentified man on an unidentified ship. If something goes wrong, you'll get blamed."

She gave him a sad smile. "I'm already getting blamed for a lot of things, Miles."

"You don't need this too," he said. "Besides, I don't want a record of this request."

DeRicci's smile widened into a real smile. "You're sneaky, Miles."

He smiled in return.

Then her smile faded. "If you were going to be that sneaky, you didn't have to tell me. You could have just done it."

"I considered it," he said. "I just want you to approve—or maybe to know—that I'm going to recommend that this ship arrive at the port. We expect a third attack. This might be the beginning of it."

"Oh, no," Talia said around her thumb. Flint reached over and removed her hand from her mouth. Her thumb was bleeding near the cuticle.

DeRicci looked at Talia's hand, then at Flint's face. DeRicci's expression became calm, even though Flint could tell from her body language that she wasn't calm at all.

"Letting this man in might also be a way to prevent the third attack," DeRicci said, more for Talia's benefit than for Flint's. "You wouldn't come to me if you thought this was going to go badly. You think this man can help us."

"If he is who he says he is," Flint said. "He contacted me using an old method and he's said the right things so far."

Talia clasped her hands together. Now she was biting her lower lip. Flint couldn't look at her any longer.

"But you're still worried," DeRicci said.

He had to be honest. "I have no idea why this man was listed as dead. If he is dead, then he could have been tortured before he died, and given up all kinds of information."

Flint tried not to think about that, even as he said it. Because if Zagrando was dead, and they (whoever they were) had information on Flint, then they also knew about Talia.

Talia brought her hand to her mouth, then seemed to rethink the motion and lowered her hand again.

"But," Flint said, "I'm clinging to the idea that someone wouldn't contact me over something important unless I was the only contact they had on the Moon. You wouldn't let him in with this flimsy information without my vouching for him, right?"

The *right* was also for Talia's benefit.

"Right," DeRicci said. "Do what you have to."

"Is this smart?" Talia asked.

To Flint's surprise, DeRicci smiled. "I don't know," she said. "But we have to take risks at some point. Or we're just going to sit here and wait for the next attack. I'm tired of doing that. I want to take action, even if it is not the wisest plan."

Flint didn't find that reassuring. But he wasn't going to argue with DeRicci. In that kitchen, Flint had already come to the conclusion that he wanted this man who called himself Zagrando to arrive on the Moon.

Flint wasn't going to argue with DeRicci's reasons for agreeing to it. Even if she was showing signs of fraying around the edges.

So was everyone else.

So was Flint.

They had to figure this all out—and soon.

7

RAFAEL SALEHI REACHED INTO THE CLOSET IN HIS SUITE ON S³'S FASTEST space yacht. Even though the ship was fast, it had still taken longer than he expected to reach the Moon. The yacht was approaching Moon space now, and he was nervous.

He wished he had more belongings to gather. He wished he had more space in this luxury cabin. He wished he had something to distract himself.

He hated being nervous. It made him feel weak.

Salehi never used to be nervous. He used to have balls of steel. He could go into courtrooms against impossible odds and turn a jury in his favor. He could charm a humorless judge into laughing, and that laughter would often guarantee a case went in his favor.

He could face down some of the most vicious defendants in this corner of the universe and convince them to act reasonably so that they could beat whatever charges they faced.

He used to be a much greater man than he was now.

Maybe that was part of his nervousness. The death of his friend Rafik Fujita at the hands of Alliance authorities had galvanized Salehi into action, brought him back from the disillusionment that had hit several years ago.

And now the murder of Torkild Zhu by the City of Armstrong Police reminded Salehi how much he had forgotten.

Half of the responsibility for Zhu's death rested on Salehi's shoulders. Salehi hadn't considered the atmosphere on the Moon when he hired Zhu to start S³ On The Moon. All of the Moon's communities had been ravaged by explosion or the possibility of explosions. Almost every citizen knew someone or was related to someone who had died in the past year.

The Moon had been a dangerous place before S³ decided—*Salehi* decided—to represent the Peyti clones who had tried (and mostly failed) to initiate a second bombing nearly two weeks ago.

Salehi had known that decision would be controversial on the Moon and inside the Alliance. He just hadn't realized the degree of anger that would come at S³. He hadn't thought it through.

Maybe Zhu's death was more than half Salehi's fault. He shouldn't have set up the situation in the first place.

He should have hired guards and made certain that Zhu understood security was a top priority.

But Salehi hadn't even thought of that, so he had had no way to counsel Zhu.

And now it was too late.

Zhu was dead.

And if Salehi and his new team weren't careful, they could die on this job as well.

Salehi wiped his damp palms on his khaki pants. He took a deep breath, and reminded himself that he was here for the love of the law. He was going to change clone law forever.

Those Peyti clones might be totally reprehensible, but they had once been living, breathing, functioning members of society. No one had known they were clones. And had they continued producing, being good little lawyers with strong practices and good reputations, no one would ever have known they were clones.

Then they chose to act on some command—some plot, some plan—and tried to blow up the very people they had worked alongside for decades.

And at that moment (actually, just a little earlier), the entire Moon figured out that these lawyers weren't individuals under the Alliance law definition.

They were clones, and as such, they were property.

The very idea that someone could go from person to property in the space of a few hours upset Salehi. What no one seemed to realize was that the Peyti clones would receive more appropriate punishment if they were treated as individuals under the law rather than as property.

They would be imprisoned forever. They would have to think about what they had tried to do each and every single day of their long remaining lives.

And for lawyers, for individuals trained to follow the law along its jagged edge, for individuals who were once considered officers of the court, that punishment would hurt much more than non-lawyers could ever expect.

Or maybe Salehi was being too sympathetic to them.

He removed all five suits that he had brought with him to the Moon. He would have an assistant order more clothing for him once he settled in. Because he was going to stay here a long time.

Now that Zhu had been murdered, Salehi wasn't just going to get justice for some mass-murdering clones. He was going to get justice for Zhu.

It was the least Salehi could do, since it was his carelessness that had gotten Zhu killed.

Salehi set the suits on his clothes carrier. When he was ready, it would fold everything into a tight ball of material that he would put in a small bag, along with some personal items he always brought with him when he traveled.

The suits and the rest of his clothing had nanofibers that pressed everything and made them look crisp, no matter what happened to them—something he had relied upon back in the days when he practically lived in the courts around Athena Base.

He was ready for this. He was ready for all of it.

He had spent the last week holed up in the library of this ship, preparing arguments for the clones. Technically, he was working for the government of Peyla. They wanted those clones dealt with because the Moon's policies were interfering with all business run by the Peyti.

Some of the Peyti lawyers he had brought with him even argued that the Moon's actions were a de facto way of kicking the Peyti out of the Earth Alliance.

And some bigots on the Moon probably felt that the Peyti should be tossed from the Alliance, given what those clones had done.

He grabbed his shirts out of the closet and tossed them on the carrier. Then he opened the box that contained his shoes. He grabbed the dress shoes and some athletic shoes, but he left the sandals. The Salehi who loved Earth's deserts and had his office on Athena Base mimic their conditions wasn't going to the Moon.

That Salehi was careless and thoughtless and hadn't paid enough attention to his work. That Salehi was lazy and uninterested in most things.

He was leaving that man behind, and going back to the lawyer he had once been. The lawyer who had taken his family's moribund firm and rebuilt it into an Alliance powerhouse.

The legal community in this part of the galaxy wouldn't know what hit them.

His links chirruped. He hadn't realized he had set them on *notify except for emergencies*. That was his default link setting when he was deep in researching a case, and he apparently hadn't reset the links as the ship's destination approached.

The message was from the cockpit. His tension rose.

Yes? he sent.

We have a problem, sir. The Moon won't let us into their space. We're not cleared to land on the Moon.

What? he sent. This made no sense. Of course they should be cleared. He had never encountered this situation in his decades of work at S^3.

They're telling us that, as a mixed-species ship, we need some kind of documentation that no one here has ever heard of. We need you here, sir.

Damn straight they needed him in the cockpit. This wasn't about being a mixed species ship. This was about S^3.

He set his shoes beside the bed. He would finish packing when he solved this.

The authorities in the Port of Armstrong had no idea who they were dealing with.

And he would show them, in a way they wouldn't forget.

8

BERHANE MAGALHÃES SAT IN THE FIRST CLASS COMPARTMENT IN THE TRAIN from Littrow to Armstrong, elbow on the small table in front of her, a fist over her mouth, as she stared at the passing grayness of the Moon.

She didn't really see it, the regolith, the rocks, the bright lights of the Growing Pits in the distance. She'd taken this route so many times since she started her work that it felt normal to her.

After she got past those first few minutes of entering a train.

Berhane had been on a train—Armstrong's citywide inner-dome train, the Express—when someone had bombed the city four years before. Her mother had died in that explosion.

Berhane thought of it every single time she stepped through a train's doors. It didn't matter that the Express wasn't nearly as fancy as this train. The Express was designed for short distances, while this was a bullet train, designed for travel between domes.

The trip from Littrow to Armstrong only took thirty minutes, but after the news she had just received, she needed privacy.

Her ex-fiancée, Torkild Zhu, was dead. Murdered, maybe by the police.

She'd heard from her father while she was supervising some cleanup in the devastated part of Littrow. Her father sounded shocked, something she would have thought impossible; he hadn't even sounded like that when he found out Berhane's mother had died.

After hearing the news, Berhane forced herself not to think about it. She had to finish briefing the new volunteers on the things they would discover inside the ruined section of Littrow. She always started her newest volunteers in Littrow, mostly so that she could oversee their work, and so that she could make her little "this is hard but important work" speech.

Four months ago, she had founded the Anniversary Day Victims' Identification and Recovery Service, and immediately hired Dabir Kaspian away from Armstrong Search & Rescue to run the business. She did fundraising, mostly, and handled the bigger things, like opening branches in all nineteen affected domes.

But one day per week, she went to Littrow and did hands-on work, donned an environmental suit, had some bots trail her, and used the equipment to scrape the DNA from the rubble, searching for the faintest traces of human DNA.

Her company found the Anniversary Day victims and, more importantly, identified them. So far, her company had identified nearly fifty thousand victims Moonwide—a drop in the bucket, considering the millions killed—but, as Donal Ó Brádaigh constantly reminded her, she was comforting each family whose loved one she found.

The days were wearing but worthwhile. The entire company made her feel like she was finally doing the work she was meant to do.

But she could find little comfort in that today.

She squinched up on the luxurious, high-backed chair, kicked off her shoes, and tucked her feet underneath her thighs. She still stared out the window, seeing her own narrow features reflected. Her black hair was boyishly short, something that had shocked Torkild the last time she had seen him, not quite a week ago.

Tears threatened. She shouldn't be mourning him. She shouldn't even be sad about him.

He had treated her badly throughout their relationship and had ended it in public, on Anniversary Day, just before news of the bombings struck. Which would have been memorable enough if it weren't for the fact that he was showing complete insensitivity.

Her mother had died exactly four years earlier. The "anniversary" being commemorated on that day was that of the Armstrong bombing, which had killed her mother and had, in its own way, inspired Berhane's entire company.

Because for years, *years*, Berhane had expected her mother to walk through the door. Berhane had expected her mother to show up, claim she'd had amnesia or had been in a coma or something. It wasn't until her mother's DNA had been found that Berhane had finally gotten peace.

And Torkild had never understood that. He always thought grief was something to be overcome.

Berhane wondered if he would have appreciated the irony of having her grieve for him.

She wasn't sure she appreciated the irony of it.

Especially since it forced her to admit that despite their history, despite the way they had treated each other, she had loved him.

She had thought the love was gone, murdered by their behavior, his and hers. But it remained, underneath, like the regolith beneath the bullet train, covered over, but still there.

She leaned her head against the back of the seat, glad she was alone in first class. She had bought this seat with her own money right after talking to her father. She wasn't going to charge a first class ticket to ADVI-RS, no matter how much she needed the privacy right now.

She could afford the ticket, of course. She was only recently coming to terms with the fact that she was incredibly rich. She always had been, but she had once thought of that as her father's money, something that had nothing to do with her.

Yet Berhane was extremely wealthy in her own right, and she was now using that money in a way that made her feel less like a spoiled rich girl and more like an important person.

Her father didn't approve, of course. He didn't believe that charitable foundations were worth anyone's time, except as a public relations obligation, but he had soon realized if he didn't stop complaining about her work, he would never see her.

It was only after she had started working for charities—first with Armstrong Search & Rescue, and then with ADVI-RS—that she realized how much alike her father and Torkild were.

And how very different Donal was.

She wondered what he would say when he learned about Torkild's death. Donal had grown to hate any mention of Torkild. With his reactions and his occasional comments, Donal had helped Berhane understand just how dysfunctional her relationship with Torkild had been.

Maybe that was why she had been so angry in her last meeting with Torkild. She had said some things that appalled her, things that in the past she would have apologized for.

But, on that day, Torkild had made it plain that they no longer had any common ground. And he had been right.

He had been rehired by the law firm that had kept him off the Moon for nearly a decade: Schnable, Shishani & Salehi, also known as S^3. Rafael Salehi had hired Torkild to start a branch of S^3 on the Moon, and that branch was handling the defense of the Peyti clones that had tried to blow up the Moon not two weeks ago.

A tear ran down her cheek. She wiped at it, then ran a finger over the moisture accumulating under her lower eyelids.

She had been so mad at Torkild. He didn't seem to understand how devastating that second attack had been. Even though only a handful of Peyti clones had been successful—all of them outside the various domes—the *idea* of the attacks, of the Moon's continued vulnerability, was bad enough.

And then Torkild felt that those crazy Peyti bastards needed a *defense*.

Berhane's father said that was probably what had gotten Torkild murdered. Everyone was saying that the police did it, and that didn't surprise her. Everyone was mad at S^3. She had been furious with Torkild when she learned what he was doing.

She felt like he was betraying everything and everyone they had ever known. Certainly all of the dead, whom she had come to represent.

Especially since she had lost two of her volunteers at their day job in the Growing Pits during the Peyti Crisis. They had been meeting with the Peyti clone lawyers over some contractual matters when the lawyers activated the bombs in their masks and had blown everyone to bits.

Berhane closed her eyes for just a minute.

She had never told Torkild that she had nearly died during the Peyti Crisis as well. She had been running late for a meeting with the lawyers who were drawing up some documentation for the next fund-raiser she had been planning. Those lawyers included one of the Peyti clones.

The meeting had been delayed because of her and, it turned out, only the Peyti clone lawyer had been in the conference room when it got sealed off and the environment got changed from Earth Normal to Peyti Normal, deactivating the bomb.

Berhane saw that damn clone lawyer just afterwards, and stared in his big eyes, wondering how she had ever trusted him. Then she had turned away, shaking with fury, determined to let the police handle the bastard, because she knew she couldn't deal with him at all.

Especially after she heard about the collateral damage from the Peyti Normal environmental change, and the successful bombings outside the domes.

Torkild didn't seem to care about all those new deaths, all those lost souls. He seemed to think that the Peyti clones deserved a defense, as if what they had done was defensible.

She had told her father that, and he had chuckled. *Young Torkild will get his head handed to him,* her father had said. *Clones aren't individuals under the law. They're property. And no piece of property has the right to a defense.*

She opened her eyes. The train was closer to the Growing Pits now. Their lights illuminated the Moon's harsh surface.

She hated agreeing with her father. She didn't think of the Peyti clones—or the human clones that had bombed the Moon on Anniversary Day—as anything other than monsters. Only monsters did such horrible things. Those monsters had no value to the universe.

She couldn't understand why Torkild hadn't seen that.

She sighed. It was a watery sound.

He'd still be alive if he had listened to her. She had offered him a job with ADVI-RS. She needed lawyers to represent the victims to the insurance companies, in lawsuits against the cities, and to help with all of the estate issues, especially for those whose loved ones had essentially vaporized.

Sure, ADVI-RS couldn't have paid him one-tenth what S^3 was paying him, but that hadn't been the point, at least to Berhane. He would have had the chance to do some good, instead of representing monsters.

She had no idea why Torkild had wanted to represent monsters. He had given her some crap about being a society of laws, and when she had pressed him, he had said, *There's a lot to dislike in the Alliance system, but there's a lot to like. We get along with thousands of alien species. We have cultural exchanges and economic cooperation because of this 'crap' you're talking about. That means, sometimes, you have to abide by laws you don't believe in. It also means that sometimes you have to make sure that a group of bad individuals get the best treatment possible under the law.*

The response had made her sick, just sick. He seemed to think that the Peyti clones were equal to the people they killed. Maybe even more important than the people they killed.

She had blurted, *You can't believe that.*

And he had looked at her oddly for a moment, as if contemplating her statement. Then he had given her a half-smile, the half-smile he used to charm her with.

You know, he had said, *I actually do.*

He *had* believed it. He had believed it enough to keep working at the firm, hiring new lawyers from off-Moon, doling out injunctions to law enforcement, and generally acting as if everyone agreed with S^3's position.

And it had gotten him killed.

She had accused him of all kinds of terrible things that day. The thing she had said that bothered her, even before she had heard of his death, was that she had accused him of caring more about money and prestige than about people.

And after she had left, she realized that if he cared about prestige, he would have joined her, not S³.

Because these days, everyone was on the side of the victims and no one was on the side of S³.

Everyone who knew about S³ On The Moon actively loathed them. No one wanted to be associated with them. She had gone to Torkild in the first place because her friends had asked her to reason with him.

She had thought, even before she went, that she couldn't reason with him. For their entire relationship, she had catered to him. Then he had ended the relationship and left the Moon. When he returned, she had mostly avoided him and then, at the end—

She swallowed hard.

At the end, she had treated him as badly—or worse—than he had treated her.

He had refused to fight with her that day. He had claimed he understood what she was doing. He had been *nice* to her, and she had accused him of all kinds of terrible things.

She put her head in her hands, feeling a sob in her throat. But surprisingly, no tears came now.

Torkild was dead, which was hard enough to handle. She would never see him again, never get a chance to apologize, never get to talk to him.

She should have warned him about all of the anger at him and S³.

She should have told him how high passions were on the Moon. Torkild had never been good at understanding how the average human being reacted to anything.

He wouldn't have understood just how hated he and S³ were.

Berhane? The contact came through her company link. It was Kaspian. He had probably heard about Torkild.

She sat up and wiped at her eyes. She left the visuals off. She didn't want Kaspian to know how upset the news made her.

You there, Berhane? We have a problem.

She straightened her shoulders and swallowed hard before answering. *I know about Torkild.*

Zhu? What about him?

She felt startled. How could she know this before Kaspian did?

He's dead. You didn't know?

What'd he kill himself? Kaspian made it sound like that had been the recommended option. No one who cared about Berhane liked Torkild.

No, she sent. *He was murdered.*

Silence. For a moment, she thought the link had broken. And then Kaspian sent, *I'm sorry, Berhane. I was being really insensitive. He was* murdered? *By who?*

They don't know, she sent. *My dad says the reports are that the police killed him.*

Again, silence. Obviously Kaspian's first response wasn't something he wanted to share.

I'm sorry, Berhane, he sent again.

Yeah, she sent. *Me too.*

Followed by the third silence. The train was slowing as it approached the Growing Pits. Accidents along this route decades ago had mandated a change in a train's speed as it went through here. It had to be able to sense something in its path and have enough time to stop.

The longest part of the thirty-minute trip between Armstrong and Littrow was this section by the Growing Pits.

So, she sent when it became clear that Kaspian had nothing more to say, *why did you contact me?*

I need you to talk to the labs. That response came quickly. Clearly, he was more comfortable discussing this. *We're getting weird results.*

The labs handled the DNA identification. Most of the labs she was working with were off-Moon. The on-site labs were swamped with official business or understaffed due to all the tragedies.

What kind of weird results? she asked.

I think they're false identifications, Kaspian sent, *but I don't know for sure. I initially worried that one of our volunteers was tampering with the DNA, but these results are coming from sites all over the Moon.*

Berhane wiped her eyes again, her brain clearing. She needed something like this to focus on so she wasn't thinking about Torkild.

I'll be in the office in about twenty minutes, she sent. *We can talk then.*

Good, Kaspian sent. *Because I don't like this. I don't like it at all.*

9

NOELLE DERICCI WAITED UNTIL FLINT AND TALIA LEFT THE OFFICE, AND then sank down onto the couch. She wanted to pull the scrunched-up blanket over her head.

She was losing track of all the threads of the investigation. Just today, everything had moved forward. She had spoken to Wilma Goudkins about doing an off-books investigations of Jhena Andre and of Mavis Zorn at the Impossibles.

DeRicci had new information from Bartholomew Nyquist that he was getting from one of the Peyti clones who had tried to bomb the Moon, a lawyer they all knew, named Uzvaan. And, DeRicci was certain, there were dozens of other breakthroughs as well.

This new contact, the one Flint had told her about, made her queasy. Well, queasier. Her stomach was beginning to hurt her in general. She wasn't certain if that was because she'd been eating junk the last six months or because she hadn't been eating enough or because she was under so much stress some part of her was going to break—and her stomach had volunteered.

She bowed her head and let the queasiness overtake her. She was exhausted and overwhelmed, and despite the help, felt very alone in the middle of this crisis—these crises.

It didn't matter how much Flint protected her from the political consequences of the decision they had just made, if this contact was going to harm Armstrong, word would get out that she had allowed him to enter. Not that that mattered to her. She often said she was the least political person she knew—even though she had somehow become the most important leader on the Moon.

Even if something went wrong and no one found out, it would still matter. Because DeRicci would know she had let this man in.

And the mistake would weigh on her for the rest of her life.

She burped again, started to run a hand along her stomach to activate a chip that soothed the stomach, and then stopped. She couldn't remember how many times she had done that already today, and at some point, she would overuse the technology and it would stop working.

Maybe it already had.

She took a deep breath and leaned her head back. There was more to the contact than Flint or Talia was letting on. That man had some connection to their shared past. Clearly, that meant he had something to do with Talia's relationship with Flint.

The man had been a police officer at the Valhalla Basin Police Department. He would have known something about the death of Flint's ex-wife. DeRicci had known Flint for years. He didn't trust easily.

Something in the interaction with Flint and this VBPD detective made Flint trust the man. And made Talia care about him. Because she had seemed shocked to hear that the man was presumed dead.

DeRicci had relied on Flint's word when she made her decision. She had meant what she said about taking risks. Something else was coming; she could feel it in her bones—or maybe in her stomach.

And she didn't really know what kind of action she could take to stop it.

She felt like the bad guys—whoever they were—were ahead of her. And if they were Earth Alliance officials, then they probably were ahead of her. They had access to the same information she did, and they had similar training.

They had known what she would do before she had done it.

She stood up, which sent a stab of pain through her stomach. She activated the soother after all.

She would deal with her own discomfort when this crisis was over. Right now, she had things to finish.

She needed to update her lists of the various investigations she was supervising. She also needed to continue her own internal investigation.

She was using the program that Flint had set up during the Peyti Crisis to scan faces here on the Moon. It infuriated her that the Peyti clones had been in plain sight the whole time. She hadn't thought, after Anniversary Day, to look for a large subset of clones already on the Moon.

She had thought of it now, but the parameters were so much larger. She had no idea if she was looking for human clones or alien clones. And some aliens were so very alien, she wasn't certain if the program would work.

She had broadened the scope, but that slowed the program down. And she wasn't someone who could tinker with things and make them better.

Even before this new contact, Flint was following more promising leads. DeRicci didn't want to interfere with his work there. And she wasn't sure who else she could trust to tweak the program.

Maybe it wouldn't take Flint long. Maybe she could ask him when he returned.

If all went well with this new contact.

She hoped it would. Because right now, she was stretched just about as far as she could go.

She wasn't sure she could make it through one more crisis.

She wasn't sure any of them could.

10

MARSHAL JUDITA GOMEZ STOOD IN THE ARRIVALS AREA OF THE PORT OF Armstrong, feeling disoriented. She had spent months traveling to the Moon, and now that she'd arrived, she could barely accept that she was here. She had not traveled with this kind of goal before—and to achieve it made her feel uneasy.

She knew she wasn't done; she had come to the Moon to talk with Noelle DeRicci, who as head of Security for United Domes of the Moon, seemed to be the only representative of the Moon's government. Gomez had actually had one of her crew, Neil Apaza, research who the best person to contact was, and Apaza had concluded that Gomez's initial instinct had been right—no one else on the Moon had the kind of political reach that DeRicci did.

Apaza had wanted to come with Gomez. So had Lashante Simiaar. Like Gomez, Simiaar had taken a leave of absence from the Earth Alliance Frontier Security Service. The EAFSS had no idea that the two women were actually moonlighting, investigating the attacks on the Moon from all the way out in the edges of the Alliance.

Gomez's ship, the *Stanley*, had encountered the PierLuigi Frémont clones fifteen years before, in a strange circumstance on the far side of the Frontier. After the Anniversary Day attacks, Gomez realized that no one had ever acted on the reports she had filed about that enclave of clones.

Had someone acted, Anniversary Day would never have happened.

In her long travels to the Moon, Gomez had investigated the clones and other things that had bothered her about the Anniversary Day attacks. She had convincing evidence that the attacks on the Moon had originated within the Alliance—and because she was convinced, she couldn't send that information along her links.

She needed to convince Security Chief DeRicci in person.

And now that Gomez was facing the moment, she felt uneasy. Here she was, a EAFSS Marshal near retirement, coming to the Moon with a fantastical story of betrayal within the Alliance.

She had to approach DeRicci correctly, so that the woman didn't dismiss her out of hand.

Which was why Gomez was going to see DeRicci alone, and why she hadn't contacted DeRicci before arriving on the Moon.

Gomez didn't want to give DeRicci the opportunity to put off a meeting. Gomez needed DeRicci to hear her out immediately.

Particularly since another set of clones whose original had been a mass murderer had tried to destroy the Moon a second time.

Whoever—whatever—was after the Moon clearly wasn't willing to give up after one or two tries.

Gomez had visited Armstrong at several points in her career, but the last time was decades ago. She remembered it being busy and full of aliens from all over the Alliance.

The port seemed busier now—the crush of people was intense. They wove around her as they hurried to whatever their final destination was. But she saw very few aliens, and the ones she did see looked like they were heading to the departures area or were waiting near the arrivals lounge for someone else.

There had been some odd bumps before arriving—the port wanted her ship, the *Green Dragon*, to declare whether or not it was a multi-species vessel. The pilots had simply declared them a human-only ship without consulting Gomez.

Simiaar found out about it before Gomez, and gave them a tongue-lashing, reminding them that no one had those rules inside the Alliance.

But the crew Gomez had put together hadn't been inside the Alliance in years except for short stops near the Frontier, which was why they didn't know Alliance protocols.

Instead, the crew operated on Frontier protocols, which were to do whatever the port authorities asked for, if the ship really had to land in a particular site.

Gomez knew that the Moon was on edge, but some of the changes here disturbed her greatly.

She had always thought of the center of the Alliance as the most civilized place in the universe. To see that some of the basic tenets of civilization were being ignored here or deliberately flaunted really upset her.

Just like the fact that some in the Alliance were involved in these attacks disturbed her as well.

She allowed the port map to activate inside her links. She would follow the map to the nearest exit, and then she would take whatever kind of public transportation that existed in Armstrong directly to the Security Office.

She needed to give all of her information to DeRicci and then offer assistance.

It had all seemed so easy when Gomez had laid it out for her crew on the *Green Dragon*. But, as Simiaar had pointed out, it wouldn't be easy at all.

No one in the Security Office had reason to trust Gomez, especially with the outrageous information she was bringing them.

She had enough evidence to make them believe, if they only listened.

And listening would be the hardest part of all.

11

THE COCKPIT ON S³'S SPACE YACHT SHOULD HAVE BEEN MORE ACCURATELY called a bridge. It housed eight people easily and had more equipment than the environmental control room in S³'s main offices on Athena base.

Salehi had only been up here a few times, and each time, he felt the breadth and power of this particular ship. It made him feel like a master of the universe, which was probably why Domek Schnable bought it. Schnable, whom Salehi privately called Schnabby, was the oldest named partner at the firm. Schnabby reserved many large purchases—like space yachts—for himself.

Not that Salehi or the other name partner, Debra Shishani, cared. Schnabby had a great sense of luxury combined with a practicality that showed itself well in this ship. Fast, but comfortable. And clearly expensive, because Schnabby—hell, everyone at S³– knew that money talked.

Lefty Wèi, the ship's pilot, was standing behind the control panels, looking through the clear windows at the Moon, looming large enough to be a presence in front of them. Hundreds of lights gathered around the Moon's exterior—ships of all types, inside the Moon's protected space.

Wèi had a virtual screen active above his pilot's chair, showing all of the ships in 2-D, but he wasn't looking at it. His copilot and his navigator were monitoring their own screens.

"What's this, now?" Salehi asked as he stepped across the yellow line that Wèi had painted along the edge of the cockpit, ostensibly to bar "civilians" from his domain. Wèi preferred to be called Captain Wèi, but Salehi refused, given the fact that Wèi had never served in the military and he wasn't really in charge of this ship. "We're a mixed-species vessel? What the hell's that?"

"Apparently, some new regulation established by the Port of Armstrong," Wèi said, arms crossed. "I have sent you all the documentation they want. Looks like it violates all kinds of laws that pertain to open Alliance ports, but I'm no lawyer."

Salehi was, but space law wasn't anywhere near his specialty.

"Fortunately," said a voice behind Salehi, "you are ferrying a ship filled with lawyers."

Salehi turned. Uzvuyiten, the Peyti lawyer whom the government of Peyla had asked to join S³ on the clone case, stood just inside the door. He was acutely attuned to the moods of others, no more so than on this trip. He knew that his mask made humans nervous, even though the humans on this ship knew he had nothing to do with the attempted bombings on the Moon.

His sticklike arms were at his sides, his damaged fingers mostly hidden by the human-style suit he wore. He had maintained formal dress throughout this trip, ostensibly because that was who he was, but Salehi knew that Uzvuyiten was doing it primarily for the others on the ship. He wanted them to know he was on their side in all things.

Even among the high-powered lawyers on this ship and in S³, Uzvuyiten was among the most subtle and manipulative, which often made him the smartest person in the room.

"Have you sent the port a passenger list, complete with species designation?" Uzvuyiten asked Wèi.

"Of course not." Wèi was clearly insulted by the question, which made Salehi glad that Uzvuyiten had asked it. Salehi had planned to ask the same thing just before Uzvuyiten entered the cockpit.

"Then how do they know this is a multispecies ship?" Uzvuyiten managed to ask the question without it sounding accusatory.

"Perhaps they don't," Salehi said. "Perhaps the new policy is to send every new ship this message and let it self-identify."

Uzvuyiten inclined his head toward Salehi, silently complimenting him on that thought.

"Have you self-identified?" Uzvuyiten asked Wèi.

"I don't even know what that means," Wèi said, looking at Salehi. Apparently, Wèi was one of the humans who now had difficulty with the Peyti. Or perhaps Wèi was still feeling insulted.

"How did you respond to their multi-species demand?" Salehi said, both clarifying and asking the same question.

"I contacted you," Wèi said. "I didn't contact *you*."

The second *you* was directed at Uzvuyiten. He shrugged his bony shoulders, then adjusted his mask, which—oddly enough—looked like a threatening move, even to Salehi.

Perhaps Uzvuyiten had intended it that way.

But Wèi probably didn't. Because his gaze was on Uzvuyiten's hand. Uzvuyiten's fingers had been damaged long ago, bent backwards between the last knuckle and the tip of the finger. The damaged section glowed blue, and brought out the weird blue edges of Uzvuyiten's gray eyes.

Salehi frowned at Uzvuyiten. Was he monitoring all shipwide communications or just communications that came to Salehi? They would have to discuss that later.

"You did not contact me." Uzvuyiten's tone made it sound like Wèi was a particularly poor student who had finally gotten an answer right. "I've been expecting this, so I've been monitoring in-ship cockpit communications since I'm not privy to your communications outside of the ship."

That last part was for Salehi. Uzvuyiten was explaining why and how he got here.

Whether or not he spoke the truth was another matter entirely.

"You've been expecting a problem and you didn't tell me?" Wèi asked.

"One of the reasons I'm here is that the Peyti have been consistently denied access to the Moon since the Peyti Crisis," Uzvuyiten said. "We've been wondering how so many got turned back before arrival at the port itself. I think we have just answered that question."

He looked at Salehi as he said that last. Salehi had thought all the Peyti had trouble once their ships landed, not before landing.

"And here I thought they were coming after us because we're S³," Salehi said.

"S³ is well known for its human bias," Uzvuyiten said. "Which is one reason I am here."

That sounded accusatory as well. Or maybe Salehi was just feeling sensitive.

S³ did have a human bias. Most of their cases involved humans, primarily because human law within the Alliance was easier for humans to understand and work around.

"We'd already discussed the Peyti problems." Salehi didn't like Uzvuyiten's tone any more than Wèi had. "You weren't going to come with us to the Moon. You were going to work from the ship."

Uzvuyiten shrugged his shoulders again. It looked so odd to see him do that. Schnabby would have said it looked like a coat hanger suddenly took on a life of its own.

Salehi forced his partner's cutting voice from his mind.

"I've changed my mind," Uzvuyiten said. "You need me."

"Yes," Salehi said. "You were going to work—"

"No, my dear Rafael." Uzvuyiten could sound so unctuous when he wanted to. "We are beginning to understand why the Peyti are having trouble on the Moon. You could protest that, with a bit of understanding. Or we could test the system each step of the way."

Salehi bit back irritation. He had enough to deal with. He had to plan his case for the Peyti clones, and he had to make certain that the local prosecutor went after Zhu's murderers. Salehi knew that the Peyti government wanted him to pursue the discrimination against the Peyti that had just started on the Moon, but Salehi believed that the courts weren't the best venue for the one-on-one discrimination. He was better off using a different strategy, one that included media coverage and the involvement of other species from within the Earth Alliance.

"You really want to do this now?" Salehi asked Uzvuyiten. "Because we have a lot on our plates."

"We do," Uzvuyiten said. "But this is part of what we have on our plates."

"You're not going to be able to get into Armstrong, no matter how hard you try," Salehi said.

"Ah, but I will create a record that we can then pursue. Decorated attorney, barred from entry to the heart of the Earth Alliance—which his government is a founding member of. We would have more evidence than we know what to do with, my dear Rafael."

Salehi hated the way Uzvuyiten was talking to him right now, but he knew that Uzvuyiten was doing it for effect. And it was working, of course, because that was the kind of lawyer Uzvuyiten was—the kind who knew exactly how to irritate the people around him into action.

"We can gather evidence," Salehi said, "but I can tell you now, Uzvuyiten, I won't have time to pursue this case, with everything else I have to do."

Uzvuyiten bowed slightly. "I am aware of that, Rafael. I am also aware that before he was so brutally murdered, Torkild Zhu hired some good lawyers from Earth herself, not to mention a few young lawyers who want to get their hands dirty. I propose to use them to handle this case, not you. Your time is best served handling the clones."

"You'll be diverting resources," Salehi said.

"I'll be setting up a different side to the same case," Uzvuyiten said. "Since the discrimination and illegal behavior is starting outside the very entrance to Moon space, I think we'll have more than enough to do."

"None of which concerns me." Wèi spoke for the first time in a while. He'd been watching the interchange. "I want to know how we handle this contact from Armstrong's Space Traffic Control."

Salehi normally would have glanced at Uzvuyiten. They would have consulted and figured out the best approach. But Salehi was too annoyed.

Besides, Uzvuyiten had forgotten that he was here as a guest, because the Government of Peyla wanted a Peyti near the clone case. But the Peyti government believed that they couldn't bring a lawyer here and get a good hearing, and circumstances were already proving them right.

Uzvuyiten could play all the games he wanted with the Port of Armstrong, but that wasn't going to help the case that interested Salehi the most.

Salehi said to Wèi, "Tell the port that under Alliance law, the passenger composition of an Earth Alliance vessel is protected information. If they are searching for a fugitive or for some kind of contraband material, they may examine the ship and its passengers once we arrive. Otherwise, we have every legal right to enter the Moon's space, and petition the port for landing."

Wèi frowned at Salehi. "That'll piss them off."

"Fine," Salehi said. "We're S³. We're already pissing them off. We might as well remain consistent."

"You don't want to play their games?" Uzvuyiten asked.

"We play along, we have no legal grounds to appeal their decision." Salehi kept his voice calm even though he was irritated. Uzvuyiten knew all of this. "We proceed the way that we would have proceeded before this year. If they want to arrest us, fine."

"They won't arrest *us*," Wèi said. "They'll arrest *me*."

Salehi gave him a withering look. "If you're so frightened, *Captain*, then don't leave the ship."

Wèi moved back to his ornate captain's chair, turning his back to Salehi. "It's just weird, that's all."

"What's weird?" Salehi asked.

"All of this," Wèi said. "It's like we're leaving the Alliance or something."

"Indeed," Uzvuyiten said from the doorway. "Captain, you are onto something."

Legally, he was onto something, but at the moment, Salehi wasn't going to agree with Uzvuyiten. Salehi was too annoyed.

He had expected some territorial issues with Uzvuyiten on the various cases. Salehi just hadn't expected them to start so quickly.

"Let us know if anything else comes up," he said to Wèi. "Otherwise, I expect to hear from you just before we land."

"You're an optimist," Wèi said.

"No," Uzvuyiten said. "He's just going to give me a good talking to."

"Yes," Salehi said as he headed toward the door. "I am. We're going to discuss how S³ is handling these cases, and how you, as a consultant, can help or hurt us."

"I am not going to remain on this ship for the duration of your stay here," Uzvuyiten said. "If you do not like what I'm going to do, then we'll make that strictly my responsibility."

Salehi felt his cheeks heat. Uzvuyiten had outmaneuvered him. Uzvuyiten wanted a case that he could handle for himself and the Peyti government without S³ involvement, and he had just designed it.

As they stepped out of the cockpit, Salehi said, "All right, tell me honestly. This is why the government of Peyla insisted that you consult on the clone case, isn't it? So that you, one of the most upstanding members of Peyti society, can be denied access to the Port of Armstrong."

"It's simply a side benefit," Uzvuyiten said.

"It's the point of the entire trip," Salehi said. "I'm here on a wild-goose chase for your government. The representative of S³, who is handling a case that's a real loser, while the famous Peyti lawyer creates a case all his own, one that he'll win easily in the Multicultural Tribunals, should things go that far."

"You give us too much credit," Uzvuyiten said as he headed down the corridor.

Salehi resisted the urge to grab Uzvuyiten by his thin arm. Salehi was well aware how delicate the Peyti were in comparison to humans. He didn't want to hurt Uzvuyiten physically, even by accident.

"No, I didn't give you enough credit at the beginning of this trip," Salehi said. "I should have seen that your government had a secondary agenda. S³ is the perfect cover for you people because we're so well known as a human-oriented law firm."

"You're well known as one of the best law firms in the Alliance," Uzvuyiten said. "And you, Rafael, are known as one of the most creative legal minds of our generation."

"Flattery and money got you here, Uzvuyiten," Salehi said. "But you can stop now."

"My dear Rafael—"

"And you can stop that too," Salehi said. "I would probably have been quite amused by this situation under normal circumstances. But these aren't normal circumstances. Zhu's dead, and the Moon's a dangerous place for all of us—especially you. You're a Peyti lawyer. Have you thought that through?"

"Yes, I have," Uzvuyiten said. "I'm an old Peyti lawyer, with a fantastic reputation all over the Alliance. I'm well liked. If something happens to me here, well, then, it'll show just how bad things have gotten on the Moon, won't it?"

Salehi stared at him. "You think they'll attack you."

"You think they won't?"

"I wanted you to stay on this ship for that reason," Salehi said, "and that was *before* Zhu died. Don't do this, Uzvuyiten. You're taking too many risks."

"And I would say that you're not taking enough," Uzvuyiten said. "But I think you are taking risks. The wrong kind."

"What does that mean?" Salehi asked.

Uzvuyiten shrugged and then made his way down the hall.

"What are you saying?" Salehi asked.

"S³ On The Moon?" Uzvuyiten said. "Thinking you can ride the backs of a million dead to change clone law? You're too arrogant, Rafael."

"I am?" Salehi said. "What about you?"

"We're talking about my people here, Rafael," Uzvuyiten said. "That's not arrogance. That's survival."

"The Peyti aren't threatened," Salehi said.

"Maybe not at home," Uzvuyiten said. "But our place in the Alliance is. And I'm here to protect it. Or die trying."

He continued down the corridor.

Salehi watched him go, and then sighed.

Uzvuyiten seemed to think he could be a martyr to the cause, not realizing they already had one.

Salehi returned to his suite.

He had always known this was going to be an interesting trip. He just hadn't realized how interesting.

Or how dangerous.

For all of them.

12

THE SHIP ARRIVED SOONER THAN FLINT HAD EXPECTED.

He had just entered the port when he got the first contact from Murray Atherton of Space Traffic Control.

Your boy just arrived.

No explosions, then. Flint let out an audible sigh of relief, which made the new kid standing behind the west security entrance look at him with suspicion. To be fair, the new kid behind the west security entrance to the port looked at everyone with suspicion.

The port was no longer the place it had been when Flint worked there just seven years before. It looked older, battered, filthy in a way it had never looked before. All effort had been turned to security, and with that effort, most of the funds, as well.

So cleaning bots had been reprogrammed to sniff out all kinds of toxins and explosives; the human security staff had been beefed up to the point of ridiculousness; and, most disturbing to Flint, the entrances had been set up to separate people by species. Humans had their own entrance, as did the Disty and the Peyti. Other species often were lumped together by size, with little consideration for species tolerance or the way that the species might travel.

Lately, Flint had tried to come to the port as infrequently as possible.

He slipped through the first round of security, which checked him for weaponry and explosives. Ahead, he would have to go through a decontamination unit to make certain he wasn't bringing any biological hazard into the port, never mind that Armstrong's environmental systems swept for biological hazards continually, and it would be nearly impossible for someone to bring a known biological hazard—the kind that would cause mass deaths—into the port.

But he wasn't one of the people making the decisions for the port, and he never had been.

The new kid—whom Flint spotted by his attitude and his creased and shiny uniform—continued to stare at Flint as if he had sprouted horns or something. And then Flint flushed. The kid was looking at Flint because Flint was as blond and pale as the Frémont clones. White skin, blue eyes, and blond hair were recessive traits—a sign of inbreeding, his ex-wife Rhonda had said to him in one of their epic fights—and uncommon in almost all human communities.

Flint tipped an imaginary hat to the kid and kept going, contacting Murray while crossing the expanse between the first check-in point and the second.

Is he out of the ship?

Not yet, Murray sent. *The suits are going in first. There's no identification on his ship, you know. What you sent me, I can't confirm it by the ship itself.*

That didn't surprise Flint. He was about to say so when he had to step into the decontamination unit. It was an old unit, clearly moved from the arrival terminals.

Security might have improved here, but not enough to make the port more secure.

The decontamination unit was large enough to hold a tall, fat man or a Sequev. Flint stood in the center as lights washed over him, checking him for a thousand different things.

He made himself take a deep breath. He'd been running since he left the Security Office. Talia remained there, under protest. She wanted to know what was happening. But he didn't want to bring her into what could be an extremely dangerous situation.

She didn't entirely understand, although she said she did. She made him promise that he would tell her if the real Zagrando was dead.

Flint would have anyway, so the promise was easy.

The lights intensified. A sign in a dozen languages appeared across his right eye, telling him to stretch out his arms and his legs. So, even though the decontamination unit was designed to seem non-invasive, whoever decided that it needed to be moved to this part of the port had added instructions to make the unit seem invasive.

If this were a different day, he would mention that to Murray. But Flint was pushing his connection to Murray. Murray had done Flint a lot of favors since Flint left Space Traffic. Most of them had occurred when Flint was a detective, but still. Murray let Flint bend more rules than Flint wanted to contemplate.

Murray had complained about this one, however.

You realize that you could be letting in yet another terrorist, Murray had sent when Flint contacted him.

I do, Flint had replied. *Lock this guy down until I get there. And be ready. He said someone was after him.*

We'll monitor anyone on his tail, Murray sent.

Clearly, Murray was following instructions to lock the man down. Flint had warned him that the ship might be contaminated and would need to go to quarantine. And when the ship was still about ten minutes out, Murray had contacted Flint to complain that the ship had no registration and no computerized identification. When Space Traffic had tried to contact the pilot, an automated response answered, broadcasting that the pilot was in distress.

Murray hadn't liked that.

Flint didn't either. If the port had been one of those places that wasn't cautious, a "sick" pilot could cause a lot of port employees their health or their lives.

Flint stepped outside of the decontamination unit into a large open area with high ceilings. Once upon a time, this had been the entry, without all the security. Now it was the place where the people who had gone through the different entrances mingled as they headed toward the terminals.

...'s fine. Word is that the passenger isn't. You there, Miles? Murray had clearly been trying to communicate with Flint while Flint was in decon.

I'm going through your lovely damn security, Flint sent.

Hustle your ass to Terminal Five. I'm getting word that your boy is injured, maybe dying.

What? Flint sent. He hadn't expected that. *I thought you said he was fine.*

I said the ship *was fine. Nothing on it except one passenger. Lots of laser weapon scarring. And he's been shot up real bad. They're taking him to the Medical Unit. I'm told you gotta hurry if you want to see him alive.*

Flint cursed, then took off at a run. It was hard to maintain any kind of speed. The crowd was thick, and getting thicker. Some people were hurrying, but most were meandering.

Human security officers stood every few meters or so, watching him run as if he were fleeing arrest. Within seconds, he had bots keeping pace with him, obviously monitoring him.

I caught the attention of Port Security, Flint sent. *Call them off.*

Some kind of wheeze made it through the links. Clearly, Murray had set the communication to audio for that single sound. Because then he sent, *Like Space Traffic has control of those amateurs.*

Well, it'll do us no good if one of those amateurs kills me, Flint sent.

Nothing I can do, Murray sent. *Try not to look suspicious.*

While running, Flint sent. He wished he still had his police badge. He should have thought this through and asked DeRicci to give him some kind of identification.

But he hadn't been thinking, just reacting. He hurried, rounding corner after corner, weaving in and out of the throng as he ran to the arrivals area.

There, his passage got easier. Almost everyone was human. Flint had never seen anything like it. Usually there were so many different species the place looked like one of those unity vids the kids watched their first week in school. But this wasn't unity. This was like traveling to some of the ancient cities of Earth, where aliens weren't welcome.

The shock of the change almost made Flint slow down.

Has he made it to the Medical Unit? Flint sent.

Just now. They're expecting you. Flash your palm as you go through the terminal entry. I greased the way for you there, at least.

A small miracle. Flint wondered how Murray pulled that off, then decided not to ask.

The doors to the Arrivals Terminal ran as far as the eye could see. People generally couldn't go into the Arrivals Terminal; only staff could. Flint veered to the small kiosk on his left, where some of the Traffic staff worked. He held up his palm, and the door opened as if he were still employed by Space Traffic.

He sent a thank-you to Murray, but didn't say any more.

Everything was feeling like an effort. Somehow he had gotten out of shape in the last few months. Or maybe longer. Maybe since Talia had come into his life.

The back corridor threaded past the windy hallways that regular passengers had to take to leave the Arrivals area. Above Flint, cameras tracked his every movement. He had lost the bots, but he knew smaller cameras the size of an eyelash were tracking him as he ran.

Right now, if this went south, the only person who would get into trouble was Murray. Flint hoped it wouldn't happen that way—Murray was trusting him, and Flint was trusting a dim memory of a man who had saved Talia's life—and a contact made through a link that hadn't been used in more than three years.

Flint finally reached the double doors of the security entrance to the Human Medical Unit. He slammed both hands on the doors, and they opened for him.

He stepped into a cacophony of sound. A woman wailing as she leaned against the wall, a baby looking up at her from a nearby bassinet. A man clutching his left arm and moaning in pain. Two women shouting at someone in blue medical gear.

Flint stopped at the main desk, and held up his hands for the virtual identification as he said to the young man sifting through some holoscreens, "Miles Flint. I'm here to see the patient they just wheeled in from Terminal Five."

The young man looked up, glanced at Flint's identification (which calmed Flint some), and said, "I was waiting for you, Mr. Flint. Come with me."

Flint hadn't expected that. He had expected instructions.

The young man led him to a room just off the main area. "You have to suit up."

"Why?" Flint asked. "I thought he was injured, not contagious."

"He's got laser burns all along the lower part of his body. It's amazing he's alive. And he's barely conscious, but he's conscious enough—according to our equipment—to legally refuse treatment until you arrive."

The young man handed Flint a thin disposable suit—not a standard environmental suit, but a medical suit, one that allowed a full range of movement but didn't allow any contaminates through the thin fabric, in either direction.

"You can slip it on over your clothes, but hurry," the young man said. "The longer you delay, the less chance this guy has of surviving."

Flint's mouth went dry. The suit was one piece, designed big. He pulled it on, and then it attached itself like a second skin. The attachment was vaguely painful, and pulled at his face and hair. Fresh oxygen circulated into his nostrils and made him feel more awake than he had in weeks.

"Where is he?" Flint asked, expecting his voice to sound different. But of course it didn't.

"Through those doors," the young man said. He stepped out of the way.

Flint had to go through a double airlock to get to an antechamber that he had never seen before. The lights were down except underneath the bed, making the patient look like he was glowing. Two medical professionals hovered around him.

"I'm Miles Flint," Flint said to them. "I understand this man was waiting for me."

"Flint?" The voice sounded familiar, but Flint didn't know if his memory was playing tricks on him.

He activated one of his memory chips. He'd thought to download some of the information he had gathered at Valhalla Basin as he drove to the port, and now he compared that single word to Zagrando's voice from years ago.

"Yes." Flint walked to the bedside. The man on it didn't look injured—at least from the chest up. But from the chest down, he was a mass of bloated red and black skin.

Flint suspected that if he weren't wearing the suit, the stench in the room would be almost unbearable.

"Miles Flint," the man said again, as if he couldn't believe it. "I need to talk to you."

The voice print matched. Flint never had any of Zagrando's DNA. He supposed he could get Murray to run it against the DNA on file for the dead man, but Flint wasn't sure if he wanted the authorities to know that Zagrando was here.

Of course, it didn't matter if they already knew who he was.

"Who is this man?" Flint asked one of the medical personnel.

"His identification says he's Isamu Vidal," she said. "He says you know him."

Flint, you have to get them out of here. I have to talk to you alone. That message came through the same old link that had started this conversation.

Can't we do this on the links? Flint asked.

Don't want a record, came the reply.

There might be recordings in here.

I'll mumble. You can lean over.

Talia would tell Flint not to do that, that this was the point of the entire mission for this man, to contaminate Flint somehow. Only Flint had no idea how or what it would gain. Besides, Flint's system just told him that the voice matched.

"I need to speak to him alone," Flint told the woman medical tech.

"It's not advised," she said. "He's in bad shape, and we—"

"He won't talk otherwise," Flint said, "and he came here specifically to see me. The sooner you get out of here, the faster you can get him into surgery or whatever you're going to do to save his life."

The woman looked at the other tech, who shrugged.

"You have two minutes," the woman said, then led the other tech out of the room.

"Thank you." Zagrando didn't speak as softly as he said he would.

Flint came to his side. The man's dark skin was gray, and his eyes were sunken.

"Why do they list you as dead?" Flint asked.

"It's complicated." Zagrando's voice shook. His eyelids drooped for a moment, and then he seemed to catch himself. "I'm not sure how long I can stay awake. I'll tell you the full story when we have more time, but here's what you need to know."

Flint leaned in.

Zagrando took a deep breath. His hands gripped the side of the bed. His eyelids drooped again.

"Iniko," Flint said. "What do I need to know?"

"Oh." Zagrando looked at him. "I forgot you were here."

Flint's heart started pounding. The man was near death, and he needed to say something. Flint wasn't sure he'd get it out.

"They sent me undercover to find out how easy the clones were to track," Zagrando said. "Took weeks and weeks. I couldn't find them. Then when they realized I was on the wrong track, they tried to kill me."

Flint was confused. He couldn't follow exactly what Zagrando said. "Who sent you?"

Zagrando blinked at Flint. "I came here of my own accord."

This wasn't going to work. The man was too ill. But Flint decided to try one last time.

"I need you to pay attention, Iniko." Flint made his voice just a bit harsh. "You said someone sent you to find the clones. The Anniversary Day clones?"

"Yes." Zagrando blinked, his eyes opening wide. He seemed to be alert, at least for the moment.

"Who sent you?" Flint asked.

"I was undercover for the EAIS. Thought I was working for them. Should've known." His eyes drooped a third time.

Flint wanted to shake him awake, but refrained.

"Should have known what?" Flint asked.

"They used a clone to kill me. You know that? It's why I'm dead. Should've been a clue."

The door opened and the woman entered. "I'm sorry, sir, you have to leave now."

Flint's stomach clenched. He didn't look at her. "A clue to what?"

"Wasn't working for Intelligence. Working for them." Zagrando's gaze flicked to the woman, but Flint wasn't sure Zagrando saw her.

Flint wasn't sure Zagrando saw anything.

"Sir." The woman took Flint's arm. "You have to leave. If you don't leave, we'll escort you out."

Flint kept his feet planted firmly on the floor. One last question, and then he'd go. If he had some solid information, he could work with it.

"Who were you working for?" Flint asked. "Give me a name."

"Ike Jarvis, bastard." Zagrando gave Flint a weak smile. "Killed him. Looks like he killed me too."

"Not if we can help it." The woman pulled Flint away, and this time, Flint let her.

She escorted him out of the room. As the door closed, Flint said, "Keep me apprised on every detail of his treatment. I want him to have the best of everything. I will pay for the difference between the standard care and the high-end treatment. Got that?"

"You'll have to let billing know," she said. "But we will keep you apprised."

Then she went back into the room. So did two other people, and some equipment Flint had never seen before.

He had to take care of Zagrando's expenses, and then he had a name to follow.

Ike Jarvis. Earth Alliance Intelligence.

And Jarvis just might be dead.

Flint glanced at the closed door. He hoped Zagrando made it through. The man clearly had a lot to say, and Flint wanted to hear it all.

13

ANNIVERSARY DAY VICTIMS' IDENTIFICATION AND RECOVERY SERVICE had three different offices in Armstrong. The first was what Berhane called the "show" office, the one that potential donors met her in, and the one where she brought in professional charity teams to help her with fundraisers.

That office was nice, but not too nice—she didn't want the potential donors to think the organization was wasting money on office design.

The second office had been a closet. It was outside the dome, in a warehouse where she and Kaspian stored their equipment and everything that Berhane ordered—like up-to-date environmental suits. Because the Moon was in such dire straits, almost all of their supplies came from Earth.

The third office was where she usually worked. It was in an unfinished building not too far from the warehouse. In fact, if she wanted to apply for special permission, she could walk through one of the dome's airlocks to get to the warehouse.

That walk would require an environmental suit and two weeks of testing to get the permission, but she could do it, and she had even toyed with it in the beginning, just so she could avoid taking the train.

Fortunately, she had realized that was silly before she learned that she would spend half her life on trains.

She sat in the third office now, filling out documentation while she waited for Kaspian. He wanted to present everything to her, because he worried that the problem with the DNA was their fault. When he let her know he was leaving his office in the warehouse, he had added that he believed they needed to redo training.

He thought the DNA problem was because all (or most) of their volunteers were misusing the equipment.

This office was spartan. It had gray floors and gray walls. The construction company hadn't installed any design features yet, and she had discouraged it from doing so. She wanted the building done, but she didn't need any fancy stuff.

The documentation she was working on annoyed her. It was for her father. He had provided all of the office buildings and warehouses that housed ADVI-RS, which he did to prove his charitable bona fides. He was already using his involvement with ADVI-RS in pitches he made to investors in his company.

Even though Berhane was a majority shareholder in her father's company, she couldn't just move resources to ADVI-RS, much as she wanted to. Her father wanted a wall of documentation to separate the companies.

Believe me, Berhane, he had said, *you don't want ADVI-RS to have the slightest affiliation with any for-profit company.*

She was beginning to understand that. But she didn't like the fact that he required the documentation before he did anything. She figured he could take the action and they could back-date their documentation to account for it.

Or maybe her irritation was simply a cover for the sadness she had been feeling since she learned about Torkild. The first thing she had done when she returned to her office wasn't to contact Kaspian and tell him she was here; the first thing she had done was download the media reports on Torkild.

He had died in the street in front of his office, kicked to death, it seemed, after getting his morning coffee. Some reporter had gotten a shot of the coffee cup rolling along the sidewalk, coffee spilling from it.

Clearly, the reporter was using that from some security camera footage, because there would have been no reason for a reporter to have been onsite at the moment of Torkild's beating and death.

It had broken her heart. She'd had to stop listening to the reports after just a few minutes because of the way all of the reporters were characterizing Torkild—an opportunist, a man who chased money for money's sake—almost all of the things she had accused Torkild of the last time she saw him.

And of course, all of the reports mentioned his connection to her and her father.

The door banged shut.

She started. She hadn't even heard the door open.

She looked up. Dabir Kaspian still had his hand on the doorknob.

Kaspian was tall and unnaturally thin. He worked at twice the speed of anyone else, slept only a few hours per night, and didn't eat enough to cover all the energy he expended. She tried to get him to take better care of himself, but he told her he would do that when the crisis ended.

Which crisis, she had no idea. She suspected Kaspian liked the overwork and the feeling of exhaustion. It made him feel important.

He gave her a half-hearted, somewhat apologetic smile. "I'm sorry about Zhu," he said.

"Thanks," she said this time. She didn't want to talk about Torkild with anyone ever again. If there was a ceremony for Torkild, she would go, but she wouldn't let the rest of the city know how devastated his death had made her. "Let's talk about this DNA thing."

Kaspian nodded. He tucked a loose strand of his long, gray hair behind an ear. He needed to redo the ponytail he had started wearing a few months ago, when he declared himself too busy to tend to his grooming.

"May I?" he asked, and then, without waiting for her answer, he commandeered the office computer system, opening a half a dozen holographic screens all at once.

Faces filled them, with old identification marks at the bottom of the imagery. She hadn't seen some of those marks since she was a child, looking through family images she'd found stored in an unmarked file in the computer system of her childhood home.

"What's this?" she asked, as she stood up. Kaspian had placed the screens too high for her to comfortably see them from her desk.

"These," he said, "are some of the identifications that have come from the DNA we've gotten from the various bombing sites."

Berhane frowned. "I'm confused. These identifications are old."

"Not only that," Kaspian said, "These people died forty, fifty, sixty years ago."

She didn't touch the screens. She knew the files would tell her who these people had been, but she wasn't ready for that. Not yet.

"Were there some…cemeteries…in some of these domes?" she asked. She knew her Moon history. A few of the early Earth colonists had actually buried their dead before it was outlawed, and one or two of the domes had allowed the practice to continue for certain religious sects.

"That's the first thing I checked," Kaspian said. "Even if that were the case, though, it wouldn't help with the other problem."

"What's that?" she asked.

He took a deep breath. "Some of this DNA has showed up in more than one dome."

"I know," she said. "You mentioned that we're having the problem with all our volunteers."

"No," he said. "I mean that DNA from the same person has shown up in more than one dome. Which is why at first I thought we were dealing with tampering."

She felt cold. "By our volunteers?"

"Yes," he said. "But it's never the same volunteer who gathered the sample, and often the volunteers used different equipment."

Berhane's chill worsened. "You're not here because of procedures, though, are you? You wouldn't come in person about something we could change with a simple agreement."

"That's right." Kaspian glanced at the screen and sighed. "I don't think this is about our volunteers."

Berhane didn't like what she was thinking. "You believe this is another cluster of clones."

"Yeah," he said. "I'm afraid I do."

14

PIPPA LANDAU SAT ON THE EDGE OF THE BED IN HER HOTEL ROOM, HANDS clasped over her carry bag. She had sat here since she registered, feeling her heart pound, questioning everything she was doing.

The room was larger than she expected, with a big bed, soft coverings, and a lovely sitting area. The bathroom off to the side was a religious experience.

She had never been in a hotel room this nice off Earth. But then, when she had been traveling outside of Earth, she had been incredibly poor. She wasn't rich now, but she had money, enough to make this trip without hurting her children's inheritance if she didn't survive.

She was terrified. And weirdly, that terror was freezing her in place.

When she was young, she hadn't frozen in place when she was terrified. If she had, she never would have escaped Starbase Human. She wouldn't have had her quiet, comfortable life and her marvelous children.

She wouldn't have survived.

Her fingers tightened on her bag. She had unfamiliar clothes inside, along with familiar shoes and, of all things, a pillow. So middle-aged midwestern woman, that pillow. Not something Takara Hamasaki would have brought with her off Starbase Human.

(Although she had brought a pillow off the starbase. Pillows and blankets and dirty clothes and all kinds of things that she had stored in the crappy space ship she had dumped at her very first chance.)

Pippa made herself take a deep breath. She needed to find Takara Hamasaki within herself, the persona she had abandoned decades ago. The woman she had become in the intervening years was too comfortable for a survival instinct.

Pippa was halfway there. She had cut and colored her hair. She wore different clothes than Pippa Landau would have worn while teaching school.

She was sitting *here*, in Armstrong, after taking a shuttle from Illinois. It would be ridiculous to stop now.

She stood up, because standing made her feel just a little less overwhelmed. She looked at the public network screen attached to the hotel wall, but she didn't walk over to it.

She had researched who to contact while she was still at home. She had come up with only one name. Noelle DeRicci, the woman who headed the United Domes of the Moon Security Office. It seemed the other heads of the Moonwide government were dead or had abandoned their posts.

That probably should have scared Pippa off when she had been in Iowa, but it hadn't.

It sure made her nervous now.

She took a deep breath and put a hand to her ear, just like all of her kids had done when they got their first links as young teenagers. Her links weren't very sophisticated. The encryption in them was designed for families, not for high-level government work. And the encryption was also designed for short bursts of information, not long conversations or large amounts of data. Designed to aid a bank transfer or send a message to a medical professional or to let children know that they needed to come home because their father wasn't going to make it through the week.

Her eyes welled. She missed Raymond. He hadn't known any of her history, and he probably would have been furious when he found out she was a Disappeared and hadn't told him.

But he had always been steady in a crisis. He had known how to handle everything, even the momentary lack of courage that was affecting her right now.

The very thought of him, his lanky, sturdy frame, his broad, sun-reddened midwestern face, calmed her.

She had loved him. She had had three beautiful children with him.

She had a legacy.

She could do this and not regret the life she had lived.

She opened an encoded link and sent a message to the woman who had been listed as DeRicci's assistant, Rudra Popova.

My name is Pippa Landau, Pippa sent. *I am a longtime Disappeared. I have information on the history of the Anniversary Day clones that I believe you need. I'm taking a huge risk contacting you. Please do me the courtesy of letting me speak with Noelle DeRicci as soon as possible. Thank you.*

Pippa brought her hand down. It was shaking.

Her link only brought silence.

Somehow she had thought she would get an immediate response, even if that response was automated. But she didn't.

She looked at the edge of the bed, the spread wrinkled from her moments of indecision.

She wasn't going to sit back down there. That was a defeat.

She would wait up here for an hour, and then she would get something to eat from one of the nearby restaurants.

If she hadn't heard from the Security Office by then, she would contact them again. She would keep doing so until they responded.

No matter how long it took.

15

FLINT TOOK THE ELEVATOR TO THE TOP FLOOR OF THE SECURITY OFFICE. He hated standing in that little box. It made him feel restless.

He was being pulled in eight different directions. He had been trying to get back to his office to investigate the leads he had received earlier in the week, and then he'd gotten derailed by personal events. He had just settled those when Zagrando contacted him.

Now that Flint had spoken to Zagrando, Flint wanted to investigate Zagrando's (albeit truncated) information. But Flint also felt odd about leaving Zagrando alone with the medical authorities.

It wasn't so much that he didn't trust them—although that was a factor. It was that he worried he would lose Zagrando to some Earth Alliance official without anyone ever knowing.

Flint had already asked Space Traffic's Murray Atherton to keep an eye on Zagrando, saying that Zagrando had information essential to solving Anniversary Day, and he would only give it to Flint. Flint warned Murray that someone might be coming after Zagrando, and under no circumstances was Murray to allow anyone to take Zagrando without contacting Flint first.

Of course, as he did that, Flint didn't use Zagrando's real name, but the alias he'd arrived with.

So far, no one had come after Zagrando, either on a space ship or inside the port. Murray had stationed a number of space traffic cops near the port's medical facility, and some near Zagrando's room. Everyone in Space Traffic was on alert for a ship that might arrive in obvious pursuit of someone. Flint wanted to make certain that no one followed Zagrando here.

He had looked at the trajectory of Zagrando's ship once it got close to the Moon; it appeared as if no one had followed him. But Flint knew that only time would tell.

The port was relatively safe—as safe as it could be, given what was going on these days on the Moon. He never thought of the port as a dangerous place. These days, he thought of it as a potential escape route.

He had told Talia that a number of times. If things looked particularly bad in the dome, she was to go to Flint's ship, the *Emmeline,* and wait for him there. If the dome was being harmed in anyway, she was to take the ship off the Moon.

He had told her that he would let her know when the situation warranted that. He didn't think anything rose to that level on this day, but he also knew that it could.

Which was why he had decided to ask for Talia's help with Zagrando. She would be as safe here, with the police protection and the *Emmeline* nearby, as she would be in the Security Office or with him while he was working in his office. Or so he liked to think.

Besides, the help Flint needed with Zagrando was risky in a different way. He could only trust Talia with this particular mission.

He hoped she was up for the task.

She was still in the Security Office. Even though he knew she was doing better, he had worried that the improvement was just temporary. Now, he had to believe what Talia had told him before he left; that she was doing better, and that she was willing to work.

He didn't contact her on his links. Instead, he had gone directly to the Security Office. As he rounded the corner from the elevators, Popova waved at him from her desk.

"I have a question for you," she said.

He glanced at the kitchen. He wondered if Talia was still there or if she had moved to a different part of the building.

"Make it fast," he said.

"Have you heard of a woman named Pippa Landau? She says she's a Disappeared."

Flint turned toward Popova so fast that he nearly lost his balance. "She *what*?" he asked.

"She says she's a Disappeared."

Flint frowned. "People don't admit that."

"I know," Popova said. "That's why I thought you might know her. Maybe she has come home after a Retrieval Artist found her or she was in the news and I missed it...?"

Flint shook his head. "In theory, I'm retired. I haven't watched that kind of news closely since Talia moved in with me."

"So, you don't know her." Popova sounded disappointed.

Flint gave her a wry smile. "Believe it or not, I don't know every single Disappeared in the Earth Alliance. Why are you asking?"

"Because she contacted me just a few minutes ago, and said she was a Disappeared, and she had important information for me, and she was taking a risk contacting us." Popova tapped a finger against her desk. "I haven't responded. I don't know how to handle this at all. Do you think you could find out if she's what she says she is?"

"No," Flint said. "I've got much too much to research as it is, and all of it seems to be tied to the Anniversary Day attacks. I will tell you this, Disappeareds never identify themselves that way. Either she's a fraud or she thinks this information is so important she has to reveal herself to give it to you."

Popova now tapped all of her fingers against the desk. The drumming sound was arrhythmic, and drove Flint slightly crazy.

"I'm not sure what to do." Her gaze met Flint's. He'd never heard Popova say something like that.

"Check out the name she gave you," he said. "If she gave you her real name, her history should stop at some point in the past. If she gave you the name she's been using recently, then you should find some kind of record, which should give you a sense of what kind of person she is."

"And then what?" Popova asked.

"If her history stops, you know she's telling the truth. If she has an entire lifetime's worth of history, then you need to judge it on its merits. If you only have a year or two of recent data, ignore her. If you have decades' worth, and she's managed to stay out of trouble, then I think you should invite her here under heavy guard, and see what she has to say."

"What if she's a bomber or something?" Popova asked.

Flint reached over and took her hand, stopping the tapping. "That's why I'm suggesting she come here. She doesn't need to come to this floor. Meet her in the lobby. She has to go through more security to get into this building than she has to go through almost anywhere else in Armstrong. If she's carrying something or she looks suspicious, then don't let her up here. Trust the guards downstairs and the systems inside the building. You'll be fine."

Popova squeezed his hand. Her fingers were cold and a little clammy. "I'm sorry," she said. "There are days when nothing seems easy. This is one of them."

He understood, but he felt that if he said that, he was patronizing Popova.

"Talia still in the kitchen?" he asked.

"She's moved to the room you two sometimes use. She asked for a tablet. I gave one to her. Is that all right?"

Flint was cheered to hear that news and worried at the same time. He had no idea what Talia would be working on.

"Thanks," he said, pivoted, and headed the other way down the hall. Behind him, he heard a chair squeak as Popova sat back down.

The empty office he and Talia had used in the past was just beyond the elevators, around the corner. The door was open. Talia sat in her usual chair—although Flint wasn't exactly certain about that as a definition of sitting.

She had her knees over one of the chair's arms and her back propped against the other arm. She rested her head against the top of the chair. The tablet was propped against her thighs.

When she saw him, she grinned. "I'm setting up so that I can help you with whatever you need." She sounded just a bit too cheerful, as if she were compensating a bit too much. But he would take it at the moment. "I decided to start with finding Detective Zagrando's history. He's listed as dead in every database you know."

"I know," Flint said. That disturbed him, but Zagrando had said it was all complicated. And the fact that the man had worked undercover for Earth Alliance Intelligence might have explained the subterfuge.

"Is it him?" Talia asked, clutching the tablet to her chest.

"I'm ninety-nine percent sure it is." Flint felt the need to leave at least a small margin of error.

"Is he going to be okay?"

"I don't know," Flint said.

Talia hugged the tablet harder. Her eyes were big, her expression solemn.

"Do the databases say how he died?" Flint asked.

"It's weird," Talia said. "That's why I was digging into it. He was called to Valhalla Basin's port on some case, alone, and then he got murdered in a room by some perpetrators. They all got caught, but he died pretty horribly. His body was recognizable, though."

Flint frowned. "If that had happened here, the body would have been autopsied."

"It was," Talia said. "There were some strange things."

"You read the report?"

She smiled a little and shrugged.

He almost smiled in return. His daughter had come back to him. He had missed her.

"What's strange?" he asked.

"His weight, for one thing. Standard VBPD procedure. A monthly health check, including weight and height and general fitness. His general fitness was less when he died, although his heart was stronger and some of the health problems his enhancements had compensated for were gone."

Flint wanted to grab the tablet and look at the results, but Talia kept it close. Apparently, she wanted to watch him as she told him the news.

"But his weight was way off. Like forty pounds off. And he would have had to lose that in two weeks. That kind of weight loss usually means an illness, not an increase in health, at least that's what my poking around this afternoon told me." Talia's gaze met Flint's.

He knew the look. It meant she had a theory.

"What are you thinking?" he asked.

"They ran the DNA," Talia said. "Standard test, just to make sure, even though he still had his badge in his palm and all of his enhancements and stuff, plus his face was recognizable."

"But…?" Flint asked.

"But there are all these weird aspects to the death. He didn't put up much of a fight. He had a weapon and they disarmed him. Plus, he went into this room without backup, and he'd been the one called to be there. Like it was a set-up."

"That happens," Flint said.

"I know it does," Talia said. "So I looked at the standard DNA tests that VBPD runs. It's pretty cursory in cases like this."

"What are you saying?" Flint asked.

"The body's gone, so we can't recheck. But think about it, Dad. He's thinner and his heart is healthier and he doesn't have some of the problems that his enhancements were designed to compensate for and he goes into a trap without backup and he loses his weapon right away—I remember him. He was older than the guy who found me in that closet, and he was *sensible* and sturdy and I had the sense that he never did something without thinking about it."

Flint had had that sense of Zagrando too. In fact, Zagrando had made Flint uncomfortable on Valhalla Basin because Zagrando had the kind of gaze that took nothing for granted. Zagrando had known more about Flint in ten minutes than Flint had ever found out about Zagrando.

"He wouldn't have gone into that room alone," Talia said. "I'm convinced of it. And he wouldn't have lost forty pounds in that short a period of time. Not even enhancements allow for that. If they do anything, they make you look thin until you *are* thin."

Flint knew that as well. "You're saying…what, Talia?"

"I'm saying they killed the clone," Talia said. "The real guy is here. The clone wouldn't have known about us, Dad. We're just a case in his past. We're not something just anyone would know."

Flint frowned. In his haze, Zagrando had muttered, *They used a clone to kill me. You know that? It's why I'm dead. Should've been a clue.*

And now, Talia had found things that indicated Zagrando had spoken the truth.

Flint felt odd. He had his daughter back, and he also felt uncomfortable with what she had found. He sat down in a nearby chair. "The simplest thing to do is to check this man, see if he's a clone."

"I know," Talia said. "But you can't ask anyone to do that, Dad. Not right now. Everyone is crazy about clones."

There was sadness in her voice. She had run into that with her therapist, and it had been ugly. Flint had had a terrible conversation with the man. Flint hoped that Talia's conversation hadn't been quite as nasty.

"He said his so-called death was complicated," Flint said, more to himself than to Talia.

"He did? What else did he say?"

"Not much," Flint said. "He was too ill. He gave me a name, and then the doctors carted him off into surgery. Which is why I'm here."

He paused, uncertain now if he should ask her to leave the Security Office.

Talia's expression brightened just a little. She clearly wanted to do something. That pleased him.

He would let this be her choice. She had shown an interest, after all.

"I have Murray at Space Traffic keeping an eye on Zagrando," Flint said. "Murray assigned a lot of cops to watch the medical unit. And they're looking for ships that might be in pursuit."

Talia was frowning. "He's in the port still?"

"They're operating on him onsite. He was in too bad of shape to be taken away. I'm afraid someone will move in on him while he's under. I'm also worried that he might wake up, need to talk to me, and no one contacts me." Flint paused.

Talia's eyebrows went up as she considered all of that.

"I'm also worried that under the influence of whatever drug they have given him, he'll say the wrong thing. I could go back to the port, Talia, but it means I'll either be doing research there or I'll be doing nothing important."

Talia's fingers tightened on the tablet.

"If there are traffic cops," she said, "I could go. I know I need to get to the *Emmeline* if something goes really bad. And if someone tries to harm him, there should be protection nearby. I don't mind, Dad."

Flint's heart was pounding. He did mind. He didn't want her in danger again. But he wasn't really convinced that watching Zagrando was dangerous.

And she understood Flint's fears.

"If you're willing, then I'd like you at his side." Flint swallowed hard. He was actually nervous. "Let me know when he wakes up, make sure that no one identifies him or tries to take him off the Moon. If he has to talk, you record it and then contact me. Can you do that?"

"Yeah," Talia said. "I don't have to get him out of there if something goes wrong, do I?"

"No," Flint said. "You leave that to the authorities."

Talia shrugged. "Then it's just sitting, right?"

"And making certain you call him by the right name, and making sure that no one kicks you out of the area. You have to be by his side until I come back."

"I can do that, Dad," Talia said. "As long as you tell me what name he's registered under."

"I will," Flint said. He extended his hand for the tablet. "No research into Zagrando's past while you're there, either. You have to read a book or play a game or do something while you wait. Nothing out of the ordinary for a kid your age."

"Wow," Talia said with a bit of a smile. "I'll have to imitate a real person."

"You can do that," Flint said. "I have faith in you."

She still hadn't handed him the tablet, so he took it. Then he stood and helped her up. He pulled her into a hug. She leaned into him for just a minute, then stepped back and eyed the tablet.

"I can work encrypted," she said.

"Not there," he said.

She sighed. "Can I go there now?"

"Yeah," Flint said. "And promise me you'll stay in touch. If I tell you to leave fast, you will."

"I promise," she said, and almost skipped out of the room.

He watched her go.

He hoped he was making the right choice, both for this investigation and for his daughter.

He would contact Murray Atherton to make certain that Talia was protected—as best as anyone could protect her.

Then Flint took a deep breath and willed himself to let the worry go. He couldn't control everything, no matter how much he wanted to.

At some point, he would have to trust Talia again.

He might as well start now.

16

Ó BRÁDAIGH WALKED PETTEWAY TO THE ELEVATOR. IT WAS FARTHER AWAY from the controls than Ó Brádaigh remembered. Everything in the substructure was far from everything else. That alone was a part of the design that Ó Brádaigh didn't like.

Petteway entered, then held the door. "You coming, Ó Brádaigh?"

Ó Brádaigh shook his head. "I always take the stairs. I see more that way."

"And exhaust yourself further." Petteway jerked his head toward the back of the elevator. "Take a rest. Come on up this way."

"I'll meet you at the top," Ó Brádaigh said. "I'm going to take the other stairs up."

"Other stairs?" Petteway asked.

"I took the north stairs down," Ó Brádaigh said. "I'll take the south stairs up."

Petteway let go of the door. "You're a glutton for punishment, Ó Brádaigh."

The door started to close. "I'll see you up there, sir," Ó Brádaigh said.

"No, you won't," Petteway said. "I'm going home. You should too."

And then the door closed tightly. If he had said anything else, Ó Brádaigh couldn't hear it.

He rubbed his hands over his arms, feeling goose bumps. They weren't caused by the temperature down here. The environmental system kept everything at a consistent twenty degrees Celsius.

He was unnerved that Petteway had had the same thoughts that he had had.

Or rather, slightly different thoughts. Petteway had thought someone could tamper with the controls.

Ó Brádaigh made his way back toward that wall. He had no idea how anyone would get into the control area, let alone tamper with them. It took levels and levels of clearance for someone to do that.

And then a shiver ran through him.

Petteway had levels and levels of clearance.

Ó Brádaigh's heart started to pound. He'd known Petteway forever.

But, then, those Peyti clones had been on the Moon, working as *lawyers*, for godssake, for decades. No one had suspected them until they went rogue.

Ó Brádaigh didn't like how he was thinking. Maybe that was how the bad guys—whoever they were—won this battle of minds and hearts. Maybe their stupid attacks managed to make everyone suspicious of each other, in a way that would nibble at what little trust existed among the disparate communities on the Moon.

Only Petteway wasn't part of a disparate community from Ó Brádaigh. Petteway was a co-worker, his *boss*. They'd had beers on more than one occasion. Petteway had given Ó Brádaigh the needed cover and time off to deal with Fiona after the first Armstrong bombing. It had taken months to get his life in order again, and Petteway had let Ó Brádaigh have the flexibility he needed to tend to his baby daughter and his own broken heart.

Ó Brádaigh didn't like that he had even a moment of suspicion against his boss. The man wouldn't have treated Ó Brádaigh so fairly if he were a bad guy, would he?

Ó Brádaigh walked back to the nanowall. It looked flat again, undisturbed. Petteway would be upset if he knew Ó Brádaigh was having these thoughts. And what would Petteway think if Ó Brádaigh went into the control room to double-check?

Would Petteway suspect something off about Ó Brádaigh? Or would Petteway see the behavior as a sign of mistrust? Which it was, of course.

Ó Brádaigh's cheeks heated.

He hated what he had become.

But he couldn't just leave this alone. He had to see what was going on inside the control room.

If that got him fired, well, then, he would move up the chain of command and argue his case. They couldn't fault him for protecting the dome.

He hoped.

He took a deep breath and placed his hand on the access panel, sending the control room his own personal passkey.

Error 5221

Entrance Off-Line

The message appeared across his eyes and on the door itself.

His heart rate went up. Had Petteway just denied him access to the control panel?

Then Ó Brádaigh remembered: access to the control room wasn't determined here or through links. There were other controls elsewhere in the substructures, designed to make it almost impossible for an outsider to figure out how to tamper with the system.

And Ó Brádaigh had seen Petteway go up the elevator. He couldn't have denied Ó Brádaigh access.

The access had to have been changed earlier, if Petteway had done it. Or it had just been changed now from a different location.

Ó Brádaigh tried again. He got the same message. His heart rate increased more, and his palms grew damp. He wiped them on his pants.

His clearance couldn't have been revoked or he wouldn't have been able to get into the substructure. And the clearance system was set up so that even if clearances were revoked, the revocation never took place while someone was in a protected space.

There were too many ways to trap a person down here, even accidentally. The changes in clearance happened outside of secure levels to prevent someone from dying down here.

Ó Brádaigh glanced toward the stairs. For a moment, he wondered if that system had just been overridden.

There was only one way to find out.

He jogged toward the stairs, and placed his sweaty palm on the panel. The door said hello to him like it always had, and then swung open.

He didn't leave—he wasn't ready to leave. He held up a finger as if he were still with another person and had just forgotten something, then headed back to the control room.

He tried again, and kept his palm on the access panel. He got the error message again. He stared at it.

Error 5221
Entrance Off-Line

Entrance Off-Line. He'd never seen that before, in all his years working for the city. He hadn't even seen it during Anniversary Day.

He checked the database of codes that he had in one of his chips. Error 5221, when applied to a control room, did mean the entrance was offline. Offline meant several things, but it didn't mean that the person trying to get in had no access.

He scrolled through the meanings and found several that alarmed him.

The door was broken. The entire control system was damaged. The access panel was broken.

It went on and on.

He slipped his fingers against the edge of the door. If the door was broken, it might have been broken *open*. So he tugged.

Unauthorized Access
Use Entry Passkey and Try Again

He expected to get that message if he had tried the door without using the passkey. So that was working.

He wondered if Petteway had had trouble accessing the room. If he had, wouldn't he have told Ó Brádaigh?

Had this problem cropped up since Petteway was in the control room?

Ó Brádaigh started to open an encrypted link to Petteway and then stopped. This was the moment in which Ó Brádaigh decided whether or not he trusted his boss, the man he had known for decades.

Ó Brádaigh's throat was dry, his face flushed, his heart pounding.

He felt the risk as if Petteway were standing right here.

And, after a moment, Ó Brádaigh shut down the link. If he hadn't seen Petteway here not ten minutes ago, Ó Brádaigh would have opened the link as a matter of course.

But he had seen Petteway and now the control room wasn't responding properly. And Petteway had said nothing about it.

Ó Brádaigh cursed under his breath.

He wasn't sure who he could trust. He was also aware that he was down here alone, after his shift ended, and if someone reviewed the security footage, they would think he had acted suspiciously.

Any other man would have walked away and saved this for another day. But he couldn't.

He needed to investigate, and he needed to do it now.

17

"DID YOU CHECK TO SEE IF THE DNA HAS CLONE MARKS OR SOME KIND of trademark?" Berhane asked.

Kaspian stared at the faces floating around him on the various holoscreens. Berhane didn't glance at them, not at the moment. She would deal with the faces—the *identities*—after she and Kaspian finished their discussion.

"Yeah, I had our labs check," he said. "No clone marks, no trademarks, nothing. I didn't have them check for shortened telomeres, but I'm not sure, given the samples we're using, how reliable that would be anyway."

His comment on telomeres made her think. She didn't like seeing these long-dead faces, and she really didn't like the implication that yet more clones were on the Moon, plotting something evil.

But she didn't yet know if that was true. She grabbed one of the chairs and leaned on its back, staring at the floating faces. A few of them looked vaguely familiar, but she didn't trust that. All faces looked vaguely familiar once someone placed that suggestion in a person's brain. She wasn't going to rely on her gut sense.

"Did the same labs come up with the same identifications?" she asked. "Meaning, did one lab—"

"Did one lab only identify one of the old identities, did another only identify the other identity, and so on?" he asked. "Oh, God, I wish. But the answer is no. The DNA comes from different parts of the Moon, from different volunteers, and was collected at different times. That's what took so long to find this. And, I'll be honest, I didn't find it. One of the lab techs found the first set."

Berhane frowned. "What do you mean?"

"He asked if we had some kind of error in our routing system. Because he claimed he had already tested some of the samples."

Berhane ran a hand over her face. She thought about that for a moment. "Do we have an error?"

"No," Kaspian said. "First of all, the samples were in varying degrees of decay. Some were covered in regolith from the Moon's surface, some had smoke damage, some included bits of destroyed building—I mean, if we were sending the same samples, they should have been the same on all levels. They should have been from Littrow or the same building and they should have had the same contaminants. They didn't."

Berhane's heart was beating hard. If there were more clones, then what did that mean?

"How many samples have you found?" she asked.

"Enough to disturb me," Kaspian said.

She shook her head. That wasn't a good answer. "There are cloning operations all over the Moon—all over the Earth Alliance, for that matter. Legitimate cloning operations."

"Those clones would have had some kind of tag in their DNA," Kaspian said curtly, as if she hadn't been listening. She knew he had addressed that, but she couldn't quite accept what she was seeing. She didn't immediately want to go to the worst case.

"Could that tag have been destroyed?" she asked.

"I don't know," he said. "I'm not a scientist."

"Did you ask?"

He glanced at her, then took a deep breath, obviously trying to contain his irritation. "Yes, yes I did."

"And what did the labs say?"

"They said anything's possible, but chances are, if they can use the DNA to identify someone, then the DNA sample would still have its clone marks."

She didn't like that at all. She bit her lower lip and looked at the floating faces. All male, yet again. She wondered if that was some kind of pattern, or if she was reading something else into this entirely.

"If these clones were supposed to set off another attack," she said slowly, "how did they die in this one? Wouldn't they have known?"

Kaspian raised his forefingers and tapped them against his lips. "I don't know the answer to that. You would think they wouldn't have died."

"Unless they were suicide bombers," she said. "Unless the bombs weren't set off by the people we thought."

"These people we're finding now," Kaspian said, "they couldn't have set off the bombs. There were too many surviving witnesses, too much evidence pointing to those Frémont clones. At least that's what's in the press. We have known for months who set off the Anniversary Day explosions."

Berhane nodded. This wasn't making sense. She made herself take a deep breath.

"Let me try this again," she said. "These clones we've found, who are the originals? I mean—"

"There are too many originals to give you a quick answer," Kaspian said. "I can give you names here, but I'd be looking them up, just like you would."

"No," she said, thinking it was hard to be clear about these matters. "I mean the originals. You've already examined them, who they were, right?"

"Yes," he said.

"And were the originals mass murderers like Frémont?"

"No," Kaspian said. "They aren't even murderers. They lived pretty quiet lives. They're not famous in any way, at least that I could tell."

"How many of them are there?" she asked.

"Originals?" he asked.

She nodded.

"We found one hundred different originals who had been cloned," he said.

"How many clones have you found?" she asked again. This time, though, her tone was softer.

"Hundreds," he said.

She felt her breath catch. Twenty clones had damaged nineteen domes on Anniversary Day. Hundreds of Peyti clones had tried to do something similar during the Peyti Crisis.

And now, Kaspian was telling her that their small search for the identity of the dead had uncovered hundreds of clones.

"Not all of the same person," she said to herself.

But Kaspian heard. "Not all of the same person."

His gray eyes met hers. She could see how troubled he was. She was just as troubled.

"I wonder what would happen if we searched the rubble for Peyti DNA," she said. "I wonder how many of the Peyti lawyer clones we would find."

"We could do that," he said.

She nodded, but felt dismissive. She didn't want to waste resources like that, looking into the perpetrators rather than looking for victims. She had already limited what they used their precious resources for.

In fact, that had led to the first fight with Kaspian back when they set up this company. Back then, he had argued that they should search for human and alien DNA. Berhane had already felt overwhelmed, just searching for humans. She agreed that ADVI-RS would set aside all organic materials—or at least as much as they could—until they had more lab space.

But she had been looking at limited funds, limited time, and limited numbers of volunteers. She had made the hard choice four months ago to only look for human remains. Even that was daunting, given the millions who had died.

"I don't want to search for the Peyti clone lawyers," she said. "We have a mission. We can't get sidetracked."

"The mission is no good if we're going to get attacked again." His voice trembled just a bit.

The entire city was on edge—the entire *Moon* was on edge—after the Peyti Crisis. Everyone was waiting for the next attack.

"We are not equipped to deal with this," she said. "Figuring out who those clones were and what they were doing here isn't our mission. We have to remain focused on what we do."

"If we have the information that could prevent the next attack, then we should—"

She put up a hand and stopped him. "Let's take this to the authorities. Let them deal with it."

"You want me to do that?" he asked. "Who do I take it to? Armstrong PD?"

She shook her head. Even if she were feeling kindly disposed to the Armstrong Police Department right now, she wouldn't approach them with something this big.

The only organization on the Moon big enough to handle Moon-wide information was the United Domes Security Office.

Berhane had met Noelle DeRicci once at a fund-raiser before Mayor Arek Soseki died. DeRicci had made it clear that she didn't do events for political reasons, and she had spent most of her time there cradling a drink and looking extremely uncomfortable.

It was a tenuous connection, but it was probably enough to get De-Ricci to listen to her.

Besides, Berhane was the daughter of Bernard Magalhães, one of the richest men on the Moon. That always opened doors.

Even doors that claimed to remain closed in the face of local politics.

Someone would have to deal with Berhane, and quickly.

"Get me the information you gathered," she said. "I'll take it up to the Security Office."

"This isn't something that can wait," Kaspian said. He must have thought she would go up to the office when she found the time.

"I know that," she said, hiding her irritation at his assumption. "The sooner you get me the information, the quicker I'll head up there."

He straightened his shoulders. She had never seen him stand up straight. He was taller than she had ever realized. She hadn't realized until that moment just how badly he slouched.

"I have everything now," he said with a dignity that she hadn't heard from him before. "And I'd like to come with you. You'll need me to answer the detail questions."

She stared at him for a moment. Usually she would say no. Dealing with people wasn't Kaspian's strong suit.

But she didn't need a diplomat here. She needed someone to tell the leaders of the Moon about something suspicious.

She could get them to listen—for a minute, anyway.

He could show them why they needed to investigate.

"All right," she said. "Let's go."

18

Flint returned to his office in Old Armstrong. He had only been gone part of the day, but it felt like he'd been away for months. After he closed the door, he stood for a moment in the silence.

Before he left, he had been running massive searches on a variety of Peyti-related items. He was investigating a corporation with the Peyti name that had a variety of meanings, one of which was, of all things, *Legal Fiction*. It apparently had paid all expenses for the Peyti clones' education. It had also sent the clones their masks every quarter.

Which meant that it had also sent the bombs.

Flint had compiled hundreds of addresses for the Peyti clones, and he had been in the process of checking the shipping records to those addresses when he got called away.

He had shut down the searches when he left. He hadn't known how long he was going to be gone, and he didn't want to leave systems open. This office had fantastic security, but no security was good enough to prevent a breach from a dedicated—and smart—attacker.

He ran his hand through his hair and considered his options. He had a human name now, and a connection to the Alliance. But he felt that the investigation of the Peyti clones was worthwhile as well.

He set up his systems again. He had saved his searches, even though they weren't complete. He could start them roughly from where he left off.

But he also wanted to make certain that he had one of his more powerful computer systems free. He needed to find Ike Jarvis.

That search would be even more delicate than the ones Flint was conducting into *Legal Fiction*. If Jarvis was running an illegal operation from inside the Alliance, then he would be set up to catch any potential incursions into his systems or background.

For that very reason, Flint had decided against doing his preliminary searches in the Security Office. He had debated telling DeRicci about Jarvis and then rejected that idea. He wanted to see what he could find first.

Flint also knew that DeRicci would suggest that Wilma Goudkins run the search. Goudkins worked with the Investigative Department of the Earth Alliance Security Division, but she was doing a lot of off-book searches for DeRicci. Goudkins was looking into databases that Flint couldn't easily access.

On the surface, a search for Jarvis's information would be a prime search for Goudkins.

But Flint had decided against it for several reasons. The main reason was Zagrando. Flint didn't want anyone else to know that Zagrando was here. Flint hadn't even told Murray Atherton who Zagrando was, and Murray had shown himself to be very trustworthy over the years.

Flint didn't know enough about Jarvis or Zagrando to know if a search into one man's history would lead to the other man. He didn't want to take that risk.

And, if truth be told, he wasn't certain he could trust the information he had gotten from Zagrando. Zagrando had been floating in and out of consciousness. He had lost his train of thought once in their conversation. Flint was worried that Zagrando had spoken a name that had no relationship to the Moon, and had simply been in his mind before he got injured.

Flint decided to work at his desk. He'd had enough moving around for one day.

Before he settled in, he shut off all of his links except his link to Talia and his emergency links. Normally when he did work this delicate, he shut off all of his links. But he couldn't do that right now. He couldn't leave his daughter unprotected, and he couldn't ignore the fact that something else could easily go wrong.

He sat down and started his search for Ike Jarvis. When Flint did these searches, he had learned to start with the most accessible place, and then move forward. So he opened the public Earth Alliance databases, keeping his own signature as encrypted as possible.

He needed all the official information on Ike Jarvis first.

Then Flint would find out who the man really was, and if he was at all relevant to everything that had been happening on the Moon.

19

Judita Gomez walked through the doors of the United Domes of the Moon Security Office as if she had done so every single day of her life. The ease with which she entered the building startled her. She knew that the systems here had checked her identification, but still, someone or something should have stopped her by now.

The entrance was wide and high. The doors looked like glass, but weren't. They weren't even clear. They just appeared that way, because the person entering saw her reflection, and then shadows from inside the building.

Only the shadows weren't real.

Gomez hadn't liked her reflection. She had put on weight since she left the *Stanley*. She got most of her exercise by walking around her ship, and the *Green Dragon* was tiny compared to the *Stanley*. She had thought she had put on only a little weight, and she was startled to realize she looked a bit tubby.

Then she smiled to herself. The reflecting doors were brilliant. They made the entrant focus on herself instead of the building. She had stepped inside, through obvious security that didn't seem to mind her, and into a high-ceilinged lobby that had almost no décor. No chair, no sofa, no tables, and no desks. Nothing for anyone to stand near or behind. Everything was open, and that made it all uncomfortable for her.

She almost felt like yelling, *Hey! I'm here! Make sure I'm not going to attack this stupid building!*

But she didn't, of course. Since yelling something like that would be suspicious, and, apparently, walking through wasn't suspicious at all.

She hit her first barrier just inside the obvious security. A clear wall shimmered before her, and across her vision an automated person appeared.

State your business.

She straightened her shoulders. *Earth Alliance Frontier Security Service Marshal Judita Gomez here to see Noelle DeRicci.*

You do not have an appointment.

That's right. She hated these automated greetings. All of them frustrated her, and the frustration piled onto old frustrations. Just knowing the automation existed frustrated her, even before the thing started talking with her.

Please exit the building and return when you have an appointment.

She had known it would say that. *Please let Noelle DeRicci know I'm here. This is an urgent matter.*

The avatar winked out and the wall before her hardened. Some people would have gotten discouraged here, but Gomez did not.

Then an oval-shaped face appeared in her links. The face belonged to a stunning woman with long, black hair that hung over her shoulder like a waterfall.

Are you the woman who contacted me? the woman asked.

Noelle DeRicci? Gomez asked, not certain how to respond to the query.

No, I'm her assistant, Rudra Popova. The woman looked irritated. *You did not answer my query. Are—*

I haven't contacted you, Gomez sent. *I decided I should come directly to the office. I just arrived on the Moon. You can check out the history of my ship, the* Green Dragon. *I have information that Chief DeRicci needs to hear.*

The woman—Popova—frowned. *What kind of information?*

I'd prefer to discuss that with her.

The woman's image vanished. Gomez sighed. She had no idea if she had made any impact or not.

Then the avatar returned. *Extensive DNA sample required. Test will be measured against DNA already on file. Place your hand on the barrier before you.*

Gomez did. She felt some heat against her palm, then the system told her to put her hand down.

She wondered how many people that request alone discouraged. She would wager quite a few simply walked away when they were told they needed to provide an extensive DNA sample, instead of the usual minor identity check.

Then the barrier dissolved from the inside out, slowly revealing the actual lobby. It was smaller than the one she had thought she was in.

Two human guards, one male and one female, waited for her.

"Marshal Gomez," the female guard said. "We're to escort you upstairs."

"Thank you," Gomez said.

She was certain she would pass through other security areas with tests she couldn't see. The guards flanked her. She could probably have gotten away from them, but it would have taken planning and work.

The Security Office Building didn't have the best security she had ever seen—she had run into some amazingly secure office buildings in the Frontier—but it had the best security she had seen since she arrived in Armstrong, and that included the port.

She had been startled when she left the port without going through security to enter the city. And she didn't have to go through any major security to get on the Armstrong Express, the city's public transit system.

Once she figured out who to report city matters to, she would report on the ways the city could tighten its security.

The guards led her to an elevator, but there were no obvious floors to press, and if they told it what floor they needed, they did so by links. The elevator did not telegraph what floors it was passing, nor could she feel it move.

For all she knew, once the doors closed, the elevator car remained stationary. Only the fact that the exterior looked different when the doors opened told her she had gone somewhere else.

A woman waited before the elevator doors. It was the woman Gomez had seen on the barrier in the lobby. She was thinner than Gomez expected, and her hair was more of a curtain than a waterfall.

Her gaze met those of the guards, obviously communicating with them on links, probably giving the guards instructions as to what to do next.

A male security guard came down the corridor and stopped just behind the woman.

Then the woman's gaze met Gomez's.

"Marshal," the woman said, "I'm Rudra Popova. Please forgive our mistrust. The Moon is not the place it was."

"I can only imagine what you're going through," Gomez said.

Popova took a step back, and Gomez saw that as a signal that she could leave the elevator. She stepped out, and the original guards remained. But the new guard came to her side.

"I have informed Chief DeRicci that you're here. Before she sees you, she would like to know what this is concerning."

Gomez looked at the security guard. He was staring ahead, as if the conversation didn't matter to him at all.

Gomez was prepared for this.

"Over fifteen years ago," she said, "I discovered an enclave of Pier-Luigi Frémont clones in the Frontier. I had a rather extensive encounter with them, and reported my findings to the Alliance. Nothing was done."

Popova clasped her hands behind her back. "This seems like information that you could have sent to Chief DeRicci. Is there some reason you wanted to see her in person?"

"Yes," Gomez said. "I have more information, some that I do not want to send on links."

"Please forgive our mistrust, Marshal, but none of us know you. I am loathe to send you into the Chief's office without much more vetting."

Gomez understood that. She nodded slightly.

"Whatever you need," she said in the most conciliatory tone she could manage.

"We'll need you to sit and wait right here." Popova led her to a small grouping of chairs near a desk that appeared to be in the corridor. "Thanks for understanding."

Gomez smiled as warmly as she could. She sat on the edge of one of the chairs.

She wondered what the point of this was. Because she knew they wouldn't let her so deep into the Security Office if they weren't sure she was who she said she was.

But then, the Moon had just been attacked by lawyers that the entire legal community had worked with for years. Confirming that a person was who she said she was clearly wasn't enough. Somehow they would have to divine if she meant the Security Office harm.

She had no idea how they would determine that. She hoped they had a system.

She clasped her hands together and made sure her gaze did not scan the desk or the other chairs. She had learned on the Frontier how to look almost harmless.

She found it ironic that she would need the same skill here, in the heart of the Alliance.

Where they had gotten lazy about protecting themselves—and were now paying the price.

20

TALIA SAT IN THE WAITING AREA OF THE MEDICAL UNIT AT THE PORT OF Armstrong. Until this afternoon, she hadn't known there was a medical unit in the Port of Armstrong, let alone that the medical unit had a waiting area.

It was hodgepodge of colors—gold walls, orange and green chairs, a pale blue couch that had seen better days, several scarred tables, and signs that popped up on the blank surfaces, warning her that she could be asked to leave if she violated this rule or that rule or some other behavior.

Getting in here had been surprisingly easy, but then, her father had made certain she had access to Detective Zagrando. She had to refer to him as Isamu Vidal, because that was the name all of his official identification used.

A lot of port security guards and several rookie space traffic cops guarded the medical unit. Two higher-ranked space traffic cops stood near the surgical part of the wing, clearly guarding Detective Zagrando—or Vidal, as she needed to remind herself to call him. Vidal without the Detective in front of it.

She felt safe, despite the fact that her father went over and over the escape plan with her should anything go wrong.

She didn't think anything would go wrong—not with this many police here—but she didn't know for certain. She didn't entirely understand what was going on. She figured her father would explain it to her. Or Detective Zagrando would do so when the time was right.

She hadn't been able to see him yet. They were still working on him.

The good news, according to the woman Talia had spoken to, was that he hadn't died yet. The bad news was that he needed extensive surgery and reconstruction. Every time they put nanobots into his system, they rebuilt a bit of him, but not enough to compensate for all the damage.

He's a very strong man, the woman had said. *Most people would never have survived those injuries.*

But no one could tell Talia when he would get out or become conscious.

So she sat and waited. She had a tablet from the Security Office, and the tablet's systems were encrypted, but her father had warned her that the standard encryption wasn't enough. If Talia did any research, she had to do it for items that everyone knew or no one would find suspicious.

Her father had made her uncomfortable enough that she wasn't going to disobey him, not on this one.

Besides, her mind wasn't exactly on it all.

She used the tablet to review Detective Zagrando's arrival. The port records were open, at least to family, which somehow her father had gotten her registered as. So she saw the weird little ship that Detective Zagrando had arrived in, and saw it struggle to land. Plus she saw the security vid of the medical staff getting him off the ship.

His wounds weren't obvious from the security vid, but the fact that people had to carry him off the ship showed just how badly he was injured. She had a sense—and maybe she was just putting herself in his place—that he was the kind of man who rarely wanted anyone to see how weak he actually was.

She couldn't get a lot of information from the footage—at least on Detective Zagrando's condition. So she turned her attention to the ship itself.

It hadn't been made inside the Alliance, at least according to the public sources that she used to trace it. In fact, there were limitations on its use within the Alliance. And it certainly couldn't be sold here, because it had some features that would need to be retrofitted before it followed Alliance regulations.

She had stopped researching after looking at the ship.

She was tired too, and still somewhat sad. She was glad that her father had trusted her to do this task, but she still felt out of her depth.

And beneath it all, she was angry.

Over the years, she had always assumed that Detective Zagrando, the kind man who might have saved her life, was doing great and compassionate things in Valhalla Basin. She had imagined that he saved a few other kids, and maybe got married and had some kids of his own.

Sometimes she thought he would have been promoted for all his good works, and every once in a while, she thought of contacting him to let him know she was okay.

When she first arrived in Armstrong, she thought about him a lot. She wondered if he wanted to adopt a girl whose mother had killed herself because of her crimes and if he needed help investigating stuff. She had been so mad at her father in those days; she blamed him for a lot of what happened, even though he hadn't even known she existed until he showed up in Valhalla Basin.

Eventually, she got that worked out in her head. Plus she knew deep down that Detective Zagrando had no place for her in his life. He had actually told her before her dad arrived that the VBPD job didn't leave any room for having someone special.

She couldn't exactly remember what Detective Zagrando had said or if he had actually said the words that he couldn't adopt her. But she had gotten the message all the same. And it had frightened her, because she had known already that she was alone, and in a lot of trouble, and she might not have had a future at all.

Then her dad had shown up. Detective Zagrando was the one whose behavior had let her know that her dad would take care of her. Detective Zagrando had trusted her father—maybe more than either of them realized, given the fact that Detective Zagrando was here now.

Alone. In a lot of trouble. And maybe with no future at all.

"Ms. Flint-Shindo?"

The voice startled her out of her reverie. She hadn't even heard the door to the waiting area open. Then she looked at it, and saw a very slender woman standing there. The woman had an angular face and dark, intelligent eyes. Her black hair was so short that it almost looked shorn.

"Yes?" Talia silently cursed herself. That response had sounded panicked.

"You're here for Mr. Vidal?"

"Yes," Talia said, unable to take the suspense. "Is he okay?"

"He came through the surgery. We had to do some old-fashioned rehabilitation work. We used some nanobots to rebuild his legs, but we had to add some material. It should be fine. He might want some actual reconstruction, though. He's a candidate for enhanced limbs with all kinds of special features. In fact, I would recommend it. But those aren't things we can do here."

"Um." Talia felt out of her depth. "Okay."

The woman smiled. She must have realized that Talia wasn't prepared to have these discussions.

"I'll talk to him about that in a day or so," the woman said. "When we can move him?"

"Move him?" Talia asked. She felt that fear grow. Were they taking him to prison or something? Had he done something wrong?

"He needs to be in one of the hospitals. I would recommend Deep Craters if he can afford it, because they do the best reconstruction on the Moon."

"Okay," Talia said, trying not to sound as confused as she felt.

"But it's better not to move him right now, and we have the beds. So we can keep him here for the next twenty-four to thirty-six hours."

"Okay." Talia knew she was repeating herself, but she'd never been in this circumstance before. And the woman—who had to be one of the doctors—was talking to her like she was an adult.

The woman smiled at her. "I think it would be good to have family with him."

"Me too," Talia said, then her breath caught. She'd almost added, *Wish I knew who they were.*

She knew that the woman wouldn't think anything wrong with what Talia had just said if she went to Detective Zagrando's side. She stood and smoothed the front of her pants, as if they were stained or something.

She was nervous. She hadn't seen him in a long time, and he had been really important to her, and now he was hurt. Her heart was actually pounding hard.

"Come with me." The woman held open the door.

Talia glanced at the chair she'd been sitting on to see if she'd forgotten anything. And there was the tablet, sitting on the armrest. She had nearly forgotten that. Both her dad and Chief DeRicci would have been mad if Talia had screwed up like that.

She picked up the tablet, then walked through the door, feeling a little lightheaded. She waited in the hallway for the woman to join her. The woman led her down the corridor through some more doors.

Signs appeared at eye level, warning Talia that this was the patient wing and required quiet at all times. The signs also stated that she was being scanned and if she was deemed a carrier of a whole slew of diseases or if she was actually ill, she would be asked to leave.

She wondered if they would tell her what was wrong—if something was actually wrong.

But no one said anything before the woman stopped in front of another door. It was clear, and there were windows on either side of it. The room beyond seemed small, but she couldn't see much more than the edge of the bed.

"He's here," the woman said. "If he wakes up, we'll know. He's being monitored all the time. But if something is bothering you, just say so out loud, and someone will come to the room."

What a strange way to let her know that she would be monitored at all times. But it was effective.

She thanked the woman, then went inside the room.

It smelled of almonds and something metallic. She swallowed hard, then forced herself to look at the bed.

The man on it seemed familiar—kinda, sorta—but he looked too small and too weak to be Detective Zagrando. His face was lined, his eyes were sunken into his sallow skin, and his hair was matted against his scalp.

His hands rested on top of the blanket and they, at least, looked familiar. Strong hands, square, with some scars. She remembered watching them move as he had talked to her, thinking he looked strong enough to take on the men who had kidnapped her mother.

Talia sank into the chair beside the bed, gripping the tablet hard. The woman closed the door, then nodded at her through the window and proceeded down the hall.

Talia looked at the length of Detective Zagrando. His legs were covered with some kind of healing cloth that was different from the blanket over his torso. There was a clear tent over him from the hips down. She knew it was monitoring everything, including the way the nanobots reconstructed the damage to his legs.

She made herself take a silent breath. She wanted to say, *Detective Zagrando, it's Talia.* But she couldn't. She didn't know how to address him, if he would find the name he'd been using familiar or not.

Then she looked around the room, saw panels that monitored stuff, saw all kinds of graphs and charts and images, none of which she understood. Medical things didn't interest her, so she never bothered to learn about them. She couldn't tell what was really going on with Detective Zagrando, except what the doctor told her.

I think it would be good to have family with him, she had said.

And family would be familiar with him. They'd take his hand or brush his hair back or talk softly to him.

She couldn't talk to him, not with him unconscious. She might say something wrong. And she didn't want to touch his face.

She looked at his hands, his familiar hands, and thought of holding them. She'd hugged him once, and he'd seemed surprised. That had been years ago, and she hadn't seen him in all that time.

Surely not every family member held the hand of someone who was ill. Maybe family members sat quietly while the person was really sick.

Especially if they were estranged.

And she hadn't been off the Moon in years. She'd say that if someone questioned her.

Because she couldn't touch him. It just didn't feel right.

She set the tablet on her thighs and leaned back in the chair.

She would just wait until he woke up. She would be a familiar face. Besides, she could tell her dad what was going on then, maybe send for him, make sure that they did everything they could do to take care of Detective Zagrando.

Mentally, she apologized to him for not talking to him. He would understand later. When he knew that the entire room was being monitored.

For all she knew, the links were too. She would have to be careful.

They would all have to be careful.

She'd tell Detective Zagrando that when he woke up.

She'd tell him a lot of things.

She settled in her chair, clutching the tablet, and she waited, hoping that he would wake up so she could talk to him, and hoping he would stay asleep until her dad could come.

Because for the first time in months, she was completely out of her depth.

21

THEY PILED OUT OF S³'S SPACE YACHT USING EVERY AVAILABLE EXIT. Rafael Salehi felt like he was unleashing an army of lawyers on the Moon, some of whom just happened to be Peyti.

Who was he kidding? A good third of them were Peyti, and they were all expecting trouble.

The yacht had docked in Terminal 25, where the Port of Armstrong placed its most expensive vessels. Apparently Schnabby had bought berths at all the important ports inside the Earth Alliance, including here, even though the firm didn't use the berths much.

When Salehi found that out on the way to the Moon, he decided to do an audit of the firm's books when he got a chance. Expenditures like this one, while convenient, were ridiculous. The yacht's arrival was probably the first time this berth had been used in ten years.

He was glad to have it, though. Terminal 25 provided a lot of perks to its clients, including privacy. He wasn't even certain how well the arrivals were monitored, since they were assumed to have been already vetted.

Although he expected to find out how tight the arrivals security was at any moment now.

He had traveled from Athena Base with thirty human staff, not all of them lawyers. Many of them were assistants and researchers.

Then he picked up the lawyers and legal theorists along the way, adding a smattering of former judges and professors, for another forty human passengers.

All of them were pouring out of the ship now. In theory, S^3 on The Moon had sent a dozen newly hired security guards to meet them once the group from S^3 on Athena Base left the restricted arrivals area of the port. Salehi had had Melcia Seng, who was acting as temporary head of S^3 On The Moon since Zhu's death, arrange that part of the arrivals. Salehi hoped that set-up would work.

Salehi hadn't told Seng that, in addition to the seventy humans he had brought with him, he had also brought twenty Peyti lawyers and their support staff (another forty Peyti). He had asked her to arrange housing for everyone, and more security there, but hadn't bothered with the details of Peyti versus human needs.

He figured the Peyti weren't getting off the ship any time soon, no matter how much Uzvuyiten wanted them to.

But the assault on the port, as Salehi was calling it (only to himself), was all Salehi's design. Once he found out that Uzvuyiten had wanted to make a statement, Salehi had arranged for the best statement possible.

He mixed the Peyti with the humans, grouping individuals with the same credentials together. The lawyers walked with the lawyers, the legal assistants with the legal assistants, the law professors with the law professors. He had the humans surround the Peyti.

Everyone was given specific instructions on how to behave. No one was to scream or shout. No one was to move in a threatening manner, and no Peyti was allowed to touch its mask unless ordered to do so by the space traffic cops.

Salehi was expecting dozens of space traffic cops and, so far, he was disappointed.

He had emerged from the ship first. Uzvuyiten had been second. They stood on opposite sides of the floor, just past the yellow line painted there for spaceport personnel, so that they wouldn't get too close to the ships and set off proximity sensors or security.

It was hard to get close to this ship. It was so large that it almost hid its dock. Even though the ship was classified as a space yacht, it was so big that it probably should have been registered outside of that class. The luxurious interior, the perks, and the speed, all kept it in the yacht category.

And probably some greased palms, courtesy of Schnabby.

Salehi tried to ignore the presence of Schnabby in his own mind. But it was hard: they were in a ship purchased by Schnabby, landing in a private berth bought by Schnabby, and on a mission initially vetted by Schnabby.

Although Salehi doubted Schnabby would have been able to handle the spectacle this had become.

Salehi looked across the floor at Uzvuyiten. He stood as rigidly as he could, given all of his strange health issues. His suit seemed even baggier than usual, covering his fingers and pooling over his feet.

Uzvuyiten's gaze met Salehi's. Uzvuyiten nodded. Salehi nodded in return. They had created a special encrypted link between them, in case things got out of hand.

Salehi had expected trouble by now. At least thirty staff were already crossing the floor, heading to the arrivals lounge. If the port had been monitoring the ship, then this berth should have been crawling with space traffic cops already.

But Salehi didn't want to mention that to Uzvuyiten. Uzvuyiten was spoiling for a fight—a legal fight, but a fight all the same. Salehi didn't want to make Uzvuyiten defensive before anything started (if anything was going to start).

The lawyers and the support staff kept marching forward—the S³ staff wearing suits that seemed to vary by color only, and carrying tablets that were often color-coordinated to the suits. The Peyti generally wore suits as well, which had to be Uzvuyiten's doing. Many of the Peyti hadn't worn human clothes when they were on the ship.

A few of the former judges wore legal robes. Most of those robes were an unrelenting black.

The professors and legal theorists generally wore whatever the business outfit of their dominant culture was—some wore saris, some wore kimonos, some wore rather sloppy vests with brown jackets. Everyone in this group somehow managed to look rumpled, as if just putting on the clothing had been a challenge for them.

Some of the professors seemed emboldened by the pending fight—eyes bright, shoulders back—but most hunched forward as if they expected to get hit.

Salehi didn't look at the side doors into the terminal. He didn't want to clue anyone that he was expecting trouble.

Uzvuyiten didn't look, either. Instead, they waited until the last of the support staff left the yacht and then fell in behind the group.

Which stopped moving as suddenly as if they had all received the same command.

The people in the back tried to see what was going on. The group in the middle spread outward, craning their necks as if they had a view of something.

Salehi glanced at Uzvuyiten, whose eyes seemed to sparkle. Since the Peyti's mouths were always covered by masks, it was impossible for them to mimic a human smile. So they often communicate amusement with bright eyes and shrugging shoulders.

But Salehi had never seen Uzvuyiten use that trick, so it felt odd to assume that was what Uzvuyiten's shrug meant. Sometimes Uzvuyiten used the shrug exactly as it was intended—as an I-don't-know or an I-don't-really-care gesture.

Salehi decided to stop paying attention to Uzvuyiten and hurried forward. Salehi wanted to handle the problem before Uzvuyiten got there, which shouldn't have been too hard, considering how difficult it was for Uzvuyiten to move quickly.

Salehi had to shove his way through his own people to reach the doors. The arrivals lounge doors were sealed shut, and a red announcement ran at human eye level:

Security Breach. Space Traffic Shall Arrive Shortly.

"When did this appear?" he asked Lauren Jiolitti.

Jiolitti was one of the S³ lawyers he trusted the most, which was why he had placed her near the front of the exodus. She had taken the time to clean up from the long trip, adding a strip of lime green to her hair to accent the lime green piping on her black suit. Today, her eyes were also lime green, which was both startling and off-putting.

"About three minutes ago," she said.

"Did we do anything wrong?" he asked.

"No," she said. She knew better than to volunteer that they were traveling with Peyti or had arrived with a throng of S³ lawyers. If anyone mentioned that at this point in time, they could harm the upcoming court case that Uzvuyiten was spoiling for.

Still, Jiolitti couldn't quite sound confused or surprised. She wasn't as good an actor as Salehi had hoped she was.

He scanned the front of the group. Several Peyti stood near the doors.

"Has anyone been able to enter the lounge?" Salehi asked Jiolitti.

"A few S³ legal assistants," she said, telling him without telling him that everyone who had stepped out of the berth had been human.

"Stand back, stand back."

Six humans wearing Space Traffic Control uniforms approached the group from the left side of the terminal. Four android guards, the kind that Salehi usually saw in prisons, approached from the right.

His stomach clenched. Android guards were designed to keep prisoners under control using any means necessary.

The potential for violence here had just grown.

The yacht's passengers were under instructions to follow all orders from the space traffic cops, so the passengers stepped backwards, placing a distance between themselves and the doors.

Salehi walked to the front of the group. Uzvuyiten hadn't gotten here yet.

Because Salehi didn't have a lot of time to establish himself as the man in charge, he spoke earlier than he normally would have.

"Officers," he said, using his most polite voice, "I see that there's a security breach notice. Is there trouble inside the port?"

"No," one of the officers said. She was tall and broad-shouldered, wearing some kind of armor as part of her regular uniform. Salehi recognized the armor's design. It had firing mechanisms in the wrists, easily activated with just a swipe of a finger.

She had laser pistols attached to her hips.

The other space traffic cops had similar weaponry.

Salehi's heart was pounding. "Then may I ask what the problem is?"

"State your business here," one of the other cops—a man—snapped.

"We are part of a long-established law firm, one of the most prestigious in the Earth Alliance," Salehi said, dropping into the script he and Uzvuyiten had prepared. "We are opening a branch office here in Armstrong."

"With Peyti?" A third officer asked.

Salehi was glad he couldn't see Uzvuyiten's face. Uzvuyiten must have loved that question.

"The Peyti have consistently produced the best legal minds in the Earth Alliance. We would be remiss as a law firm not to have Peyti on our staff." Salehi made certain that his hands were at his sides and visible, and his voice remained calm.

"You do realize that our most recent crisis, resulting in thousands of deaths, was perpetrated by Peyti lawyers," said the female space traffic cop.

Salehi had been prepared for this question, but he also knew there were no good answers to it. He could defend the Peyti clones, and get all of S³ banned. He could claim the clones were not lawyers, which was a lie, or he could respond with a bit of bravado.

Uzvuyiten wanted to defend the Peyti, but Salehi wasn't going to do that, not yet. He wanted to do it from the Moon, not from some space port nearby.

"I hate to say this about such a major disaster," Salehi said slowly, "but that crisis is not relevant to our staff's entry into the port."

"Excuse me?" the female cop said, and he could hear the anger in her tone.

The other cops moved forward, and the android guards shuffled sideways just enough to seem menacing.

"Everyone here has traveled for days to get to the Moon. *Everyone.* We have not had any contact with any perpetrators of crimes. Many of us have never been to the Moon before. The actions of others have no bearing on our entry to the Moon." Salehi spoke crisply.

Except in their prejudiced minds, Uzvuyiten sent him. *You forgot that part.*

Salehi ignored Uzvuyiten, as well. Uzvuyiten had pressed him to make that statement before they left the ship, but Salehi hadn't really agreed to it. He didn't want to alienate the cops further.

"Every single one of us is a member of the Earth Alliance. None of us have ever been arrested or caused any trouble anywhere within the Alliance. Moreover, over eighty percent of us are members in good standing of the Earth Alliance bar, and most of that eighty percent are so good that we're cleared to argue cases before the Multicultural Tribunals. Are you saying that solid, upstanding citizens, with this kind of background, are no longer permitted to enter the Port of Armstrong?"

Everyone was watching Salehi now. His people watched, Uzvuyiten watched, and the six space traffic cops were watching.

Or rather, five were. The sixth was glaring at him.

"I'm saying that we've been fooled before," she said. "They might look like lawyers, but they're actually killers in disguise."

Salehi gave her his most dismissive smile, the one he used to use in court when the person on the witness stand made an unrecoverable error.

"No, actually, you have not been fooled before," Salehi said, using the same reasonable tone he'd been using all along. "The port didn't do its due diligence when the Peyti clones came through. Nor did it do its due diligence six months ago when the clones of PierLuigi Frémont came through together."

She opened her mouth to say something, but he continued, not letting her get a word in.

"It's your duty, under *Alliance* law, to make certain that unsavory characters don't make it onto the Moon. You are to scan for problems with the things the passengers carry into Armstrong, and you're to scan for any diseases or other issues that they might have. One would think that twenty clones of a human serial killer would catch your attention."

She raised a finger, as if ordering him to stop. But he wasn't going to.

"One would also think that *hundreds* of clones of a Peyti serial killer would also catch your attention. But it never did. And those clones existed on the Moon, untouched and unnoticed for *decades*. Now you decide to take some action, but it's not sensible action. None of us are clones. We are setting up a branch of a highly profitable business in a community that has suffered severe economic hardship due to the two crises that you mentioned a few moments ago. And you want to block our entry."

Because we have Peyti along, Uzvuyiten sent through the encrypted link. *You need to say that.*

But Salehi didn't say that. He wasn't ready to make that argument.

"I told you before," he said to her. "We represent one of the best law firms in the Earth Alliance. Are you sure you want to bar any member of our team's entry into Armstrong?"

She finally managed to say something. "Are you threatening me, Mr.—?"

He shook his head, as if he couldn't believe her. "You know who I am, officer. You have already identified everyone in this part of the terminal. You wouldn't be here if you hadn't already run the identifications."

"All right, Mr. Salehi," she said, her voice threaded with irritation. "Are you threatening me?"

"With what, officer?" he asked as innocently as he could.

"With a lawsuit if we don't let you into the port?"

"Hm," he said, as if the idea had never occurred to him. "Do I have grounds?"

She stared at him, fury on every line of her face. "We have the right to bar anyone we want from entering the port."

"No," he said. "You don't. Under the Alliance laws you agreed to when you made this an Alliance port, you have no right to bar Alliance citizens from entering the port without just cause. Do you have just cause, officer?"

"We don't want Peyti lawyers here," one of the other officers snapped. The female officer waved a hand at him to shut him up, but it was too late.

The sentence was out there, spoken aloud, and there was no taking it back.

Salehi wanted to send a jubilant message to Uzvuyiten, but refrained. This wasn't over yet.

"And that sentiment," Salehi said softly, "is precisely why the Earth Alliance established the laws concerning the ports. No Alliance citizen can be barred without just cause, cause that will stand up in *Alliance* courts, not in local courts."

Bravo, Uzvuyiten sent.

He probably wasn't going to like what Salehi was going to say next.

"You might not like the Peyti lawyers," Salehi said, "and given what's occurred here, I don't think any of us can blame you."

Oh, I can, Uzvuyiten sent.

The rest of the staff stood very still. The other Peyti lawyers didn't move at all, as if they were afraid to make any kind of mistake.

"But fear is not just cause under Alliance law, particularly when the fear is based on appearance. Those concepts were among the first ever litigated in Alliance courts. We all find the appearance of some other species reprehensible, and we have to—under Alliance law—get past that sense, because—"

"I don't find their appearance reprehensible," the male officer said, moving around the woman. "I find them all reprehensible."

Salehi didn't look at him. Instead, Salehi looked at the woman. "You might want to ask your colleague to stop talking. I can tell you that two of the best attorneys in the Alliance are standing here right now—with incredible win records in the Multicultural Tribunals—and you are giving them so much ammunition for a court case against the Port of Armstrong that I'm not sure we would have to do more than file and present to win. This is a *prima facie* case of discrimination. And some of my colleagues here would be happy to pursue this matter in court. If I were you, I wouldn't give them the opportunity."

"Are you saying you're here to set up a court case?" the woman asked.

"Apparently, you didn't hear me initially," Salehi said. "We are here to set up a branch office on the Moon. I've told you that several times. I've told you that from the moment we started having this conversation. We have already rented offices and apartments. We will be spending quite a bit of money in Armstrong, if you let us through that port. Have you looked at the ship we arrived in? Have you noticed what berth we're standing near? Every moment you delay costs the City of Armstrong money it desperately needs to rebuild. How many other businesses are coming to the Moon these days? Not many, I would wager. Then why turn away one that is all ready to get started?"

"We don't want—" The male officer started, but the female officer waved him silent.

"You've had enough time now to vet each one of us," Salehi said. "You know who we are, and why we're here, and you have no good reason to bar our entry. So, are you going to let us into the arrivals lounge or not?"

The woman didn't move for a long moment. Obviously she was communicating with someone on her links. Salehi had no idea who it was, but he would wager it was someone with more seniority than she had.

"Go ahead," she said. "Go into the port. But let me warn you— all of you—you're not going to find a hospitable environment inside of Armstrong. You're better off opening your branch office on Mars or somewhere."

"I appreciate your opinion, officer," Salehi said. Then he stepped in front of his staff and pushed the double doors open. He waved a hand, so that everyone could walk past him. He held the door open for them, even though he didn't have to.

The people—and they were mostly human—inside the arrivals lounge looked startled at the S³ contingent coming at them. A few people moved away from the Peyti.

The officers watched the group leave the berth. Uzvuyiten stepped through last, and narrowed his strangely colored eyes as he went past. Salehi stopped holding the door and stepped inside as well.

As soon as they were away from the doors, Uzvuyiten sent a message along the links.

You should have let me handle that.

Salehi knew what irritated Uzvuyiten. He wanted the Peyti barred so he had a case. Salehi did not respond. Instead, he followed his staff through the port.

He didn't see the security guards that Seng had supposedly hired.

He hoped they would arrive soon, because the officers had had enough time to let friends who weren't wearing uniforms know that Peyti lawyers had just arrived on Moon soil.

They weren't in the clear yet. And even if they made it out of the port, they would have to be wary wherever they went.

Salehi didn't need the implied threat of those officers to convince him that the Moon was dangerous for every member of S³.

He just had to remember what happened to Torkild Zhu.

22

Ó Brádaigh had climbed the steps out of the substructure. To get into the control room that Petteway might have tampered with (*had* tampered with), Ó Brádaigh had to go clear across Armstrong to the oldest part of the dome substructure, where the main override controls were.

The Armstrong Express, the city's massive public transportation, stopped right near the substructure. And since he hadn't brought a car to work today, he took the fastest route he knew to get around town.

He stood in the center of one of the train cars, clinging to the handrails and feeling jittery.

Very few people rode the train in the middle of the day, particularly on the way to Old Armstrong. When the train went to the university, the cars were often packed, even at non-peak hours, but in other parts of the city, the train mostly went by empty.

He wanted to go to the front of the train and reprogram the controls, setting the speed even higher. But he knew he couldn't do that.

Still, he felt like he was wasting precious time.

He wished he could contact one of his colleagues, but he wasn't sure what he would say. That he suspected Petteway of tampering with the controls? That Ó Brádaigh had been in the substructure and had tried to get into the control room, even though he was no longer on the clock? That he suspected something bad was happening, but he didn't know what?

He needed to check on his own first, even though this damn ride fueled his impatience.

The main override controls had existed in Old Armstrong since the founding of the city. Over the centuries, more and more parts of the dome controls and maintenance moved to other parts of the city, but the override controls for the doors and for some other emergency systems remained here.

The propaganda issued by the City of Armstrong claimed all that remained in this site were controls for the oldest section of the dome. That propaganda was completely wrong. The controls for the oldest section of the dome stood alongside the other controls in the substructure where Ó Brádaigh had entered earlier in the afternoon.

Where he had seen Vato Petteway.

That sighting—and the fact that Ó Brádaigh couldn't access the main controls—bothered him enough that he contacted his mother to let her know he wouldn't pick up Fiona for another few hours. He couldn't let the situation remain, not because he was afraid something would happen, but because he was afraid something would happen if he didn't check.

The controls in Old Armstrong only changed access codes for the many doors and control rooms in the entire dome substructure. Some engineer, long before Ó Brádaigh's time, had decided it was safer to put the access code controls far from the doors, so that no one could change those codes on a whim.

It sounded good in theory, but in practice, it led to moments like this one, where an engineer had to leave one site and go to another just to finish an override.

After Ó Brádaigh's wife died, he wanted to streamline all of the dome controls. He had researched why one of his predecessors thought this access code idea was a good one. Turned out the engineer who designed this had been thinking about tamper prevention.

The engineer thought that anyone who had his access blocked to the control rooms would search around those rooms for ways to change the codes. Frustrated that he couldn't find the access controls, the saboteur would give up.

Ó Brádaigh didn't believe the give-up part of this, but he did think that one aspect of the separated controls made sense: If someone had to act quickly, he needed a partner at a different location. Generally, it was hard for saboteurs to have more than one person who could access the control panels and rooms for the domes. Having two probably thwarted several attacks.

If no one knew about the way the panels worked—no one outside the dome engineering staff in Armstrong. The other domes had a much less elaborate system, but none of those domes covered cities as large as Armstrong or as well known throughout the Alliance.

As the train swayed its way through the city, Ó Brádaigh got more and more nervous. *He* was acting like a saboteur, going into the substructure on his time off, investigating things without permission.

If Petteway was exactly what he seemed—a good man with a stressful job—then he might think Ó Brádaigh was doing something wrong.

It felt like Ó Brádaigh was doing something wrong. He wasn't trusting anyone, and that felt odd for him.

But he worried. He kept thinking that if others had been observant before the Peyti Crisis, they would have seen how oddly those clone lawyers were behaving. Or maybe someone in the port would have wondered why twenty clones of a human mass murderer were laughing as they made their way into the City of Armstrong six months ago.

Ó Brádaigh shuddered and looked at his city. His daughter's city. The place where his wife had died.

He'd been doing his best to rebuild it. He wanted to stay here. His family was here. His life was here.

And, if he took Fiona to Earth or some other part of the solar system, he felt like he would be running away from his home. He didn't want to do that.

But if he didn't calm down, he might have to, no matter how it felt to rebuild.

Or how deeply he was falling in love.

He didn't want to tell Berhane how obsessive he was getting about the dome. She might have understood; she might have suggested therapy. She might have decided he was no longer worth her time.

He gripped the railing tighter as the train rounded a sharp corner and headed into Old Armstrong. Everything seemed a little duller here, a little grayer, the dome a weird yellow as its exterior aged poorly.

Even though the dome here looked worse than the rest of the dome, it was stronger than other sections. The original materials the colonists used to build the dome were the strongest used on the Moon. They were also impossible to replicate. The colonists had used materials brought from Earth, materials now restricted because of scarcity and also because of toxicity in some parts of the manufacture.

Still, Ó Brádaigh wished that all of the dome could be as strong as the dome here.

The train stopped at a platform that looked older than the dome, even though it wasn't. The stop was maybe a hundred years old, but like so many things in Old Armstrong, it hadn't been maintained.

The dome engineers didn't want it to look fancy. They wanted everyone to ignore this site.

Ó Brádaigh waited until a few passengers moved out of his way, then stepped off the train. A woman stepped off a few meters down, looked at him as if he startled her, and then scurried to the nearest side street. She probably lived near here and was surprised to see someone else disembark at her stop.

Which meant that if something went wrong, she would remember him.

He took a deep breath. This was his last chance to change his mind.

The train's doors closed. Then it slowly left the stop. He waited until the cars passed, then let himself into a small building near the end of the platform.

He hesitated before opening the door to the stairs.

If something did go wrong, *all* of his behavior would be suspect. *All* of it. He froze for a half second, then decided he could do only one thing.

He had to register as at-work again. Who would tamper with anything if they admitted they were onsite?

He used his standard link access, and clicked his at-work status to on. Because he had worked ten hours already, the system asked him why he had returned to the job.

Saw something out of the ordinary, he sent. *Need to check it out. Have been denied access to standard control rooms, so am seeing what the problem is.*

Honesty: the best policy, as he repeatedly told Fiona. He hoped it would help him.

He placed his palm on the door handle, and it opened. He had to go through two more layers of security to reach the stairs leading down to the substructure.

He slowly made his way inside, the jittery feeling remaining.

Something was wrong. He could feel it.

He just didn't know what to do about it.

23

IKE JARVIS TURNED OUT TO BE A MAJOR SURPRISE—AND THAT SURPRISE was just in the public records.

Flint ran a hand over his face, eyes tired from scanning information that flowed to him from a variety of sources. He looked over the screen he had stationed at eye level and saw his other searches proceeding, some flagging information he would have to look at.

At the moment, however, he maintained his focus on Jarvis. Who, on the surface, didn't seem like much of anyone.

According to the easily accessible information, Ike Jarvis was a mid-level staff operations operative. He handled a lot of covert operatives, mostly working in Earth's Solar System. Although the public information didn't say so, Jarvis handled operatives who embedded with corporations whose headquarters weren't based in the Alliance or who sheltered much of their money outside of the Alliance.

Before that, Jarvis had worked as a targeting officer, and had some success outside of the Alliance. He had been decorated for a still-classified op that targeted pirates working at the edge of the Alliance.

The public information didn't directly state the target, but Flint had done enough of this research to know the codes and the hints that allowed him to glean a greater understanding than the simple facts should have allowed.

The interesting part of Jarvis's public history mentioned his loan to the Earth Alliance Security Division's Investigative Department. He had done a lot of work in Earth's solar system, and some of that work had centered on the Moon.

Once Flint saw that information, he was relieved he hadn't had De-Ricci assign Goudkins to researching Jarvis. For all Flint knew, Goudkins had worked with Jarvis.

The Jarvis loan had occurred in the middle of his targeting service with the Military Division Intelligence Service. Given that division's love of secrecy, Flint wondered if Jarvis was doing two jobs—one on loan for the Security Division and the other for the Intelligence Service.

If Zagrando didn't regain consciousness soon, Flint would have to do some research to see if that was when Jarvis's handling of Zagrando began. Flint had a hunch that it was.

Flint opened a small window on his screen and mapped Jarvis's timeline. According to that, Jarvis was still working on the Moon, or connected to the Moon, when Flint was finishing his detective's exam. Flint was still at Space Traffic then. He might have seen Jarvis, but not known who he was.

The images of Jarvis that Flint found—and there weren't many of them—seemed unfamiliar.

He almost contacted DeRicci to see if she remembered an Ike Jarvis, and then changed his mind. Flint wanted this research as complete as he could get it before bothering her.

As he started to dig, he hacked into Jarvis's government file. The hack was a low-level job, and Flint went through a backdoor that he had used countless times before. He knew this wouldn't set off alarms—or at least, it hadn't in the past.

So he was startled when something red flashed along his vision. He almost shut the entire search down, when he realized what the red flash was saying.

New update on the status of Ike Jarvis.

Flint knew better than to follow the lead directly. When he had trained new computer investigators years ago, he had showed them how following leads like that often enabled the established systems to detect the hack.

Instead, he logged out of the search, and logged back in to a different area in the government database, staying away from the intelligence database entirely. He searched for recent updates on military employees and found Jarvis almost immediately.

There was just a bit of information on Jarvis, with the promise of more information to come.

Jarvis was identified by his service number first, name second, and no listing of his position. He had been identified as part of a crew of a ship that had exploded in Earth's Solar System hours before. Cause of the explosion was unknown.

A single sentence caught Flint's attention.

Authorization for the ship's mission not yet verified.

Flint stared at that for a long moment. He'd seen such things before. Often, unverified information disappeared from news updates when the mission or the job became clear to the system. Then the system could properly filter the information to the right database.

The notice of Jarvis's death was automated, and the system had flagged an anomaly. The anomaly was that ship.

So Flint followed that trail, and paused when he understood what the ship was.

It was a vessel that looked like it was part of the Black Fleet.

The ship had belonged to Jarvis's old mission, the one where he targeted Black Fleet ships at the edges of the Earth Alliance.

In other words, this mission hadn't been part of his official job.

Who were you working for? Flint had asked Zagrando.

Zagrando had said, *Ike Jarvis, bastard. Killed him. Looks like he killed me too.*

Zagrando had destroyed that ship. Zagrando hadn't mentioned anything about his injuries except to say that what happened was "complicated." Clearly Jarvis was part of that complication.

And it was, as Flint had hoped, a promising lead instead of some confusion on the part of Zagrando.

Another promising lead.

Flint allowed himself a brief moment of excitement before he leaned forward and started the difficult task of digging deeply into the life and history of a man whose entire career was based on secrecy.

Flint had no idea if he could do this without giving himself away, but he was going to try.

And he was going to try fast.

24

IT'S HAPPENED AGAIN!

Odgerel woke out of a sound sleep, head pounding, klaxons echoing, voices screaming.

It took her a moment to realize all of the noise came through her emergency links.

She was alone in her bedroom, sprawled sideways on the mattress, her arm pushed up against the elmwood frame. She sat up, holding the covers tight against her chest.

"Lights," she told the house.

Slowly, the lights came up to a level she once called drowsy. They were amber, set to comfort her when she got near the time to sleep.

She allowed no screens in her bedroom, nothing except the antique bed, so old that the last person she had brought in here had blanched when he discovered she was actually using it. The front of the frame was designed to look like the entrance to the gardens she so loved in Beijing's Forbidden City.

Matching end tables rose from the floor as the lights came up just a bit more. Those were modern, just like the images painted on the wall. All of them were simply designed to look ancient.

The noise in her links continued. It took her another moment to realize that the noise was directed at her, and not a general emergency response.

She blinked. She was getting too old for this sort of thing; she did not wake quickly any longer, no matter what the emergency.

She sent a general query into the noise. *What is happening again?*
Bombings.

The word was simple, but it echoed from a thousand sources. She tried to isolate them, and couldn't. She then commanded her links to show her the first message to get through her sleep blocks.

It had come from Mitchell Brown, the newest employee at the Earth Alliance Security Division Human Coordination Department. Even though he had been at headquarters for a very short time, she already had a fondness for him.

He could see things that others could not.

She filtered the noise down, kept the visuals off, and set the link on audio only.

Brown, update me.

Sorry to wake you, sir, he sent, *but Hétique City was bombed a few hours ago. An entire swath of the city has been destroyed.*

Hétique City. Hétique City. She had to think about it for a moment. The name was familiar, but her brain didn't fire as quickly as it used to.

She liked to blame that on the depth of her sleep, but she suspected it was one of the first signs of aging.

And then she remembered. Hétique. There was some kind of government facility there.

What part of the city? She sent.

The clone factory, and some other Alliance buildings, he sent. *That's all we have.*

Clone factory. She sighed. Now she remembered. Hétique City had housed much of the Earth Alliance's human cloning capability for decades. Much of the cloning had moved off-site, especially some of the sensitive clone projects, but routine cloning for inside-Alliance operations still happened at the old facility.

How bad is the damage? she sent.

We don't know, Brown sent back. *We're just starting to get footage now.*

Was it attacked by clones? she asked. She was already trying to figure out if it had been attacked by the same mysterious operatives who had gone after the Moon.

We don't know that, either, Brown sent. *The attacks seemed to have come from orbit, and what we can see of the ships—well, they look remarkably dissimilar.*

She nodded. She wasn't sure the different types of ships meant anything. *Loss of life?*

We don't know that, either. The attackers hit during their night, and there are some reports that some of the clones were stolen. Most of the workers were in their homes, asleep, when the attacks happened. And I don't know if you've been to Hétique City, but the residential parts were several kilometers from the clone factory.

So, she sent, trying to cut through his excitement, and the dearth of information, *minimal loss of life?*

I'm not going to make that claim, sir, he sent.

She could monitor everything from here, but that would disturb the tranquility of her home. She had set up her home as a haven, a sanctuary, since her job was so very stressful.

I'll be at the office within the hour, she sent him. *I'll expect a full update when I arrive.*

Yes, sir, he sent and signed off.

The noise in her links began again, and she muted them. She probably shouldn't have done that, given the fact that there was yet another emergency within the Alliance, but she needed the silence so that she could think.

Besides, the screaming panic from her own people was disturbing the serenity of her bedroom. She couldn't afford to have this room in particular associated with the stress and terror of another attack inside the Alliance.

She pulled back the covers and slipped out of bed, her bare feet touching the warm wooden floor. She would get herself a bite of breakfast, since that would probably be the only food she would get for hours, and then she would go to the office.

Her head was still pounding—all that noise and worry, the klaxons, the alarms—had had an impact.

She needed to center herself before she could guide her people. They expected her to be an ocean of calm, a font of wisdom, the decisive leader who understood more than they ever could.

Sometimes, she wished all of that were true.

Especially in emergencies like this.

25

J<small>HENA</small> A<small>NDRE</small> <small>STEPPED OUT OF THE MEETING AND INTO THE CORRIDOR.</small> S<small>HE</small> was shaking with fury.

She sent an encrypted message along her links. *I told you* never *to contact me. Ever.*

The moment she sent that message, she regretted it.

She hadn't gotten this far by being careless.

It showed just how angry she was that Claudio Stott had contacted her without a good reason. Fortunately, they worked in the same division—sort of.

She could figure out a way to lie about that message if she had to.

She just hoped she wouldn't have to.

Chances were, no one would ever know about the message. She had the best encrypted links in the entire Earth Alliance Security Division. She was always changing and updating them, but she knew that sometimes the best links were not enough. She had completed dozens of successful investigations of Security Division employees simply by monitoring their links. Security Division employees always thought they knew more than anyone else about personal security.

Those employees were always wrong.

And now she was in the middle of the same situation, all because Stott had panicked.

I'm getting out, Jhena, he sent. *They found us.*

Now, he was simply repeating what he had said earlier, and she found that just as irritating as the fact he had contacted her.

She walked farther down the corridor before contacting him again.

The corridor was wide, and done in pale blues. The carpet was soft beneath her feet, and the walls designed to absorb sound.

She was in an unfamiliar part of the division. The meeting had been called without her permission, which was happening more and more these days.

Someone would get it in their head to investigate an important personage, and she would have to meet that someone on their turf.

She hated that. She was in charge of investigating employees of the Security Division, and therefore she should choose where the investigation happened.

At some point, she would have to reclaim her own place within the division, and that meant reclaiming her power, even on small things such as where meetings took place.

If she still cared enough when that happened.

If she cared at all.

She straightened her shoulders, trying to calm herself. She had to figure out a way to deal with Stott without drawing attention to herself.

The problem was that she didn't know enough about this area physically, and stupid her, she hadn't checked it out before deciding to attend the meeting. She had no idea if this section had been upgraded to include the latest technology, the kind that listened in on every single link transmission.

She had to act as if it did.

And she had to keep her expression neutral. She knew she was under surveillance. If she acted at all suspicious, some lower-level security personnel would walk past her, their investigative chips set so that they could detect elevated hormones or the presence of flop sweat.

She probably had elevated stress hormones, and she knew she was covered with flop sweat. She had never bothered to get one of those enhancements that prevented sweat, thinking them counterproductive—the human body sweated for a reason.

But sometimes that reason was complete fury tinged with a bit of panic.

Damn Stott for contacting her here and marking it as an emergency.

She opened the links again to tell him that he needed to calm down, and realized he hadn't stopped sending.

…if they stole records, we're screwed, Jhena. Imagine what they'll find…

Idiot. He was breaking every single directive she had ever given the group.

She had thought him an ally once. She had also thought him smarter than he turned out to be.

By then, she had already compromised the group by involving him.

He was in the center of everything, and now he was about to destroy it all.

I have no idea why you've contacted me, she sent. *Clearly, your division is having issues. Resolve it through the chain of command. You have no right to contact me directly.*

And then she blocked him.

She wanted to grab the wall and close her eyes for a moment, but she didn't dare. She had to look like she was dealing with the meltdown of an old friend, not a colleague who was going to destroy everything they had ever worked for.

And she still had no idea what had set him off.

She walked back to the conference room. The meeting had to do with some high alert notice every employee in Alliance government had received because of the Moon bombings.

When the meeting began, the sense of controlled panic in that room had amused her, even though she couldn't show it. Every employee in the Security Division seemed to believe that more attacks were imminent, and that the entire Alliance was at risk.

They were right.

They just didn't understand why she had chosen the Moon as the prime target.

And she wasn't about to explain it to them.

Even now, when the attacks hadn't quite gone as expected.

Initially, she had hoped for more destruction on the Moon. Then, when the lawyers and the architects and the money people would have felt it was safe enough to show up and repair the Moon, the Peyti clones would initiate another attack. The third attack would come shortly thereafter, destroying what remained of the domes and anyone who responded, and making the Moon a desolate place.

The Alliance would scramble, because there would no longer be an easy way onto Earth.

And everyone would panic, searching for the perpetrators. Or, as they were calling her and her team now, the masterminds.

She loved that word "masterminds." It made her seem much more powerful than she was.

She took a deep breath and reminded herself that even though the attacks hadn't quite gone as planned, the Moon was still on edge. And the third attack would come soon.

She had seen nothing to show that the Alliance—or, indeed, the thorns in her side on the Moon itself—had any idea what or when the next attack would be.

They hadn't yet figured out that she was exploiting the Alliance's own disaster playbook: Clean up the mess, then rebuild with tighter security.

Remembering what she had done—and what she was about to do—calmed her.

She pushed open the door and stepped back into the conference room.

That sense of controlled panic felt like a buzz along her skin. She liked the way everyone looked at her, as if they were frightened of everything.

Twenty humans, all theoretically in charge of some major part of the Earth Alliance Security Division. They sat around the table like scared children, staring at her with big eyes.

For a moment, she thought the sound of the door opening startled them. Then she realized she had missed something.

Maybe it was the something Stott had mentioned.

"What happened?" she asked.

Jiannan Faizy, the head of the Human Section of the Earth Alliance Security Divisions Prisons Department, placed his hands firmly on the table. It took her a second to realize he had done that because his hands were shaking.

She didn't know everyone in the room well, but she knew Faizy. She had recommended him for the position when she was promoted out of it.

He was trustworthy—or as trustworthy as someone who believed in the Alliance could be.

"We've been hit again," Faizy said.

She frowned. The next attack wasn't scheduled for hours. Who had screwed up?

"What happened?" she asked, because she knew better than to offer information in the form of a question. That was how suspects always tripped up. She wasn't a suspect—not yet, maybe not ever—but she had to be cautious.

"They attacked Hétique City," said someone in the back of the room.

Andre didn't look at the speaker.

"What?" She wasn't sure she had heard correctly.

No one was scheduled to attack Hétique City. The attacks were supposed to be on the Moon.

Were there copycats?

"Massive bombing run," said Abija Rowe, the second in command in the Political Department of the Security Division. "From orbit, it looks like."

Hétique City. Andre kept her hand on the door, more for support than anything else. Not the Moon. Hétique City was on Hétique, where the original clone factory was.

The factory she had used years ago. She hadn't made the Armstrong clones there, but she had used the original clones of PierLuigi Frémont, created in that factory, to help her raise the Armstrong clones.

Well, she hadn't exactly, but her people had.

She blinked. She wasn't concentrating on what the group was saying.

"Orbit," she repeated. "So no clones attacked this time?"

"Clones *were* attacked," said Bosco Welker of the Legal System in the Security Division. She didn't favor him with a glance either. His nitpicky nature had annoyed her before this meeting; she didn't want to deal with him now.

"We have no idea who attacked," said someone farther down the table. "They used all kinds of different ships."

Andre was jittery now. Stott was right; someone was on their trail.

But no one in this room knew that. The brightest human minds in the Earth Alliance Security Division—at least at the System level.

She wondered what the actual Division thought of this, then decided she didn't want to know.

She willed herself to be calm. Everyone here thought the attack on Hétique City was another attack on the Earth Alliance.

She could use that.

Her *group* could use that.

In the short term, anyway.

Long-term, Stott was right. They were going to be discovered, and they needed to plan for that.

If the Alliance held together after the next attack on the Moon.

She felt a surge of gratitude to those mystery bombers in Hétique City. Judging by the panic in this room, those bombers might have made the dissolution of the Alliance a lot easier. Panicked people made bad decisions.

She saw it every single day.

She sat down in the chair she had vacated when Stott screamed across her links.

She was much calmer now, but she didn't want to show that. She wanted to add to the panic, not quell it.

"Unknown ships," she said, rubbing her hands together the way that nervous people often did. "Has anyone contacted the Military Division?"

"Do you think we should?" Faizy asked, his voice shaking.

"The sooner we figure out what's going on, the faster we can stop it," she said, thinking that the faster they acted, the more likely they were to make a mistake.

The bigger the mistakes made inside the Alliance, the greater her opportunities.

"I think we need to contact the Human Coordination Department in Beijing," Rowe said.

The last thing they needed was a cool head like Odgerel's involved in all of this.

"I'm sure they know," Andre said.

"I'm sure the military does as well," Rowe said, a slight frown creasing her forehead.

"Let's see if we can track those ships," Andre said, ignoring Rowe. "Technically, it's not my job to plan this. I'm not even sure whose job it is."

Earth Alliance Security at this level was too scattered to address this kind of attack. That was one of the reasons she had planned actual attacks to shatter the Alliance.

For years, she had studied where the holes were.

Now, she was exploiting them.

And, apparently, she had help.

"We have to know the type of ship first before we figure out jurisdiction," Welker said, bless his anal little heart. "If those ships came from outside the Alliance, then the pursuit does belong to the military. But if they came from inside, then the security police need to take this one."

"Why didn't Hétique City go after them?" Andre asked.

"I think their port was destroyed," said a woman whose name Andre always forgot.

"I guess we better find out what actually happened," Andre said, and leaned forward, her mind racing, preparing to slow the people in this room down while she scared them half to death.

She hadn't expected this day to be fun. She had thought that kind of fun would happen on the morrow.

She settled in, ready to stir up some chaos, while she considered what else she needed to do.

26

FLINT WORKED AS FAST AS HE COULD. HE HAD TO GET UP EVERY NOW AND then to answer the pings his other searches sent him. Most of those pings were questions about refining the searches.

The other searches were going through reams of information, finding hundreds of shipments to the hundreds of Peyti clones on the Moon. The searches had found the first unique spot where the shipments came from, but that had been a false address.

Flint had set those searches to find the actual address, or figure out a way to track where the masks had come from. He hated that he didn't have several assistants at the moment; he really was doing a half-assed job. He could never figure out how to set those searches to figure out which subtle piece of information was important and which wasn't.

The other searches, for the corporation with the Peyti name that could be interpreted as *Legal Fiction*, were finding a lot of false positives.

"False positive" wasn't the most exact phrase he could come up with, but that was how he felt when he looked at them. Apparently, a lot of Peyti corporations had the words "legal fiction" in their names—another sign of how upright almost all Peyti were.

Corporations *were* legal fictions, no matter what anyone said. The fact that the Peyti admitted it in so many corporate documents would have amused Flint under different circumstances.

At the moment, it merely annoyed him—and it distracted him from the investigation into Ike Jarvis.

Still, Flint had managed to find out a lot in a short period of time, things that looked suspicious once Zagrando had pointed a light on them. Flint had a hunch, though, that when Jarvis was alive, he had figured out a way to explain most of those things away—or he had the time to cover his tracks.

His death had prevented the last of the track-covering.

Someone in the Alliance had flagged Jarvis's operational accounts within the last hour. Millions were missing, most of them moved from other operations. If Jarvis had been stealing money, it wasn't showing up in his personal accounts.

But Zagrando had arrived in an expensive bullet ship that was part of a larger space yacht design. Had he taken the money? Was that why Jarvis was after him?

Zagrando had said their relationship was complicated. Who had stolen from whom? Had they both stolen from the Earth Alliance?

Flint's shoulders tightened. He had sent his daughter to watch over Zagrando because, despite it all, he trusted the man. Had his trust been misplaced?

Then Flint took a deep breath. Even if Zagrando were malicious, he would have no reason to harm Talia. Zagrando had come to talk with Flint, and Talia would let Flint know when Zagrando was awake.

Besides, Zagrando was hurt too badly to harm anyone.

No one in the port's medical unit would let him near weaponry, even if he were getting better.

Flint had made the right decision.

It was amazing to him, though, how quickly he could question his own actions, based on so very little.

He delved back into the information on Jarvis.

Jarvis's time on the Moon was sketchy. It took a lot of digging to find a mention of Jarvis at all, and then it had been a surprising place—real estate records. In the name of the Alliance, Jarvis had rented or purchased a lot of property on the Moon over a decade ago.

Flint used those addresses to track Jarvis. Flint couldn't find evidence that the man actually lived on the Moon, but he did stay in hotels near those properties.

And one of those properties showed up in police records.

A man had gone missing from one of the buildings eight years before. Digging around showed that the man was a suspect in several property crimes. But he had been flagged as dangerous.

Flint couldn't quite figure out how someone went from petty vandalism and theft—property crimes—to being flagged as dangerous.

Then he dug into the allegations.

The flagger—who was anonymous—had stated that the missing man, Cade Faulke, was a suspect in the murder of dozens of clones. Clones were considered property, and their deaths weren't considered murder. But the flagger had called Faulke a murderer and issued a warning:

Anyone who kills that many clones is probably a serial killer in the making.

Flint disagreed. Anyone who killed that many clones *was* a serial killer. He had just found a way to make certain his behavior was ignored.

He tried to find a connection between Cade Faulke and Ike Jarvis, but aside from the building and the fact that the one-man office where Faulke worked looked like some kind of cover for intelligence behavior, Flint couldn't find anything quickly.

He worried that he was slipping into a side investigation that would take precious time from the important investigation.

He stopped, stood, and walked around.

Jarvis had rented a building to a one-man employment agency staffed by Cade Faulke, killer of clones.

Jarvis, clones.

Talia thought Zagrando was listed as dead in the databases because someone had killed a clone of him to make him look dead. Zagrando had said, *They used a clone to kill me. You know that? It's why I'm dead. Should've been a clue.*

At the time, Flint had dismissed the statement. Zagrando had accused Jarvis of killing him after Zagrando killed Jarvis, so Flint just figured a clone was involved, as well.

But if there had been a clone of Zagrando on Valhalla Basin…

Flint ran a hand over his face.

He was swimming in information, in theories, in too much data and not enough context.

He needed help, and he had finally hit a place in the investigation where he could bring in help, help he trusted.

He opened one of the links he had previously shut down.

Hey, Nyquist, he sent. *Can you investigate a case file for me?*

Sure, Nyquist sent back immediately, *because I'm doing absolutely nothing with my life.*

Even though they weren't speaking, the sarcasm came through loud and clear.

It's time-critical, Flint sent.

Isn't everything? Nyquist sent back. There was a slight pause, and Flint could almost hear Nyquist's put-upon sigh. *All right. Tell me exactly what you need.*

27

It had not been the day she had planned.

DeRicci ran a hand through her hair and wondered when she had last washed it. She could barely remember when she had last slept. And she knew she had eaten because her stomach still ached. Besides, she had shared that lunch with Wilma Goudkins, and had sent her to research some of the inside-the-Alliance names that Flint needed help with.

Flint, who had his own mystery to deal with. Who, apparently, had sent Talia to deal with part of it.

And now, a marshal from the Earth Alliance Frontier Service had shown up, unbidden.

With Popova's help, DeRicci had looked over all of the information that was quickly available on this marshal. Judita Gomez had a spectacular reputation, with more commendations than almost anyone else in the marshal service.

Until five months ago, she'd had her own ship, the *Stanley*. She had taken a leave of absence ahead of a possible retirement, but she had arrived in Armstrong on a ship called the *Green Dragon*, which seemed to have been fitted out with a forensic lab, oddly enough—something the ship had to declare as it made its way into Armstrong's port.

The ship's pilot hadn't answered a question the port posed: whether or not the crew was mixed. DeRicci found that odd—not that the pilot hadn't answered, but that the port was asking questions like that now.

The port should have been just as worried about humans as it was about Peyti and other aliens. After all, the initial attack on the Moon had been by human clones, not Peyti clones. DeRicci should probably assign someone in her team to talk to the head of the port, just to make sure this behavior didn't continue.

As if talking to the Port Master was part of her job description.

She was doing a lot of things that were not part of her job description.

Like meeting with marshals from the Frontier. DeRicci wasn't even certain where they stood in the security hierarchy. DeRicci worked for the United Domes of the Moon, and Gomez was as high as a law enforcement officer got inside the Frontier Department of the Earth Alliance Security Division.

Gomez had lots of experience dealing with other cultures and had been working in law enforcement longer than DeRicci had been alive.

That alone made DeRicci respect her.

But her trip here was strange. Gomez hadn't been this deep in the Earth Alliance in a very long time. She had stopped in Hétique City for a job interview with a government-owned cloning facility, an interview dutifully logged into her record along with a query from the interviewer, stating he wasn't certain why a woman of Gomez's skills would want a security position, no matter how well paid it was.

That job application was the only real red flag that Popova had found in Gomez's record. Gomez had stopped other places, but DeRicci couldn't find a pattern. Most of those places had been resorts or vacation spots inside the Earth Alliance.

If Gomez hadn't had the *Green Dragon*, and if her chief forensic officer, Lashante Simiaar, hadn't been traveling with her, DeRicci would have thought that Gomez really was thinking of retirement.

But old law enforcement officials—particularly those with high-adrenaline jobs, jobs with an unbelievable amount of autonomy, like the ones on the Frontier—never really retired. They usually died at work, sometimes in a dangerous situation that went awry, but more often still running their ship, but not doing the hands-on stuff any longer.

DeRicci wished she looked better. She wished her office looked better. She wished the Moon looked better.

That last thought made her smile ruefully. She had to remember what had been going on the last six months.

The least she could do, however, was be courteous.

She opened the door to her office and walked past Popova's desk. Popova had gone to check on another visitor who was arriving.

DeRicci wasn't certain if people were arriving out of the woodwork because they were some kind of strange disaster groupies or because they actually believed they could help with the disaster.

She knew that Popova had dealt with a lot of them in the past six months, and even more in the past two weeks. And those were the ones that the building's security system had vetted and the security personnel that DeRicci had hired long ago believed worth Popova's precious time.

Apparently, the current visitor was worth Popova's precious time. DeRicci was just glad Popova was handling things like that. Because DeRicci had more than enough to handle on her own.

DeRicci found Gomez in a small grouping of chairs not too far from Popova's desk. Gomez was a little heavier than DeRicci expected for such a high-ranking security officer. She had a square face, lined, no obvious enhancements, and her hair was threaded with just enough silver to make it glisten in the artificial light.

When Gomez saw DeRicci, she stood and extended her hand. "Chief DeRicci, please forgive the intrusion."

DeRicci was surprised that Gomez recognized her, then realized she probably shouldn't have been. If Gomez had come here on some kind of mission, then she would have done research before she arrived, just like DeRicci had done research before coming to speak to Gomez.

DeRicci had no polite way to answer the intrusion comment, so she didn't.

"Why don't we go to my office," she said. "I understand you have some information for me."

"I do," Gomez said, "and I hope it's information that you can use."

DeRicci did too. She didn't have the time to lose on a side issue. Popova had said that Gomez mentioned finding PierLuigi Frémont clones fifteen years ago on the Frontier.

DeRicci hoped that Gomez's information was less than fifteen years old. Because otherwise, this visit would be a waste of precious time.

28

THERE WERE A LOT OF UNNECESSARY ROOMS AND DOORS DOWN IN THE Old Armstrong dome substructure.

Ó Brádaigh tugged on the hem of his shirt, feeling grit on its fabric. His face felt grimy too.

He always felt dirty when he was in this substructure beneath the oldest part of the city. The environmental systems weren't quite as efficient here. They needed a complete overhaul, and before Anniversary Day, there hadn't been money in the city budget to do the work.

After Anniversary Day, everyone forgot day-to-day maintenance.

This substructure wasn't quite as deep below ground as the one he had been in earlier that day. He'd actually had to go down several flights, cross a small landing to another set of stairs, and climb back up several more flights.

When this part of the dome had been redesigned, its pilings had gone much deeper into the Moon's surface to handle more weight. The dome had gotten heavier and the foundation stronger in the past centuries.

But the engineers kept the old control rooms up and active, and didn't move them down several flights. That would have taken some digging out and rebuilding, and no one wanted to do that.

Besides, over the past several decades, most of the functions of this old control substructure had moved to newer parts of the dome's substructure. All that remained here now were the controls to the access codes and the secondary overrides.

And even those were supposed to be moved—or, at least, they had been on the agenda to move—before Anniversary Day occurred.

Ó Brádaigh ran a hand over his face, felt even more grit mixed with a bit of sweat. He probably had some dirt lines on his skin. He probably looked a mess.

The lighting down here was an odd, amber color, probably because the light casings had browned over time and no one had fixed them. The substructure control rooms—mostly vacant—were made of perma-plastic so old that it was yellowing and peeling. A few of the really old structures, the truly ancient ones, protected as relics by the historical society, were considered to be among the oldest engineering equipment on the Moon.

Ó Brádaigh walked around all of that, his shoes brushing over the plaque announcing the historic nature of this substructure, a plaque that only engineers had seen for at least a century now.

The access code control room was an innocuous little square struc-ture built against one of the side walls. The building had once been white, but looked brown and dilapidated in the amber light.

All except for the door. The handle—and there was a real handle—glistened.

Someone had used this recently.

Ó Brádaigh slipped on the gloves he always carried, and set them to col-lect all kinds of information from everything he touched, including DNA samples and fingerprints. He wanted evidence—of what, he wasn't sure yet.

Or at least, he hoped he wasn't sure.

He broadcast his own access code, let the door scan his retina, and hoped the door didn't want his DNA as well. He didn't want to take off the gloves.

The door didn't ask for the DNA. Instead, the door clicked as the old-fashioned locks opened. Ó Brádaigh turned the knob, and entered the small room.

It was hot inside, like it always was. There wasn't enough cooling equipment in here—apparently, the long-ago designer figured the "modern" systems didn't need anything to cool them down. Ó Brádaigh had always meant to fix that and had never found the time.

He downloaded the access information from the system so that later he could figure out who had been here before. Then he looked at the access codes to see what had changed about them.

Only a handful of codes had changed. The altered codes opened the sectioning equipment and the airlocks to the engineering-only parts of the exterior dome.

Ó Brádaigh stared at all of the changes, trying to figure out the double sets of commands before him.

Then the information tumbled into place.

The codes had been changed, yes, but only for six hours. After that, they would reset.

Ó Brádaigh leaned back, careful not to touch the walls, thinking about what he was seeing. Why would anyone change the codes for just six hours? Why reset them if—

Then he let out a long breath.

The controls were in the substructure because, no matter what happened to the dome, the controls would remain untouched. The damn dome could collapse and the controls would still be down here, protected and unharmed. Even if the environmental systems shut down, the controls would still work. They had been designed that way.

So if something happened to the dome—if someone *tampered* with the dome—someone with the right knowledge could come down here and investigate what had been changed, to see what had gone wrong.

If the controls automatically reset, however, the panicked engineer (or whomever had come down here) would think that nothing had changed with the access codes. It would take a suspicious mind to double-check the code history.

Without a reason, no one would.

It had been the luck of the draw that had put Ó Brádaigh in the substructure at the same time as Petteway. It had been Ó Brádaigh's nervousness that had caused him to check the access codes to the control room in the main substructure. And it had been his tenacity that had brought him here.

He hated what he was thinking.

He was thinking that Petteway had tampered with the sectioning commands for the dome. Or had left the control room open so that *someone* could tamper with the sectioning commands in the next few hours.

If Armstrong's dome didn't section, then it wouldn't take a large explosion to kill everyone inside. A very small hole in the dome would do. In fact, a hole small enough to conceal behind a building or a car or a box would be almost impossible to find in the short few moments that anyone would have to look for it.

His heart was pounding.

He needed to let the authorities know. He'd never done that before, and he had to be careful who he spoke to.

He would do that.

But first, he needed to do something else.

He would re-established the old access codes so that the engineers had control of the dome and its sectioning equipment again.

Then he would travel back to the part of the substructure where he had seen Petteway and make sure no one had tampered with the sectioning equipment.

And as Ó Brádaigh thought of that, his breath caught.

He would need help, not just here in Armstrong, but with the other domes, too. Because if the Anniversary Day pattern ran true to form, then what happened in this dome was going to happen in nineteen other domes as well.

He made himself take a deep breath and calm down.

First, he had to reset the controls.

Then he would take action—one important step at a time.

29

BARTHOLOMEW NYQUIST STOOD NEAR HIS DESK, WISHING TO HELL HE'D gotten some sleep the night before. He'd been doing too many things at once, and now Miles Flint wanted him to look up a case file, see what exactly was left out, and figure out how—or if—that case was connected to an Earth Alliance Intelligence officer named Ike Jarvis.

Yeah, sure, easy. Something Nyquist could do in an afternoon—if he weren't already handling a delicate murder case and trying to find time to interrogate one of the Peyti clones in prison.

Technically, Nyquist wasn't supposed to talk to the clones. S³ had issued an injunction against all interrogations of the clones without lawyers present. It had been done in the name of the Peyti government for some damned reason Nyquist didn't want to think about, but knew he had to.

So, he had gone into the Armstrong's euphemistically named Reception Center and told them that he had to see Uzvaan, the clone who had tried to kill Nyquist personally—and who, just the day before, had been such a good lawyer that Nyquist had recommended Uzvaan's services to Nyquist's former partner, a human woman who had been involved in the Anniversary Day bombings.

Ironies of ironies. Nyquist was the only police official with legitimate access to one of the clones, based on the previous case, because Uzvaan was still the lawyer of record for Ursula Palmette, the former partner.

But a real case had taken Nyquist away from all of that, a case that had its own irony built right in. Nyquist was the only detective that Andrea Gumiela, the chief of detectives, trusted to handle the murder of the S³ lawyer who had handed out the Peyti clone injunctions to every single law enforcement agency a week after the Peyti Crisis.

Gumiela wanted that case wrapped up quickly, before one of S³'s senior partners arrived on the Moon and took over all of the cases.

Nyquist wasn't sure he could act that fast. He knew who murdered Torkild Zhu, but Gumiela wanted an airtight case that would go to court. And that, dammit, would take time.

As would Flint's request.

Except that Flint said his request might lead them directly to the masterminds of this entire mess. Nyquist had thought Flint had enough to do, researching the information that Uzvaan had given them, but apparently not.

Flint had acquired yet another task.

Something had led to an eight-year-old case file with a flagged and missing perpetrator—and Flint wouldn't say what that something was. All Flint would say was that he was buried in information, and Nyquist was the only person he could trust to investigate this new lead.

How marvelous for him. For all of them. As if Nyquist didn't have enough to handle.

He towered over his desk and looked at the chair longingly. One little nap. And lunch. He might have had lunch, but he didn't remember. Up until a few days ago, he was the guy who brought lunch to everyone in the Security Office. Plus he had taken care of DeRicci when she stumbled into his apartment for her four hours of sleep.

He had been worried about her for weeks. What would happen if he got just as overwhelmed?

Then he sighed. "Got" was the wrong word. He *was* just as overwhelmed. Like her, he had been unwilling to admit it to himself.

"Hey, partner."

He looked up. Savita Romey had walked into the Detective Unit. She was smiling at him.

His heart was pounding. Until a week ago, he had thought her the most attractive woman he knew. She was still attractive, which irritated him. His heart shouldn't have done that school-boy skip when he saw her—not because she had changed, but because he had.

Like everyone right now, she was a bit ragged. Her dark hair needed a trim, and she had shadows under her eyes. She wore an oversized t-shirt with the name of her son's high school basketball team and the dates for the moon-wide championship they'd won just before Anniversary Day emblazoned across the front.

She had been wearing a variation on that outfit off and on since the attack.

But she hadn't been wearing that outfit when she and two of her colleagues had kicked Torkild Zhu to death for representing the Peyti clones.

Nyquist swallowed back bile. He still found her attractive. But he was no longer *attracted* to her. Now he found her disgusting.

And he didn't dare arrest her until he had the kind of evidence that would hold up in court.

"Savita," he said, because he couldn't bring himself to flirt with her any longer.

"Tired, partner?" She clearly recognized that his tone was off.

"We're not partners on this one, Savita," he said, mostly because he couldn't stomach the conversation. They had partnered on two cases—the Whitford case, which had nearly cost Nyquist his life, and Arek Soseki's murder on Anniversary Day, in the hours before everyone realized that the attack on the mayor hadn't been an isolated event.

"Not for lack of trying," Romey said. "I hear that the barriers to interviewing the Peyti clones might go away soon."

It was an open door, one he could walk through and get her to confess. He was recording the conversation, and thought it odd that the very act of recording it felt like a betrayal.

"Where did you hear that?" he asked.

She shrugged. "Around. You haven't heard?"

He didn't respond to that. He couldn't, really.

But she didn't wait for him to say anything. Instead, a small, secretive grin touched her lips.

"The lawyers got a message to back off," she said, and then she waited.

Her gaze challenged him. She raised her chin. He had worked with her long enough to recognize her tells.

She knew. She knew he was investigating that case. Investigating was one thing. But only Nyquist and Gumiela knew his mandate was to get the perpetrators into court.

"I had heard that," Nyquist said. "I also heard that only baby lawyers were left at S³. They're out of their league."

"Thank God," Romey said. "Now maybe we can interrogate those clones."

Did she know he was already interrogating a clone? Did anyone here? He hadn't told anyone, but that didn't mean the prison staff hadn't reported back into the Armstrong PD.

"We gotta figure out who is doing this," Nyquist said, changing the topic slightly. "I still think another attack is coming."

She made a dismissive sound. "If the damn lawyers had let us interrogate the clones the way we wanted to, we would know what the next attack is going to be."

She was feeling him out, trying to see where his sympathies were. Every cop knew that a detective could run a real investigation or he could run an investigation to satisfy the brass.

She clearly wanted to know which kind of investigation Nyquist was running.

"That assumes those clones actually know what's going to happen next," Nyquist said. "I suspect that the clones are just tools. You generally don't tell your tools how you plan to use them to build a wall."

"Or how you plan to tear one down." She walked around some chairs and stopped next to him. Too close, in fact. So close that had she done this before the Peyti Crisis, he might've leaned in to her.

Now, it took all of his strength to stand next to her without backing away.

"I get the sense you're not into this investigation," she said.

He wasn't exactly sure which investigation she meant. The investigation of the Peyti Crisis? Anniversary Day? Or of her?

No sense in lying to her, whatever investigation she meant. "Honestly," he said, "I'm way over my head."

She raised her chin even more, so that her face was close to his. It was as if she were trying to see his thoughts.

"Yeah," she said after a moment. "That's why sometimes you have to ignore things in the name of justice."

"What's justice, Savita?" Nyquist asked.

"We serve and protect, Bartholomew," she said. "That's our job. Sometimes detectives forget that. They get so wrapped up in the investigating, they forget about the serving and the protecting. You'd remember if you had kids."

That made him bristle. He hated it when people said things like to that to him, even when the circumstances weren't charged.

"Are you saying I don't care about the right things because I'm childless?" he asked.

She opened her mouth to answer, but he leaned in to her, so close that he could kiss her if he wanted to—which he most decidedly did *not* want to do.

"I love this city," he said softly. "I love the Moon. I *hate* what's happening here. All of it. And what it's turning people into."

She leaned in just a bit more. Maybe a centimeter separated their lips. "What's it turning people into, Bartholomew?"

He could feel her breath on his face.

"Monsters," he said softly. "Amoral monsters."

The color left her skin. She pulled back. The flirting had ended.

"Is that what you think I am?" she asked.

"No," he said. "That's what I know you are."

She took one step back and tilted her head as if he had slapped her. She bit her lower lip, then let it go.

"I'm not the enemy here," she said. "There are people out there in the universe who want to kill us just for being here, on the Moon."

"And before that," he said, "there were people who wanted to kill us for being cops, and people who wanted to kill us for being human, and people who just want to kill. You think the fact that there have always been murderers in the universe justifies the taking of a life?"

She squared her shoulders. Two spots of color had returned to her cheeks.

"There are murderers," she said. "Then there are *mass* murderers. And finally, there are those who look the other way when the mass murderers decide to take over. You don't let any of them get away. Not the mass murderers or those who defend them."

That was probably as close to a confession as he would get out of her.

"And you don't let the murderers get away either," he said. "You forgot that part."

"I didn't forget it," she said. "Under Alliance law, some killings are justified. Disty Vengeance Killings come to mind."

"We're not Disty," Nyquist said.

"But we accept their vengeance," she said.

"When *they* conduct it," he said. "But I've investigated a lot of Disty Vengeance Killings, and you know what, Savita? They go after the *perpetrator,* not the perpetrator's *lawyer.*"

Her eyes narrowed. Her cheeks were flushed, her eyes glistening. She seemed hurt that Nyquist didn't agree with her.

"I just told you about that lawyer," she said, then caught herself. "All the lawyers who represent those murderers. They're as guilty as the murderers are."

"No, they're not," Nyquist said softly. "Not even under Disty law."

She pointed a finger right into his chest. Her fingertip was as hard as the muzzle of a gun.

"You're taking the wrong side, Bartholomew," she said.

"I'm doing my job," he said.

"Like the damn lawyer," she said.

"So what are you going to do, Savita? Kill me too?"

She froze for a half second, then shoved him backwards. The shove was so hard he nearly stumbled over his own chair. He caught himself.

"You're a bastard," she said, and walked away.

He watched her go. So much for being subtle. So much for manipulating her into a full confession.

Maybe he should go to Andrea Gumiela and ask to be taken off the Zhu case.

But he knew what Gumiela would say.

She would tell him she didn't trust anyone else.

Because she had told him that before, when he tried to talk his way off the case after she had assigned it to him.

Someone had to investigate Zhu's death.

And apparently, that someone was Bartholomew Nyquist.

30

PIPPA DIDN'T RECOGNIZE THE WOMAN SHE SAW IN THE REFLECTING DOORS at the United Domes of the Moon Security Office. That woman had short, reddish hair and a careworn face with a frightened expression. Pippa recognized herself only by the distressed cotton shirt she wore over dark blue pants.

The inside of the building was shadowed so she couldn't see where she was going, and that alone nearly made her turn around.

But now, the midwestern politeness, drilled into her when she married her husband, kept her going. She had contacted a woman inside this office, a Rudra Popova, who was expecting her. This Popova woman sounded a bit hesitant about meeting Pippa, but this Popova had said that Pippa should come to the building.

So Pippa had.

She stepped inside, her heart beating so hard she thought maybe she was having some kind of attack. She made herself breathe. She was shaking.

She almost felt like crouching and running, then recognized the feeling. She had spent more than a year ready to bolt at the wrong kind of glance, the wrong person standing in a corridor.

That had been when she was Takara Hamasaki. Takara was back, not the courageous woman who had rebuilt her life, but the terrified woman who had run from place to place until she finally felt safe.

Pippa half-cursed herself. She wanted the courageous part to show up, not the scared rabbit-woman.

She made herself focus on the lobby. It was empty—at least as far as she could see, and she knew she wasn't seeing all of it.

The high ceiling felt fake, the lack of furniture was unnerving because she couldn't blend in with it.

She was in the middle of the entrance and she knew everyone inside of the building could see her, and she couldn't see them.

She almost bolted again, but common sense stopped her this time: They had seen her. She was on the security feed.

It wouldn't take much work to figure out that she had been the woman who contacted this Popova person. And then the security office could track Pippa to her hotel and from her hotel to her shuttle, and from her shuttle to her home on Earth.

She was committed now.

She took one more step forward, and the wall shimmered in front of her. A gender-neutral avatar appeared and Pippa jumped.

She clenched her hands into fists, concentrating on the pressure in her fingers. She couldn't will herself to be calm, but she could will herself to be calm*er*.

State your business, the avatar sent to her.

She bit her lower lip, glad she didn't have to speak out loud. She wasn't sure her voice would work.

My name is Pippa Landau. Rudra Popova is expecting me.

The avatar vanished. The wall in front of her disappeared entirely. The lobby extended before her—a *real* lobby, with furniture, and human guards, and corridors off to the side.

That should have calmed her more.

It didn't.

The female guard approached her. The woman was taller than Pippa and muscled—real muscles, not enhancements (or, at least, it looked that way to her).

"Ms. Landau, Assistant Chief Popova will join us in a moment. In the meantime, please accompany me away from the door."

A lump lodged in Pippa's throat. She couldn't speak if she wanted to, so she nodded instead. She followed the guard to the side of the room, where there was tall piece of furniture too wide to be a podium, but not really an actual desk. Some kind of guard station.

Pippa folded her hands together, because otherwise she would have to grab the guard station for support. She didn't want to do that. DNA.

Then she closed her eyes for a brief second.

Transferring DNA didn't matter at all. Here in the Earth Alliance, her DNA identified her as Pippa Landau. Outside of the Alliance, a deep search of the DNA (not a cursory search) would have identified her as Takara Hamasaki.

The caution she felt was deep in her bones. She had to remind herself that it didn't matter, at least not today.

She was going to tell the people here—the *strangers* here—exactly who she was.

As she stood there, a shadow fell over the door. Apparently the security system had activated again.

"My God, what is this?" the female guard asked the male guard. "No one ever comes here."

He shrugged, and seemed to be watching some kind of monitor. At that moment, a ding sounded behind Pippa.

The female guard put a hand on Pippa's shoulder, and she stiffened at the touch, but didn't move away. Then she silently cursed herself. Her reflexes had deteriorated. If something had startled Takara like that, she would have been halfway across the room in a nanosecond.

"Come with me," the guard said. "Assistant Chief Popova will see you now."

Pippa's heart was pounding. She nodded again. She wasn't just acting like a scared rabbit; she knew she looked like one.

The guard led her down one of the corridors. She passed a bank of elevators, one of which had doors that were just closing now. So that ding had been an elevator? Or a notification to the guard that Pippa could hear?

The guard opened a door not far from the elevators. A woman not much taller than Pippa stood inside. The woman had long, black hair, and looked so tired that Pippa wondered how she could even stand up.

"Ms. Landau?" the woman asked.

Pippa nodded. She still wasn't sure she could talk.

"I'm Rudra Popova. I work for the Security Office here at the United Domes of the Moon. I understand that you have some information to share?"

Pippa nodded again. She tried to clear her throat, and found she couldn't. She glanced at the guard, who was watching them.

"I can take this from here," Popova said.

"Are you certain?" the guard asked. "Because—"

At that moment, Popova raised a hand, interrupting the guard. Popova's eyes glazed. She was clearly communicating on her links.

Pippa swallowed hard.

Popova's eyes focused again, but she was looking at the guard. "We have yet another visitor," Popova said. "If she makes it through the secondary vetting, take her upstairs."

"Yes, sir," the guard said. "But don't you want—?"

"I'll be fine," Popova said in a tone that was so dismissive, Pippa cringed. The guard glared at Pippa then pulled the door closed.

Popova pivoted, her hair moving around her like a coat in the wind.

"As you can imagine," she said in a much softer voice, "things have not been the same here for months."

Pippa nodded, felt stupid, and made herself take a deep breath. She swallowed involuntarily, but her throat didn't feel as constricted after that.

"I'm…um…sorry to bother you," she said, then she almost smiled. Raymond would have appreciated that remark. Midwestern to the core. Begin with an apology, partly to break the ice.

Popova didn't respond to the apology. She just looked expectantly at Pippa.

Pippa took a deep breath to say something she hadn't said face-to-face in decades.

"Here, in the Earth Alliance, I'm Pippa Landau, but really, I'm a Disappeared. I'm not fleeing alien justice. I haven't broken any laws. I'm in hiding."

Popova's expression remained impassive. Pippa rubbed her damp palms on her pants. She had always expected a more dramatic reaction when she revealed who she was—a gasp, maybe, or a look of suspicion, maybe even a sympathetic comment.

But she wasn't getting anything, just a person she didn't know at all, staring at her.

She said, "I worked on a starbase in the Frontier. The local name for the starbase was Starbase Human, because the place deliberately catered to humans. I mean, aliens could land there and all, but they weren't really *welcome*...."

Pippa let her voice trail off. She was babbling. She'd never expected to babble when she told this. In her imagination, she would speak clearly and forcefully, telling the story of her escape as if it were a grand adventure and something terrifying all at the same time.

"Um, anyway," she said, stumbling as she switched gears. "The base blew up decades ago. I mean, it *was* blown up by a bunch of PierLuigi Frémont clones."

Popova's mouth opened slightly. Finally, a reaction from her.

"I think I'm the only survivor," Pippa said, "but I don't know. I believe I was being pursued by some more of those clones, but I'm not sure. Anyway, um, I'm pretty sure that was a practice event for your bombing here. On the Moon. And I thought, maybe, you could use it to track stuff down...?"

Two spots of color had risen on Popova's cheeks.

"Give me just a minute," she said, and then she left the room.

Pippa glanced around. She hadn't looked at her surroundings before. A few chairs, a table with nothing on it, and a wall that clearly had no network built in. This room was designed for exactly what Popova had used it for—a preliminary investigation room.

Popova had closed the door, making Pippa feel like a prisoner. She paced for a moment, her heart still racing. She half expected someone to take her into custody. After all, she had just admitted to being a Disappeared, and inside the Alliance, most Disappeareds had broken actual laws—major laws, not identity laws.

But Popova hadn't said anything about arrest.

Maybe, though, she had locked Pippa inside the room.

Pippa walked to the door, and pushed it. It opened easily, revealing the corridor outside.

She kept the door open just slightly. It was a psychological thing, so that she knew deep down that she wasn't a prisoner here.

She had been terrified of being caught, imprisoned, and killed for so very long, especially after she had admitted who she was, that she was trembling.

Only she hadn't said her real name, not at all.

She smiled just a little. She had always planned to reveal that. The fact that she hadn't surprised her. The secrecy had become a reflex.

She wondered what Popova was doing. Was she checking the name of Starbase Human? Was she investigating Pippa?

Was she getting the guards?

Pippa didn't know. But she was on this path now.

She had chosen it. She had chosen to help all of these people on the Moon, even though she didn't know a one of them.

Her son had told her that the Anniversary Day bombings weren't her problem. But they felt like her problem. They felt like they had always been her problem.

She had never talked to law enforcement about the base explosion. She had never done anything to get those clones captured or stopped or the clone creators imprisoned.

Maybe if she had...

She shook her head. Raymond used to say that what-ifs didn't matter at all. What-ifs were a foolish way to self-flagellate.

Usually, she took his advice. But on this one, she couldn't stop.

Maybe if these people caught her clones, she wouldn't be so afraid all the time. Maybe the nightmares would go away.

Maybe she could really slide into Pippa Landau, and not be terrified that someone was going to drag her away in the middle of the night, taking her children too.

Maybe, maybe, maybe. As useless as what-if.

Rudra Popova leaned in the doorway. "Ms. Landau," she said, "let's go upstairs. Someone up there would like to talk with you."

Pippa nodded. She was back to being a scared rabbit again. She didn't ask who wanted to talk to her, because she knew nothing about the way things worked here on the Moon. The name would most likely be meaningless.

She was on the road now, the road created by her latest choice.

She just needed to keep moving forward, and see where this road would take her.

31

IN THE PAST HOUR, ALL FLINT HAD DONE WAS WALK FROM ONE PART OF HIS office to another. He was deep inside two searches. The search into the Peyti Corporation that might or might not be named Legal Fiction was narrowing. He found numerous references to it on law school sites and in documentation concerning the Peyti lawyers back when they were law students.

But Flint couldn't find the shipping addresses for the masks that the Peyti lawyers had received earlier in the year. The one-of-a-kind explosive masks had to have come from somewhere.

So far, every address he found turned out to be false.

About a half an hour ago, he had opened a search into the masks themselves. They had to have been made somewhere. There were a lot of companies that made the Peyti masks. Most of the information was in Peytin, so he had to have translation programs working simultaneously with the mask search.

He wished he could speak to Luc Deshin. Deshin knew more about explosives than Flint ever would, and Deshin also knew how to do a proper search for them. Deshin had given Flint a lot of information about the explosives and things to search for after Anniversary Day. Flint had valued that, even though Deshin made him uncomfortable.

But Deshin had told Flint that he had done all he could. And Deshin had done a lot. He had left the Moon to track down the clones of PierLuigi Frémont, which had led to the name Jhena Andre, a woman who worked inside the Alliance.

Flint had given that name to DeRicci, and she had assigned Wilma Goudkins to investigate Andre.

Flint had tried shortly thereafter to contact Deshin, but had been unable to do so. Either Deshin had not answered deliberately or he was out of range.

Flint had no idea where Deshin had gone, but he did know that Deshin was not currently on the Moon.

And that made Flint uncomfortable. He needed as much help as possible.

Nyquist was investigating the Jarvis/Moon connection, but that was a small piece of information, and searching for the source of the explosive masks was a large piece of information—which was thwarting Flint at the moment.

He returned to his main desk and the Jarvis search. He had found the Moon connection fairly easily. Maybe he should search for a connection between Jarvis and Jhena Andre.

Flint knew he had to explore that connection carefully. He didn't want to tip off Andre, and he didn't want to interfere with Goudkins' searches.

But he didn't trust Jarvis to Goudkins, either. Not with Zagrando's life in the balance.

So Flint started compiling a list of all the people Jarvis had worked with, both on the Moon and off. The list was extensive. Jarvis had worked with a lot of people inside the Alliance, and those were the names listed publically.

They did not include Zagrando, at least so far. And Flint had been delving for a while now.

That meant that any undercover operative Jarvis ran would be difficult to find in a casual search.

At some point, Flint would have to work with Goudkins on the Jarvis connections.

Flint set up a program so that the computers would put together a list of Jarvis's known interactions, and leaned back.

That lack of focus—the sense of too many things to do at the same time—was driving Flint crazy.

Or maybe it was the fact that he wasn't finding what he wanted quickly. He wasn't used to being this cautious in his searches. When he searched for a Disappeared, he had set protocols to protect the Disappeared, but he often didn't care if he attracted the notice of whoever maintained the database he was searching in.

This time, he was acutely aware that most of the databases he was digging through were attached to the Alliance, and the attacks were coming from a faction inside the Alliance.

He had no idea what kinds of protections they had placed inside their databases. He would have placed extensive hidden tripwires, things that would never be obvious to the searcher, but which would notify of anyone poking around in the databases.

Flint had to assume that whoever he was looking for was just as smart about this stuff as he was.

He ran a hand over his face, then sighed.

No word from Talia yet on Zagrando's condition. She would let Flint know the moment Zagrando woke.

Flint thought about contacting her, then decided against it. He needed to continue his search, and Jarvis was his best lead.

Instead of looking for connections, maybe his finances would reveal something.

Flint leaned forward and began another search, this time into the monies in Jarvis's personal accounts.

Flint half expected to find a man who enriched himself off the sale of clones, but Flint didn't find anything like that. Jarvis had no hidden wealth, no living above his means.

All the search of Jarvis's finances showed was a mid-level Alliance civil servant who was barely making it from paycheck to paycheck.

So how did he get a Black Fleet replica ship? He couldn't have paid for it himself. It had to have been part of one of his operations.

But he hadn't worked on targeting of the Black Fleet for years. Flint felt confused by this detail. There was no name on that Black Fleet replica ship, at least that Flint had been able to find.

Still, there had to have been a crew and a history—*something* that would lead to the one piece of information that Flint needed.

He didn't know right now what exactly that piece of information was, but he would know it when he saw it.

And he hoped he would see it soon.

32

GOMEZ FOLLOWED DERICCI THROUGH DOUBLE DOORS THAT OPENED INTO an office. The office would have been impressive—if it weren't for the piles of self-cleaning food cartons on one desk, and the dirty clothes that peaked out behind the other. Tablets covered a few chairs. A blanket, scrunched up against the arm of one couch, looked like it had recently doubled as a pillow.

Signs of stress, everywhere, and none clearer than on the face of the chief herself, Noelle DeRicci.

DeRicci looked nothing like the vids that Gomez had seen of her. The woman before Gomez was thinner, older, with lots of gray in her curls. Those curls were matted, whether from inattention or a recent nap Gomez couldn't tell. The blanket suggested a nap, but the food cartons suggested inattention.

"Forgive me for being blunt," DeRicci said, "but I'm pressed for time here. I know you told my assistant that you have information we need. Before I hear about that, I want to know why you were looking for a job in Hétique City."

Gomez felt a frisson of surprise. She hadn't expected that piece of information to show up in a vetting.

"I wasn't," Gomez said. "I used my status as on-leave and an old posting the cloning factory in Hétique City had made on law enforcement sites to get into the factory itself. I was following a lead."

"What lead?" DeRicci's voice was flat. She was obviously tired, but still sharp.

Gomez appreciated that.

"Some PierLuigi Frémont clones originated there decades ago," Gomez said. "I wanted to see if that factory was the one that made the clones that attacked the Moon."

DeRicci's eyebrows went up dramatically, which was clearly an affectation, done for Gomez's benefit.

"Why would you care?" DeRicci asked.

She hadn't been kidding when she said she was going to be blunt.

"Because," Gomez said, "I think I could have prevented all of the attacks on the Moon years ago, if I had only followed up."

DeRicci leaned her head back as if she hadn't expected that answer. "Followed up?"

"I sent some injured PierLuigi Frémont clones from a moon in the Frontier to hospitals inside the Alliance, expecting that my division would follow up, interview the survivors about the strange situation they had been in, and stop whatever was going on. Instead, those clones were warehoused in the Alliance prison system. Shortly after I found him, he and the rest were killed."

DeRicci's expression didn't change.

Gomez wondered if her words had been too dramatic. Maybe she should have led into the Alliance involvement. DeRicci probably had no idea that there was an Alliance connection to the attacks.

The silence hung between them what seemed like hours.

Then DeRicci sighed. "How long ago was this?"

"About fifteen years," Gomez said.

DeRicci cursed. "Who plays this kind of long game? And why? What has the Moon done to these people?"

"I don't think it was the Moon," Gomez said. "I think these attacks are aimed at the Alliance itself."

DeRicci didn't seem surprised by that either, although she did say, "Well, it's sure looking personal to me."

Gomez nodded. "I understand that. It's personal to me too. I thought I was working for some kind of justice out there on the Frontier. I believed in the system, and the system failed so badly that you've lost millions here on the Moon. And I'm connected to it. I could have stopped it."

DeRicci let out a snort. "If I had a credit for every time I said that..." She swept her hand toward the couch set-up on the far side of the room.

Gomez walked toward it. DeRicci followed.

They sat down together.

"I want to hear what you have to say," DeRicci said. "I need to hear it all, without recriminations."

"Recriminations?" Gomez asked.

"Yes," DeRicci said. "You were out there, doing your job. Someone inside the Alliance wasn't doing theirs."

"Or someone was actively thwarting these cases." Gomez wasn't going to let DeRicci misunderstand this. Gomez firmly believed someone was trying to tear down the Alliance from the inside.

"Yeah," DeRicci said softly. "Do you have a name of who that might be?"

"No," Gomez said. "But I know where the clones were made. I have the name of that company—and it's not an Alliance-based company. It's in the Frontier. And I think with the right tools, we can find out who owns it."

DeRicci folded her hands together. "Why haven't you already investigated that?"

Blunt. Gomez was beginning to like that.

"It took the acting commander of my ship, the *Stanley*, months to gain that information. He had to go deep into the Frontier." Then, because Gomez had learned long ago that no one inside the Alliance knew how big the Frontier was, she added, "The Frontier is five times the size of the Alliance, you know."

DeRicci didn't seem angry at being told a fact that could be easily looked up. Gomez liked that about her as well. Not everyone in authority could know everything, and it was the comfortable leader who accepted what she didn't know as well as what she did.

"I hadn't known the Frontier was that big," DeRicci said. "Just that it *was* big."

"Nuuyoma got the information to me just before I came here," Gomez said. "Combined with everything else I've found and the Peyti Crisis, I felt you needed all of this information sooner rather than later."

"You said 'my ship.' You're going back when this is over, aren't you?" DeRicci didn't wait for an answer. "Leaving like that must've been hard. You made quite a commitment to get me this information."

It was Gomez's turn to be blunt. "No offense, Chief, but the commitment isn't to you or the Moon. The commitment is to the Alliance. The more information I got, the more I became concerned about what's going on inside our government."

"But you came to me," DeRicci said.

Gomez nodded. "You've suffered through these attacks, and you don't work for the Alliance. That makes you trustworthy in my book."

For the first since Gomez met her, DeRicci smiled. "That must be some book."

Gomez smiled in return. "Yeah," she said. "When this is all over, I'll share some chapters with you."

"Deal," DeRicci said. "You've got yourself a deal."

33

EARTH ALLIANCE INVESTIGATOR WILMA GOUDKINS SAT IN HER FAVORITE chair in front of the system she always used for investigations. Her heart was pounding as if she had run the Moon marathon.

She was doing extremely risky work, and she knew it.

Fortunately, she was deep inside her own ship, with a non-networked system that was hard to hack. She had armed the ship's doors so that anyone even attempting to enter would have difficulty—not that anyone else had access.

She worked here alone, and she often did her best work here.

The problem was that the system she used was networked with the Earth Alliance's Security Division. She just hoped no one was monitoring her work.

For the past few hours, she had been investigating names for Noelle DeRicci instead of doing her job with the Earth Alliance Security Division. Goudkins had argued to her partner, Lawrence Ostaka (the asshole), that she really was doing work for the Security Division by helping DeRicci, but Ostaka had made a fair point: some of the things that Goudkins was doing now compromised her job.

The fact that she didn't care had as much to do with her sister's death during Anniversary Day as it did with the fact that Goudkins believed—deep down—that there was a cancer inside of the Alliance, and for some reason, it was attacking the Moon.

With just a few hours of investigation, she had discovered that Jhena Andre had ordered the hold on any investigation of the PierLuigi Frémont clones. Andre was so high up inside the Earth Alliance Security Division that Goudkins couldn't even figure out exactly how Andre outranked her. Andre didn't seem to do much connected with the Anniversary Day attacks, but what she did seemed suspicious enough, especially when combined with the fact that she'd also had access to pure PierLuigi Frémont DNA from the day the man had killed himself inside an Earth Alliance prison.

The problem was that Andre could flag any investigation inside the Earth Alliance system without someone as low-ranking as Goudkins even noticing the flag. And Goudkins had been using Earth Alliance Security protocols to do her investigation.

Goudkins had taken some precautions. Part of her job was to investigate misbehaving Earth Alliance officials, so her little ship had all sorts of layers of security that usually made it invisible to someone who was watching their back.

The problem was that the people she usually investigated didn't have the reach that Andre did.

Goudkins had focused her initial search on Andre as if Andre were a candidate for a high-level job. Goudkins deliberately did *not* search for any connection between Andre and clones, Andre and PierLuigi Frémont, and Andre and the Anniversary Day investigations.

Eventually, Goudkins would have to do all of that. But she wanted to bounce what she had found off someone else before she did.

That someone would probably be Noelle DeRicci.

But Goudkins didn't want to leave her ship just yet, and hurry back to the Security Office. She wanted to check one other thing.

DeRicci had also assigned Goudkins to investigate Mavis Zorn. Zorn had been one of the Peyti clone lawyer's mentors at the Impossibles. From the information that Goudkins had discovered earlier this afternoon, Zorn's legal career had been a second career, begun when she was seventy and continuing until her death ten years ago.

The Impossibles were part of the Alliance Justice Division, which was not part of the Security Division.

But Goudkins had a hunch.

There was a big legal department inside the Security Division. That Legal Department, which some mistakenly called the Justice Department, prosecuted crimes and often determined whether or not a species had violated another species' laws. Most members of the Alliance who didn't travel or who hadn't really had much experience with the legal system didn't realize that legal violations often weren't as simple as they seemed.

Sometimes an alien could violate another culture's laws, but in arresting that alien, the other culture then violated *that* alien's rights. It could be a complete nightmare.

Goudkins had initially considered becoming part the Alliance legal system—even going back to school to join the Security Division's Legal Department—but when she realized how complicated and difficult it could all be, she decided against it.

Zorn, on the other hand, had worked in the Impossibles, where the Security Division's Legal Department's lawyers often trained. The prosecutors generally won their cases in the Impossibles. It was the budding defense attorneys who had the most difficulty there.

And all young attorneys coming into the Impossibles spent some time in defense. Including that Peyti clone lawyer. And Zorn had protected him against failure.

Goudkins dug into Mavis Zorn's resume. It didn't take much to find what she had done from law school to the Impossibles.

She had interned at a major law firm during law school. She had paid her own way through that law school, so she didn't have to go to the Impossibles at all after she graduated, and she didn't. She returned to that major law firm for one year. It was difficult to see what she had done for them, since she was a first year associate, who probably did everything some senior attorney thought amusing and/or important.

But Zorn left, even though she was on a career track, and she went into government service.

"There it is," Goudkins muttered, and then she smiled. The piece she'd been looking for. It wasn't quite a firm confirmation, but it was close enough: Zorn had gone from her high-paying law firm job to working for the Earth Alliance Security Division Legal Department.

Since Zorn's law career was her second career, she didn't need the money that so many associates needed to repay bills, even if they had served in the Impossibles to get their school loans repaid. Zorn could afford a lower-paying civil service job, one done for the love of government rather than the desire to earn a small fortune.

Or perhaps Goudkins was projecting. She smiled a little more broadly. She had also gone into civil service instead of the private sector. The choices in the Earth Alliance government, when viewed from the outside, seemed a little more black-and-white.

Only when a person became a member of the civil service did she learn that no decision was ever completely black-and-white.

Goudkins wondered if Zorn had ever learned that, had ever been disillusioned by it.

Goudkins would never find out, not unless she found something personal that Zorn recorded or wrote. And Goudkins didn't have the time to search for that—at least at the moment.

She dug deeper into the files. Zorn had started in the Security Division's Legal Department Human Division and, according to her files, served with distinction, whatever that meant. Then she got transferred to the Joint Division. Usually transfers came with a promotion, but she didn't get one. It seemed she had requested work in the Joint Division, where she would work with aliens.

Goudkins wasn't sure if that was odd or refreshing. Because Andre had repeatedly refused to serve with other species. Zorn had requested the opportunity to do so.

Goudkins looked a bit more, and paused, staring at the information on her floating screen. Zorn hadn't just requested a position with the Joint Division. She had asked to work in the Human-Peyti section of the Legal Department's Joint Division. Human and Peyti lawyers worked side by side there to handle issues that concerned both of their various governments.

Goudkins put a hand to her mouth, her index finger resting on her lips. Her heart was pounding. She made herself take a deep breath.

She couldn't get ahead of herself. That was the worst thing an investigator could do. She would find what she assumed was there rather than what was actually there.

But she had just found a connection between the Alliance Security Department and Peyti lawyers. A *direct* connection.

If only Goudkins could find a connection with Andre—or, at least, a direct connection with Andre. Because Andre was working in the Security Division at the same time as Zorn.

Goudkins made herself get up from the station and walk around the small research area. Zorn's position in the Impossibles might have been as simple as a woman deciding that she was better off using her skills to help Peyti lawyers with the difficulties of the Impossibles.

But why wouldn't a Peyti do that?

And, more importantly, if Zorn had worked directly with the Peyti *for years*, she should have seen the obvious: that the Peyti clones all looked alike. Most humans rarely looked past the mask, but Zorn would have.

She would have seen dozens of Peyti clone lawyers come through the Impossibles; more than that, she would have recognized them for the clones that they were.

And she had helped at least one of them deal with the Impossibles.

Had she helped the others?

Goudkins sat back down, feeling reinvigorated.

It wouldn't be hard to find out.

34

Ó BRÁDAIGH'S HANDS WERE SHAKING AS HE RESET ALL THE ACCESS CODES. He wiped sweat from his eyes. The little room was too hot, and his nervousness didn't help matters any. He double- and triple-checked himself, knowing that his mistakes could cause some kind of situation he could barely imagine. But he had to take that chance.

Technically, he hadn't been cleared to do this. He could almost imagine himself defending his actions to someone in authority.

I'm supposed to fix something that's gone wrong. Fix first, ask permission later. That's my job. I'm sure it's in the job description.

As if he actually knew. He'd never checked his job description. He'd been a dome engineer since he got out of training. He'd even apprenticed here.

And he needed the work. What would happen to Fiona if someone indicted him as a terrorist? His mother would take care of her, but it wasn't the same thing. Ó Brádaigh and Fiona were close; he was all she had, all she remembered. She'd never really known her mother.

The codes had only changed for the sectioning equipment and the entries to the engineering workspaces for the dome. Ó Brádaigh didn't want to think about what that meant, but he had to.

Best case: It meant nothing.

Worst case: Someone was going to prevent a huge part of the dome from sectioning, from protecting itself. Maybe the main part, with all the government buildings.

That was what he would do if he were a bad guy. And he would make sure there wouldn't be any way to override it.

Ó Brádaigh forced himself to concentrate, but it was hard. He was trembling all over.

When he was certain the codes were properly reset, he let himself out of the little room.

The air in the substructure was cold compared to the air inside that room. He shivered, blaming the cool air, knowing deep down that it wasn't the air at all. He ran a hand through his hair, felt the sweat beaded against his scalp, and tried to ignore how hard his heart was pounding.

All the while he'd been working, he tried to think about who he could contact for help, who would be the fastest and solve the problem, not who was the proper authority.

His brain had been working so fast that he actually had to stop more than once and force himself to concentrate on the task before him. He hoped he had stopped the problem right at the start, but he had no way to know.

By the time he finished, he had (again) ruled out contacting his colleagues in dome engineering. He might need them, but he wouldn't be the one to organize them. Because Ó Brádaigh would have to go through Petteway, and he couldn't do that.

As Ó Brádaigh stood in the substructure, feeling the cooler air dry the sweat on his body, he almost contacted the Armstrong Police Department, then stopped himself.

They couldn't help with the other domes. Sure, someone at APD could contact the other domes, but the information would get lost in the bureaucracy.

He needed to contact the United Domes of the Moon Security Office, and he had no direct way to do it.

He opened emergency links and was startled to learn that, while the Armstrong Police had a direct emergency contact, the Security Office didn't.

So he sent his message with bells and horns and flares, flashing red lights, and the panic he felt deep down.

Dome emergency! Dome emergency!

He didn't exactly know what to say, so he added not just his name, but all his degrees and his commendations, everything he could think of as part of this contact.

I have evidence of dome tampering and I think it might be Moonwide. Please, someone answer me! Please!

No one was. He cursed, then moved forward. He couldn't wait for them to answer.

He put the message on repeat and ran across the floor of the substructure to the stairs. He needed people everywhere. Someone had to investigate the dome itself, to see if there was something off about it.

He could tell whoever answered him where the weak points of the dome were.

Because if a dome engineer was resetting the codes, then a dome engineer had helped set up whatever damage was aimed at the dome.

The problem was that dome engineers spent their entire careers thinking about dome damage. There were—literally—a thousand different ways to destabilize the dome.

The question was, which one was the easiest or the most effective.

Then, as Ó Brádaigh mounted the stairs, he realized he was asking the wrong question.

Which damage scenario required some dome sections to be shut off?

His mouth went dry as he realized the answer.

Hundreds of them.

And the problem was that every single one would be instantly—and fatally—effective.

35

MARSHAL GOMEZ HAD BROUGHT NOELLE DERICCI AN AMAZING AMOUNT of information. DeRicci just wasn't certain what it all meant.

DeRicci sat on her couch, listening intently. At some point, she had grabbed her wadded-up blanket and clutched it against her stomach, as if the blanket could block the spread of bad news.

Someone—or rather, a bunch of someones—hated the Moon enough to plan these attacks *for decades.* These someones had hidden information all over the Alliance and beyond, and even had a practice attack in the Frontier decades ago.

Then these people casually destroyed clone after clone if those clones did not meet some exacting standard. Gomez had stumbled on this, and had gotten some clones imprisoned, nearly preventing the Anniversary Day attacks fifteen years before they happened.

DeRicci found herself wondering how many other chances authorities had had to stop these attacks and somehow missed the opportunities or had the opportunities blocked.

Gomez looked both enervated by all of this, and sincere. When she finished recounting her trip and all of the puzzling things she had encountered, and after she had sent back-up files to DeRicci, DeRicci asked the first question that had come to her mind.

"Have you heard of a woman named Jhena Andre?"

Gomez shook her head. "Should I have?"

"She's the only person we can find who is linked to the slow-grow Frémont clones. but she hasn't been selling the DNA. She's been sitting on it, as far as we can tell. I have people investigating her now."

"Who does she work for?" Gomez asked.

DeRicci gave her a thin smile. "The Alliance."

Gomez frowned, and as she did, the door to DeRicci's office burst open. Popova let herself in. Her cheeks were flushed as if she had hurried across the building.

"There's been another attack," she said, then waved her arms and brought up half a dozen screens. Some of them were still processing the facial program that DeRicci had been working on. Popova hid that work in the background, and showed images of burning buildings.

Gomez stood up. "That's Hétique City."

Popova gave her an odd look. "Yes, it is. How did you know?"

DeRicci stood too, letting the blanket fall. Her heart was pounding. Maybe it *was* no longer about the Moon. Maybe this was all the proof they needed that the attacks were about the Alliance.

Gomez's face had gone gray.

"I'm not liking this," she said to DeRicci as if Popova weren't there. "I investigate something, and then it gets wiped out. That happened with the imprisoned clones and now here."

DeRicci forced herself to focus.

"Where was the attack, exactly?" she asked Popova. "The city or some other part of Hétique?"

"The bulk of the explosions happened in an industrial park," Popova said.

"On the edge of the city?" Gomez asked.

"Yes." Popova was really frowning at her now, as if Gomez were disturbing her.

"That's the clone factory," Gomez said to DeRicci.

"Do you think there was information at the factory that got destroyed in these attacks?" DeRicci asked. "Information that we could use?"

Gomez nodded, her gaze still on the burning buildings, the loop of destruction that showed up over and over again in the visual feeds.

DeRicci didn't need to see more destruction. She'd seen enough of it on the Moon. She had empathy for the people on Hétique, but she couldn't let scope of the disaster sink deeply into her consciousness.

Still, she had to ask.

"How many dead?" she asked Popova.

"No one knows yet. The attacks happened at night, and most of the workers weren't at the factory."

"But people lived onsite," Gomez said softly. "There were children…"

DeRicci closed her eyes. She didn't want to think about any of that. She needed to keep her mind on the Moon.

"Do we know how this attack happened?" she asked Popova.

"From orbit," Popova said. "That's what they're saying now."

DeRicci's gaze met Gomez's. That wasn't the way that the Moon's attacks had happened.

"Were there clones involved in the attack?" Gomez asked.

"Not that we can tell," Popova said.

Gomez was frowning. DeRicci could feel the tension in her own face as well. This wasn't adding up.

Not an attack *with* clones. An attack *on* clones. Or the factory. Gomez was right. This was some kind of cleanup.

"This is a lead," DeRicci said. "We need to investigate this place from a different angle."

"We don't have anyone," Popova said. "And besides, we just got some more information. I have a woman in the lobby who saw the Frémont clones attack nearly five decades ago. She's—"

"Where was this clone attack?" Gomez asked.

Popova looked startled that someone had interrupted her. Or rather, that someone who wasn't DeRicci had interrupted her.

Popova glanced at DeRicci, silently asking if she should tell Gomez. DeRicci nodded.

"It was on the Frontier. Some place called Starbase Human?"

Gomez whistled as DeRicci cursed softly.

Gomez took a step toward Popova, as if unable to contain herself. "How is this woman connected?" Gomez asked.

"She says she's a Disappeared," Popova said. "I was going to ask you, Chief, if our Retrieval Artist friend should—"

But she couldn't finish because Gomez was already talking over her to DeRicci. "Nuuyoma said that the old Frémont clone was looking for a woman who had vanished after the attack. I'd like to talk to her, Chief."

DeRicci felt a little off-balance. She glanced at the burning ruins of yet another destroyed city, and found—sadly—that the images focused her.

"Rudra," DeRicci said, "does this possible Disappeared have any current information?"

"She's been living on Earth for twenty or thirty years or something like that," Popova said. "So, most likely, no."

"She might not have current information," Gomez said, "but she might have *valuable* information."

"If we had the time to get it out of her," DeRicci said.

"You don't, but I do. And I have someone on my staff who can investigate Hétique City for you, if you would like."

DeRicci wasn't sure how much she wanted to trust Gomez, at least not this early in their relationship.

"If you don't mind, see what you can find out from this woman," DeRicci said. "I think I know someone who can look into Hétique City."

Gomez gave her a knowing glance, then said, "If you need more information or help, I have an information whiz as well as one of the best forensic scientists in the entire Alliance on my ship."

"Noted," DeRicci said, then realized that sounded curt. "Thank you. I've got to handle one crisis at a time, though."

Gomez nodded. She looked at Popova. "You want to show me where this Disappeared is?"

"I've sent a map to your links," Popova said. "I'll let her know to expect you."

Gomez glanced at DeRicci.

"I'll talk to you shortly," DeRicci said to her. "Thank you for doing this."

"Let's hope she has real information," Gomez said.

DeRicci nodded. Then she waited until Gomez let herself out.

Popova started, "I think we should have Miles Flint investigate this possible Disappeared—"

"He's got enough to do," DeRicci said curtly. She had known that was what Popova had been thinking, and she wished Popova hadn't brought it up again. "I want to know what's going on with Hétique City, at least as far as the Alliance is concerned."

"I suppose I could—"

"No," DeRicci said. "We're all stretched here. I think we should see if Goudkins' partner can help us with this."

"Ostaka?" Popova asked. "Goudkins said he doesn't want to help us directly."

Goudkins didn't like Ostaka. It was pretty clear that Popova didn't either.

"This wouldn't be helping us directly," DeRicci said. "It would get us all information."

"I think he'd say no," Popova said.

DeRicci sighed internally. Obviously, Popova couldn't finesse this line of inquiry, so DeRicci was going to have to do it.

She needed to talk to Ostaka, and she needed to do it now.

36

THE ENTIRE ROOM OF TWENTY HIGH-LEVEL ALLIANCE SECURITY OFFICERS were panicked—and Jhena Andre was having trouble keeping a smile off her face.

She was tweaking them, pushing them, forcing them to think about what else could go wrong. And they were. Who knew that bureaucrats at this level had such fantastic and gruesome imaginations? She certainly hadn't. She should have pushed these people years ago. Her attacks might not have followed the Earth Alliance Emergency Response Playbook so closely then.

Half of the people in the room were leaning across the conference table, arguing with each other about who held jurisdiction. A quarter were staring forward, investigating on their links or with some screens that they carried with them, trying to see what kind of ships had attacked Hétique City. Another quarter was trying to find out where the next attack was going to be.

The Moon, idiots, she thought but didn't say. *Wait a few hours. There will be an attack on the Moon.*

She listened to the arguments. It sounded like the ships were not some coordinated military power, but different vessels from different parts of the Earth Alliance, maybe even some from outside of the Alliance.

If she were actually worried about this attack, she would have directed these nincompoops to see which ship had arrived first and from where.

But if she had to guess based on what she already knew, and what had been happening the last few months, she would guess that these ships had come from some criminal organization, one that finally discovered where the Alliance clones that got embedded into those organizations had been made.

Bye-bye huge long-term investment in stopping the Alliance's great criminals. Hello, panic.

She just loved this panic.

Then a red light flared over her right eye. She blinked, startled. Earth Alliance alerts were sent across the left eye because some doofus had believed that most people's dominant eye was their right.

She frowned, then remembered: she had set up her own personal alerts along her right eye.

Emergency alerts.

She stood. "I have to deal with something," she said to no one in particular, and then she stepped into the corridor.

It took her a moment to find where the alert came from and when she did, her knees actually buckled. She reached for the wall and held herself up, silently cursing at that moment of physical weakness. It would show up on the security feeds, and someone could trace it.

But the reason for the reaction wouldn't be as obvious to an outsider as her conversation with Stott might have been.

Because this alert told her that someone had found Mavis Zorn.

Andre let herself into a darkened office. The office smelled faintly of vanilla and sweaty socks. She moved away from the window and the door, and stood near the closest wall, with her back to the wall across from her. That way her face wouldn't be visible on security feeds.

Andre's heart was pounding. She hadn't expected anyone to find Mavis Zorn. The only reason Andre had put a security alert on Zorn's information was because Andre had put a security alert on all of the major players in her group.

Zorn had been very important. She had been one of the few willing to work with non-humans. Her willingness to deal on a day-to-day basis with the Peyti allowed the group to create the second "event" on the Moon.

It had been Andre's idea to use non-human clones for that event, but she had initially thought it impossible to execute. No one in the group wanted to deal with aliens. Aliens were the root of the Alliance's problems, after all.

Well, aliens and the founders of the Alliance. If the Alliance had been set up properly, then none of this would have been necessary. The founders should have decided that aliens had to abide by human laws, human ethics, and human morality. There was enough variation among humans to satisfy most alien legal scholars.

But Andre had watched the old debates and read the old documents. Even though the majority of humans had put that idea forth, it hadn't gotten adopted into the Alliance. The aliens threatened to walk, and the corporations, already a serious force in human-alien relations, saw billions leaving with the aliens.

So the "Earth" Alliance became a joke. It should have been called the "Alien" Alliance, because alien laws and alien morality trumped human laws and morality all the damn time.

Andre had lost both of her parents to alien laws, and the Earth Alliance had backed those rulings up—*allowed* the deaths to happen as if her parents had actually done something wrong. In the decades since, she'd lost countless friends the same way, and saw even more lives destroyed by the so-called justice inside the so-called Earth Alliance.

She had been only twenty when she realized the Alliance had to be taken apart and reconstructed. Eventually, with the help of others who had had similar upbringings, she realized that only a hard blow to the Alliance itself, one that dissolved so many of its assumptions, would allow her group (and others who believed the same way) to rebuild the Alliance according to *human* values and laws.

A real *Earth* Alliance.

If there were no aliens anymore, so be it.

She had loved the way that the Moon responded to what they were calling the Peyti Crisis. Blaming the Peyti. Exactly how it should be when something went wrong inside the Alliance.

The non-humans should have been blamed.

Zorn had agreed with that, but somehow she could still summon the strength to put up with aliens and alien law. Maybe because she had become a lawyer when she was Andre's age now.

Zorn had been one of the driving forces inside their group, and had remained so until her death. She had been the wise one behind so many of their systems—limited contact, meetings in isolated places with no tech allowed, and Andre's personal favorite: no name for the group.

The moment you name the group, Zorn had said, *it not only becomes traceable, it also becomes a legal entity. When people belong to that legal entity, their behavior becomes tainted with the association. When you say "group," you could mean anything from a group of friends to an actual organization.*

Andre, who had become the leader early because she had more of a vision than anyone else had, took those words to heart.

She rested her forehead against the cool wall. Zorn had died more than a decade ago. There were people inside the group who hadn't even known her or known of her involvement. She had been dead so long that she shouldn't have been relevant to any investigation.

Unless one of the damn Peyti clones talked.

Andre closed her eyes for just a moment. Those damn alien screwups. They should have all died in the attack, but their attack fizzled—thwarted by that security chief on the Moon. Or maybe thwarted because the Peyti were not competent to pull off something that complex, even with all of the hand-holding her group had done.

It should have been as simple as getting a message on the links at the exact right moment, activating the mask bomb, and dying along with everyone else in the vicinity.

Instead, most of the damn clones had been *arrested.*

Then Andre had hoped that some good people in the Moon's various law enforcement agencies would kill the Peyti clones out of anger, but that hadn't happened either. Some goody-two-shoes law firm decided to work with the Government of Peyla to protect the stupid clones.

Alien and cloned. Why anyone would *ever* defend creatures like that was beyond her.

And Andre hoped, if the last attack went off without a hitch, she wouldn't have to worry about it.

She let out a deep sigh. She didn't like the fact that *someone* had found Zorn. Someone with Earth Alliance Security credentials.

That meant the investigation was closer to Andre than she had initially thought.

She made herself stand up, straighten her shoulders, and calm down.

Even if they caught her—even if they *killed* her—the last attack would happen.

Even if they caught her—even if they *blamed* her—the last attack would destroy every dome on the Moon. They would forget about her. The crisis would be too big.

And Hétique City had helped her. The Alliance now believed the attacks were moving away from the Moon.

The more distracted the authorities were, the greater the chance Andre had to escape.

If she needed to escape.

She swallowed hard, regained her composure, and decided she was done with her meeting. She would go back, let those panicked imbeciles worry about Hétique City and the end of the universe, and tell them she had to deal with a minor personal emergency.

Then she would track whoever was tracing her.

Maybe she could stop this new investigation in its tracks.

All she needed to do was try.

37

BERHANE THOUGHT SHE AND KASPIAN WERE GOING TO BE STUCK IN THE lobby of the United Domes of the Moon Security Office forever. What was Noelle DeRicci thinking, having only two human guards?

They seemed to be busy, too, ushering people to and fro, ignoring both Berhane and Kaspian as they stood inside the smaller-than-expected lobby, after they had been cleared by the first part of the system.

When Berhane used her links to try to contact Security Chief De-Ricci directly, she got a user-not-authorized message. The link Berhane had tried to use wasn't the standard entry-level messaging system for the Security Office. It had supposedly been DeRicci's direct link.

But either DeRicci had shut down that link or too many people had been trying to contact her.

Berhane had already told several avatars that she and Kaspian were here on important business, business that couldn't wait, but those avatars didn't seem to care.

Which wasn't entirely true: they had cared enough to let her into the main part of the lobby, just in time to see some mousy woman with out-of-place short orange hair be led into a back area.

Since then, Berhane and Kaspian had waited.

He'd paced around the lobby at least five times, touched the blank walls as if trying to see if there was some kind of entertainment screen, and peered over the guards' station. The remaining guard, a man, studiously ignored both Kaspian and Berhane.

When Berhane tried to talk to the guard, he'd said, *I only do as I'm instructed. I have not yet received instructions concerning you.*

Well, she was thinking she'd issue some instructions concerning him. Two guards weren't enough. This entire entry into the building was somewhat ridiculous. She and Kaspian had enough time to set off all kinds of bombs—although, to be honest, she wasn't certain if the security that allowed them into the building had already checked them for things like weapons and explosives.

Kaspian finally stopped pacing, and stood just a bit too close to her.

"This is working well," he said snidely.

She agreed. Her father would have been making a scene by now. Her father and Torkild both.

Maybe she should too.

Berhane walked over to the guard.

"Look," she said. "We have some really important information that can't wait. I don't know what it'll take to get in to see Chief DeRicci, but we need to talk to her now."

"I know," the guard said. "Your friend already told me that."

She glanced over her shoulder at Kaspian. He had spoken to the guard briefly, but quietly. She had thought Kaspian had simply been checking to see how long they had to wait.

Apparently, Kaspian's method marked the difference between a loud scene and a quiet scene.

"Do you know who I am?" Berhane asked.

"The system says you're Berhane Magalhães, head of the Anniversary Day Victims' Identification and Recovery Service," the guard said.

She wasn't sure how he managed to sound so very uninterested.

"Yes, I am," she said, "and we've found some information in doing the recovery work that needs to get to the chief right away."

The guard sighed. "I've already sent your information upstairs twice. They're having a busy day."

So was she, and she had just wasted an hour waiting in a *lobby*, for no good reason.

"I'm also the daughter of one of the richest men on the Moon," she said, hating that she had to pull rank. "My father is putting billions into rebuilding the domes. If he were here—"

"If he were here, he'd have some kind of hissy fit that would impress the local politicians," the guard said. "The thing is that Chief DeRicci doesn't care about politics, and you can't impress her, except with information."

Berhane felt the frustration rise. She closed her hands into fists.

"Well, impress her with this," Berhane said. "We think we've found the next clone attackers."

The guard's head snapped back. His gaze met hers directly for the very first time. "What?"

"We believe we know who the next attackers are. We've found evidence that points directly to them, and we need to talk with the Chief *now*."

The guard looked momentarily confused. "We have no protocols for this," he said. "You'll have to give me a minute."

"I've given you *sixty* minutes," she said, clipping her words just like her father would. "You get a *maximum* of five more. After that, my partner and I will figure out another way to attract attention, even if it means setting off some alarms."

The guard held out his hand in a "stop" gesture. "Oh, lady, you don't want to do that. Believe me."

"I will, if—"

"Just give me a minute. I'll make sure someone talks to you, okay?" He looked panicked, even as his eyes glazed while he sent some message along his links.

Berhane held her ground. She wondered if he was saying he had a crazy woman here, who was making the wrong kinds of demands.

Then she shook off the thought. She was here on legitimate business with a legitimate concern.

Just because she wasn't used to standing up for herself didn't mean that her doing so offended others.

She glanced over her shoulder at Kaspian. His lips were turned up in a small smile.

He approved which, for some reason, she found reassuring.

She nodded back, then turned her attention to the guard and the elevators beyond him.

She hadn't been bluffing. If someone didn't talk to her in the next few minutes, she would go past this guard station and up a flight of stairs.

She was going to talk to Noelle DeRicci, no matter what it took.

38

It took another fifteen minutes of searching Jarvis's finances before Flint found something really strange.

Jarvis had requisitioned millions for an operation shortly after Anniversary Day. Alliance protocols required the requisitioning employee to list what the money was for, and when or if it would be returned. On undercover operations, like this one was supposed to have been, the money (which was significant) had to be returned or accounted for within a week.

The money had been requisitioned months ago, but the operation was still marked as open.

Flint had almost missed that, because it seemed so standard. But the money had been requisitioned shortly after Anniversary Day, and the amount was a lot.

Flint couldn't find exactly what kind of operation that Jarvis had requisitioned the money for. Flint wasn't certain if he should have found it, or if the code for undercover operation was enough for the Earth Alliance.

That might become something to investigate.

At the moment, though, Flint was following the money. The money always told an interesting tale. And this money was no exception.

The amount had been backed by the Earth Alliance Currency Department, something Flint had initially overlooked when he first noticed the missing funds. He had continued searching for incriminating information on Jarvis, before his brain ordered him to circle back to the Currency Department.

The fact that the Currency Department was involved was unusual. Not the kind of unusual that a computer search would find or even flag.

Computer logic would figure this: Jarvis worked for Earth Alliance. He had been handling a vast sum of money. That vast sum of money had to be guaranteed by someone within the Earth Alliance.

Any search by a computer wouldn't find the different divisions to be an anomaly. Which was probably how the transfer was designed. Nothing flagged it, except Flint's unruly brain.

He had seen a name—Pearl Brooks—and had done a quick check, as he always did when he was searching, to see if the name belonged to a real person or was an alias of some kind.

Brooks was a real person who worked for the Currency Department. High up in the Currency Department, in fact.

Flint had glanced at that, glanced away, moved deeper in his search, and that was when the information hit his brain.

Currency Department? Why would the Currency Department be financing a Security Division op? The Security Division had an extensive budget. All operations, overt and covert, came from that budget.

Earth Alliance Treasury Division would give the Security Division its operating budget, but through the funds designated for that Division, not from Currency.

The Currency Department handled exchange rates and the money supply inside and outside of the Alliance. Handling exchange rates inside the Alliance was the most important part of the Currency Department's job. Many of the alien governments maintained a local currency for use on their home worlds. That money had to be converted into Alliance credits for any purchases, travel, or businesses done outside of the home worlds.

And Flint didn't even pretend to understand how the money supply was determined. He'd never had to know.

He felt a frisson of excitement. He had found an important link: Brooks and Jarvis. Flint had to check on procedures with Goudkins, but he knew in his gut that this was the thing he had been looking for.

He had known there was a conspiracy inside the Alliance, and it had covered its tracks. He had found hints of it before, but never something so blatant.

As Deshin had said to Flint, and as Flint had kept in mind ever since, operations like Anniversary Day cost a fortune to pull off. Add the Peyti Clones, Legal Fiction, and the entire second operation, and the expenses were off the chart.

No small group could fundraise its way into that kind of money. And Deshin had repeated that most criminal enterprises with Anniversary Day kind of money didn't have the leadership at the top that could manage a plan conducted over decades. There was no guarantee that the leadership would remain in place that long.

Factor the Peyti Crisis into all of this, and the expense got too much, even for the large (if loosely associated) organizations like the Black Fleet. No criminal organization would spend its money this way.

But a rogue political organization hidden inside a real organization with nearly unlimited funds—that might be possible.

Flint would have to check with someone who knew finance better than he did, but he suspected that someone with a criminal bent could figure out how to skim a fraction of a percentage off the float inside any currency exchange. If Flint was right, doing that in an organized and somewhat hidden way would net billions. If that money wasn't being moved into a separate bank account, then it wouldn't get flagged.

The money would be moving from one Alliance account to another, and the movement would seem innocuous.

Flint had just seen how the computers ignored it in his search for Jarvis's funds.

Flint smiled. He had finally figured out how an operation of this size received funding and remained relatively hidden. He wondered if the participants in the organization were hidden in the same way. That would make them impossible to see—until someone figured out a way to catch a glimpse of them.

Then their appearance would become not just clear—but obvious.

Flint paused for just a moment to allow that feeling of movement, of *finally* going forward, sweep over him.

Then he delved deeper into the research, hoping he found the masterminds behind the attack before they found his searches.

He knew it was only a matter of time before they did.

39

LAWRENCE OSTAKA HAD TAKEN OVER THE TOP FLOOR CONFERENCE ROOM to run his investigations. Initially, he and Goudkins ran their investigations from here, but since the Peyti Crisis, Goudkins had helped DeRicci.

DeRicci hadn't been in the conference room for longer than a moment since then. The room smelled of coffee and spicy cologne, and the faint odor of someone else's office, instead of the neutral scent of a little-used conference area.

Ostaka sat at the head of the large table, all kinds of equipment scattered around him. DeRicci recognized some of it, and didn't recognize the rest of it.

Ostaka looked up as DeRicci stepped all the way inside the room and closed the door behind her. He was a gray man who wore a rumpled gray suit and didn't seem to care much about his own appearance. He had taken the suit coat off and draped it on the back of his chair. A little extra weight made him look doughy rather than comfortable.

His gaze was hard, as if she had interrupted him, as if she worked for him.

DeRicci made herself smile at him. He was here on sufferance. Her sufferance.

"Have you seen the attacks on Hétique City?" she asked.

"Yeah," he said.

"Do you have any information on them?" she asked.

"Not anything more than what's been in the media. I'm searching now."

He seemed a lot more focused than she would have expected. During the Peyti Crisis, he had viewed the problem as something DeRicci had to handle, not something that concerned him.

It had been one of the things that had greatly angered Goudkins.

"Would it help to use some of our systems?" DeRicci asked.

His eyebrows went up. One of the terms that allowed the Earth Alliance investigators to work in this conference room was that they couldn't have anything more than standard access to the Security Office's systems. DeRicci had been adamant about that, although she had broken that rule when Goudkins had joined them during the Peyti Crisis.

"It might," Ostaka said, and she could tell: he was trying not to sound too eager.

Had he been waiting to be included, like Goudkins was? Or did he have another agenda?

DeRicci had a system in her office that dated from the Peyti Crisis that was minimally networked. She could let him use that system.

"I think someone's blocking Earth Alliance investigators," Ostaka said. "I know that sounds weird, but I keep getting bounced back every time I try to find out what happened on Hétique."

Was he trying to explain his eagerness? Or was he just being enthusiastic? She'd never seen Ostaka be enthusiastic before.

"Maybe if my searches look like they're coming from another entity, I might get through," he said.

"Or you might be doubly-blocked," DeRicci said without humor. "After all, the Moon's been the primary target until now."

"Yes, it has," he said. "But this seems different, doesn't it?"

"It does," she said. "I'm wondering if it's something else entirely."

He nodded, then tilted his head slightly. "It's possible. You'd think that the masterminds, as you call them, would continue their focus on the Moon."

"But that's what we expect," DeRicci said.

"Yeah." His mood seemed subdued. "It is, isn't it."

He was silent for a moment, as if he were contemplating all of it. Then he added, "Maybe, when things didn't go as they expected, these so-called masterminds decided to try an attack away from the Moon."

"It's a possibility." DeRicci had thought of that too. "It would certainly confirm that the attacks were about the Alliance, and not about the Moon."

He looked startled. "You think that's what's going on?"

She had forgotten that he hadn't been in any of the conversations about motivations for the masterminds.

"I'm guessing at everything," she said. "I just want to find these people and stop them before more goes wrong."

He nodded. "Wilma thinks you're on the right track. Do you?"

DeRicci shrugged. "For all I know, there's a third attack coming and it's been planned for decades. I can hope that I'll figure it out before it happens, but I'm not going to bet on it."

His skin seemed even grayer than it had earlier. "You said *third* attack. You don't think this attack on Hétique City is the third attack?"

Apparently, she didn't. She hadn't realized it until she had spoken up. But she wanted his help confirming her hunch.

"Oh," she said, thinking quickly. "I meant the third attack on the Moon."

He nodded. "If the attacks are six months apart, then you have time."

"We only have two data points, maybe three," DeRicci said. "That's not enough to draw a conclusion. If we use the two, then you're right: there will be another attack in six months. If we add in Hétique City, then we could have another attack tomorrow."

"Or five years from now, after everyone has become complacent," he said.

"No," she said the word before she even had time to think. "When you have someone on the edge, you don't wait five years to finish them off. You do it fast."

His eyes narrowed a little. His mood seemed to shift again, but to what, she couldn't quite tell.

"Well," he said, standing up. "You want me to work on your systems?"

He made it almost sound like a repair. She was definitely going to make sure he only had access to the non-networked system.

"Yeah," she said. "I can use your help. Let's see what you can find out."

40

Ó BRÁDAIGH MADE IT BACK TO THE MAIN SUBSTATION. DAMN PUBLIC transportation. Damn him for not having a car.

I don't need a car, he often told his nagging mother. *The city is so well constructed, I can get wherever I want to go faster on the Armstrong Express.*

Except on days like today, when he needed to move at lightspeed. Plus, half his links shut down as he moved from one section of the dome to the other, something he had never noticed before.

But he had noticed it this time, because he had been constantly pinging the Security Office. As he got on the Express, he had gotten some kind of canned response, something about being in a queue.

And then nothing, as if the pinging had been shut off. He asked one of the others on the train if their links had shut down, and the man responded that they were going past some high-security buildings that had link-blocking equipment installed.

Ó Brádaigh had sent his emergency message to the Security Office again as he got off the Express and ran to the substructure.

This time, he didn't take the stairs down; he took the elevator. And he was halfway down in that cramped box when he was informed that he was in a queue again.

As the elevator doors opened, he pinged the Security Chief, DeRicci, and got a not-authorized message. He would have to contact someone at the Armstrong Police Department in a moment, or maybe contact Berhane. She knew everyone. She might get him through.

The substructure was empty this time. The cool air covered him with the faint scent of regolith mixed with the dry smell of active equipment.

He sprinted to the control room, and slammed his hand against the identification panel. This time, his identification ran, the system worked, he had a password, and he was clearly authorized.

The door clicked open.

He wiped his palms against his pants, then stepped inside. Lights came on, and the system greeted him by name.

He ignored that—for a moment. Then realized he could use the vocal feature of the system. Now that he was reinstated, he could ask the system anything he wanted.

"Vato Petteway was in here earlier," Ó Brádaigh said. "What did he do when he was inside this room?"

Ó Brádaigh knew that the simplest question brought the quickest answers. Besides, open-ended questions like that often gave him the most information.

"Vato Petteway altered the settings on the dome sections," the system told Ó Brádaigh. "Would you like to see what he has done?"

"Yes." Sweat dripped off Ó Brádaigh's face. His heart was pounding from all the exertion, but he felt calmer than he had in the past hour.

Lights flared around the small room, followed by numbers in various colors. The numbers told Ó Brádaigh what the changes were—and they were extreme.

Brilliant engineer that he was, Petteway had not shut down the dome sections. That would have needed two other confirmations from at least one other location.

Instead, Petteway changed the settings for the sections. The normal settings throughout the dome were designed to ensure that the sections fell whenever there was a breach or a hint of a breach. The sections would also fall when commanded to do so by various officials. The commands were normally set so that all it took was one official to order an area to section.

There were other ways that the sections could lower. Anyone inside this control room who had the proper identification and codes could lower or raise the sections at will. And that was just one of the extra ways the sections could fall.

But Petteway had changed *all* of those settings. He had redone the settings on what would cause the sections to lower. He didn't shut down the sections or make it impossible for them to function.

He had set the standards for dropping the sections so loose that a bomb could go off in the center of Armstrong, and the sections wouldn't come down at all.

Ó Brádaigh felt physically ill. Why would anyone do that? Everyone inside the dome would die.

Ó Brádaigh couldn't think about what he had found—not yet. First, he had to fix this. The sections had to be restored to their normal settings.

It would take him several minutes to complete the task. He didn't trust the system to reset itself. He hadn't asked the system if Petteway had tampered with things earlier in the week. Ó Brádaigh had only asked about today.

The nausea got worse.

Ó Brádaigh would deal with that secondary problem after he finished this one. He needed to reset the sections—and he needed to do it now.

41

To the human ear, all Peyti names sounded similar. Goudkins knew that the Peyti thought there was as vast a difference between the names Uzvaan and Xyven as there was between Goudkins and Zorn. But Goudkins struggled with the difference. Most humans did, even those fluent in Peytin.

Goudkins had resorted to whispering names out loud. She could do that because she was alone in her ship. She probably would have been embarrassed to do it anywhere else.

That damn subtlety in the names slowed down her investigation. Plus, she was probably mispronouncing everything. She finally decided to stop scanning the information while listening to it. She actually made her computer show her the translated names—and the spellings, at least, helped her distinguish between names that had seemed exactly the same to her before.

After Goudkins decided on that little trick, she realized that Mavis Zorn had mentored even more Peyti in the Impossibles than Goudkins had initially realized. Dozens and dozens of Peyti lawyers.

Goudkins was looking through their backgrounds now, but she believed that all of the Peyti lawyers that Zorn had mentored had been clones of the Peyti mass murderer Uzvekmt.

But, not all of them had received jobs on the Moon.

Goudkins couldn't track them all. She had sent information on those clones to her superior, Ava Huỳnh. Huỳnh had told her that all of those clones had killed themselves at the same moment as the Peyti Crisis started unfolding.

Now, Goudkins needed another piece of information, one she hadn't thought to ask before.

She wanted to know if all of the off-Moon clones had been lawyers who had gone through the Impossibles. Because if they had, they had probably been in touch with Mavis Zorn.

Asking about the lawyers without mentioning Zorn wouldn't set off any red flags at all.

Besides, Goudkins needed to get up and move around. The depth of the perfidy that she was finding was making her ill.

She left her investigative area and went to the ship's cockpit. She sent a message through her government links to Huỳnh, asking if she could get a piece of information.

Goudkins didn't expect a response immediately. She figured she had at least an hour before Huỳnh finished whatever she was doing and got back to her.

Instead, Huỳnh appeared on a nearby table, her hologram wearing her signature purple outfit.

"Wilma," Huỳnh said with a smile, "Lawrence Ostaka is still saying bad things about you."

Goudkins felt her stomach clench, but she rolled her eyes anyway. "He's the only person I know who can sit on his ass in an emergency and claim that it doesn't fall into his jurisdiction."

"And here I thought you two would complement each other," Huỳnh said. "I was wrong. Sorry about that."

Goudkins was sorry about it too. She didn't want to admit how much she had grown to hate Ostaka to Huỳnh.

"Just finish this assignment," Huỳnh said, "and I'll assign you a new partner when you return."

Goudkins had no idea if Huỳnh was watching her at a large size or a small size, so she made herself smile. She hoped the smile didn't look too fake.

"Thank you," she said.

Huỳnh nodded, then looked over her shoulder as if someone had entered the room or something had happened.

"Is this a bad time?" Goudkins asked.

"No, it's fine," Huỳnh said.

Goudkins hoped that was true. "I just wanted to check on something. You had probably told Ostaka, but, well, you know how things are going."

Huỳnh said, "I do," but she sounded distracted.

"I was wondering, you know the Peyti clones off-Moon? That information I sent you two weeks ago—"

"The ones related to the clones that nearly blew up the Moon again?" Now Huỳnh sounded annoyed. "Of course I do."

"Do you have information on how many of those clones were lawyers?"

"I don't have information at the moment, without checking," Huỳnh said, then looked over her shoulder again. "How quickly do you need it?"

"Sooner rather than later," Goudkins said.

"Huh," Huỳnh said, sounding a bit surprised. "I actually thought you might've wanted to talk about Hétique City."

"Hétique City?" Goudkins asked.

"You didn't know?" Huỳnh asked. "There's been another attack, Wilma. On Hétique this time. We're investigating."

"Oh." Goudkins had to remind herself to breathe. "How many—"

"I can't talk any longer. I'm about to go into a meeting. If I send that information, you'll have everything from me, right?"

"Yes, thank you," Goudkins said, but by the time the sentence was out of her mouth, Huỳnh had severed the link.

Goudkins put a hand against the wall, bracing herself. Another attack. She wondered if DeRicci knew, then realized she probably did.

Did DeRicci feel relieved that the attack was on Hétique and not the Moon? Or was she worried that things were about to get worse?

Goudkins wasn't sure how she felt about it. She headed back to her computer, but as she did, her links pinged.

She stopped in the ship's most narrow corridor and took the link without any audio or visual.

You alone?

It took her a moment to recognize that the contact had come from Miles Flint.

Yes, Goudkins answered.

Great, because I have two questions for you and something I need you to look into.

No *hi, how are you?* No *have you heard about the new attack?* Just a quick contact, with no small talk at all.

Are you familiar with the Currency Department of the Treasury? He asked.

As much as anyone is, she sent.

Should they be funding operations in Earth Alliance Security?

What? The question made no sense. She actually had to review it. *No, of course not.*

That's what I thought. Have you ever met a woman named Pearl Brooks?

No, Goudkins sent.

She authorized the Currency Department's transfer of funds to an operation run by an intelligence officer named Ike Jarvis. I'm wondering if she's authorized other operations as well.

You want me to audit someone in the Currency Department? Goudkins swallowed hard. *You realize that someone will trace that investigation.*

Yeah, Flint sent. *Hold off for the moment. But if you can check the files on Brooks, I'd appreciate it.*

I'll only check the easily accessed files, Goudkins sent. *We don't want to alert her to our interest.*

Good thinking, Flint sent. *I suspect we'll have to go deeper later, but this is a start. And thanks for the help.*

Then he signed off.

Goudkins hadn't felt as if she had helped at all. She felt like she had told him no continually. Or maybe she was just off-balance from the new attack on Hétique City.

She went back to her investigative chair. Before she started looking up Pearl Brooks, she watched a few minutes of footage about Hétique City. The destruction didn't look familiar. It seemed like a completely different kind of attack.

It seemed odd to her. But at the moment, it wasn't her concern.

Mavis Zorn, Jhena Andre, and now Pearl Brooks were Goudkins' concern. And this thing about the Currency Department had her intrigued.

Goudkins needed to calm down, and focus. She needed to think it all through.

An investigation—done right—would focus her.

She settled in, and got back to work.

42

Finally, they allowed Berhane and Kaspian to go upstairs.

Not a moment too soon, either. Berhane had just about figured out what kind of angry fit she was going to throw. She had seen her father do it and get an instant response. She had seen Torkild do it, and occasionally make the person he was screaming at angry.

And she had seen her mother charm the people who didn't let her do what she wanted.

Berhane couldn't charm, and she wasn't sure she could be insulting enough, but she was going to try.

Then the guard opened the last security barrier.

"They'll see you upstairs," he said. "Take the first elevator."

She was so astonished that she didn't walk past him immediately, even though Kaspian did.

Instead, Berhane said, "I can see Chief DeRicci?"

"Actually, you'll be seeing her assistant chief, Rudra Popova. Chief DeRicci is still in the middle of something."

Of course. But this was a start. And Berhane had heard about the legendary Popova. The woman could get anything done in one-tenth the time it would take the best assistant anywhere else.

Berhane's father had dealt with Popova just once, and tried to hire her away from the Security Office. Popova hadn't gone.

Berhane saw that as a vote in Popova's favor.

"Berhane," Kaspian said, making a get-over-here gesture with his hands. Apparently, he thought this opportunity would vanish in an instant.

She probably should have thought of that as well. She scurried past the guard, and got onto the elevator along with Kaspian. He looked at her, seeming even more stressed than he had when he'd contacted her on the train.

This is crazy, he sent to her on their private links. *Someone from this office should have seen us immediately. Imagine if we had an emergency.*

I thought this was an emergency, she sent back.

No, I mean something like we've locked the clone terrorists in our house and we need someone to get them right away.

We would have contacted the police in that instance, she sent. She didn't want to be criticizing the Security Office, even on a private link. Not when she needed them to take her seriously.

But Kaspian never handled authority well. She had agreed to bring him along because he had all of the details of the old DNA and the possible cloning, but she had done so with reservations.

Those reservations had just gotten a lot worse.

The elevator doors opened, and Berhane started to leave, but Kaspian stepped out first. He was deliberately blocking her exit. He looked both ways before he moved aside.

He had been trying to protect her. Against what, she had no idea. She would have been amused by it, if it weren't so ridiculous. Kaspian couldn't have protected her from a physical threat even if he wanted to.

The corridor was quiet. There were a lot of closed doors, and some voices from her left.

A woman appeared on her right. The woman wasn't much taller than Berhane was, but she had a long cloud of black hair.

"Ms. Magalhães," the woman said, "I'm Rudra Popova. I'm sorry this has taken so long, but there's been another attack."

Berhane's stomach clenched. "Here? In Armstrong?"

"No," Popova said. "On Hétique. Are you familiar with it?"

Berhane wasn't. But she didn't know much about the rest of the Alliance.

"Is that a moon too?" she asked, then thought the question was stupid.

"You know," Popova said as she led Berhane and Kaspian down the hallway, "I have no idea. I hadn't heard of it until today. But the attack looks pretty bad. Apparently their major city was hit."

"Why would the Moon's Security Office care?" Kaspian asked.

Berhane sent a message across their links: *Stop talking.*

To Berhane's surprise, the question didn't seem to offend Popova. "We're trying to figure out the same thing. We think maybe the attacks have moved away from here, although someone just suggested that the attack might have been designed to lull us into complacency."

"Nothing will lull us into complacency," Kaspian said, then looked defiantly at Berhane.

She didn't say anything. She agreed.

They rounded a corner, just as a woman and a man left a large room. They were in deep discussion. The woman looked like a heavyset person who had lost too much weight too quickly. Her clothes bagged on her.

It took Berhane a moment to recognize Noelle DeRicci. She looked nothing like the out-of-place person Berhane had seen at the fundraiser five months ago.

The man was gray and clearly sedentary. His hair was gray, his suit was gray, and his face—

Berhane's breath caught.

His face was one of the ones she had seen just a few hours ago, with Kaspian.

"Oh, my God," Kaspian said.

She grabbed his arm. *Shut up. They have no idea, and we'll scare this guy.*

But he's a clone, Kaspian sent back.

No kidding, Berhane sent.

DeRicci and the man ignored Berhane and went through some double doors. As soon as the doors closed, Berhane glanced at Kaspian.

He looked terrified.

He wasn't going to figure out what to do. It was up to her.

"Chief Popova," Berhane said.

"It's Assistant Chief," Popova said, "but call me Rudra. I've worked with your father—"

"I'm sorry, Rudra," Berhane said, "but who is that man who was with Chief DeRicci?"

"His name is Lawrence Ostaka. He's an investigator for the Earth Alliance Security Division."

Berhane was shaking her head. "No, he can't be."

Popova frowned. "I checked his credentials myself. More than once in fact. And in great depth. He is with the Security Division."

Kaspian cursed. All the blood had left his face.

"What's wrong?" Popova asked.

"He's a clone," Berhane said. "That's what I came to tell you."

"That Lawrence Ostaka is a clone?" Popova sounded as confused as she looked.

"That there are more clones on the Moon. We found the old DNA as we were digging through the wreckage, and we identified hundreds of dead clones."

"He's not dead," Popova said, glancing at the door.

"No, he's not," Berhane said, "but I'm sure some of the Peyti clones died on Anniversary Day too. Believe me, his face is one of the ones we were looking at just this morning."

"You identified Lawrence Ostaka?" Clearly, Popova wasn't following this exactly.

"*No*," Berhane said, grabbing Popova's arm and pulling her close. "No, don't you see? We had no idea he was here. We just have the faces and the names of the originals. He looks just like one of them."

Popova's mouth opened, then she seemed to get a grip on herself, and she nodded.

"You need to show me all of this," she said, "and you need to show it to me right now."

43

Nyquist sank into his chair. He wondered if he had raised his voice too loudly when he was speaking to Romey. He had let his feelings take over.

He ran a hand over his face. He needed to concentrate. He didn't dare make a mistake on the Zhu investigation, particularly after that semi-public conversation with Romey.

But right now, he was too shaken to concentrate, at least at the levels he needed to make a perfect case against Romey and her cohorts.

He would look up the information for Flint, instead.

The case Flint had sent him was eight years old. Nyquist had been a detective then, and going through his usual troubles trying to hang onto a partner.

He felt a moment of private amusement. He'd always gone through partners because he had been too harsh on them, because their investigative skills weren't up to his standards, and, because he had no real manners, he let his former partners know it.

Romey had had a similar approach to investigation, and she had been as thorough as he wanted.

Apparently, the only problem he had with her was her moral compass.

He shook off the thought and opened the case file.

He was stunned to see that the case was a property case, not a homicide case. He scanned through the information, uncertain why Flint wanted him to look into a property crime.

Then Nyquist paused.

The original detective on the case had been DeRicci. And she'd been working homicide at the time.

So Nyquist went deeper into the file and found that they'd been dealing with the death of a clone who, like other clones before her, had been dumped into the compost buckets near the port.

Flint had mentioned clones, but not what kind. He was more interested in the case's connection—if any—to a man named Ike Jarvis. Flint also wanted to know if the person of interest in the case, a man named Cade Faulke, worked for Earth Alliance Intelligence.

Before Nyquist dug into those names, though, he got lost in the case file. In familiar names besides DeRicci's. Luc Deshin was briefly a suspect, and DeRicci ruled him out.

Then she was forced off the case by Gumiela, who assigned the case to Property. Property actually did some work—or claimed DeRicci's work as their own—and sent a unit to arrest Cade Faulke.

By the time the unit arrived, Faulke was gone. His little office was messy, and his android guard had been disabled. No one in the area wanted to talk about where he went, which was pretty common for the neighborhood near the port.

But what wasn't common was that all of the security footage within a several-block radius had been shut off.

Nyquist dug in, searching for even casual references to Cade Faulke. Nyquist found several in older files. Faulke had served as an informant to a large number of detectives, including one Andrea Gumiela before she had received her promotion to chief of detectives.

All of Faulke's tips had been about activities inside the homes of major crime figures.

The dead clone had been embedded into Deshin's household. According to DeRicci's meticulous case file, Deshin had told her he thought the clone was the daughter of an old friend.

Nyquist leaned back.

Designer criminal clones. He'd heard a lot about them, particularly the way they were used to fight crime outside of the main part of the Alliance.

He hadn't realized that was going on *inside* the Alliance—at least to this extent—and he hadn't realized it had been going on here, on the Moon.

He almost got up and went to Gumiela's office. He could use some of this to get out of the Zhu investigation. Gumiela wouldn't want it known that a former murder suspect had been her go-to source for her most high-profile cases, particularly when that go-to source appeared to be embedding clones into households across the Moon.

But after that confrontation with Romey, Nyquist no longer wanted off the Zhu case. It didn't matter that the case would take a lot of work.

Romey had crossed a line. She seemed to think herself immune from the law.

And he'd learned that people who felt that way lost track of the line. They seemed to believe *they* were the line, and that their judgment was impeccable.

His certainly wasn't. Witness his attraction to Romey. Especially while DeRicci needed him.

He loved DeRicci, and he hadn't been able to stop his eye from wandering. Or his brain, apparently.

He went back to the file, to see what else he could find.

He needed to track down Cade Faulke, the clones, the intelligence service, and a man named Ike Jarvis.

Nyquist finally understood why all of this interested Flint. It was one of those pieces that might lead to a breakthrough in the investigation— maybe more than the Peyti corporation information that Nyquist had gotten from Uzvaan.

He felt the same kind of excitement he usually felt when he was about to close a case.

He was close to something, something important.

Something big.

Something that might lead them to whoever it was that wanted to destroy the Moon.

44

In the main conference room at the Earth Alliance Security Division Human Coordination Department, someone had stacked all of the beautifully carved wooden screens into one corner. Some of those screens were antiques. Careless handling could cost thousands in simple repairs.

Odgerel winced as she saw that. She stepped past them, trying not to frown at the lack of respect accorded to ancient things inside this room, and rubbed the knuckle of her forefinger against her forehead.

The headache had never quite left after her rather rude awakening. Her head still buzzed with the aftereffects of all the emergency klaxons sent through her links. Even a solid (if quick) breakfast and the large cup of oolong tea she had downed before her arrival hadn't eased the aches.

She didn't wake to emergencies well any more.

But she was calmer than she had been an hour before. She had taken the time to center herself, knowing that everyone around her would be panicked.

Most of them were. Her staff, while brilliant and experienced, tended toward drama.

The only other calm person in the room was Mitchell Brown. His serene presence seemed like an island in the middle of stormy seas.

Only tension lines around his eyes belied his physical composure. And those tension lines faded as his gaze met hers.

"Sir," he said, bowing slightly.

She nodded to him, and then at the rest of the staff. She had fifteen trusted department heads and assistants, counting Brown. They had gathered around the beautifully carved mahogany table that she had brought with her when she had taken over the Human Coordination Department. She had had an invisible nanocoating (removable, of course) placed on the table's surface so that no spilled beverage or sharp-edged jewelry would damage the wood.

She now wished she had had the foresight to do the same with the screens.

She pulled back her chair, carved to match the table, and sank onto the soft golden cushion. Beneath her calm, a thrum of exhaustion already threatened.

Perhaps she was getting too old for this job. When she awoke, she thought she might be too old for emergencies, but emergencies were what the job was all about.

"I had asked you, Mr. Brown, to prepare an update for me when I arrived. Have you one?"

"Yes, sir." He waved a hand over the center of the table. Semi-solid holographic images appeared, showing ships in low orbit, firing on the planet below.

Brown's information had been right when he contacted her; the ships were clearly not part of a fleet of ships. They were as dissimilar as they could possibly be—high-end space yachts mingling with weaponized cargo ships fighting alongside re-commissioned warships.

"We didn't recognize any ships except these three." He highlighted three of the ships. "I've seen two of them used in crimes before. The third has a sales record history that we could trace."

"And I assume you have." Odgerel hated it when a presenter paused for effect. Brown would learn that.

"The first two ships belong to two different organizations, the Ibori crime family, and the Kee crime family. The third ship traces back to an underling who works for the crime lord Gahiji Palone."

"The crime families are working together?" Odgerel hadn't expected that. "Why?"

"I think we have our answer in this next security footage that I will show you," Brown said. "It automatically updated at the first sign of trouble, and kept transmitting until the on-the-ground system was destroyed."

He waved his hand over another section of the table. The images were larger. Small ground-to-orbit vehicles had landed in the center of what appeared to be a large industrial complex. A pilot waited in each. Groups ran toward the vehicles. The groups appeared to be armed adults and several people holding very young children.

Brown moved the imagery forward until the ships—which had come and gone more than once—were surrounded by angry young people. He enlarged their faces.

"We believe these young people, and the children, are clones," he said. "We did a recognition search and discovered that by face, at least, they match images of several members of the named crime families on a ninety-nine point nine percent point system. We obviously don't have the DNA, but we don't really need it, since the area attacked held one of the Alliance's major clone factories."

Odgerel rubbed her eyes. They ached with tiredness. "They *are* clones. For decades, the Hétique factory has worked alongside part of the Security Department to infiltrate these families. Apparently, the families are not happy with what we have done, and are showing their displeasure."

"Then why steal the clones?" asked Eu-fùnh Pirizoni. She was one of Odgerel's most insightful division heads.

"We don't know," Brown said. "The theft looks haphazard. If I let the security footage play out, you'll see a lot of the young people get left behind, only to die a few minutes later as the attacks continue on the factory."

"It looks like a rescue," Odgerel said, more to herself than to the team.

"It does," Brown said. "But the ships used here are affiliated with Luc Deshin, perhaps the biggest crime boss on Earth's Moon."

"The Moon." Odgerel looked at Brown. He seemed as tired as she felt. "This is our link to the Moon?"

"The only link," Brown said. "The attack is different, the methodology seems different, the goal of the attack seems different. The reports we are getting now say that much of the city was not harmed, only the areas nearest the factory. The attack happened at night, when there were fewer employees, and we now know that the younger children, at least, were removed from the factory before it was destroyed."

"Should we even be calling them children?" asked Sadbhuj Barbier.

Odgerel looked at him in surprise. She didn't think he had such a hard heart. "What else would we call them?"

"They're clones," Barbier said. "They're not human."

"Then what are they, exactly?" she asked.

His lips thinned and he leaned back in his chair. He clearly realized she disliked his response. Either that, or he really didn't have an answer for her.

"Continue," she said to Brown.

He turned slightly so that he faced Odgerel directly.

"We don't know if this attack on a clone factory, done with the co-operation of at least three crime lords, is coincidental to the attacks on the Moon or if they're related. We did intercept some communications about a meeting at one of Deshin's properties recently, but we couldn't tell if the meeting was going to be held or if it had already been held."

Odgerel folded her hands together. Brown's eyes tracked downward. He clearly noted the move, but he didn't slow down because of it.

"We've had word through various departments that Deshin had been looking for designer criminal clones, which was not something he'd pursued in the past. Some of the rumors concerned the Anniversary Day bombing clones. We do know that many criminal organizations are trying to track the bombing clones' origins so that they can purchase the same kinds of clones."

"Lovely," Odgerel muttered because she had to respond to that. She had known about the search by other criminals for the maker of the Frémont clones. A successful attack of that level often served as advertising for a new weapon, and the Anniversary Day attacks were no exception.

"Deshin is known for his killings, but only as a strategy for dealing with rivals, generally those who have crossed him. He prefers shady business deals to assassination and weapons sales. His involvement in all of this is a surprise," said Brown.

"I seem to recall that we lost an operative on the Moon years ago," Odgerel said, "when Deshin fired one of the embedded clones. The operative vanished, and it was believed that Deshin had taken him, tortured him, and killed him once he had the information. Or am I misremembering that?"

"You aren't," Pirizoni said. "When Mitchell found the connection to Deshin and clones, I searched, and found that was the last mention tying Deshin directly to clones. The clone that was destroyed was the last one embedded in his organization, at least close to his family. He became quite vigilant after that."

Odgerel frowned. "So we know that Deshin was looking for the maker of the Anniversary Day clones. We know that he probably had a meeting of crime lords at one of his compounds, and the next thing we know is that the clone factory that made the clones *we* embedded into criminal organizations was destroyed."

We also know that there is an Alliance connection to some of these attacks, Brown sent her through her links, *although I haven't briefed everyone in this room on that.*

Noted, she sent back.

"We also know that Deshin is patriotic," said Jadallah Reinbrecht. He had a gift for understanding a lot of information in a short period of time—and remembering it weeks or months later, without an assist from his networks.

"Patriotic?" Odgerel asked. "To the Alliance?"

"To the Moon," Reinbrecht said. "He has steadfastly refused to leave the City of Armstrong, although he would quadruple his profits if he moved to the edges of the Alliance."

"And what do you make of that information?" Odgerel asked Reinbrecht.

"Personally? I think Deshin was going to exact his own revenge on whoever attacked the Moon. Deshin nearly died on Anniversary Day, and he lost some of his team. He's loyal to them. I think he didn't find what he was looking for, but he found something else."

"The clones we've been embedding into the criminal organizations," Odgerel said.

"So why save their lives?" Pirizoni asked.

"He didn't save all of the clones," Brown said. "The reports I'm getting list the clone casualties, not as deaths per se, but as property loss. It looks like adult clones still on site were not saved."

"Just the children," Odgerel muttered. She blinked, trying to reconcile the idea of a criminal organization led by a man who would save children. "Do you think he wants to use the children for his own criminal activities?"

"I don't know," Brown said. "We have already lost track of the rescue ships, if that's what you want to call them."

"We can identify those clones," Barbier said. "I think we put a watch for them once they become adults."

Odgerel nodded. "I'll assign that," she said, although she wouldn't assign it at this moment. She did not want Barbier handling that, even though he had come up with the idea.

"So we are now certain that the attackers of Hétique City are not the Anniversary Day attackers?" she asked.

"We're not certain of anything yet," Brown said.

"It is possible that the crime lords did attack the Moon," Barbier said. "After all, all of the four we have just named have shell corporations that could be used in the Moon's rebuilding."

"Then why the second attack a few weeks ago?" Odgerel asked.

Barbier shrugged.

"I am still of the opinion that crime lords do not have the long-term vision to handle something this large over so many decades," Brown said.

"I tend to agree. Still, we have to look at all possibilities." Odgerel turned to Pirizoni. "Eu-fùnh, please, investigate the connection between these crime lords and see if one or all of them could have worked together for the attacks on the Moon."

"Yes, sir," she said.

"I do, however, think that this attack is related to the Anniversary Day attacks," Odgerel said. "But I am guessing that Jadallah's assumption is correct: that Deshin discovered our clone factory's purpose while searching for the Anniversary Day clones, and that his connection to the bombings is as victim, not as perpetrator. We should, of course, try to find him and the property he has stolen from us, but our main focus needs to remain finding the perpetrators of the Moon attacks."

She looked at the group, feeling more energy that she had felt since she woke up.

"Proceed with the Hétique City attack as if it were an isolated event. Investigate it as if it had happened before Anniversary Day and is a crime, not a terrorist act. It's not necessary to put a lot of resources into this crime if, indeed, we would be taking resources from our primary purpose, which is finding the terrorists who are attacking the Moon. But we shouldn't lose sight of this investigation either."

"Waiting will slow us down on catching these crime lords," Barbier said.

Odgerel smiled at him. "We have been unable to 'catch them' in the legal sense for years now. I'm certain that a few months will make little difference. My orders stand."

He glared at her.

"Is there anything else?" she asked.

"No, sir," Brown said, clearly speaking for the group.

She nodded. "I appreciate the good and swift information. Please keep me apprised on all of the related investigative fronts."

Then she bowed her head slightly, and left the room.

She was relieved that this Hétique City attack was not the expected third attack. She did not want the crisis to spread beyond Earth's solar system.

But she knew that there would be another attack, and her intuition told her it would be soon.

She needed to keep her staff focused, and with any organization this large, maintaining focus was difficult.

She would guide them as best she could until the crisis ended.

If it ended at all.

45

THE SIDE ROOM THAT POPOVA HAD PULLED BERHANE AND KASPIAN INTO seemed claustrophobic and small, particularly with all the floating heads around them. Images of dozens of long-dead Moon citizens, all of whose DNA had been found in the last few months in the ruins from the Anniversary Day bombings.

Popova had turned gray, and she had tucked her hair behind her ears. She looked terrified.

Berhane understood that. Seeing this Lawrence Ostaka person had spiked her heart rate, and it hadn't slowed down. She never thought of herself as courageous, even though she had fended off a few scummy people inside the ruins while she worked.

She certainly wasn't sure what to do now.

Except that she needed to give Popova information as quickly as possible.

Kaspian had started to explain how they found the DNA, and Berhane had cut him off. Popova didn't need that, not right now. Maybe later. What she had needed were the faces of the originals for the DNA that Berhane's volunteers had found—and now as those faces floated around the room, Popova looked like her world was collapsing.

Popova pointed to another face, not Ostaka's face.

"I know him," she said. "He works with the city engineers."

Her voice was shaking. Berhane felt like she was floating, as if something had shifted in her entire world.

Popova said, "Half of these people are on staff here in Armstrong. How is that possible?"

And then she shook her head.

Berhane had had a bit more time with this, although she hated the idea that these people—these clones—were in the city. She was going to have to be the voice of reason here, at least for the moment.

She remembered how she had been the day her mother died, the way she had become calmer in the crisis rather than panicked, how she had organized everyone on that train.

She found that space in herself again.

"Look," she said to Popova, "these people have been here for years. We can take another minute or two to confirm what our eyes are telling us. Do you have samples of this Earth Alliance Investigator's DNA?"

Popova looked at Berhane as if she were speaking Disty. "We don't have any time at all," Popova said. "He's with the chief."

"And he has no idea that we know who he is," Berhane said. "Let's just make sure of this. I mean, some faces look alike."

"Not to me," Kaspian said. "That resemblance is enough to indict, as far as I'm concerned."

Berhane glared at him. She didn't have to send him a "shut up" message on the links this time. He gave her a sideways glance that she took as an apology.

Berhane asked Popova, "Can you get some of this man's DNA? If we can just run a simple clone check—"

"He won't have a clone number," Popova said.

"Yeah, I know, but there's a way to check some DNA markers," Berhane said. "We won't know if he's actually from the original that we think he is, but we'll be able to see if he was cloned."

Popova visibly squared her shoulders. She seemed stronger, as if having a plan bolstered her.

"We can do that," she said. "I know where we can get some DNA right now."

"I'll come with you," Berhane said.

Popova shook her head. "For all we know, he's monitoring his stuff. He'll wonder what you're doing there, but he will think I have something to do for my job."

Berhane bit her lower lip. She didn't want Popova to face this man alone. "If he's in that space, then come back here."

"If he's in that space," Popova said, "I'll be contacting you via links and we'll go see the chief."

"You should let the chief know what's going on," Kaspian said.

Berhane looked at him in surprise. The man who hated authority wanted an authority figure involved?

He shrugged, then said to Berhane, "You know I'm right."

"I think we're going to wait until we have proof," Popova said. "We have so much happening here that the last thing we want to do is accuse someone who is innocent of doing something wrong."

"He's not innocent," Kaspian muttered.

"But he might not know he was manufactured for something," Berhane said.

Kaspian gave her a pitying look. "Then he'll be like those Peyti clones, activated when the time is right."

"Like they had a timer inside of them?" Berhane looked at Popova. "They didn't, did they?"

"No," Popova said, hand on the door. "They knew their whole lives what day they were supposed to die and how. They could have told us at any point."

Then she made a face as if she had swallowed something bad, and let herself out of the room.

Berhane twisted her fingers together. The Peyti clones had known? For decades? And they'd made friends here?

She had been with one of Peyti clones on the Armstrong Express the day her mother had died. They had talked to each other. She had *helped* him, with his broken little arm.

He had taken her help. He had worked to *survive*.

How could anyone be so normal all the time, knowing they were part of something monstrous? How?

She'd love to think that only Peyti could be so venal, but she knew better.

She looked up at the faces floating around the room. All of those faces were human.

Still, she wanted to be wrong.

She wanted to be wrong more than she had ever wanted anything in her entire life.

46

THOSE MINUTES INSIDE THE SMALL CONTROL ROOM SEEMED TO TAKE FOREVER.
Ó Brádaigh watched each part of the system reset itself. He didn't touch
any of it until the entire process was complete. Then he checked and
double-checked.

Then he asked the system to check for him. He asked the system to
make sure the usual settings were in place. He figured if the system responded that the usual settings had been tampered with, then Petteway
had taken his sabotage to a new level—to the level Ó Brádaigh would
have done.

Ó Brádaigh would have changed the default settings too. He would
have made the system reset itself after the settings were changed, and
he would have made the default settings the *new* settings, not the
usual ones.

But Ó Brádaigh had asked that question, and the system told him
that he had just reset the system properly.

He was feeling so paranoid that he worried that Petteway had set the
system to lie to him.

But that would have required Petteway to believe that someone
would catch him, and Ó Brádaigh doubted Petteway had planned for
that. Particularly with the fact that Petteway had made the settings
change himself, and the settings change would only last a few hours.

As Ó Brádaigh finished his check, another realization hit. It was a realization he had had earlier, but it was one that hadn't really sunk in.

Only a few hours.

The attack was coming soon.

He said to the system, "Did Petteway alter anything besides the dome sections settings?"

He worried after he spoke that the question was too complex.

"He did not touch any other setting," the system answered Ó Brádaigh.

"What about things that were not settings?" Ó Brádaigh took a deep breath, and rephrased. "Did Petteway alter anything that was not a setting?"

"Petteway only touched the settings."

"Today." Ó Brádaigh said. "He only touched them today, is that correct?"

"That is correct," the system said.

"What about in the last week? Did Petteway change anything in the last week?"

"No," the system said.

"Did he alter anything in the past month?"

"No," the system said.

Ó Brádaigh could actually feel time passing. Normally, he would take the system through the questions week by week, but he didn't have time.

"What about in the past year?" Ó Brádaigh asked.

"I will show you what Petteway has done in this room in the past year," the system said.

The system showed Ó Brádaigh only a few things. Petteway entered and exited the control room at least once a month, but didn't do anything while inside. In the last few months, he entered once or twice a week, and always opened the dome sectioning commands.

It was almost as if he were trying to build up his nerve so that he could change the settings.

Ó Brádaigh shuddered. Bastard.

Ó Brádaigh focused on the clock he always had running in his left eye. He had used a lot of time checking on Petteway, and Ó Brádaigh still didn't have any help.

At some point, Ó Brádaigh would have to trust he had found everything Petteway had done.

Ó Brádaigh stepped out of the control room and closed the door. He pinged the security office again. He was told he had moved farther up in the queue.

He cursed silently.

He was going to have to use the Armstrong Police, even though he didn't want to.

He debated showing up at headquarters for just a moment, then visualized himself standing in line there while mayhem happened in his city.

So he sent an urgent message along the emergency line reserved for city engineers. He hoped to hell that Petteway wasn't monitoring the line.

Or one of Petteway's cohorts.

A police avatar appeared in front of Ó Brádaigh, life-size, wearing an official uniform from ten years before.

"State the nature of your emergency," the avatar said.

Ó Brádaigh used his identification code, then stated his position with the city. "I have found evidence of mass tampering with the dome. I need help—a lot of help. We only have a few hours before something could go terribly wrong."

The avatar winked out, and a woman he didn't recognize appeared. She introduced herself, and added, "I am a dispatch officer and I am speaking to you live. Please, state the nature of your emergency again."

So Ó Brádaigh did. Then he added, "Look, I'm in the substructure, and what I've found scares the living hell out of me. I can't get through the United Domes of the Moon Security Office, so I came to you guys. I'm afraid this is going on in every single dome on the Moon."

"Can you come to us?" the woman asked.

"No," Ó Brádaigh said. "I need to check the dome's structure, but it's too big to do it alone. I need help, and I'm not sure who I can trust."

Except Noelle DeRicci.

"I will send someone to you," the woman said.

"*No*," Ó Brádaigh said. "I need to reach the Security Office, and I need to reach it now."

"I will patch you into their emergency line, but I'll warn you, they don't have the proper setup. What can we do in the meantime?"

He was afraid of scaring half the city. He was afraid of tipping off Petteway's equivalents in the other domes.

But there was one thing the police could do, at least until he had a real plan.

"I need dome inspectors," he said. "That falls into your jurisdiction, right? I need inspectors outside and inside the dome, checking every centimeter of it, looking for explosives—small and large. The way this attack was set up, a tiny hole in the dome would have been catastrophic. So even a small charge, something the size of a fingernail, should be cause for concern and should be removed. Can you set that up?"

"With approval," she said.

"Get it," he said. "I'm willing to talk to whomever you need. And please, get me to the Security Office right now."

"Absolutely," the dispatch said. She looked scared. He hated seeing someone whose job it was to remain calm look terrified. "I'm going to get everyone here in dispatch to work on getting you through as fast as we possibly can."

"Thank you," he said, and hoped it would be fast enough.

47

FLINT WAS WORKING SIX DIFFERENT SYSTEMS AT THE SAME TIME. HE HAD become so restless, he was walking around his small office, checking each piece of information as it arose.

He was tracking the money that Ike Jarvis had used for his last illegal operation. The money that had come from the Currency Department.

Flint didn't have the right kind of clearance to compare other Currency transfers within the Alliance, and he didn't want to tip his hand—not yet. He hoped Wilma Goudkins could find out more for him, or in the very least, find out more about Pearl Brooks.

What few things Flint had found were fascinating. Jarvis had spent millions on several different operatives with the same mission designation as Iniko Zagrando. The mission had come about after Anniversary Day, and it seemed cobbled together.

Whenever Flint looked for something else in the files that was as sloppy as what he had seen on this final mission, he found nothing.

He suspected—although he didn't know—that something had frightened Jarvis, and made him worry that his own cover was blown.

Hey, Flint, you see what's going on in Hétique City? The message came from the private link he had with Nyquist.

Flint hadn't been paying attention to anything outside of his research. *No. What should I know?*

Take a look. Realize that the Alliance and some folks here think it's the third attack.

Flint froze. He glanced at his systems, information pouring through them like water. The third attack, somewhere other than Earth's Moon?

The attack had to be devastating.

He made himself focus on Nyquist's words. *But you don't?*

You won't either after we talk. Just look first.

So Flint did. He opened yet another screen, saw the media coverage, saw a destroyed city without a dome, saw images of an attack that had come from orbit, and saw a crawl on one side with the names of the dead. That aspect was ghoulish. He hoped someone had done proper familial notification before putting up the names.

He watched for a moment, while downloading the latest information along the public network, his stomach clenched.

He knew what those people in Hétique City were going through—the confusion, the terror, the change that happened in a single moment. He closed his eyes for a moment, took a deep breath, and calmed himself.

Then he opened his eyes, turning his back on the images of destruction. He contacted Nyquist again. *They sound convinced it's the third attack.*

Settle in, Nyquist sent. *I'd come visit you, but I have some personal matters to attend to here.*

What do you mean, settle in? Flint asked.

I mean, I got a story to tell you.

Flint stuck his hands in his back pockets and resumed pacing. *Okay, I'm ready.*

So, you send me after a guy named Ike Jarvis and a very old case involving clones and our mutual friend Noelle.

DeRicci? Flint was startled.

She was the initial detective on the case. Seems a woman got herself killed and stuffed in a composter, only it wasn't a woman.

Flint tried to follow. *What was it?*

A clone, Nyquist sent. *And not just any clone. A clone made from the Mycenae family, and embedded into Luc Deshin's family as a nanny.*

Deshin fires the nanny one morning and in hours she turns up dead. Noelle investigates until the department realizes it's a clone, and moves the case to Property.

Flint felt a piece of information just fall into place. DeRicci had never liked Deshin. Obviously, they had run into each other in this case, and she had formed her opinions then.

Deshin hadn't remembered her—or if he had, he had never told Flint.

Then the case had been taken out of DeRicci's capable hands and sent to the black hole of the Armstrong PD, the Property Division.

I suppose they never followed up, Flint sent, feeling discouraged.

Surprise, surprise, they did. They go to the clone's handler's place to arrest the bastard because they—and Noelle—believe he's been murdering clones. Noelle calls him a serial, although Gumiela got into the file and calls him a serial in the making, because we all know that a serial killer isn't a serial killer until he kills an actual human.

Flint winced. He was so glad that Talia hadn't heard that.

Anyway, this handler, Cade Faulke, does a disappearing act—only he wasn't a Disappeared. Witnesses say a group of people took him out of the building after disabling his android guard. He wasn't seen again.

Do you know what happened to him? Flint asked.

Found some information, buried deep in Property's files, that a man named Otto Koos led the team that took Faulke away from his lair. Recognize that name?

No, Flint sent.

Head of security for Deshin Enterprises until that very year. Until that very week, in fact. Now, here's where it gets interesting. There was a rescue of clones in Hétique City a few hours before the bombings started. The clones were children, and some of them resembled Deshin's kid Paavo.

Flint frowned, trying to follow. Deshin was very protective of Paavo. It was one of the few things that Flint liked about the man. Paavo wasn't a clone, was he?

Flint didn't say any of this. He decided to wait until Nyquist was done.

Nyquist hadn't stopped sending. *And, the ship that was in orbit when those kids were stolen from the clone factory? That ship was purchased at the very fringes of the Alliance by one Otto Koos.*

Flint tilted his head. Clone factory? No one had mentioned a clone factory. That suddenly made sense. Paavo wasn't a clone. The boy's DNA had been stolen.

What clone factory? Flint asked, deciding now was the time for questions.

Oh, did I forget that? Nyquist sent. *The raid today on Hétique wasn't aimed at the city. The city was collateral damage. The clone factory got destroyed. It's an Alliance clone factory and guess what gets made there?*

Flint knew better than to sarcastically ask *Clones?* but he was tempted.

What? he asked.

Designer clones, made by the Alliance to embed into criminal organizations. What I'm seeing, which isn't in the media, is that a few of those ships can be traced back to other crime families. This factory was the target because of the clones being embedded in the organizations, not because of the Moon.

Flint thought about that for a moment. It made sense.

You want to ask your friend Deshin about that? Nyquist added.

Flint almost said that Deshin had left the Moon to track the Anniversary Day bombers, but didn't. Deshin had gotten some of the information that Flint needed, and then had made it clear that he wasn't participating any longer.

Right about the time the planning for an attack of this scale would have happened.

Flint cursed out loud, glad the conversation with Nyquist wasn't audible.

Deshin's fingerprints were all over this. He had brought in the other organizations, then saw that there were children who were related to Paavo. Of course, Deshin couldn't kill them.

Even if he didn't think they were human, he wouldn't have been able to view footage and see children dying, children who looked like his son.

I don't want to talk to Deshin right now, Flint sent. He didn't like the idea of the attack at all, even if some of the clones had been saved.

Well, here's the thing, Nyquist sent. *Jarvis was hip-deep in clone making. The original Frémont clones were made at that facility—*

The ones that led to the Moon bombing? Flint asked.

No, experimental ones from something before Frémont died. All Alliance stuff, which I don't pretend to understand and can't access in depth, but I know you have sources on it. Here's what I know, though. This Jarvis? Besides the clones, he was active on the Moon for years. He knew how important the Moon is, and how to infiltrate systems.

Flint thought about that for a moment. Ike Jarvis. No wonder Zagrando had risked his life to come here.

You're thinking that Jarvis helped mastermind the attacks on the Moon? Flint sent.

Naw, Nyquist sent, surprising Flint. *He's not old enough.*

Flint blinked, realized that while he was putting some of the pieces together well, he wasn't assembling others at all. Of course Jarvis hadn't been old enough. Some of the planning started before Jarvis had been born.

I do think he helped facilitate it, Nyquist sent. *And I think he used some of it to do some of his own dirty work—and to turn a blind eye to bad stuff his operatives were doing. Like Faulke, killing clones as a hobby.*

Flint shuddered again. He wondered how often that happened all over the Alliance, and then decided he didn't want to know.

Do you have information as to who Jarvis is tied to? he sent.

That kind of crap is your job, Nyquist said. *I found Jarvis, Koos, and an operation here, thanks to your little case number. What I find fascinating is that the case ties Jarvis, the Alliance, clones, and killers with one neat little bow. You got your connection, Flint.*

Flint frowned. He wasn't sure why this was "his" connection and not "their" connection.

What can you be working on that's more important than this? Flint sent.

I got to deal with some dirty cops, and it's not fun on top of everything else. I hope I can wrap it up in the next twenty-four hours or something, Nyquist sent. *But for the moment, I'm the go-to-honest-cop on this assignment. I guess being a lonely asshole is perfect for this kind of work.*

And then he signed off without waiting for Flint's response. Flint had never heard Nyquist be quite that bitter before, and he wondered what Nyquist had run into.

Flint thought of contacting him again to simply say thank you, but he knew that Nyquist would hate that. Besides, every minute counted here.

Flint moved to one of the screens running the Jarvis information, and started isolating the names of everyone that Jarvis had worked with in his long career. Flint was going to cross-reference those with names he'd run into in his investigation.

He glanced over at the screen showing the destruction of Hétique City, then shut it off. If Deshin were involved…

Then he shook his head. Of course, Deshin had been involved. The man might've cared about his family, and he might've cared about others, but he had just been part of a small army killing innocents.

Flint understood DeRicci's antipathy. He'd let Deshin's charm disarm some of his caution.

Of course, Flint and Deshin had been using each other. Deshin had gotten Flint enough information to move forward on this investigation. And, apparently, some of the information Deshin had received had benefitted him as well.

Flint swallowed back some bile and returned to his work, forcing himself to concentrate. He needed complete focus here. He needed—

Suddenly, alerts went off on every screen and in his emergency links. His heart rate spiked. He only had a few alerts set, and most of them concerned Talia.

The alerts informed him of a systems breach—a major systems breach, a devastating systems breach.

Flint shook his head slightly, shut down the warning bells and the bright blinking visuals and opened the alerts, reminding himself that if Talia were in trouble, the information wouldn't come to him as a systems' breach. This had to be old, from some system he had set up years ago—or from his system here.

He opened the alert, realized it wasn't an old system or his system in his office, but something he had forgotten he had done.

He had set backdoor alerts inside the Security Office. He had boosted their systems when the building was built, and after DeRicci got hired, and then again, after Anniversary Day.

This was the old alert. It shouldn't have been triggered first. The new alert was state-of-the-art. The old alert—

—had gotten missed by the person or persons who breached the system. They had shut down the other alerts.

Flint went through the alert, using the back door he had set up then, and hit a wall. At the same time, he tried to contact DeRicci through his links and got a notification that he was not authorized to contact her.

He had his own system search for a way into the Security Office, and he was told, repeatedly, no matter what contact he tried, that he was in a queue and it would take time to reach someone.

His palms were sweating. He tried to reach Popova directly, and was once again told he wasn't authorized. He tried both DeRicci and Popova through private emergency links, and got nothing at all.

He contacted Nyquist, *Something's going wrong at the Security Office. I just got an alert that their systems were breached. Notify someone at Armstrong PD. Send officers to the Security Office. I'm heading there now.*

Got it, Nyquist sent back.

Flint glanced at all his systems, thought again about the work he'd lose if he'd shut it all down, then realized he needed to take this particular hack as a sign of what could happen even in his well-protected office.

The Security Office had the best system security in the city, and someone had still gotten in.

Now Flint was going to have to figure out how to get into the building as well—and then figure out what to do.

He went into his back room and got two laser pistols. He put the small one in his ankle holster, which he hadn't used since he left the force, and attached the holster to his right leg. Then he put the other pistol in another holster, which he attached to his hip.

His racing heart had slowed down. Somehow, he had reconnected with the man he had been when he worked for the Armstrong Police Department. He knew that working methodically was his best choice.

He let his own links continue to ping the Security Office, hoping someone else got there and solved this quickly. Then he shut down all the systems in his office and let himself out.

Once he had locked everything down, he ran to his car.

He needed to get to the Security Office—and he needed to do it fast.

48

THAT WAS TWICE. RUDRA POPOVA FELT A SURGE OF ANGER AT HERSELF. Twice she had melted down in a crisis. The first time had been on Anniversary Day, when she had seen images of Arek Soseki's body splayed on the sidewalk in front of O'Malley's Diner. She had loved Soseki, hadn't told him because they wanted to keep their relationship secret until after the election, and then he was gone—such a vibrant man, gone.

And now, a betrayal in their midst—and it was her fault. She had checked and double-checked and made sure the staff had checked Lawrence Ostaka's credentials, but had anyone here ever thought to check for clone markers? Of course not.

She hurried down the hall, listening to her feet whisper against the carpet, thinking the overweight, rumpled asshole could hear her every move. He probably had the conference room booby-trapped or something, his stuff protected.

He had sat in that space for weeks and watched them scurry around, trying to protect the entire city during the Peyti Crisis, and he hadn't lifted a finger to help. Why hadn't any of them seen that as a red flag? Why had they accepted that as normal?

Because Goudkins had, and Goudkins was helping them. She knew everything they were doing. *Everything.*

Popova took a deep breath, knew she had to stop panicking, panicking would ruin everything. And she had to be stealthy.

For all she knew, the chief was just debriefing Ostaka or they were having a private conversation. Nothing bad was going on in there. It couldn't be.

Just because everything had changed for Popova didn't mean it had changed for Ostaka—if she didn't reveal herself now. She had to be careful, and normal at the same time. She had to be innocent if he was already back in the conference room.

She stopped at her desk, got the little device the Security Office used to measure stranger DNA. Everyone on staff had gotten one of those back when the office opened, and Popova had never had to use it before. The systems downstairs and throughout the building—hell, the systems at the port, the systems on locked doors, the systems all over the city—always checked DNA, and confirmed someone was who they said they were.

She had laughed when she got this little device, back when Arek was alive, when Celia Alfreda thought this office was going to be her little police force, long before Anniversary Day.

I have no idea why I'm going to need this thing, Popova had said, holding it. *It's a waste of money.*

At least it was simple to use. She had tested it on herself that day, and sure enough, she had been who she said she was.

Now, she needed to use it on something Ostaka had touched—and only Ostaka.

She glanced both ways, saw no one else in the corridor, realized that the very movement alone—that glance—probably looked suspicious. Her face heated.

She was awful at this.

She snuck down the corridor, reached the conference room, and let out a small sigh of relief. He wasn't in it.

Then her stomach clenched. He wasn't in the conference room, which meant he was still with the chief.

Popova hoped the chief was all right.

Popova pushed open the door, hating the windows that opened the entire conference room to the corridor. She had initially put Ostaka and Goudkins in this room for the windows, so that Popova could monitor them if she had to, back when she'd been suspicious of both of them. Then she ended up trusting Goudkins (had that been a mistake?) and forgetting about Ostaka.

How stupid was she, anyway?

Popova was shaking. She was no hero, and she knew it. She could organize heroes; she couldn't be one.

But she had to do this. She didn't trust Berhane Magalhães to do it, and she didn't like the man Ms. Magalhães had come with. Not that Popova didn't trust him. She actually did. He was just an idiot, and she couldn't give this job over to an idiot.

Well, not that she was much better.

She glanced into the corridor, saw she was still alone, and collected herself. She walked to one of the side counters, pretending to be looking for something, all the while scanning the room using her peripheral vision.

Networked machines—not networked to the Security Office, but, in theory, to the Alliance (Popova shuddered. The Alliance. They had known for a while that the Alliance was involved. Dammit). The tablet she had given Goudkins for work here in the Security Office, with most of the important systems blocked off. (Why didn't Goudkins have it? Had Ostaka taken it from her?)

A mug, filled with some liquid. A plate covered with scaly leftovers.

And a jacket crumpled against the floor. A suit jacket, gray and undistinguished, like everything else Ostaka wore.

The jacket had fallen off the back of his chair.

Still, Popova picked the jacket up and shook it out, making sure it was big enough for Ostaka. It was.

If he saw her with it, she would simply say that it had fallen and she was replacing it. She ran the device along the lining of the jacket, and down its edges, watching the device record the sloughed off skin cells and tiny hairs it collected.

She had more than enough. She probably had too much.

But she made sure the device went all the way to the hem of the jacket before quitting.

Then she looked out the windows again, saw no one—where were the guards? Where was the rest of the staff?—and dropped the coat behind the chair.

She had to kick the coat's edges so that it bunched up the way it had before. She slipped the device into the pocket of her pants, then went to the sideboard again, as if she were still looking for something.

If Ostaka was monitoring her from his links, he would be suspicious now. She should have put that coat on the back of his chair.

Or not. She had no idea. If he had seen that device, he would be suspicious anyway.

She swallowed hard, clenched her fists to hold back the panic, and then made herself walk to the door.

She half expected him to jump out at her from the corridor.

He didn't.

She couldn't see him at all.

She thought again about warning the chief, but knew if she had it wrong, the chief would be mad. Besides, Ms. Magalhães had been right; he'd been here for months. What could another few minutes matter?

Popova snuck back to the office where she'd left the other two, device pressing against her thigh.

She had to figure out what she was going to do if Ostaka turned out to be a clone.

She always worked better with a plan.

It was time to devise one.

49

FOR THE FIRST TIME SINCE HE'D GOTTEN THE ASSIGNMENT TO INVESTIGATE Zhu's murder, Nyquist was happy he had Andrea Gumiela's ear. Because he contacted her immediately about the situation at the Security Office, and she didn't question him, she didn't make some snide comment about his relationship with DeRicci, she didn't even say she'd get back to him.

She sent, *We're on it*, and he knew, he *knew*, that they were.

Nyquist got the message almost immediately that all officers in the vicinity of the Security Office should head to that building. The announcement didn't make the knot in his stomach go away, but it made him feel better. It made him feel like something was going to get resolved.

Still, he couldn't stay in the station and wait to hear what the officers did. He had to get there.

If something happened to DeRicci…

He didn't want to complete that thought, and yet he couldn't get it out of his head. He had to see her, and he had to see her now.

He tried to contact her, and he kept getting kicked back from the system, something telling him that he wasn't authorized to speak to her. It made him mad at first, even though he knew the Security Office's system had been compromised.

Of all the people who weren't authorized to speak to DeRicci, it wouldn't have been him. It would *never* have been him.

He tried contacting her on their private links and got nothing at all. That scared him even more than the unauthorized message. Why would her links go silent? Even her emergency links didn't work—as if they didn't exist at all.

That—that moment when he realized that the links were completely gone and he had to contemplate a world without DeRicci, because he couldn't stop himself, that—that got him running before he even realized he was moving. He was down the stairs and across the parking structure, heading for one of the squads because the damn things were faster than his car, if he could even find his car in this distracted state.

The squads didn't have a governor like regular cars, nothing regulated how fast a squad car could go except the limitations of the car.

So he grabbed a new one, slid his hand across its exterior as an authorization, and felt guilty for a moment, because he was probably taking the squad from some deserving officers who could actually do something important, but he didn't care.

He had to get to that Security Office. He had to know what was happening with DeRicci, and he couldn't wait for anyone to tell him. He had to see it with his own eyes.

He slapped the dash, the identification in his palm and his DNA and the warmth of his skin bringing the thing to life.

Out loud, he gave the squad the Security Office's address, and said, "I need to get there at top speed."

Then he slipped on the restraints, slamming backwards in the seat as the squad car left the parking structure faster than Nyquist believed possible.

He just hoped it would be fast enough.

50

Ó Brádaigh had just decided to leave the substructure when he had a horrible thought: what if someone besides Petteway tampered with some other part of the dome? And how would Ó Brádaigh know?

He stood still for just a moment, looking at that control room. He wondered if he could get the system to answer a question about tampering without using the word "tamper."

If he had changed the system, he would also have taken the word "tamper" out of its vocabulary.

He took a deep breath, and as he did, the dispatch reappeared in front of him.

"We are unable to reach anyone at the Security Office," she said to him. She seemed to have more of a grip on herself than she had had earlier. "We're investigating that now."

Ó Brádaigh swore. "Look, we have a major emergency here, and I'm only one guy. Do you—"

"Dome inspectors are already suiting up," she said. "We'll have them cover everything."

"I need to talk to someone with authority," Ó Brádaigh said. "No offense, but I don't think this is isolated to Armstrong's dome. If something is happening here, it's happening all over the Moon. That's why I wanted to reach the Security Office—"

"Hello?" A male voice echoed in the substructure.

Ó Brádaigh's heart nearly pounded out of his chest. He hoped to hell that voice didn't belong to Petteway.

"Hello?" another voice shouted. That voice was female.

"You watch everything I do," Ó Brádaigh said to the dispatch. "If someone comes after me, then you need to get someone on this. There're others in the substructure and they shouldn't be here—"

"I'll monitor the area," the dispatch said.

Two uniformed officers ducked under one of the low ceiling beams. They were holding their weapons at their sides. Ó Brádaigh wanted to tell them that the laser shots from their pistols would ricochet horribly down here, but he didn't—not yet.

"What are you doing down here?" Ó Brádaigh asked, trying to sound authoritative. Not even the police had easy access to this site. He wasn't sure how they'd gotten here.

"Are you Donal Ó Brádaigh?" the female officer asked. She was taller than Ó Brádaigh and more muscular. She looked like she could throw him across the substructure without using much effort at all.

"Yes," he said, deciding there was no reason to lie to her.

He expected her to say that he had to come with them, that they thought he was breaking some kind of law.

"We're going to check your ID," she said. "Can you extend your right hand?"

"I wouldn't be down here if I didn't have the proper identification," he said.

"We beg to differ," the male police officer said. He wasn't quite as tall as his partner, but he looked as strong.

"Just let us see your identification, sir," the female officer said. "Please."

The "please" decided Ó Brádaigh. It was filled with tension, the kind of tension that came from a person who was barely holding it together, who knew what the stakes were, and how bad things could get.

Ó Brádaigh had been overthinking everything, and he knew he could overthink this. After all, these cops could be filled with tension because they were going to do something to him, to facilitate Petteway's plan—whatever the hell it was—or they could be filled with tension because they knew something bad was about to happen.

He extended his right hand. The female cop took it in her left and then holstered her laser pistol. She held her right hand over his palm.

He could feel her shaking ever so slightly.

"He is who he says he is," she said out loud.

The male officer let out a small sigh.

"All right then." The dispatch spoke from behind Ó Brádaigh, and she wasn't talking to Ó Brádaigh. She was talking to the officers. *She* had sent them, and she hadn't said anything about it.

She hadn't trusted him.

Somehow, that made him feel better.

"We have a serious problem here," the dispatch said to all of them. "You two do whatever it is Mr. Ó Brádaigh needs. We're going to have to take some kind of action. I'll make certain we facilitate it from up here."

The female officer looked at Ó Brádaigh. "Someone has been tampering with the systems?"

"Worse than someone," he said. "My boss, Vato Petteway. He changed all the sectioning controls. If something happens to breach the dome, no sections will fall. He set the controls for only six hours, so I think whatever's going to happen will happen soon."

The male officer swore. "What can we do?"

"We're going to need as many people as we can get," Ó Brádaigh said. "I don't even know what we're looking for. I fixed the sectioning commands, but that doesn't solve the problem. Look, something's going to breach the dome, and I don't know what that something is."

"We'll send someone to pick up Petteway," the dispatch said. "He'll tell us what's going on."

"All he has to do is wait a few hours," Ó Brádaigh said. "And then whatever he's planning will happen anyway."

The female officer glanced at her partner. "Should we notify the population?" she asked softly.

"And what? Have them panic?" Ó Brádaigh asked. "Where would they go?"

"They could suit up," the male officer said.

"Or they could panic and stampede the trains," Ó Brádaigh said.

"This is way above my pay grade," the female officer said. "Someone needs to figure out what to do."

"That's why I've been trying to get through to the Security Office," Ó Brádaigh said.

"We can't reach them," the dispatch said from behind him.

"Maybe, maybe in person?" Ó Brádaigh said to the dispatch. "Maybe the links are just down."

He hoped.

"We're sending teams there now, but we can't count on the Security Office," the dispatch said.

"The acting mayor or *someone* with authority," Ó Brádaigh said. And the right kind of brain. He knew how things worked, not how to get people to do something.

Then he looked at the two officers before him.

"I don't need you down here," he said. "You need to do whatever it is you do. I'm okay. I just need to figure out how to resolve all of this."

As if he could. He let out a shaky breath. The officers hadn't moved. But the dispatch's image was frozen. Clearly, she had frozen it while she handled something else.

"Hey," he said, sending the message to the dispatch through his links at the same time. "I need to talk to the chief dome inspector. They're going to need to do an emergency surface sweep, and they'll need my help."

"What's an emergency surface sweep?" the female officer asked.

Ó Brádaigh didn't answer her. It wasn't her business. But that made him realize that there hadn't been a surface sweep of the entire dome in as long as he could remember. And when there were surface sweeps, they happened during Dome Night, when no one outside of the city's engineering and inspection staff would notice.

The dispatch moved slightly, and then frowned. She was paying attention now.

"That could cause the panic you're worrying about," she said.

"Again, not something we can solve," Ó Brádaigh said. "The assistant mayor or the chief of the United Domes has to warn people, and make it sound like they're checking because of an asteroid hit or something. Something minor, okay? Just something that needs to be checked."

He didn't know why he was the guy on all of this. Someone else should have taken point. But the limited time had put him in charge.

"Can you get me the chief inspector?" Ó Brádaigh asked.

"In just a moment," the dispatch said.

"Look," the male officer said to Ó Brádaigh. "We've just been assigned to protect you and help facilitate your travel through the city if you need to get somewhere else. They can't find this Petteway guy, and they're worried he might come for you when he realizes what you've done."

"Great," Ó Brádaigh muttered. And then his heart rose in his throat. "I need to do something."

He held up a finger, holding them back, and sent a message along his family links.

Mom? Mom, are you there?

To his great relief, she answered, *You coming home any time soon?*

No, he sent. *Look, if my boss Vato Petteway shows up, don't let him in. And you and Fiona are going to need to suit up.*

What? his mother sounded surprised. *Have you ever tried to put a four-year-old in an environmental suit?*

Of course he had. He did once a month, making sure that Fiona had a suit that fit.

Make it a game, Mom, he sent. *For the next six hours, okay?*

Six hours? Donal, that's ridiculous—

Mom, just do it. Your lives could depend on it.

Even though he couldn't see her, he could feel the panic coming through the links.

Should I be telling my friends? she sent.

The choice between panicking people and not panicking them. *There'll be an announcement soon,* he sent, hoping he wasn't lying. *Once you hear that announcement, let your friends know. Until then, just take care of yourself and Fiona for me, please. I can't work here if I think something will happen to you two.*

He hoped she would listen. His mom was usually good at listening.

This doesn't sound good, Donal, she sent.

I hope it's nothing more than an inconvenience, Mom, but I can't be worrying about you two, okay? Do it for me. Please.

I will, she sent, and he let out such a large sigh of relief that the two police officers standing near him turned toward him simultaneously.

He turned his back on them. *Thanks, Mom,* he sent and signed off.

He had to make one more contact. He had to let Berhane know what was going on. Or at least, that she had to get out of the dome—any dome.

He pinged her links and got nothing. She had given him a private link, but it didn't seem to work.

His shoulders tightened. Had she blocked him somehow? He wouldn't know why.

So he tried her emergency links and again, got nothing. Nothing at all. As if she didn't exist.

He felt dizzy and he had to remind himself to breathe.

She was probably in one of the damaged domes somewhere and her links had disconnected. Or in a building that blocked link contact.

Still, the emergency links should work.

He couldn't focus on it. He had to solve this. Only a few hours left, and his daughter was in the dome. He had to think of Fiona.

He turned, looked at the officers who were watching him closely, and shook his head. "I'm okay."

Then he wished he hadn't said that. He wasn't okay. He was worried.

He set up his own system to ping Berhane every few minutes.

He would reach her soon.

He had to.

51

POPOVA HAD NEVER FELT SUCH STRESS WHILE WATCHING SOMEONE ELSE gather information. She had brought her device back into the small office near her desk, and had given the device to Berhane Magalhães and her friend, Dabir Kaspian.

Magalhães took the material before Kaspian, which made Popova feel better. She trusted Magalhães, but Kaspian seemed to have an agenda.

Popova had decided, when she was in the conference room, that she would trust her gut instincts from now on. She had hated Lawrence Ostaka on sight, and she had never trusted him.

If she had acted on that instinct, she wouldn't be standing here now, watching Magalhães's face scrunch up with concentration.

"I found artificially grafted telomeres," she said to Kaspian. "What do you find?"

"The same," he said.

"What does that mean?" Popova asked, twisting her hands together.

Magalhães looked up at her. "He's a clone."

Popova made a small involuntary sound, and then her cheeks heated. She had to be the most calm person here, and she was the least calm.

"I have to let the chief know," she said.

"I wouldn't tell her in person," Kaspian said.

Popova glared at him. He was right though. He clearly saw how upset she was, and figured she wasn't calm enough to make the right decision.

She opened her private link to the chief.

Chief, I need to talk to you now, without Lawrence Ostaka in your office. It's critical.

She highlighted, alarmed, and underscored the word "critical."

And then her message bounced back at her.

"What the hell?" Popova muttered.

She sent the message again, and again, it bounced. Then she examined it.

The message didn't technically bounce at all. It never got out of her personal system.

Magalhães and Kaspian were both watching her. Popova frowned at them, that panic rising all over again.

"Send me a message across your links," she said to them. "Right now."

Magalhães tilted her head slightly, then shook it. Kaspian actually slammed the heel of his hand against his ear, as if he could knock some sense into his links. (Maybe he could knock some sense into his own mind. Popova willed that thought away; it wasn't constructive.)

"My links don't seem to work," Magalhães said, sounding confused. "I've never encountered this before. There's usually a message."

She was right: When links shut off, there usually was a message that something external was blocking them. Popova empathized with Kaspian, even though she didn't want to.

This link blockage felt like a personal malfunction, only she knew it wasn't. Because they had the same problem she did.

She had to tell the chief right now. And she had to do it carefully.

Then Popova frowned.

"Have you two seen anyone else from the Security Office since you entered this room?" she asked.

"No," Magalhães said. "Should we have?"

Probably. Someone should have checked on them. Had Ostaka blocked the links and sent the staff away?

Popova felt chilled.

"I have one other question," she said, wishing she didn't sound as panicked as she felt. "Were there any female faces in that DNA you found?"

"Female…?" Magalhães asked. "Why?"

"Please," Popova said. "Just answer me."

"No," Magalhães said.

"But that doesn't mean anything," Kaspian said. "There's no way to know if we've found all of the clones."

Popova decided she hated him. She hated his precision and his fussiness, the way he had to contradict everything. She hated him because she couldn't afford to hate Ostaka at the moment.

"I'm ninety-nine percent positive we've found all the clone originals," Magalhães said.

Popova would have to accept that, and ignore Kaspian.

So, she spoke only to Magalhães. "Three rooms down from right here, there are two women. One of them is Marshal Judita Gomez. Tell her I need her in the chief's office immediately. Tell her that the situation is probably dire, and that our links aren't working and that the man in there is a clone. Can you do that?"

"Yes," Magalhães said.

"What do I do?" Kaspian asked.

"You keep the other woman in that room calm," Popova said and managed to add without sarcasm, "You can do that, right?"

"Of course," he said with his irritating precision.

"Where are you going?" Magalhães asked.

"I'm going to the chief's office and, I hope, I'll separate her from that clone. But I have no idea what's happening there, so…" Popova let her words trail off. She wanted to tell both of them she would be fine, but she had no idea if she would be fine.

"So," she said, finishing lamely, "wish me luck."

"*Good* luck," Kaspian said.

She smiled at him. She actually appreciated the good wishes. She wasn't superstitious, but she needed something to hold onto right now.

Because she had a hunch this day was about to get a lot worse.

52

FLINT ARRIVED AT THE SECURITY OFFICE ONLY TO FIND DOZENS OF SQUAD cars parked haphazardly all over the road. Cops milled around the outside of the building, some touching an almost invisible barrier, others conferring, a few waiting along the edges of the sidewalk as if unable to move without orders.

Flint parked half a block away and ran to the building's front door. It was shut as well, and the windows were dark, clearly dimmed from the inside.

Nyquist was peering at the building, hand shading his eyes from the glare of Dome Daylight. Three tactical officers stood nearby in deep conversation, but Nyquist was ignoring them.

Flint hurried to his side, and asked without preamble, "What, exactly, is going on?"

Nyquist didn't move. He continued to try to see in the building. But he said, "The entire building's in lockdown. No one on our team has ever seen anything this sophisticated. Nothing can get in or out, including link contact."

Flint let out a breath, then felt a surge of irritation. He had warned DeRicci about this, that the various systems she had installed and she had let Celia Alfreda's people install when they built the building's security might cancel each other out.

"Get me someone from the United Domes," Flint said.

Nyquist dropped his hands as he turned to look at Flint. Nyquist's irritation was plain in his scarred face. "What?"

Flint didn't care how irritated he was. "I can access one of the security panels if I have an active United Domes security clearance. It has to be governmental. Mine isn't."

"Can't the police do this?" Nyquist asked.

That irritation was back. They had to move, and move quickly, and Nyquist was questioning him.

Flint said, "You're all welcome to keep trying, but in the meantime, get me someone in the United Domes government."

"I'm not the guy who usually does this stuff," Nyquist said, and then seemed to realize what he was saying. "Besides, I think they're all inside that building. Noelle's been complaining about that for months, that she's the only representative—"

"But she isn't, though, is she?" Flint snapped. "There are councilors and representatives all over the Moon. They might have gone back to their domes, but that means that there should be some here in Armstrong, and if there aren't, then there should be one or two in Littrow."

"That's a half an hour away," Nyquist said.

"No kidding." Flint knew Nyquist was upset, and he knew Nyquist wasn't the kind of man who usually took orders, but Flint didn't care. He needed to get into this building's security system.

Flint walked around the barrier that had fallen over the sidewalk until he found some of the police computer techs. Two were officers he had trained a long time ago.

At least the department had put their best people on this.

Flint stopped beside Kaz Issassi, who had opened a virtual window near the building's barrier. Of all the people Flint had trained when he first joined the police department, Issassi had been the most talented.

Her fingers moved across lines of light, things he couldn't read because he was standing in the wrong position compared to the virtual window—one of the security measures he had installed.

"Finding anything?" he asked.

277

She started. She had been lost in her work. She glanced over her shoulder and smiled when she saw him.

"Thank God," she said, "someone who actually knows what they're doing."

She didn't look down the line at the other techs, but he knew what she was talking about. Of the eight techs he could see, only two others could handle something this complicated.

"Catch me up," Flint said.

"This isn't an outside hack," she said, and she was speaking softly. "The system's been altered, and in a very deft way. I had to search to find anything at first. It's mostly changes to the protocols. Instead of deleting them and replacing them, or inserting a worm or a virus or a new program, whoever did this used the existing programs and made them something other than what they were intended to be."

Flint felt cold. "You think this came from the inside?"

"I know it did," Issassi said. "And it took a lot of time. Someone couldn't have done this in an afternoon."

Flint didn't like the sound of that. Because if it took weeks to program, then it would take an equally long time to reprogram. Unless…

"Can we reset the system?" he asked.

"Not from out here. The system is designed for outside attacks, not an inside job. So everything about this system uses identification codes or locations to approve any changes. It doesn't matter if you can spoof the system or use a code that you know might work from the inside. You actually have to *be* inside."

Flint nodded. He remembered that from when he had tweaked the system. He had seen that information go by him, and hadn't thought much about it.

Hacking the system from the inside was nearly impossible. It would take weeks just to break in. He had dismissed any inside hack as a near-impossibility.

He silently cursed himself. He knew that most security breaches were caused not by someone getting lucky or having incredible programming skills, but by an error in the assumptions of the security system's designer.

He had compounded the error by failing to flag it.

Even though he had given himself a way in should something go wrong, he hadn't planned for this. That way in was predicated on the idea of an outside hack, not an inside breach.

"How much of the system has been changed?" Flint asked.

"Everything," she said. "The access points, the codes needed, the ways the system protects itself, it's all been changed from the inside, and every time I try to touch it, I get knocked out of the system. Here, you try."

Flint shook his head. "I don't know what you've done, and I don't want to make things worse. Just give me a quick tour."

She did. She went through all of the pieces she had touched. Flint moved behind her and watched. He didn't recognize anything anymore. Everything he knew about the system was wrong. He wondered if the outside access was wrong too. Maybe he wouldn't need the United Domes identification.

Then he remembered: he had set up the emergency access outside of the security program. It had been an add-on that he had designed, with only a few people who knew how to run it.

He just hadn't trusted the security system DeRicci had. He had also figured he would be trying to dismantle any outside hack, and he wouldn't be in the office when he did it.

He was glad for that; it would probably give him a way in.

He hoped.

He sent a message to Nyquist, *Have you found me someone from the United Domes government yet?*

They're scattered to the winds, Nyquist sent back. *The nearest I can find is in Littrow, and he doesn't want to come here. Says we can solve it ourselves.*

Flint cursed. *Get him here or have the Littrow Police arrest him and bring him here. Right now.*

You say that like there is a Littrow Police, Nyquist sent. He had a point. The Littrow Police Department was small and mostly useless.

Do what you have to, Flint sent.

The easy way into the system wasn't going to work. With what he was learning, his back-door might not work either. He was going to have to hack his own system.

"Do you think that whoever did these changes also altered some of the internal security protections?" Flint asked.

"Of course they did," Issassi said. "That's what I'm running into."

"No," Flint said. "This system has redundancies upon redundancies upon redundancies. Do you think whoever altered this knew about all of the redundancies?"

She grinned at him, then turned back to the virtual screen.

"There's only one way to find out," she said.

53

THE CURRENT NEWS FROM HÉTIQUE CITY CONFLICTED WITH THE INITIAL assumptions. DeRicci frowned at the images of the ships that had attacked the city from orbit. Some of them seemed familiar.

Ostaka worked on the minimally networked computer that DeRicci had had in her office for the past several weeks. DeRicci had checked the security on that particular machine before giving it over to Ostaka. He had worked hard on it ever since.

When she asked him what he was finding, he would say "Not much," and continue working. When she had pressed him about five minutes before, he confirmed what she had already found: that the information coming out of Hétique City was contradictory.

Then he swore.

The word seemed like an unconscious utterance. His fingers were flying over the keys, and he was leaning toward a virtual screen as people did when they used their own links to interface with the system—something she had not approved.

Clearly Ostaka was one of those people who, when given permission to do one thing, thought it was permission to do a dozen things.

"Hey," DeRicci said. "I didn't—"

The door burst open, and Popova pushed her way in. She looked terrified.

"Chief, all our links are down and I have to tell you—" She glanced sideways at Ostaka as she spoke, and then choked.

DeRicci looked in the same direction. He was reaching for something inside his shirt.

Popova walked farther into the large room.

"You have to leave," she said to DeRicci. *"Right now."*

DeRicci wasn't going to leave Ostaka alone in here. "Why are our links down?"

"I don't know. We just found out, but *please*, come with me. *Please.*" Popova gave Ostaka another terrified look. He kept one hand on the computer he was working on.

DeRicci sighed. She had seen Popova panic before, and it wasn't pretty. There was probably a glitch in the security system, and one of the techs could fix it. But Popova without links was like most people losing their hands.

DeRicci walked toward the door. "Come on, Lawrence," she said. "Let's see if we can solve this."

He grabbed her and pulled her toward him. He had a laser pistol in his left hand and he put it to her temple.

"We don't have to solve anything," he said. "You're either going to wait until I'm done, or I'm going to kill you."

Popova screamed and put her hands to her mouth. No help from that quarter.

DeRicci had to mentally switch gears. Ostaka was trying to hold her hostage? Really?

He was out of shape, and the hand holding the laser pistol trembled. His arm, pulling her tight against him, was trembling as well.

It was all DeRicci could do to keep from shaking her head in disgust.

She elbowed him in the gut while raising her other hand to grab his gun wrist. She pulled him forward, over her shoulder, slamming him against the floor.

He let out a cry of pain as the breath left his body. Somehow he managed to hold onto the pistol.

She put a foot on his wrist.

"Get me some cuffs," she said to Popova.

Popova hadn't moved.

"Rudra," DeRicci said. "Get me some cuffs."

"Where? I…."

DeRicci would have sent the location across her links, but Popova had been right: the links weren't working. "Weapons cabinet near the east window."

She hadn't opened that cabinet in months, maybe years, so she hoped there were cuffs in it. Popova glanced at the cabinet as if it were miles from her.

Ostaka moaned. He rolled over and tried to grab DeRicci's ankle. She bent over and smacked him in the face so hard that his nose gushed blood, ruining her only pair of shoes that hadn't fallen apart in this crisis.

"Rudra," DeRicci said. "Hurry."

Popova looked at Ostaka as if he were coming after her. She sidled to the cabinet, pulled it open, and grabbed cuffs.

Then she scurried toward DeRicci, handing them to her.

Ostaka wasn't fighting any more. He was choking on his own blood and whimpering.

DeRicci slammed her heel on his wrist, breaking it. His hand opened involuntarily, and she kicked the gun away.

"Take the pistol," she said to Popova.

Popova looked horrified.

"For godssake, Rudra, you're all I've got here. Take the damn pistol." DeRicci didn't watch to see if Popova followed her command.

DeRicci bent over and grabbed Ostaka by his broken wrist. He screamed. DeRicci pulled him upright, then yanked his arm behind his back. He screamed again. She flicked on the cuffs and attached one above his broken wrist.

Then she pulled his other arm back, and attached the other cuff to his wrist, making him lean sideways. His nose still dripped blood, and he was sobbing.

DeRicci cursed him.

She looked up at Popova, who was holding the laser pistol properly—thank heavens DeRicci had insisted on weapons training for the entire staff—pointing it at Ostaka.

"You stay there," she said to Popova, and then went to the weapons cabinet herself.

DeRicci pushed the door aside, leaving a bloody handprint on the fake wood. She grabbed more cuffs and two laser pistols. Then she considered before pulling two more out of the cabinet.

Popova would be her weapons' bearer until DeRicci figured out exactly what was going on.

DeRicci returned to Ostaka, cuffed him at the ankles as well, and pulled him against the mound of trash.

"All right, you bastard," DeRicci said to him. "Tell me who you really are and what the hell you've been doing."

He looked up at her, his swollen nose beginning to bruise. He spit out some blood.

He was probably in shock. DeRicci wasn't even sure he had understood her.

So she leaned toward him.

"Talk now, asshole," she said. "Or I'm going to make sure you learn what pain really is."

He blinked at her and let out a frightened sob.

And then he started to speak.

54

ANDRE HAD LOCKED EVERYONE OUT OF HER OFFICE AS SHE TRIED TO FIND whoever it was who had found Mavis Zorn. Andre had to be careful with her searches. She didn't want to seem interested, particularly since the person searching Mavis Zorn's name had already attached it to Andre's.

Andre's office was the largest in this building, maybe even the largest in this part of the division. She had a couch and three chairs, all Earth antiques—built for humans back when humans thought they owned the galaxy. She had imported her desk at great cost from an antique dealer on Earth, and had had to struggle to find the matching chair.

The chair, unfortunately, was uncomfortable, and the desk was so old it couldn't be networked without destroying its value, so Andre did much of her work standing up, working off a virtual screen.

This time, however, she had hauled out an actual computer, one that she had brought into this section herself, and she was researching on a network normally assigned only to undercover operatives. That way, no one would question the searches she ran. Undercovers did all kinds of crazy things all the time.

She was deep in the system, tracing the pings, following the signatures, when a red light flashed across her eyes.

She felt a surge of irritation. If this was Stott again, she would cut him off. She had no idea how she was going to do it, but she would. She would absolutely destroy him.

She didn't want to see who had sent the alert—hell, she didn't even want to see what the alert was. She had already calmed Stott, and even if it wasn't him, it was probably some other idiot panicking at the wrong time.

The alert brightened, taking over her vision, and she cursed. If she didn't do something with the damn alert, it would probably start making siren noises or activating one of the nerves in her face.

So she opened the alert, and frowned.

She didn't recognize the name of the sender, Lawrence Ostaka, but she recognized his face. He was one of the hundreds of clones who was taking part in the third attack. She had chosen the originals for that third attack herself, and she knew the names of each of the one-hundred originals in the procedure.

Ostaka's name came with an Earth Alliance Security clearance, as an investigator, and she opened a separate screen and accessed his information. He was originally off-Moon, but had managed to get himself assigned to the Moon right after Anniversary Day. It had taken some finagling on his part, but he had ended up in the office of security for the United Domes of the Moon.

Andre let out a *hunh* of appreciation. The man had ended up in the very office that had given Andre fits for the past six months. The only people with brains on the Moon, she had privately called them.

They had thwarted parts of the first attack, and nearly aborted *all* of the second. They wouldn't be able to stop the third—it was too massive—but if they knew what was ahead—

She made herself focus on his message. It was panicked, sent from the Office of Security for the United Domes of the Moon. *Found me. Can't finish lock-out. They have the names of Andre, Starbase Human—*

And that was where it ended, as if he were interrupted mid-send. She frowned at it, heart pounding, knowing the message for what it was—a get-out warning. She had made certain the upper-level team managers knew how to warn most of the important staff in the group when it was time to get out.

She had been warned.

She played the message again, saw his terrified features, saw him reach into his shirt, saw him glance over his shoulder before the message stopped.

Then she deleted the message, scrubbing it off her system.

She almost walked away, but she paused for one moment. He wasn't supposed to send messages to her. The only reason this one came through was because it was on the alert network.

But she had access to everything her people did—at least in theory. So she went back to the system she'd been using, and looked to see if there were more messages from Ostaka.

There were dozens, going all the way back to his posting in the Moon's security office. The most recent came shortly before the alert.

I've altered everything in the system here, he had sent to his handler. Andre assumed that "here" meant the security office. *I'm activating the protection protocols now. It should be impossible for anything to get in or out of their system. I'll keep my connection to you open, just in case, but I'm not anticipating problems. In fact, DeRicci just invited me to her office, so everything just got easier.*

And then, apparently, it broke down.

Andre shut down his message and scrubbed it, as well. She had seen that name—DeRicci—so many times since the first attack that she wanted to meet the woman. One of the brains on the Moon. Either that, or one of the luckiest people in the history of the human race.

Too bad Andre hadn't met DeRicci before the Moon attacks. A person like that would have been valuable. Andre wondered if DeRicci were corruptible—or had been. She certainly wouldn't be now.

Andre closed the computer, then packed it in a carry-all. She had to clear her office. She had an escape plan, and it looked like she would need it.

She supposed she could bluff it out here, but she wasn't sure she wanted to.

After all, there wasn't anything this DeRicci could do, even if she caught half the clones on the Moon. In a few hours, the last attack on the Moon would devastate all the domes, and take everyone's attention away from the so-called masterminds, and place it on rebuilding, recovery, or perhaps, on deciding whether or not the Alliance was even necessary.

Andre had time to escape. If she did it right, no one would ever find her.

The only way to do it right was to remain calm.

Sure, they had captured a clone named Ostaka. He was a mid-level manager of the attacks, but he didn't know everything. He knew some things that would set the so-called good guys on her trail, but even that might not have been enough.

And it sounded like he had done the important work.

Andre had believed for months now that if the Security Office on the Moon were neutralized, the attack would work.

She simply hadn't believed it possible to completely neutralize that office.

It seemed like this clone had managed the impossible.

Her luck was holding.

But luck, as she had learned, favored the prepared.

The final mission was underway.

55

GOMEZ HAD FINALLY WON THE TRUST OF POOR PIPPA LANDAU. THE WOMAN sat at the edge of her chair, looking terrified and out of place, even in her own body. She had confessed that she had cut her hair and wore different makeup than she had on Earth, and that she wasn't wearing her usual clothing.

But she hadn't completely recovered the persona she had lost when she Disappeared decades ago. She was rubbing her hands on her knees, and when she reached up to adjust the hair that no longer fell to her chin, the sweat stains from her palms dotted the fabric of her pants.

Gomez felt for her. Landau—or Takara Hamasaki, as she had once been known—was doing something she had vowed she never would, something that could possibly get her killed even now.

Gomez respected the amount of courage it had taken Landau/Hamasaki to leave her comfortable home on Earth and travel to the Moon, simply to impart information that might or might not help in the investigation of Anniversary Day.

Gomez still hadn't gotten enough information from Landau to know if that decades-old experience would provide anything valuable or not.

Then the door to the room banged open. A tiny woman with close-cropped black hair burst inside.

"I'm sorry," she said. "The links aren't working. Rudra Popova sent me for Marshal Gomez. She says that the chief is in trouble in her office and needs your help right away."

Landau gasped audibly, but Gomez didn't have time for her. Gomez stood, reaching for her laser pistol at the same time. Her hand closed on air. She had forgotten that she had left the pistol on the *Green Dragon,* figuring it would be easier to get into the security office without it.

"Stay here," she said to Landau. "Someone will come for you."

Gomez had no idea if that was true. As she followed the tiny woman out the door, she said to the woman, "Get some guards up here. We're going to need to protect the people on this floor. Make sure one of those guards is in front of this door."

"I don't work here," the woman said plaintively, "and I haven't seen any guards since I arrived."

Gomez cursed and pushed past her, Landau nearly forgotten. Gomez ran to DeRicci's office, pulled back the door—

And saw no one.

She stepped deeper inside, moving stealthily, and then DeRicci popped up from behind that mound of trash.

DeRicci's blouse and pants were soaked in blood, and some of it had sprayed across her face. She grinned at Gomez, eyes glittering happily.

"Hey, Marshal," she said. "Welcome to the party."

Gomez stepped around one of the desks and saw a man splayed on the floor. He had been in the conference room earlier, although he looked nothing like the rumpled but comfortable person who had been behind that desk.

Gomez recognized him by his thinning hair and, of all things, his government-issue shoes.

Dried blood covered his mouth and chin. His nose was swollen and his eyes were turning black-and-blue. Someone—DeRicci, probably— had broken his nose.

DeRicci had two laser pistols on her hip. A movement toward the back of the room revealed Popova, looking like a lost child. She was clutching two more laser pistols as if they might bite her, and there was a third on a desk near her. One of her hands clutched at least four laser cuffs.

"What did I miss?" Gomez asked. She felt a brush of air touch her back and turned just enough to see the woman who had fetched her.

"This idiot just pulled a laser pistol on me," DeRicci said. "He seemed to think he could hold me in place. Either he forgot that I was a cop or he thought I was too out of practice to take him. He learned."

Gomez grinned. She stepped deeper into the office, saw an open cabinet near one of the windows, with more weapons inside.

She turned to the woman who had fetched her. "I think we're going to need some privacy here."

"No, you're not," the woman said tightly. "You need me. You all need me and my partner. This guy is just one of the your problems. There are hundreds of others."

"What's she talking about?" DeRicci asked Popova.

"Clones," Popova said. "More clones. My guess is this guy just initiated the third attack, and we don't even know what it is."

56

It only took the dispatch a moment to patch in the chief inspector for Armstrong's dome. Ó Brádaigh had always hated Gary Lombrozo. The man had made Ó Brádaigh's life a living hell on more than one occasion. Lombrozo was fussy, precise, and unimaginative. He hated change of all kinds.

Ó Brádaigh wiped his sweating palms together, then glanced at the officers assigned to guard him. The female officer was looking around the substructure as if she had never been here before, studying the sturdy beams and the lighting. The male officer watched Ó Brádaigh as if still expecting him to do something wrong.

"What do you want?" Lombrozo said, his nasal voice echoing. It almost sounded as if he were standing inside the substructure, instead of his life-sized face floating at eye-level.

"I have credible evidence that someone is going to tamper with the dome," Ó Brádaigh said. "We're going to need to an emergency surface sweep, and then your people are going to have to inspect the entire dome. Someone tampered with the sectioning, so that it wouldn't come down even if there's a breach, and—"

"You don't give my department orders, Ó Brádaigh," Lombrozo said.

This was why someone else needed to be in control of what was going on. Ó Brádaigh wasn't good with people, he really wasn't. And his relationship with Lombrozo was terrible at best.

"Look," Ó Brádaigh said. "It was Armstrong PD that contacted you, right? They know how important this is—"

"Based on your lousy word? Ó Brádaigh, you're the worst engineer in the city, and I have no idea why they keep you on, but whatever you think is an emergency, isn't."

The female officer now stared at the floating image of the chief inspector. She stepped closer, so that she was in his line of vision.

"Forgive me, sir," she said to him. "I'm Armstrong Police Officer Karen Kobani. The Armstrong Police Department believes we have a credible threat here, and that all action must be taken immediately."

Ó Brádaigh could have kissed her. The male officer beside her nodded.

Lombrozo turned his head slightly as he looked at the scene in that substructure. "Men like Ó Brádaigh can't tell me how to do my job, Officer. Just because he says we need an emergency surface sweep doesn't mean we do. Do you know what'll happen in the city if we do something like that unscheduled?"

"Sir," Officer Kobani said, "do you know what'll happen to the city if you fail to do a sweep, and something blows through the dome?"

Lombrozo's lips thinned. "Ó Brádaigh, you send me all the information you have, and I'll consider your request."

Then he signed off.

"Son of a bitch," Ó Brádaigh said. He had no idea what to do. He needed that sweep.

"Is he always that big an asshole?" the male officer asked.

"We're on opposite sides," Ó Brádaigh said. "He's an inspector. I'm the one who does the work. He likes the power his position gives him."

"Can you initiate an emergency surface whatever?" Kobani asked.

"Yeah, but he's right," Ó Brádaigh said. "The dome programs will shut off. The entire interior will go dark. The city will know something's up."

Kobani shrugged. "I say you just do it."

"And then what?" Ó Brádaigh asked. "Inspectors need to be monitoring the surface, to see what's going on. If there's a hairline fracture or something, I might miss it."

"We need to get the department on this," the male officer said to Kobani.

"I wish we could reach the Security Office," Ó Brádaigh said. He ran a hand over his face. "I'll do the emergency sweep, but it'd be better if the inspectors ordered it."

"Who's his boss?" the male officer asked.

"I don't know. The city, I guess." Ó Brádaigh had no idea how all the departments worked.

"Maybe the acting mayor could help," Kobani said.

"It's not our decision. We just gotta impress on these people that this is an emergency, and someone else can light a fire under that guy's ass," the male officer said.

Ó Brádaigh nodded. He glanced at the control room. He didn't want to do this on his own.

But, he realized, he had no choice.

57

FLINT STOOD NEXT TO ISSASSI AND OPENED ANOTHER VIRTUAL SCREEN. Sometimes it was better to work beside someone and share information rather than work in isolation.

He would rather work beside Talia, whose thought processes he understood almost better than his own, but he didn't want to bring her into this.

She saw the Security Office as a safe place, and he didn't want to alter that perception. She was still at Zagrando's bedside, and it was the best place for her. With luck, this entire crisis would be past before she ever found out about it.

Chaos continued around him—police officers whose names he didn't know were talking out loud on their links; a few tactical officers were trying to figure out if there was a vulnerability in the building's barrier; two officials were arguing over who was in charge.

Several people went up to the windows and peered in, just as Nyquist had done. Flint wasn't sure what the point was behind that. Were they worried that no one was inside?

His stomach jumped at the very idea and he willed the thought away, but not before another followed on its heels. He hoped everyone was still alive in there.

He didn't want to think about what he would do if DeRicci were gone.

He made himself focus. He had a gift for remembering details of systems he set up, and he had set up so much inside this system that it felt like one of his own.

The changes were as visible to him as they would have been if someone had highlighted them in gold. And as he looked, he had a realization: Whoever had done this hadn't been a gifted programmer. Whoever had made these changes had learned enough about systems to change them, but not to design them.

"Hey, Kaz," Flint said softly, "I think only one person did this."

"If that's the case, it took 'em a long time." The light from the virtual screen illuminated her face. She was frowning in concentration.

Flint nodded once, putting that piece of information in his mind to use later. Whoever did this had to have had access for Issassi's "long time," and not a lot of people had that.

There was a pattern to what this person had done. Flint could see the edges of it.

He worked, for how long, he didn't know. He was losing track of time, like he often did when he was digging into systems. And then he saw it.

The hacker—or alterer—or whatever this person was—had changed things in the same order. If he changed an entry code to one part of the system, he then worked his way through that part of the system as if he were walking from front to back in a room, instead of fixing all of the entry codes at the same time.

"Kaz," Flint said. "Look."

He showed her what he had found. She grinned at him, her expression victorious.

"Idiot," she said—about the hacker, not about Flint. "We don't reset by item, we reset by date."

She was right; they had to find the first access date. Flint switched everything on his screen, querying the system, asking it when this user first appeared.

The date he received was a month after Anniversary Day. Flint tried to remember when he had beefed up the system. It had to be earlier than that.

He couldn't get deep enough into the system to check his alterations. If he reset too early, those alterations would be lost.

But did it matter? The system was inaccessible, and if he managed to fix the system, then he could repair what he had destroyed.

"Can you find what date this person entered the system?" Issassi asked.

"I got a date, but I don't trust it," Flint said. "Let's do this: let's use a date we can be certain of."

She glanced at him, her fingers still working even though she wasn't looking at what she was doing.

"What date?" she asked.

He smiled. "Anniversary Day," he said.

"But, how do we know this person wasn't already in the system?" she asked.

"Because I made some alterations after Anniversary Day, and I would have noticed changes this inelegant," Flint said.

"We don't have the authorization to reboot the entire system. Not now," she said.

"Oh, but we do," he said. He had just checked. His outside security protocol, the one very few people knew about, seemed completely untouched. In that protocol, he had given himself the ability to reboot the entire system.

He had thought of it as the doomsday option, because he had known, even then, that it would wipe the system clean.

He opened a third window, found his little protected part of the Security Office system, and took a deep breath.

"You ready, Kaz?" he asked.

She widened her black eyes slightly. They expressed what she couldn't say out loud. She wasn't sure this was going to work. She was afraid it would make everything worse.

There was only one way to find out.

Flint initiated the reboot—and waited.

58

DeRicci grabbed a cleaning cloth from her desk and wiped off her face. The cloth smelled faintly of garlic and polish. Popova made a circular motion in front of her left cheek, indicating that DeRicci hadn't gotten everything. She wiped again.

She wasn't really doing it to get rid of the blood. She was doing it because of the iron smell that the blood had coated her with. Only the spray on her face wasn't the problem.

The problem was her clothes, soaked in the blood from Ostaka's nose. They were extra-heavy. She rummaged behind her desk for something to change into.

Her adrenalin flowed, her hands moving faster than they usually did. Even with the adrenalin, she could feel a pulled muscle along her spine. Picking up a man of Ostaka's weight and flinging him, even when done properly, really wasn't something she had done of late.

Heck, it had probably been five years or more since she had dropped someone. She was rather pleased to know she still could.

Gomez had taken the laser pistols from Popova. The woman who had said there were hundreds more problems had come farther into the office. It had taken DeRicci a second to place her.

That was Berhane Magalhães, Bernard Magalhães's daughter. They had met at some long, stupid, boring fundraiser for something, and

DeRicci's impression of the young Ms. Magalhães was that she was one of those rich, sincere types who wanted to give money to every single cause that caught her fancy.

DeRicci had no idea why she was here.

Ostaka had closed his eyes. He hadn't said a word since Gomez had come into the room, and DeRicci wasn't sure he was going to say more.

What he had said alarmed her: he had shut off all access to the building.

"We need to get everything back online," she said to Popova. "And where the hell is the rest of the staff?"

"I sent them away," Ostaka mumbled. Apparently, he was going to talk.

"Away where?" DeRicci asked, making sure she sounded as angry as she felt. Asshole. Ruining her building. She had trusted him.

"Middle of the building. Told them there was an emergency. Then I locked down the floor."

Gomez's gaze met DeRicci's, and DeRicci could almost hear her thoughts. Something was happening today besides this lockdown.

But DeRicci wasn't going to assume that.

"Did you decide to mess with our systems today because I let you into my office?" she asked.

"No," he said miserably. Then shook his head, winced as if it hurt, and said, "I mean, I took some liberties, yes, but I didn't do it because you were dumb enough to let me in here."

She wanted to hit him again. She came closer, fist clenched. It wasn't just for effect—or maybe it wasn't for effect at all.

"Then what was so important about today?" she asked.

Gomez watched it all, expression impassive.

Ostaka opened his eyes as far as he could. He even attempted a smile. "You'll find out."

DeRicci wasn't going to play games. She was going to make him talk. Enough playing.

As DeRicci took a step toward him, Berhane Magalhães spoke up.

"I think we need to deal with all the others," she said. "If he's doing something today, they probably are too."

Popova nodded. "She showed me a lot of clones, Chief."

Gomez looked back and forth between them. "We should see this."

DeRicci took a step back. She was angry—she had been angry for months—and she finally had someone to direct her anger at. No wonder her control and focus had slipped a little.

"You're right." She took a deep breath. "Rudra, do you know how to access the emergency lockdown on the lower floors?"

"I'm already on it," Popova said. "It's a little more complicated than I expected."

In other words, this jerk had tweaked things to make it hard for Popova to fix from up here. DeRicci wished Flint were here, but she'd already tried to use her links after she had hit Ostaka. The links weren't working.

"Show me what you have," she said to Magalhães.

Magalhães glanced over her shoulder. "Can I bring my partner here?"

"We don't have time to bring in someone from the outside," DeRicci said. "I need to know—"

"He's in the next room," Magalhães said.

"Go," DeRicci said. She sighed, then looked at Gomez. "Any good with computer systems, Marshal?"

"I'm afraid not," Gomez said. "But I can probably get this one to talk, if you like."

DeRicci felt reluctant to give up Ostaka. That emotion alone was a warning sign.

"Sure," DeRicci said. "See what you can do."

Ostaka winced even before Gomez got to him. She yanked him up by his collar and shoved him against the desk buried under the trash.

"It'll be in your best interest to tell us everything," Gomez said.

He shook his head. "I no longer have a best interest."

Just like the Peyti clones. DeRicci would wager everything she owned that this fool had been on some kind of suicide mission.

Magalhães returned with a skinny man who looked like he needed a good meal. His long hair was pulled back into a ponytail.

"Did Berhane explain to you how we got the DNA?" he asked.

DeRicci had no idea what he was talking about.

Popova looked at all of them from above a floating screen. "Chief, they found some information on clones. Ms. Magalhães runs one of the search and recovery efforts in the domes."

"Thanks for the context, Rudra," DeRicci said. "You found—"

"Old DNA, out of place." Magalhães spoke over her partner. "These people had died decades ago, so we didn't know how they kept appearing in the destroyed parts of the dome. I can tell you how we found it all later, but you need to see this. These are the originals."

She nodded at the skinny man. He raised a dozen screens around the room, and faces appeared.

DeRicci recognized half of them. She'd seen them around Armstrong—not dead people, but living people. One of the originals had Ostaka's face, albeit an older, fleshier version. She recognized others from some of the city planning meetings she had attended in the past few months.

Her breath caught.

"The thing is," the skinny guy said, "the pattern repeated over and over. It wasn't like we found only one person's DNA in one dome. We found versions of these originals in most of the dome sites we've worked."

"Obviously something is going to happen today, and these people are involved," Gomez said. "How the heck are we going to deal with that?"

As she said that last, she shook Ostaka. He winced again, but didn't say anything at all.

DeRicci was just staring at the faces. No wonder she hadn't found anything. She had set her searches to find large clone patterns, figuring the Peyti Crisis was the new model for clone attacks. Not twenty clones of one person, as she had seen on Anniversary Day, but hundreds.

Although she had set up a different search for the port, searching for smaller groups of clones who had come in together on a transport, as they had done before Anniversary Day.

She hadn't been imaginative enough.

"These originals," she said to Magalhães, "they were born on the Moon, weren't they?"

"Yeah," she said, "and that's about all we can find in common between them."

If DeRicci had to guess, she would have guessed that the clones had come in as children or had come in at different times, or maybe were even cloned here, in some illegal operation.

She didn't have time to worry about the how. She needed to worry about whatever was next.

Ostaka hadn't grown up on the Moon. He had come here.

"I assume you have a higher rank than all the other clones," she said, appealing to his vanity.

"In life or in the Earth Alliance?" he asked.

Fascinating response. She wished she could mention that to Gomez on a link, but the links were still down.

"In general," DeRicci said. "You know who the players are."

"I don't know those people," he said.

"But you knew they existed," DeRicci said.

He shrugged, then grimaced. She had hurt him badly.

"Let's preserve him," she said to Gomez. "He'll lead us to the masterminds once today is over."

"We won't be here when today is over," he said.

DeRicci grinned at him. "You have consistently underestimated me, Lawrence," she said softly. "And I just heard you do it again."

59

THE MASSIVE SECURITY SYSTEM FOR THE UNITED DOMES OF THE MOON Security Office disappeared from the screen Flint was working on. The entire screen had gone dark as the system rebooted.

All down the line beside him, techs stepped back from their screens.

"What the hell?" someone asked.

Issassi glanced sideways at Flint. She was biting her lower lip so hard, she had drawn blood. She didn't seem to notice.

One of two things could happen. The system could harden, and he would never get in this way. Or it could completely disappear, leaving the Security Office vulnerable.

Then he mentally shook his head at himself. The Security Office was already vulnerable. Even if the security shut down, the office would be better off than it had been when he arrived.

And his "one of two things" estimation was just wrong. A million things could go wrong. Attempting to reset the system, back to a date before Anniversary Day, might trigger something, some kind of internal worm or something that he had no idea about. Because he hadn't been able to check.

So he listened to the techs, fretting and worrying and wondering what they had done, not telling them what he had done, and he watched the blackness on his screen.

Then the screen lit up, and a cheer went up around him. For a moment, he thought the techs were cheering, and then he realized it was the hardened police officers.

The shield around the building had disappeared. Police officers streamed forward.

Issassi extended her hand. She grinned at him.

"It worked," she said.

"Yeah," he said. "Now we have to repair whatever the hell this person has done."

But first he sent a message along his links to DeRicci. *Hey, haven't been able to reach you. Are you all right?*

He got an immediate message back. *Miles? Is that really you?*

Yes, he sent. *Are you all right?*

Oh, yeah, she sent, *but can you get here right now? We're having trouble with our systems.*

He smiled—really smiled—for the first time in hours. *I'm already here. We're in the systems now.*

Great, she sent, *because I really need your help with something else. Can you come upstairs?*

Yeah, he sent. *I'll be right there.*

"Think you can handle this?" he asked Issassi.

"Yeah," she said. "I'll do everything I can. Where are you going?"

"I'm needed inside," he said.

She nodded. "I'll clean up this mess as fast as I can."

"I'd rather you be accurate," Flint said.

"Point taken." Her head was already bent over yet another screen. He could tell from the way she leaned that she was using her own links to access some of the information.

He hurried past her. Relief mixed with worry as he headed toward the main door of the office. Relief was winning out, though. If someone had been trying to imitate DeRicci, they would have never gotten that level of command correct. DeRicci was all business. Clearly, she had to be.

He entered the main door, saw that the security system had rebooted to its pre-Anniversary Day level. It greeted him by name (something he had gotten rid of) and welcomed him into the building (something else he had gotten rid of).

Several police officers complained as he slipped through. They felt their badges should let them in. At least that rudimentary level of security existed. Clearly, the system was confirming who they were before allowing them access.

He ran across the lobby floor, startled that no humans were there to greet him. And since the elevators were automated, he decided he wouldn't get on one. He still had no idea what was working and what wasn't.

As he took the stairs, he sent DeRicci another message. *I'm coming to your office, right?*

Oh, yeah, she sent. *And ignore the mess.*

He had been ignoring the mess for months. He wondered what she meant by that, then figured he would find out soon enough.

60

BEFORE Ó BRÁDAIGH EXECUTED AN EMERGENCY DOME SURFACE SWEEP all on his own, he decided to try Berhane one last time. He didn't want her to panic when the dome went dark.

He was probably going to panic enough for the both of them. He would have to trust computers that might've been tampered with to tell him the sweep worked. He would rather have had the city's fifty inspectors monitor their dome areas, and their own systems, than trust the overall system that Petteway had touched.

For all Ó Brádaigh knew, Petteway had set something to blow when there was a surface sweep.

Ó Brádaigh took a deep breath and turned to the two police officers who were assigned to guard him. "You both are making sure the city knows that Lombrozo wouldn't cooperate?"

"We're past that," the male officer said. "We're working our way up the chain of command, seeing if we can bypass that tight-ass for good."

"Thanks." Ó Brádaigh wished he could believe that the work the officers were doing would help. But he wasn't sure anything could.

He'd already warned his mother. But he still needed to reach Berhane.

Berhane, he sent on his private links. *Oh, please, Berhane, answer me this time.*

Donal? It was her.

He gasped with surprise. Kobani looked at him.

"I got ahold of my girlfriend," Ó Brádaigh said by way of explanation. Then heard himself. That was probably the first time he had ever told anyone that Berhane was his girlfriend.

"You don't have a lot of time here," Kobani said.

Donal, I'm in the middle of something, Berhane sent. *Can I contact you in a while?*

Berhane, listen, he sent. *I'm probably not supposed to tell you this, but you should put on an environmental suit. I'm not sure we're going to make it through the next few hours, and if you have a suit on—*

What? What's going on, Donal? She sounded surprised, but not panicked like his mother had.

I found evidence that someone's messing with the dome, and I can't reach the Security Office. Armstrong PD is trying to help, but we're running into problems at every turn. I—

I'm in the Security Office, Berhane sent. *Let me patch you through to the chief.*

Ó Brádaigh looked at the officers in surprise. They frowned at him. He must've been making a spectacularly strange face.

I'm going to go to full visual, Berhane sent.

Okay, go.

She appeared before him, a life-sized hologram so real he wanted to put his arms around her. He couldn't see behind her—wherever she was appeared to be whited out—but he got the sense that she wasn't alone.

She looked on either side of him, obviously seeing the officers.

"Where are you?" Berhane asked.

"I'm in the substructure where the dome controls are," Ó Brádaigh said. "The officers here are guarding me. We're in trouble, Berhane."

"You are or *we* are?" she asked.

"We are," he said. "The Moon. The next attack will happen in the next few hours. I just happened on my boss, altering the commands for the sections."

The Chief of Security for the United Domes of the Moon appeared beside Berhane. They were about the same height, but the chief appeared to be covered in blood.

"What happened there?" Ó Brádaigh asked the chief. "You look injured."

Berhane glanced at the chief, who waved her hands in an it-doesn't-matter gesture.

"Tell me exactly what you found," the chief said.

So he did. He explained the problems with the sections, the trouble he'd had with the chief inspector for the domes, and the fact that the smallest crack in the dome could cause a catastrophic dome failure. Everyone would die.

"And it's not just this dome," he said. "I think it's going to happen in other domes on the Moon. We only have a few hours to stop this, and I haven't been able to tell anyone."

"You've told me," the chief said. She looked over his shoulder, as if seeing someone else arrive. Her expression relaxed for just a moment. Then she turned her attention back to Ó Brádaigh and nodded. "I'll make sure the other domes know, and I'll override that chief inspector. We're going to get moving on this immediately. Tell me what else we need to do."

His knees had gone weak with relief. Finally, someone who could actually help.

"We have to do the sweep," Ó Brádaigh said, "but that's just the beginning. We need people inside and outside the dome, seeing if there's anything on them. A surface sweep will take care of a problem on the exterior, but crap sticks to the inside of the dome all the time. In Armstrong, at least, the interior surface sweep capability is minimal. It only searches for flaws in the surface, not for stuff sticking to the surface."

"Meaning what?" the chief asked.

"Meaning I could place a small explosive the size of a fingernail on the interior, and the sweep won't catch it. It's one of those things that the engineers and the inspectors know, but the general population doesn't.

The problem is that I'm afraid Petteway has been running this thing, and he's an engineer, a damn good one."

The chief nodded. "What can we do from the inside? Bots? The kind of nanocleaners that someone would use on the exterior of their house? Would any of that work?"

"It might," Ó Brádaigh said. "That's outside my area of expertise. I need someone to consult with."

"We may have leads on that, as well," she said. "Is there anything else?"

"Yes," he said. "Whatever breaches the dome might not be something small. For all I know, someone has set up a large explosive on the roof of a building somewhere. Or inside a building. Anything's possible, chief, and we only have a few hours. That's the tough part. Plus, I don't know who to trust."

"Can I send him the images?" Berhane asked the chief.

Ó Brádaigh looked from one to the other of them. He had no idea why Berhane was in the Security Office, and he didn't know what she meant by images.

It appeared the chief didn't, either. She was frowning at Berhane.

"The Old DNA," Berhane said. "The originals. Can I send those to him, because if I do, then he might know who he can rely on."

"It's worth a try," the chief said to her.

The officers had moved closer to Ó Brádaigh. They glanced at each other, then looked at him. He wished they were watching the area around him, but he didn't say that.

"We're going to send you images of one hundred people," the chief said to Ó Brádaigh. "They're the originals for clones that we believe are planning this attack on the Moon. We already caught one. Maybe we can find some of the others this way."

"Are all of these images possible clones?" Ó Brádaigh asked.

"I have no idea," the chief said. "We'll have to proceed as if they are. At some point, with only a few hours to go, we're going to have to trust, at least a little bit. Can you do that, Mr.—"

"Ó Brádaigh, sir," he said. "I'm Donal Ó Brádaigh."

"Mr. Ó Brádaigh, you have probably saved millions of lives today," the chief said.

"I haven't saved anyone yet, Chief. But I'm going to do my damndest."

"We are too, Mr. Ó Brádaigh," she said with great passion. "We are too."

61

MILES FLINT HAD ENTERED THE OFFICE WHILE DERICCI WAS SPEAKING to Donal Ó Brádaigh. DeRicci held it together until she finished talking to Ó Brádaigh, and then she hurried across the office.

She stopped for a half second. She wanted to hug Flint, but wasn't sure she should. She was covered in Ostaka's blood. She didn't need to coat Flint in it, no matter how happy she was to see him.

He looked at her for a moment, as if trying to see if the blood were hers, and then wrapped her in his arms. They held each other tightly for a long moment.

She couldn't remember if she had ever hugged him before, but it felt right to hug him now.

"That sounded awfully serious," Flint said as he pulled back. Her shirt stuck to his. She eased them apart.

"It's worse than serious," she said. "We've got to act fast."

She felt like she could do that, now, with Flint here.

And then more people came into her office, some she didn't recognize. At their heels, Bartholomew Nyquist. She hugged him too. She had gone to every extreme today—from beating the crap out of Ostaka to holding the two men in her life.

"I was so afraid something had happened to you," Nyquist said in her ear.

"Well, it's been exciting," she said as she pulled out of the hug.

He saw the blood and blanched.

"It's not mine," she said. "It's his."

She pointed with her thumb over her shoulder.

"Look," she said to the dozen people who had come into her office—cops, Nyquist, Flint, and her own security staff, released from the lower floors where Ostaka had held them. "I don't have time to brief you people. Marshal, can you get them up to speed?"

"With pleasure," Gomez said from beside Ostaka.

Flint frowned at her, and DeRicci realized he had never met Gomez. Neither had Nyquist. Well, they'd meet her now. DeRicci didn't have time for formal introductions.

"When you're done, Miles, I'll need you to tweak one of our security programs—you'll understand why—and I need someone good repairing our own systems. Bartholomew, we need Armstrong PD rallying the citizenry. We're going to need everyone searching for suspicious anythings."

"Meaning what?" he asked.

"I'll explain," Gomez said.

"No offense," Nyquist said, "but I have no idea who the hell you are or why I should trust you."

"You trust her because I do," DeRicci said.

"That's not a reason, Noelle," Nyquist said. "That Earth Alliance investigator—"

"Fooled all of us, Bartholomew, including you. Now shut up and listen, because we probably have less than four hours to save this stupid moon, again."

She took a breath. Just stating the number of hours left made the panic she'd been living with for so long gnaw at her. She willed it away.

"I've got to talk with the heads of the various domes, and for that, I need you, Rudra. We need to get them all, and we need to get them all at once."

"Do you want to change your shirt, chief?" Popova asked. Always practical, that one.

DeRicci almost agreed, and then she shook her head. She needed to impress on everyone how very important it was to act quickly.

"No," she said. "And I need the images of those originals. Now, the rest of you, give me a minute, because I'm going to need to think how to present all of this."

Normally, she would kick them all out of her office, but that wasn't going to work. Instead, she moved to the couch, and started outlining her presentation in her head.

She had to talk about the dome sectioning, the possible breaches, the multitudinous clones—it all sounded impossible. There was no way they were going to reach everyone.

Then she took a deep breath. One thing at a time. The domes first.

She looked up at her team. "We're going to need to section our dome, just in case. Rudra, that's first. Then get me the leaders of the other domes. Just send out the order, all right?"

"Are people going to have warning this time?" someone asked.

DeRicci didn't notice who questioned it. "Give them five minutes. Sirens, blaring lights, all that stuff. Let's give people time to clear intersections and get to the part of the dome they need to be in. Quickly, though, all right?"

Half the people in her office nodded their heads. Flint didn't. He was leaning toward Gomez. Nyquist was gesturing. He was clearly still trying to figure out who she was.

DeRicci turned her back on the crowd. She had to trust them to act.

She would tell the other dome leaders that they needed to section immediately as well.

She needed to tell them to examine their domes, that the threat was pretty clear, albeit difficult to thwart. She would also need to send the images of the originals to the dome leaders, but she wished she had a shorthand to help them search for the clones inside their domes. Before, she'd had one image. This time she had a hundred—literally.

She looked over her shoulder at Magalhães and that skinny guy she had arrived with.

"Did you notice any patterns with those originals?" DeRicci asked. "Anything at all?"

"Nothing we can use," Magalhães said.

DeRicci let out a breath.

"They're male." The voice cut through all of the chatter. DeRicci didn't recognize it. She looked near the main door. A strange-looking, middle-aged woman in clothes that didn't quite fit her stood near the wall with her arms crossed.

"I told you to stay in the other room, Pippa," Gomez said to the woman.

"You were gone for a long time," the woman said. "And you left the door open. I've been watching from the hallway. The faces, the originals you pulled, they're all male."

DeRicci hadn't noticed that but Magalhães nodded. So did the skinny guy.

"They are," the skinny guy said. "All that means, though, is that we might've missed the females."

"Or it might mean they're all male," Gomez said.

"Originals?" Flint asked.

"In a minute, Miles," DeRicci said. She wasn't going to get sidetracked. She frowned as she considered what the group had just told her. She'd been thinking about clone patterns for a long time. The serial killers were a pattern. The Peyti clones embedded in society were a pattern. These people were embedded too, but they weren't based on serial killers. They seemed to be clones of good citizens. But why males?

Then she realized the answer didn't matter. What mattered was acting with the knowledge they all had, and searching for more knowledge at the same time.

"What we have is this," she said, "we have one hundred originals, all human, all male, all born on the Moon. We use that. If we miss, we miss, but I'm pretty sure we have what we need."

Everyone was looking at her. She felt stronger than she had in weeks, maybe months.

She had only a few hours, but a few hours were more than she had had during the Peyti Crisis, and definitely more than she had had during Anniversary Day.

A few hours was a damn luxury.

Or, at least, she had to convince herself of that.

And she had to convince everyone else too.

62

It only took a few minutes for Marshal Judita Gomez to catch both Flint and Nyquist up on what was going on. It would have taken less time, but Nyquist had decided not to trust her, and was quizzing her about all kinds of things.

Flint finally had to send a message across his links, warning Nyquist to tone down his inquisition. They only had a short time to act, which meant they even had less time to learn what was going on.

They didn't know Gomez, but DeRicci had been right: they had to trust her. Her identification checked out—not that it mattered. Ostaka's had as well.

Ostaka still leaned against the desk piled in trash, his head down. Flint suddenly felt a surge of irritation.

"Did someone block that guy's links?" he asked Gomez, jerking his head toward Ostaka.

She cursed, and turned to one of the security staff. "Put a link blocker on that man."

"I need to check with—"

"Put the link blocker on," Flint said. "And right now, no checking. Just do your job. As the chief said, we have a very short window here."

The man nodded, then went to a nearby desk where Flint knew a stash of individual link blockers hid. He had put some of them there himself.

"I hope we didn't start something else," Nyquist said.

"We need to trace his contacts," Flint said, and then he shook his head. Nyquist was the person best suited to do that, but he had a lot of other things to do as well, maybe more important things.

He did, too. Now that Gomez had told them what was happening, he needed to tweak the program he had used to find all of the clones during the Peyti Crisis. He had already decided he would open a second version of that program and search for more human clones, without the criminal background.

And he probably needed a third program, searching for alien clones, which was ever so much harder.

He sent a message along his links to Kaz Issassi. *I need you in De-Ricci's office.*

He wished he could send for Talia too, but he wanted her away from all the trouble. Right now, he needed to concentrate. He had to believe she would be all right.

He moved to the computer system he usually used in DeRicci's office and began his work. Immediately, he got thousands of hits on the already-known clones.

"Noelle," he said, "there's no way we're going to be able to arrest all of these clones. No city on the Moon has the manpower for it."

She waved a hand at him to shut him up. She was talking to the mayors and acting mayors of every domed city on the Moon.

"That's a problem," Gomez said from beside him.

"We're going to have to release the information to the citizenry," Flint said. "They're going to have to isolate these people."

"Great," Nyquist said. "Do you realize what we'll be unleashing? We're giving people the go-ahead to maim or murder their neighbors. And there's going to be a lot of misidentification, a lot of panic—"

"You have a better idea?" Flint snapped.

Nyquist's lips thinned. He clearly didn't.

"I can release names and identification for most of these clones," Flint said. "I've been comparing citizen records. We know who these people are, we just don't have the ability to arrest them."

"No android police in Armstrong?" Gomez asked.

Nyquist looked at her, clearly horrified. Flint wondered how long she had been away from the heart of the Earth Alliance.

"In most cities, androids are only allowed as guards in prisons," he said.

Gomez nodded. "All right, then. I say release the names. If we get false arrests, and lose a few lives, it's better than losing millions of lives."

"Or a dome," Flint said.

"Do we give everyone who commits murder today a pardon as well?" Nyquist asked.

His words echoed around the room. For some reason, most of the chatter had ended just before he spoke.

Flint shuddered. He was approving something he didn't believe in. He hoped to hell no one pointed out that the murder of clones wasn't considered murder in a single city on the Moon—not unless those clones had had a status change, like Talia.

"No," Flint said. "We tell people to isolate these folks, but we don't tell them that we're having them search for clones. That'll cut down on some of the violence."

"You have a lot more faith in humanity than I do," Nyquist said. "Particularly panicked humanity."

Flint knew Nyquist had a point, but they couldn't control everything. "We're going to have to tell them that if they kill these people, they'll harm the investigation into whatever's going to happen in the domes. Tell them they'll be destroying information."

Nyquist shook his head. "Who is going to make this lovely announcement?"

"Me." DeRicci had turned toward them. "You folks didn't make it easy to talk to the heads of the domed cities. You were awfully loud. Anyone hear of link communications?"

"Sorry," Flint said.

"Don't be," DeRicci said. "The heads of the domes are all panicked, and it's all they can do to check the dome equipment and get their sections down. I'd already decided that I would send the information about the clones, and you two have just helped me with the wording. We're going to tell everyone on the Moon that we know who the next attackers are, and they've been living among us, just like the Peyti clones did. Smart people will realize they're dealing with clones. Everyone else will simply act."

"Do you want to do this by dome?" Flint asked.

"Meaning what?" DeRicci asked.

"I've got names and images. It would take nothing to isolate where they live, and when Officer Kaz Issassi gets here, we should be able to find where these people actually are."

"You can do that quickly?" DeRicci asked.

"I can do part of it quickly," Flint said.

"Then do it," she said. "We need to move *now*."

63

THE ENTIRE BUILDING SHOOK, AND DOZENS OF LAWYERS LOOKED AT EACH other, clearly startled. Salehi grabbed a nearby desk, only to feel it scoot away from him.

He had forgotten: he was on the Moon, and nothing here was bolted down.

"What the hell was that?" he asked Melcia Seng. She had run S^3 in the days since Zhu's murder.

She shook her head. Her dark eyes were wide, her back stiff. "I have no idea."

"It's the dome sectioning," said one of the private security guards who stood near the door. He was a beefy man with a jowly face. Salehi had taken one look at the guards he had hired after Zhu's death and had decided to find a different firm. Half of these guards were out of shape, and the others seemed too small to be effective.

"Dome sectioning," Salehi repeated.

"The domes section when there's a potential threat," said Uzvuyiten. "Haven't you lived in a domed community, Rafael?"

When Uzvuyiten used his most sarcastic tone, he seemed even more condescending than usual.

"No," Salehi said. "I haven't."

He had lived a lot of places, mostly on space stations or starbases. He'd also lived on Earth for several glorious years. But never in a domed community.

"The dome sectioned on Anniversary Day," said one of the lawyers that Seng had brought with her or that Zhu had hired. One of the lawyers who was already in the S³ offices when Salehi had arrived half an hour ago.

After he and his staff had their initial dust-up in the Port of Armstrong, they made their way through the city with little incident. Cars Seng had hired for them brought them directly to S³'s offices, as Salehi had instructed.

Once they arrived, he wondered if they should have gone to the apartments that Seng had rented for them first, giving everyone a chance to freshen up. He had noticed a thread of tension running through the entire group, probably from the port encounter, and he wanted to ease it.

He had been about to announce a break until the next day when the building had shaken.

"Shouldn't we get some kind of announcement when the dome sections?" he asked.

The security guard shrugged. "There's warning bells and stuff for people near the sections, sometimes, if there's time."

"Anyone monitoring the media?" Salehi asked. "Do we know why the domes have sectioned?"

"There's just been an announcement about some kind of dome check," one of the staffers said.

The guard glanced at another guard, seemingly uneasy.

"What does *that* mean?" Salehi asked.

But before the guard answered, images flooded Salehi's eyes. The images came through his emergency links.

If you are near these people, blared an androgynous voice, *detain them. They plan to attack the Moon in the next few hours. Make sure they have no weapons or explosives and no access to their links. Notify authorities once the prisoners are secure. Time is of the essence here.*

Then the message repeated itself, and strangely, it did not warn the people who received it to take care of themselves.

The images continued scrolling, and one of them lit up as his links registered a match.

The guard who had told him about the sectioning.

The guard looked alarmed. He glanced at everyone, then bolted out the door. Half a dozen associates followed, along with Salehi, who was closest.

He sprinted, reached the guard, and tackled him, sprawling across the tile floor, feeling the skin scrape off his elbow.

Others landed on top of him. The guard grunted with each landing, and Salehi actually empathized. He was amazed he could still breathe.

"Get up, get up, get up." Uzvuyiten's voice acted like a command.

The people on top of Salehi peeled off. He couldn't move quite as easily.

"You," Uzvuyiten said to someone Salehi couldn't see, "do as the instructions we all received say. And add a link blocker for good measure. And you, see if we have any other miscreants lurking in our building."

He stopped beside Salehi, whose weight still held down the guard.

You really didn't think that through, did you? Uzvuyiten sent through their links.

Salehi noted dozens of other feet around them, realized that even if the guard tried to run, he wouldn't be able to.

So Salehi slowly stood, hearing his beleaguered back crack. *Think what through?*

Tackling this creature, Uzvuyiten sent.

I hadn't done that since college, Salehi sent. He had played a variation on an ancient Earth sport when he'd lived in California, and he had learned the art of the tackle then.

I'm not speaking of your barbaric take-down of this creature, Uzvuyiten said. *I am referring to our future.*

Future? Salehi sent. He wiped off his pants and looked at his elbow. Scraped raw. It ached, although that would fade soon. The nanohealers he had were already repairing the damaged skin.

We are probably going to end up representing this creature.

What? Salehi sent.

He's a clone, Uzvuyiten sent.

A clone. Of course he was. Salehi had seen the images and acted, but Uzvuyiten was right. The images were of clones.

The irony reached him, and he shook his head. Then he stepped aside. He could bet that Uzvuyiten was the only person on the entire Moon who was thinking about the upcoming legal cases.

But Salehi took Uzvuyiten's point. Salehi nodded at one of the associates he had just met.

"Do what we were instructed. Find a way to detain this man, and notify the authorities."

And then, because he couldn't help himself, Salehi looked at the security guard.

"What were you supposed to do? Kill a bunch of lawyers?"

Rafael! Uzvuyiten sent. Salehi didn't have to see Uzvuyiten's to know he was turning blue with anger.

"I already did my job," the guard said. Then he grinned. "Wait a few hours. You'll see. They can't get to all of us."

Salehi felt a chill.

He hoped he was seeing bravado and nothing more.

He hoped that this damn security guard was wrong.

64

GOUDKINS HAD GOTTEN LOST IN HER OWN INVESTIGATION. SHE WAS following the trail of public information on Pearl Brooks, which turned out to have more information than Goudkins had ever expected.

Brooks had a public record, starting with the death of her father. He had run afoul of the Disty over a business dealing that he and his wife, Brooks's mother, had participated in. Brooks and her mother escaped, but her father had died in a Disty Vengeance Killing.

Brooks's mother died the same way a few years later, putting Brooks in public care. She was smart enough, and a good enough student, to get the Alliance to fund a high-end education, as long as she worked off her debt.

Once in public service, she never left it.

Goudkins had sat at her computer as she got lost in Brooks's life. The girl had been old enough to understand what happened, but young enough to believe that a Disty Vengeance Killing wasn't justice. She hadn't learned the difference between Alliance law and true justice, and she had been on record before her education claiming that Alliance law was wrong.

Then she got her scholarships and shut up.

Goudkins thought there had to be more to the story, and she would find it. But at the moment, she had also used her in-network system to search for an affiliation between Andre's department and Brooks's. The only thing Goudkins had found so far was an occasional transfer of funds from Brooks's Currency desk to Ike Jarvis, which was suspect enough.

Goudkins doubted the transfers would hold up if an Alliance regulator saw them.

Then an automated announcement from the port came across her links.

The dome in the City of Armstrong has just sectioned. If you have business in Armstrong, you must delay it until the sections rise again. All ships will remain grounded unless they receive special clearance or if the situation worsens. The port has its own section, constantly activated, so you are protected here.

Goudkins' breath caught. She was about to send a message to De-Ricci when another message broke through the protections Goudkins had placed on her ship.

The message had come from the United Domes of the Moon Security Office, and it blared across the walls of her ship. It hadn't broken through the protections she had placed on her own emergency links though. It didn't have to.

It had her attention.

Faces after faces scrolled before her, along with a warning to find these people and detain them until the authorities could arrive. Since Goudkins was alone, she nearly deleted the messages, until a face caught her attention.

A younger, thinner version of Ostaka's face.

She ran the images back and isolated that face. It belonged to a man who lived in Gagarin Dome. He worked in their police department, which made Goudkins wonder how anyone could detain him.

She let out a breath, though, and then had her system compare that Gagarin Dome police officer's face with Lawrence Ostaka's face.

The system told her the faces matched.

She was shaking. She asked the system to see if there were other, similar faces.

She found a dozen more of all ages, from twenty-five to one-hundred-and-twenty-five, in a dozen different domes around the Moon.

And, according to her system—her excellent system, with top-notch facial recognition—those faces belonged to the same person.

She replayed the warning message from the Security Office. There was no mention of clones. Had the security office gotten the names from somewhere else? Did DeRicci know she was dealing with similar faces, similar people, or had she just sent the entire mess out as quickly as possible?

The message had said something about an urgency.

Goudkins sent a message across her links to DeRicci, and flagged it high priority and top secret.

Chief, these faces you sent, do you realize that fourteen match Lawrence Ostaka's face? We might be dealing with clones here. And if he's involved with the masterminds, that would explain all of his behavior.

Goudkins stood as she sent that message. She had to get back to the Security Office. If Ostaka was doing something, she could stop him. And if he needed to be arrested, she could detain him in her ship. She had the authority to deal with him.

No one else did.

We know, DeRicci sent back. *He's in custody, and he's been neutralized. And yes, we're dealing with clones.*

I'm at the port, Goudkins sent. *I'm not sure I can come to you, but I'm going to try.*

Stay where you are, DeRicci sent. *We're overrun with help here. But see if you can track down Jhena Andre in real time. We're going to need to find her before she gets away.*

Done, Goudkins sent.

She hoped. She was shaking. That bastard, Ostaka. Everything he had said, everything he had done, made sense now. He wasn't just an asshole; he had actively worked to destroy the Alliance.

And she had probably helped him.

She ran a hand over her face and realized that, with the depth of her anger, it was probably good she wasn't anywhere near the man.

She couldn't be trusted to keep him in good physical condition after his arrest.

She sat back down and called on all of her training to get back to her investigation.

She wasn't going to simply find Jhena Andre in real time. She would find Brooks, too.

Once Goudkins found them, she would send that information to the Alliance.

And then she stopped. She wasn't sure who to trust.

She needed to figure out if Huỳnh had worked with Ostaka, if Huỳnh was one of the bad guys too. Because if she wasn't, she might know where to take the information.

And then Goudkins stopped. She couldn't trust Huỳnh. Huỳnh didn't have the power to arrest Andre or Brooks. They both outranked her.

Goudkins would have to go to the top, the very top, when she had the information. She would have to go to the Director of the Earth Alliance Security Division Human Coordination Department—if there was no link between her and Andre.

Goudkins had to do fast research—and some of that included work on the woman everyone knew as Odgerel. The stories about Odgerel were legion: she was difficult to work with, and she hated leaving Earth.

Her antipathy to aliens put her in Andre's and Brooks's camp. But Odgerel's reputation for integrity negated some of Goudkins' suspicion.

She hated this. She hated not knowing who to trust.

She hated the betrayal and the traitors in their midst.

She would ferret them out, no matter what it took. And she would find someone to capture Andre, if it was the last thing she ever did.

65

TALIA HAD GOTTEN TWO MESSAGES—THE FIRST FROM THE PORT, MENTIONING the sectioning, and then the second with the faces, and she had hurried to the door of Detective Zagrando's hospital room, peering out. In the hallway, people were running and yelling. Mostly, she was hearing *Stop! Grab him! Don't let him get away!* but she couldn't see who they were stopping and grabbing.

She didn't recognize any of the names that were supposed to be in Armstrong, and she felt like it didn't concern her, since she was in the port's hospital wing.

But clearly, some of those people were here.

She clutched her hands together. She could give it all up, and sink back into that depression she'd been in after the Peyti Crisis, or she could take action, but she wasn't sure what kind of action to take.

The last time she had run toward something, she had watched someone die.

So, she stood in front of the door, and watched as people in scrubs ran one direction and then another. She realized after a moment, they were chasing a doctor, but it wasn't a doctor who had worked on Detective Zagrando, thank heavens.

She didn't see any of the space traffic or security officers. She had to assume they were trying to catch those people as well.

Talia let out a small breath, then realized the message had come from the Security Office. Which meant that they were finding stuff, without her.

Dad, she sent along her links. *Did you see those faces? Should we be going to help the chief?*

Her father answered immediately. *I'm already here, Talia. We have it under control.*

Should I come there? she sent.

Are you still in the hospital wing of the port? he sent.

Yes, and before you ask, Detective Zagrando is still unconscious. They're keeping him here for another twenty-four hours, I think. But they just grabbed a doctor outside of my room, and it's a little weird. So I'm not sure exactly what's going on.

There was a half-second of silence before her father sent, *Did you know that doctor?*

No, Talia sent. *I'd never seen him. Why?*

Just checking, her father sent too quickly. He had clearly been worried that the doctor would see her or maybe Detective Zagrando.

Am I the detective's protective detail? She sent. She didn't feel like a protector. She wasn't really up for it. She had no idea how to fight anyone.

No, her father sent. *I think he'll be fine as long as he doesn't reveal who he is.*

And then he added, with emphasis:

Talia, if things get worse, if you hear an evacuation order or anything, you go to our ship, and get in it. Leave the Moon if you have to. Do not wait for me.

Right now, they're saying ships can't leave, she sent.

They'll send an order if ships need to leave, he sent. *Listen for it.*

She hated hearing that. *Dad, I can't go without you—*

I'll be fine, Talia, he sent. *I'll come to you. But I can't work if I know you're in danger.*

She glanced at the detective. He was still unconscious, even with all the noise and chaos in the halls.

Should I bring the detective too?

She could probably change the controls on his bed so that it would float ahead of her. Even if she had to hack it.

If you can, her father sent. *If there's time. But if he slows you down, you have to leave him. Do you understand, Talia?*

Tears pricked at her eyes. She wouldn't leave Detective Zagrando to die. She couldn't have someone else's death on her conscience.

But she wasn't going to tell her father that.

I understand, she sent. *Should I go now?*

We just sectioned the dome, he sent. *And we're investigating a few things. If we don't find what we're looking for, I'll send you a message. It might be automated. It'll tell you that it's time to leave. You leave at that very moment, got that? Promise me.*

She took a deep breath. The third attack. Something was going on, and her dad didn't want to tell her over links.

He wanted to save her life. He couldn't come for her this time. They needed him at the Security Office.

Talia, he sent with even more urgency. *Promise me.*

I promise, she sent. *I'll go to the ship right away, and I'll leave the Moon if you tell me to.*

Thank you, he sent. *You're everything, Talia, you know that, right? I love you.*

Oh, Dad, she sent. *I love you too.*

And then he signed off. She wanted to contact him again, but she didn't. He was trying to save the city, trying to save the Moon.

He could do it, she knew he could. If she didn't bother him.

From the hallway, more yelling. "There's another one!" a woman screamed, and more footsteps, running swiftly.

Talia grabbed the door and eased it closed.

She would wait to hear from her father. And in the meantime, she was going to investigate the capabilities of that bed.

She wasn't going to leave Detective Zagrando behind.

She was going to get them both out if she had to, and she was going to be prepared to do it fast.

She just had to figure out how.

66

It hadn't taken Flint long to tweak the human identification program, and he was filtering all of the information from it to others around DeRicci's office. He was still modifying the program to accommodate the general alien population, which was turning out to be more complicated than he expected.

He was toying with giving it to Issassi while he worked on some other aspects of the program. Plus, he had also been tracking Ostaka's contacts, and he'd hit something that startled him.

Just before he shut down the last of the access to the Security Office, Ostaka had sent a message to someone in the Earth Alliance Security Office, and that message had been flagged as also-read by Jhena Andre. Flint had felt a surge of excitement when he saw it.

He would love to get his hands on that woman.

The message was damning:

I've altered everything in the system here. I'm activating the protection protocols now. It should be impossible for anything to get in or out of their system. I'll keep my connection to you open, just in case, but I'm not anticipating problems. In fact, DeRicci just invited me to her office, so everything just got easier.

Flint was about to tell DeRicci about it when he saw a second message. This one went over something called an alert network. But most interesting about the message was that it went directly to and had also been viewed by Jhena Andre.

This message was even more damning:

Found me. Can't finish lock-out. They have the names of Andre, Starbase Human—

And it ended there. But what was best about it, what made Flint nearly shout with joy, was that Ostaka hadn't had time to encrypt that message. It had gone directly from the Security Office to Jhena Andre.

He glanced at Ostaka, who had slid back to the floor. The man looked miserable, his face still swollen. Either someone had shut off his nano-healers or he hadn't had very good ones. Not that Flint cared.

Noelle, he sent to DeRicci. *I have something.*

She looked up at him, startled. She was still trying to convince two of the dome leaders to take care of their domes. But those leaders were more concerned with the announcement that DeRicci had sent dome wide, identifying the Moon's attackers. Apparently, that announcement was leading to violence, just like Nyquist predicted.

Can you tell me or do you have to show me? she sent.

I have a direct link to one of the masterminds, Flint sent. *She's not on the Moon, but we can arrest her, if we know who to contact.*

DeRicci didn't look joyful like he expected. She looked overwhelmed. The Alliance had never been her specialty.

You'll have to tell Gomez, she sent. *I can't deal with it right now. When this crisis is past, yes, but not right now.*

Flint nodded. He didn't have the time to set up an encrypted link to Gomez, one that she would accept.

"Marshal," he said. "I need you."

Gomez had been talking with the Magalhães heir. The woman had proven extremely valuable, and she wanted to do more work to find out if there was other "old DNA" as she called it.

Flint hadn't had a lot of time to pay attention to that conversation.

As Gomez made her way over, Flint leaned closer to Issassi. She was working closely beside him, so they could double-check each other's protocols. Working like that on something this important actually made him feel better.

"Do me a favor, Kaz," he said. "While I'm talking to the Marshal, see if our prisoner managed to contact anyone while we forgot to lock down his links."

Issassi shot Ostaka a quick glance. He wasn't looking at anyone. "Okay," she said softly.

Gomez reached Flint's side in a matter of seconds. She peered at the screen floating in front of him, but that wasn't the screen he needed her to see. He was still modifying his programs even as he waited for her.

"What've you got?" she asked.

Send me a way to reach you as privately as possible, Flint sent on the system links.

She immediately sent back a coded, encrypted message so private his system told him to reject it because he hadn't approved any communications from her.

He instantly approved it, and then sent her a message.

I found one of the masterminds. I'm not telling you this verbally because I'm not sure who we can trust, even in this room. I feel a bit uncomfortable trusting you with this, but Noelle wants you to handle it.

Gomez peered at the screen as if the code could tell her something. *Is the mastermind on the Moon?*

Earth Alliance Security Division, he sent. Not *the one on Earth.*

Gomez's gaze met his, and he could tell: she was truly startled.

We need to act fast, because this was a real-time communication, unencrypted, from Ostaka to a woman named Jhena Andre. You're going to have to pull a lot of strings—and the correct ones—to get her arrested. They can't kill her and they can't let her kill herself. Am I clear?

Absolutely, Gomez sent. *I'll take care of it immediately. I know exactly who to contact to get this done.*

Flint wished he felt reassured. He wished he knew this woman better. She seemed competent, but he would rather work with his friends.

And then he mentally chided himself. He had worked with Luc Deshin, of all people. And Deshin had been the one who initially got him Andre's name.

They just hadn't been able to tie her to anything.

But they could now.

I'll send the communications to you to confirm, along with the links they traveled and the second one's unencrypted path.

Gomez nodded.

Flint added, *I don't have time to deal with this effectively right now, but I'm afraid if we don't handle it quickly, Andre will vanish. If we find her—*

We find her associates, Gomez sent. *We can shut them all down.*

Flint felt a bit of relief. Maybe DeRicci was right; maybe Gomez would be just fine.

One step at a time, Marshal, he sent back. *Let's get Andre first.*

I'm already working on it, Mr. Flint, Gomez sent. *We're going to get these bastards. I promise.*

Good, Flint sent. *I'm going to let you handle that. I'm going to make sure they don't get a third victory. I'm going to make sure that they have the worst day of their lives. Starting right now.*

67

BEFORE Ó BRÁDAIGH EXECUTED THE EMERGENCY SURFACE SWEEP, HE contacted ten of his colleagues. Most of them were women, since it looked to him like there were no women in that list of people that the chief had sent him.

Lombrozo had been on that list. The officers had gotten the list too, a little after Ó Brádaigh had. They apparently ordered someone to remove Lombrozo from his position or arrest him or something.

The problem was that Ó Brádaigh recognized at least a dozen engineers and a handful of inspectors in that list of people. He told the officers, but he couldn't do anything about it. Not right now.

He could feel the time passing. He had a clock counting down at the very edge of his left eye, and even though it was driving him nuts, it was keeping him focused.

He had asked the other engineers—the ones he sort of trusted—to go into the various substructures and check his work. He'd also asked that the inspectors get teams to monitor the dome.

He couldn't monitor the dome, even though he wanted to. He was back inside the control room, hoping to hell that Petteway hadn't set anything up secretly and somehow disabled the notification.

The surface sweep scared the crap out of Ó Brádaigh. Normally, they prepped for a week before running a surface sweep. Usually nearby businesses like the Growing Pits were warned that stuff might fall off the surface of the dome, and trains were rerouted or at least prevented from being anywhere near the dome while the sweep was underway.

No one wanted debris falling on delicate machinery or people or other smaller domes, and that was always a risk with a surface sweep.

Now, he was conducting one with no warning at all.

He hoped everyone outside the dome would be all right.

Ó Brádaigh activated the sweep. The system asked him three times if the sweep was necessary. All three times, he stated that the sweep was an emergency.

His hands were shaking as he watched the program kick into gear. He stayed in the control room, and used their small screens to watch the progress of the sweep across the kilometers of dome.

First step, shut off all the non-essential dome programming, like the daylight changes. That would upset people all by itself. At least, the people who weren't already freaked out by the sectioning that Noelle DeRicci had ordered.

Then the dome would darken, and anomalies would show up as light or as redness depending on what was going on along the Moon's surface.

If real sunlight was streaming onto the Moon, the dome sweep program would use the light to help find breaches. If this part of the Moon was in darkness, other programming would kick in.

Ó Brádaigh let the sweep program handle this part of it. He had only initiated a dome surface sweep once in the past two years, and he didn't remember all of the protocols.

He had to rely on the computers, on the system, on the dome itself.

His stomach clenched. He tried not to think about Fiona, his mother, and Berhane, but of course, they were the only things he could think about.

He focused on the darkness covering the small replica of the dome before him. He looked at the numbers scrolling to his left, the sweep program in its most basic form. And he watched the microimages of the sweep on his right.

He made himself concentrate on those things.
Because the sweep was underway.
He couldn't stop it if he wanted to.
And he most definitely did not want to.

68

THE REDS AND GOLDS OF DAWN CARESSED BEIHAI PARK. ODGEREL LOOKED at the multicolored eastern sky. It made her tired.

Usually, she started her day at dawn with a walk from her home to the office. On this day, she'd not only been awake for hours by the time dawn lit the sky, but she'd already had more news than she could process.

And now, word from a marshal of the Frontier, a woman with a decades-long career who, in theory, had taken a leave of absence.

It was clear that she had not. Odgerel investigated her along one public network while listening to her on a private link.

Marshal Judita Gomez had applied for a job at the clone factory in Hétique City before the bombings. The personnel office had thought she wasn't serious about the interview and, instead, had been trying to investigate something.

If Gomez's private ship weren't already on the Moon when the bombings of Hétique City had occurred, Odgerel would have been suspicious of Gomez's motives. But until these past few months, Gomez hadn't been deep inside the Alliance in years.

And a quick search of her records showed some contact with the Frémont clones that anyone would have found disturbing.

Besides, Gomez was the second person to alert Odgerel to possible treason by Jhena Andre, whom Odgerel had met once, and hadn't liked—not that it mattered. Odgerel often didn't like subordinates in her department.

Gomez had also sent images of one hundred originals for clones known to be on the Moon. One of them, Lawrence Ostaka, also worked for the Security Department.

Odgerel tried not to let such details disturb her, although they did.

She had sent for Mitchell Brown. Since there were at least two traitors in her division, she wanted someone she could trust.

And even before she sent for Brown, she compared his visage to those of the originals, and she had one of her departments rerun his DNA, searching for hidden clone tags or shortened telomeres.

The department had found nothing.

She heard him approach before she saw him, his shoes making a slight squeak against the path. He had barely been in Beijing for a month, and he still had not absorbed local custom.

Although, as he came up beside her, he handed her a cup filled with her favorite lemon-lime drink. She usually had that mid-afternoon to refresh herself, but mid-afternoon seemed a long way away.

"Did you see the information I sent you on Jhena Andre?" she asked him quietly.

"It's legitimate," he said. "Once you look at her, you see a lot of irregularities in her behavior."

"You seem eager to believe ill of one of our more valued employees," Odgerel said.

"The office received another warning about Andre about two hours before you contacted me," Brown said. "I was going to assign someone to investigate, and then we had to deal with Hétique City."

"Where did the other warning come from?" Odgerel asked.

"One of our investigators, Wilma Goudkins," he said.

Odgerel's hands tightened against the cup. The chill of the liquid had leached into the cup's surface. "She partners with Lawrence Ostaka."

Odgerel had forwarded the images to Brown and other members of her team. She wanted any of those clones inside the Alliance caught and detained.

"Ostaka filed a complaint against her," Brown said, "claiming she was too sympathetic to the Moon and wasn't doing her job. In light of who he actually is, that complaint now reads like a recommendation."

Odgerel sipped the drink, its sweet bitterness somehow refreshing, even as the sun rose above the trees.

"We have to hope that this is not some kind of trick to get us to take her seriously," Odgerel said.

"I considered that. But I also realize we have time," he said.

Odgerel turned toward him. He was ever so slightly taller than she was.

"Time?" she asked. "Marshal Gomez said another attack on the Moon is imminent."

"And we have to trust those on the Moon to handle that problem," Brown said. "My sources claim that there are only a few hours before the next attack hits, and no matter what we do, we can't resolve anything in that time."

Odgerel forced herself to study the pinkish hues along the green leaves. She loved dawn. No fake dawn of a dome ever compared.

She could not let the idea of another Moon attack upset her now. Nor could she think about the implications to the Moon, to Earth, and to the Alliance.

Right now, she had to remain in the moment, and the sunlight, beautifully pink and golden, helped her do that.

"What kind of time do we have?" she asked Brown.

"Time for an apology," he said.

She had not expected that answer. She looked at him sideways. "Apology? To whom?"

"Jhena Andre, if need be," he said. "We arrest her now, isolate her, search for known associates. If we are wrong, we apologize and release her. If she sues us, we can argue the heat of the moment. After all, another attack is imminent."

Odgerel smiled ever so slightly. Brown was devious. She hadn't expected that of him, and she liked it.

"Order Andre's arrest. Turn her life upside down. Find everything she has ever done, every person she has ever spoken to, see if we do indeed have a traitor in our midst."

Brown nodded. He started to move away, but Odgerel caught his arm.

"Make certain that everyone who comes in contact with Andre is not connected to this originals list or to any of the investigations. Make sure they have never had contact with her before. And make certain they keep her from contacting anyone or harming herself."

"Yes, sir," he said, in a tone that made her think he had already thought of that.

"If she dies in this arrest," Odgerel said, "I will hold you personally responsible."

He nodded, his expression serious. "I would do the same in your position," he said.

He had meant the words to comfort her, but they did not.

Perhaps she couldn't be comforted. She had known that there were traitors inside the Alliance, but to learn they had been operating from within her precious division disturbed her more than she ever wanted to admit.

She knew that for weeks, maybe years to come, she would see a lot of dawns from the wrong side of the night. Sleep would become a luxury.

She had housecleaning to do, and decisions to make.

Awful decisions.

Life and death decisions.

She hated making them, but she had done it before.

She knew she could do it again.

69

DARKNESS MOVED ACROSS THE TOP OF THE DOME. DERICCI WATCHED the change through the floor to ceiling windows in her office, as she continued to argue with the leaders of the other domes. They were furious at her for releasing the faces without running the information through them first, without giving them a chance to warn their police or security departments.

The fact that some of those faces showed up in their police departments seemed beyond the leaders. And as she argued with them, wishing she had more time, she watched the programs shut off in Armstrong's dome. First, Dome Daylight vanished, and the dome became clear.

This part of the Moon was tilted away from the sun, but hadn't entirely gone dark yet. Some rays of light hit the dome, just not enough to compensate for Dome Daylight.

Then a shadow darkened the outside of the dome, and even though DeRicci knew that the shadow was part of the emergency surface sweep, it still startled her.

All surface sweeps were done during Dome Night. Although they were visible to the naked eye, most people didn't notice because the dome was in darkness anyway. She had watched one from this very office when she first became chief of security.

That seemed like a hundred years ago.

Around her, half of the people in her office stopped working and looked at the shadow spreading across the top of the dome. She wanted to tell them to get back to work, but she was too hooked into her conversation with the dome leaders.

She made herself turn away from the windows, moving the images of the leaders with her as she did, because she didn't want to focus on the dome. Still, she could see the shadow through the windows of the other side of the large room.

And the lights in her own office had gone up because of the darkness outside.

She glanced over at Flint, whose head was down. He and the technical officer from the Armstrong Police Department, a woman he had introduced as Kaz Issassi, were consulting with each other, and then they'd do something on a screen in front of them, and then they'd consult some more.

After that initial moment of alarm as the shadows crept along the surface of the dome, everyone had returned to work. Even Berhane Magalhães seemed busy. She was talking to the skinny man she had brought with her, and the strange-looking middle-aged woman was standing just outside their conversation, head down, seemingly listening intently.

DeRicci made herself focus on the conversations she was having. And then two of the mayors looked startled, almost frightened. And behind DeRicci, someone cursed.

"What?" she asked, but she wasn't sure she knew who she was asking.

Popova opened a large screen in the center of the room. Apparently, she had made the noise.

On the screen, images appeared. DeRicci recognized the damaged spires of Sverdrup Crater in the distance. The image she was watching seemed to be from some kind of security camera. To one side, she saw the massive Shackleton crater, where energy companies thrived but no city existed, and prominently, near the front of the image, the bubble of the small dome of Crater de Gerlache.

Sverdrup had been one of the twenty cities targeted by the Frémont clones, but Crater de Gerlache had been too small. DeRicci had declined the opportunity to visit there. Sverdrup had freaked her out enough. She didn't like that part of the Moon; it was in perpetual darkness, and even with everything the cities had done to combat that, she had been unable to forget it.

"What is this, Rudra?" she asked. Two of the mayors had disappeared from her line of vision. Another cursed.

And then the image from the security camera changed. As she watched, the dome over Crater de Gerlache exploded outward and upward, illuminating the rocks and Moon's surface all around it, the explosion reflecting in the clear spires of Sverdrup's remaining towers.

DeRicci's knees buckled, and she caught herself on her desk. "Did that just happen? Or was that a propaganda video?"

"It happened," someone said softly.

"But," DeRicci said stupidly, "it wasn't one of the twenty domes."

She had sent a message to all the leaders on the Moon, but she hadn't spoken to everyone. She thought the same domes would be targeted, not *all* the domes.

The debris fell around Crater de Gerlache, but where the city had been, there was only darkness. The top of the dome had disappeared. Correct that: the *dome* had disappeared.

"How many people live in that city?" she asked. She mentally corrected herself on that too. *Lived.* How many people *had lived* in that city?

"Forty-five thousand," Popova said quietly.

Someone swore, but the rest of the room was quiet. Then the strangely dressed woman, the one who had been talking to Gomez said plaintively, "I thought we had hours, still."

"Me, too," DeRicci said, feeling cold.

"Mr. Ostaka over there sent messages all over the Moon before we shut off his links," said Issassi. "He sent several to Crater de Gerlache."

DeRicci turned toward him. Despite the evidence of the battering she had given him still swelling his face, Ostaka was smiling.

"Son of a bitch," she said. "Find out who else he contacted—which other domes—and warn them. Rudra, warn *all* the domes, say an attack could be imminent. And…"

She took one menacing step toward Ostaka. He cringed. The movement seemed involuntary, not theatrical. He wasn't doing it for show. He was terrified of her.

"Get this asshole out of my office. Put him in custody, and make sure his link blocker still works."

No one moved.

"*Now*," DeRicci said, "before I kill him with my bare hands."

Nyquist stepped forward, even though he didn't work for DeRicci, grabbed Ostaka by the arm, and said, "You're going to wish you hadn't survived this day," as he led Ostaka out of the room.

DeRicci looked up at the image, which someone was replaying. Her stomach was churning.

They had run out of time. They had just lost forty-five thousand people, in an instant.

She didn't want this third attack to succeed, and it looked like it was going to, no matter what she did.

70

FLINT COULDN'T THINK ABOUT THE DEAD, THE PEOPLE WHO HAD JUST DIED in front of his very eyes. He didn't have the time or the luxury. Everyone in this room—everyone on the Moon—had just learned that the domes could blow at any moment.

He hoped to hell the other dome leaders had at least sectioned their domes. That would decrease the deaths, make certain that not everyone in the domes died.

Unlike Crater de Gerlache. The crater hadn't protected its people. The crater itself had probably reinforced the power of the explosion, and rained down hell on them, even as the oxygen sucked out of the city's layers and the environment vanished.

He took a deep breath, forced those thoughts away, and came up with—

Luc Deshin.

In one of their very first meetings just before the Peyti Crisis, Deshin had talked to Flint about explosives, and tracking explosives, saying it was hard for him to find what was happening.

Flint had let that investigation go as other things happened. Besides, he thought the attackers were opportunists, like the woman whom they had thwarted in Armstrong on Anniversary Day, using whatever was available to make bombs.

Then, after the Peyti Crisis, where it became clear that those explosives had arrived with the masks, Flint had dropped that part of his investigation altogether.

But Deshin had said explosives were all over the Moon, easily available. Construction sites, mining operations—

Flint was leaning forward before he could even think about what he was doing. He searched the old security footage from Crater de Gerlache, stuff that had already been uploaded before the city vanished, and then scanned in on the *interior* of the dome.

This explosion was in a crater, and the city was layered, if he remembered correctly. It would have been hard to explode upward—it would have taken longer for something from below to harm the dome.

He assumed, anyway. He was no engineer.

But before he bothered the one engineer they all seemed to trust, Flint would do a bit more digging. He opened another window, silently queried one of the information gathering surfaces, and moved the footage of the Crater de Gerlache bombing onto it.

What explosive would cause that kind of result? he asked.

The question seemed so bloodless. And as the system gave him options, names of different kinds of charges, he looked at the interior of the now destroyed dome's surface.

Something small, placed along the sections, and where the dome sections met in the very center of the dome.

Something small, and on the inside, not the outside.

He looked at the list of explosives that the query had found for him. His heart was in his throat.

All of the previous attacks had been uniform. The same kind of clones executing the same kind of event, using the same (or similar) kinds of equipment. Even the Anniversary Day bombers used the same system—they had taken what they could from the cities they had gone to in order to make their bombs.

But these clones had had time. They could have all used the same explosives, and they had jobs that allowed them to attach those explosives to the parts of the dome where they would do the most damage.

If the sections didn't go down, then the dome would explode outward, just like it had done in Crater de Gerlache. Even if the sections went down, if the explosives ran all along the mechanism, each section of the dome would be destroyed anyway.

"Noelle," he said, "I have got to talk to your engineer."

DeRicci whirled toward Flint. "My engineer?"

Clearly she was thinking of something else, focused on the entire Moon, not the city of Armstrong.

He needed to focus on the Moon too, but he also needed that engineer.

"He means Donal Ó Brádaigh," the Magalhães woman said.

"Did you find something?" DeRicci asked.

"Yes," Flint said, "and we need to deal with it right away."

71

Ó Brádaigh watched the sweep finish its fifth run across the dome. He saw nothing and neither did all of the other people he had assigned to monitor the sweep.

More importantly—or maybe as important—the computers found nothing either. There were no weaknesses in the dome's surface, and nothing out of the ordinary covered it. Just Moon dust, and debris from a dozen meteoroids that had hit the dome since the last official sweep several weeks ago.

Ó Brádaigh wasn't sure how he felt about that. He wanted to find something, in part because he knew something was going to happen. He wanted to discover it in time.

Then he got an alert from the United Domes of the Moon Security Office. Before he could even step out of the control room, a man he'd never seen before appeared before him.

"I'm Miles Flint," the man said. "I work with DeRicci."

Ó Brádaigh had heard of Flint, but he couldn't remember in what context.

"We just lost Crater de Gerlache," Flint said, his tone even.

Ó Brádaigh's breath caught. His chest ached. They had lost a city? Already? He'd thought they still had a few hours.

"I've looked at the footage," Flint said, "and I think I know what we're dealing with."

It took Ó Brádaigh a moment to understand what Flint said.

"I'm going to send you my work. It'll be easier for you to digest," Flint said, "and you might see a few errors. But in short, we're looking for explosives along the section lines and in the very center of the dome where everything meets. On the *inside* of the dome. I think we even know the explosive, but you can double-check me on that."

And then he dumped all kinds of information along Ó Brádaigh's links. Ó Brádaigh staggered backwards, nearly hitting the control room wall.

He couldn't think about the destroyed dome, even though he was seeing it on the images that Flint sent, a series of small explosions, the debris floating *out* of the dome, not into the dome, the light and fire blazing against the darkest part of the Moon.

A series of small explosions, concentrated on the dome's weakest points, guaranteed to destroy it all at once.

And the kind of material that could be applied to the dome's surface.

Ó Brádaigh would double-check, that was the kind of man he was, but he had a hunch Flint was right.

They knew what they were dealing with.

They knew how to solve it.

And they had also run out of time.

72

WITHIN TEN MINUTES, DeRICCI HAD HEARD FROM Ó BRÁDAIGH. HE had confirmed Flint's work. They had found the type of explosives, and where they were on the domes.

DeRicci had no idea if the explosives were on timers or if they hand-detonated. She had no idea if something would set them off randomly, although sectioning Armstrong's dome hadn't done it.

Now getting rid of those explosives was out of her hands. She had to trust the city engineering and inspection staff, the bomb squad of the Armstrong Police Department, and all of the equipment inside and out-side of the city to get the work done.

Magalhães offered to contact her father, one of the major builders in the city, to get his explosives experts working on the interior of the dome as well. DeRicci didn't feel comfortable with that, even though she knew that Magalhães's father had access to the same clone information that DeRicci did.

So DeRicci corrected a mistake she had made during the Peyti Cri-sis. She sent Magalhães's father and all of the construction and mining experts *outside* of the domes, to handle smaller units like the Growing Pits and the train stations and the warehouses and the living quarters for some of the mining areas, anywhere that living creatures gathered and could possibly die.

And DeRicci sent urgent information to all of the other domes. *All* of them, every single dome on the Moon, and she hoped to God those idiots running the places would take immediate action.

It looked like the destruction of Crater de Gerlache had inspired several of them to section their domes. Now those leaders had to stop blaming people and solve the damn crisis.

It was out of DeRicci's hands, even though she didn't want it to be.

She encouraged Marshal Gomez to let the Earth Alliance Security Division know what kind of explosives they were dealing with, and what kind of attack, just in case this was the first plan that wasn't Moon-oriented.

DeRicci believed it was, but she didn't know.

She didn't know anything.

All she could do was direct people to solve this crisis for her.

She did a few more things: In addition to isolating the clones, she ordered citizens to look for suspicious packages or to contact the police if it looked like there was something in one of the clones' homes or offices that might harm the city.

DeRicci wouldn't put it past these creatures to have backup explosions planned.

After all, Ostaka had been damned determined to make this work. He had encouraged his cohorts in Crater de Gerlache to act ahead of schedule. He had sent messages to Gagarin Dome as well, but they either didn't get through or they were ignored.

Nothing else had blown up.

Yet.

73

WORD OF THE FIRST DESTROYED DOME ON THE MOON REACHED JHENA
Andre in her bedroom. She was digging her go-bag out of the closet,
changing out a few items before she headed to the port. She had a reser-
vation on a shuttle flight to the nearest large city, and it had been easier
to book than she had expected.

She had altered the information in her file to reflect a death in her
family, not that she had any close family or that anyone had died. But the
alteration would last as long as she needed it to—just a few days.

By then, she would be on the Frontier, heading toward her new home.

She took a moment to look at the footage coming from the Moon.
She actually turned on some human news programs with real anchors
talking about the crisis, just to hear their tone of panic.

So what if someone had released the trigger a little early? So what if the
other domes had an hour or two of warning? As that Ostaka man in the
Moon's Security Office had noted, DeRicci and her crew were close to figuring
out what was happening, and they probably were dealing with the warnings.

Not that it mattered. Soon they'd either be dead or handling so much
disaster that they wouldn't remember anything about the information
they had received early.

Andre smiled softly. The final leg of her plan was underway. The Alliance would buckle under this stress. The destruction of every dome on

the Moon would cause everyone to rethink the devil's bargain they had made, particularly when Andre released her one and only manifesto, reminding everyone how many humans inside the Alliance had died because Alliance law made it legal for non-humans to kill them.

If Andre actually believed in the eye-for-an-eye thing that had been part of humanity for millennia, her actions against the Alliance still wouldn't come close to making up for all the Alliance-caused deaths.

If she were being honest with herself, the deaths on the Moon were also Alliance-caused. If those people hadn't lived in the heart of the Alliance, they wouldn't have died there either.

She grabbed her jewelry from the small safe she had in the back of the closet. To anyone who investigated her, the jewelry—as miniscule as it was—would represent all of her wealth.

The rest of the money she had made over the decades grew in several accounts in the Frontier.

She put the jewelry next to the unnamed doll she'd had since she was a little girl and sealed the go-bag closed. She would get rid of almost everything in that bag on her second stop, where she would completely redo her look.

She needed a makeover anyway. She was no longer a government employee. Now, she had officially become a mastermind.

She smiled, slung the bag over her shoulder, and silently said goodbye to the small room. Then she walked through the living area and pulled the door open to the stairs—

To find two dozen laser rifles pointed at her. Her heart rate rose.

She hadn't expected this despite Stott's warning.

But she recognized most of the people in the hallway, and standing on the stairs.

She smiled at them. "Did I do something wrong?" she asked cheerfully.

James Noya stepped forward, holding cuffs. She had trained Noya, hand-chosen him herself. She had had dinner with him and his wife just two days before.

"Jhena Andre," he said in a voice she had never heard before, "you are under arrest for treason, and mass murder."

Her eyebrows went up. Treason and mass murder? She hadn't expected that at all. Maybe for a connection to criminals, conspiracy or something. But treason and mass murder?

"James," she said softly. "You know me. You know I would never—"

"I suggest you come with us willingly, Jhena," he said. "Because we can use lethal force if we need to."

She felt the blood leave her face. No one smiled back at her. They were all looking at her like they had never seen her before.

She remembered how people had done that to her father, after they realized he hadn't lost his wife, but that she had died in an Alliance-sanctioned legal murder.

Lethal force. These people were going to kill her, if they could.

And she could choose right now—live? Or die?

She took a deep breath. She could defend herself. The Alliance was wrong about almost everything.

She dropped her go-bag and extended her arms, wrists together.

"You're making a mistake, Jim," she said quietly.

He put the cuffs on her, the orange light burning her skin.

"No," he said. "I made my mistake years ago. The day I decided to trust you. I'm going to regret that day for the rest of my life."

Then he grabbed her by the elbow and pulled her forward. She stumbled toward the stairs. No one met her gaze, but the rifles followed her movements as if she were going to try to escape.

She didn't send any messages along her links. That would implicate others. She just moved forward.

Maybe this would be better than a manifesto. A trial, with news coverage. Analysis of who she was and why she had done what she had done.

Examination of the difficulties for anyone without money living inside the Alliance.

But she had money.

She could defend herself—and she would.

And the entire universe would be watching.

74

IF SOMEONE HAD TOLD FLINT THAT THE NEXT TWO HOURS WOULD PASS quickly, he wouldn't have believed them. But the hours did indeed fly by.

He and Issassi developed the program to search for clones of all the common species found in the Moon's cities. They found twins and triplets and a handful of clones (no more than four) of the same original, but they didn't find another mass grouping of clones like they had found among the Peyti during the Peyti Crisis or among the humans of this last grouping who were doing their best to sabotage the Moon.

From the reports flowing into the Security Office, almost everyone Flint had identified as a possible attacker had been isolated, if not arrested. Flint had heard stories of violence, but tuned them out as best he could, trying not think of any of the deaths—especially the ones tied to Crater de Gerlache.

It was looking more and more like their initial impression was correct: No one had survived in the entire city.

But no more bombs had gone off either, not anywhere on the Moon, not even outside the main domes in places like the Growing Pits. The explosives attached to Armstrong's dome had been deactivated, although they hadn't been removed yet—some said that was a delicate process too—and no one found anything on the street level or in buildings.

Armstrong PD and every bot they could find were going through abandoned buildings now, scouring for any anomaly.

Similar things were going on in every single domed community on the Moon, and maybe elsewhere. DeRicci had sent the images of the clones throughout the Alliance. If others, like Ostaka, worked off-Moon, they would be located and dealt with.

Plus, Marshal Gomez had reported that Jhena Andre had been arrested, and officials were combing through her contacts now. Flint knew how these investigations went. Contacts would lead to more contacts, which would lead to more contacts, and eventually, someone would talk.

The entire conspiracy would break down in a matter of days.

He shook the tension from his shoulders. His stomach growled, and he remembered he hadn't eaten anything since that morning. He looked at Issassi, who was still focused on the program. She was rerunning it, making sure they hadn't missed anything.

"Hey!" someone said from behind Flint. "It's been seven hours."

He frowned, not sure what the person was talking about.

But the chatter throughout the office stopped. Everyone either checked their internal clock or some clock nearby.

Flint looked at the open screen to his left. He had set a timer to monitor the six hours they had from the moment that Ó Brádaigh said he had found the countdown.

The timer had stopped, and Flint hadn't even noticed.

Six hours. Ó Brádaigh believed, they all believed, that the reset done by Ó Brádaigh's boss indicated the timing of attack.

Flint's gaze met DeRicci's. Her eyes were lined with tears, but he knew her: They were happy tears. Popova clapped her hands together and put them in front of her mouth. Nyquist, back from wherever he had taken Ostaka, almost smiled.

And then, toward the back of the room, a rumble started. It took Flint a moment to realize it was an actual cheer—a sound of joy. It had been a long time since he'd heard anything like that on the Moon.

People started clapping and yelling and jumping up and down, and a few burst into tears. Nyquist walked to DeRicci's side and enfolded her in his arms. Issassi wrapped her arms around Flint and kissed him, startling him. He couldn't remember the last time someone had kissed him like that.

She pulled back, surprised, and he laughed.

He *laughed*.

The relief was so heady he wasn't sure what to do with it, how to deal with it, where to put it.

They had survived. They had stopped the final attack. They had saved the Moon—the Alliance—their entire universe.

The masterminds were being rounded up, and the threat was over.

It was *over*.

He wasn't sure he actually believed that. He knew they had a lot of work ahead of them, but he also knew it was work they could do.

Work *he* could do.

His laughter melded into the general din. He doubted he had ever felt this good in his life.

He needed to contact Talia. He wished she were here. She had probably never seen him like this.

But she would.

Oh, dear God, she would.

And that—not this—would be the best moment of his life.

Although this moment was damn close.

TWO DAYS LATER

75

DeRicci set her tablet on the seat in the first class compartment on the bullet train. She rubbed a fist against the window, noted that there was Moon dust on the outside, and frowned. She turned to the porter—she still wasn't used to first class porters—and asked him to activate the window's self-cleaning protocol.

She had decided to take the train to Sverdrup Crater, and the remains of Crater de Gerlache. She wanted to see her Moon. Each city along the route, each dome, and every single rock and grain of Moon dust. She wanted to see what she had saved.

She didn't tell the porter that, but Nyquist knew. He was leaning against the compartment door, arms crossed.

"I think you should wait a few weeks before doing this," he said for the umpteenth time.

He had fed her the last two days, and let her sleep in, even though she had a mountain of work to do. But she hadn't yelled at him. She knew she needed the rest.

The real food he had given her on a regular basis had settled her stomach, or maybe it was the nerves, finally settling.

She was devastated at the death toll, truly devastated, which was why she was going to Crater de Gerlache. She wanted to see it for herself. She wished they had saved the city.

But she also needed to see the ruins so she could know, deep down, what her entire Moon had faced. And she had chosen to travel slowly, because she knew that seeing her Moon would heal her in ways that no amount of sleep and excellent meals ever could.

She knew she had lost part of the Moon, but she had saved most of it.

And she was smart enough to know what a victory that was.

She still didn't have a full concept of the odds they had faced. Reports kept coming in of arrests throughout the Alliance. As of that morning, more than ten thousand people—all human—in various parts of the Alliance had been arrested as part of the conspiracy to bring down the Alliance. The Peyti government had started investigations of some of its citizens as well, and just an hour ago, the first Peyti had been arrested.

His name was Uzven. Gomez, who had told DeRicci about the arrest, said she had worked with him unsuccessfully fifteen years ago when she had first come across the Frémont clones. Gomez had no idea if Uzven had been working for Andre's group back then, but his mistranslations and screw-ups had caused Gomez problems, and had probably cost some of the clones their lives.

Nyquist was still looking at DeRicci, his expression dark.

She smiled at him. Smiling was easier these days.

"You could come with me," she replied for the umpteenth time.

He sighed. "Tell Gumiela that. I've got to finish the case against Romey, plus we're dealing with a new set of S³ lawyers, including one of the firm's partners. Those bastards were in the middle of the last crisis—they even had one of those clones in their law office—and they're still crying clones' rights."

DeRicci shrugged. She wasn't going to listen to any tales of woe about lawyers or clones' rights or murder. She was going to sit in this train compartment, have a nice meal, and watch her Moon go by. If Nyquist didn't want to do that, then fine. He could finish his investigations and deal with all the lawyers he wanted to.

DeRicci had more than enough to deal with herself.

"They'll be waiting for you when you get back," she said.

He shook his head. "I'm also helping Gumiela figure out how to process the overzealous."

That was his term for the citizens who were "overzealous" in their detention of the clones throughout the city. There were no cases of outright killing, which actually surprised DeRicci, but some of those clones had been badly beaten.

DeRicci had no leg to stand on in that matter. She still wanted to pound Ostaka's face into the ground every single time she thought of him.

"You just don't want to come," she said.

Nyquist's smile faded. "I don't want to see Crater de Gerlache."

She started to tell him that he didn't have to, but before she could get a word out, he added,

"And I know I can stay in the train or in a hotel in Sverdrup Crater or wherever you're staying. I just—would rather bury myself in work."

She had tried to tell him just once that while she viewed the deaths in Crater de Gerlache as a failure, the bombing had also provided the solution. Those deaths had saved the lives of everyone else on the Moon.

And he had shaken his head.

"I think we would have figured it out in time," he had said.

But DeRicci didn't. She knew that the explosives had been the missing piece. Everything had come together quickly after that.

He didn't have to agree with her. He probably never would.

But he was standing here, disagreeing with her, because of the way the tragedy had unfolded.

She leaned over and kissed him. "If you don't get off the train now," she said, "you will come with me whether you want to or not."

He stroked her cheek with his right hand. "Let's do something special when you get back."

She smiled, and leaned her forehead against his. She wasn't going to make any promises. A normal night at home would be special, at least to her.

She hadn't had one in over six months.

But she wasn't going to spoil his mood.

"I'll see you in a week," she said.

He kissed her again and, as was his way, left the compartment without saying good-bye.

She sank into the comfortable chair, and looked at the window again. The Moon dust was gone. She could see every detail through that window.

She smiled to herself. A week ago, she would never have thought she would be able to take a small tour of the Moon.

A week ago, she thought she might be stuck in that hell of searching for the third attack forever.

A week ago, she thought she would never succeed.

But she had. The Moon was here. The Alliance was intact.

She was taking a victory lap.

And she deserved it.

76

Pippa Landau sat at a large table in the crew's mess on the *Green Dragon*. She had just finished talking with her son. He had sent her panicked messages all during the crisis two days ago, some of which she never received because she was in the Security Office when it had been blacked out, and some of which she hadn't answered because she was too fascinated by the competent people working hard to save lives.

When she finally reached Takumi, he was frantic. He called her inconsiderate and self-centered and stuck in the past. Maybe only the last was true.

She still hadn't told him she was a Disappeared. She might have to, if she decided to stay on the Moon to help with the investigation. Right now, Marshal Gomez and her crew had no idea where to put Pippa, but they knew they needed her.

The marshal told Pippa that she held the key to the operation conducted by the masterminds on the Frontier.

Pippa wasn't sure if she held a modern key or an ancient one. She knew that there was a lot of information trapped in her brain that she hadn't thought about in years.

In the short conversation she had had with the marshal before everything went wrong two days ago, Pippa had given up details she had never spoken about, and the marshal thought they were significant.

Since then, two other people had debriefed Pippa, but none had asked questions as insightful as the marshal's.

Pippa knew she would help dissolve this cabal that had tried to destroy the Alliance. She had a personal reason, of course. Apparently, someone in the Frontier was still searching for her. But she could return to her old life and never be found.

Instead, she wanted to stay. She had lost a lot of friends on Starbase Human, something else she had never admitted, and she had lost herself there.

She couldn't reclaim Takara Hamasaki—she had changed too much for that—but she could revive and acknowledge her. And maybe even tell her children about Takara one day.

Once Pippa had put it all into perspective.

She got up and made herself some coffee. She still had to wait—everyone on the ship was dealing with details she wasn't privy to—and she didn't mind. She felt useful in a completely different way than she had when she taught or when she raised her children.

Now, she felt like she was contributing to the Alliance, not just to her small Iowa town.

Pippa had no idea if she would go back to that world. She suspected she would.

But she was going to have an adventure first, and she was going to stop hiding. She had been ashamed of her past.

She was no longer.

She only wished that Raymond was still alive so she could tell him all about this. She had no idea what he would think about it, which might have been why she wanted to talk to him.

She missed him.

She missed her children and her grandchildren.

But she was sitting on a spaceship after explosions and a major crisis. Her life had come full circle.

She loved that.

And she was looking forward to the future—for the first time in years.

77

GOMEZ HADN'T EXPECTED THE JOB OFFER. ODGEREL CONTACTED HER that morning; the security division—the *entire* Earth Alliance Security Division (not just the human division of the Investigative Department)—wanted Gomez to lead the task force that would bring the Anniversary Day criminals from arrest through trial to convictions.

It would take a decade at least. They wanted Gomez to steer an entire department, because they believed the criminal side of this was so vast that it would take an entire department to handle all of the details.

Ten thousand arrests and more on the way. Not counting what Gomez—or someone—would find on the Frontier. The things Pippa Landau had told Gomez about the way business used to be conducted on the original Starbase Human made Gomez think that there was an entire wing of this treasonous enterprise that never touched Alliance space at all.

The idea of handling this massive investigation with all of its moving parts intrigued her. The idea of running a bureaucracy did not.

Gomez hadn't told Simiaar yet. Simiaar was working with Dabir Kaspian on the DNA found in the Anniversary Day sites. Simiaar was running all sorts of tests with rubble from the ruin, not just looking for old human DNA, but for alien DNA as well.

One of the labs had asked Simiaar if she wanted to open her own lab here. Kaspian was trying to talk Berhane Magalhães into starting a side organization that searched for non-human dead from the various crises.

Everyone had opportunities now, and it startled Gomez. She had thought she was throwing away her career when she left the *Stanley*. Instead, she had the chance to start a whole new one.

She was in her quarters, mulling over Odgerel's offer. In typical fashion, Odgerel had given Gomez only a few hours to consider a massive lifestyle change.

Gomez loved the Frontier. She loved running her own ship. She could continue doing that forever—

If only she could trust that the Alliance would follow up on the information she found and properly handle the people she arrested. But she still couldn't trust that, and it bothered her.

This department that Odgerel wanted her to lead could change the culture of the Security Division forever. They both knew it.

What Gomez had to determine was if she could handle all of the petty politics, the infighting, and the day-to-day grind.

Then she sat on the edge of her bed and laughed at herself. Of course she could handle that. She had run a large ship with no backup in the wildest parts of the known universe.

She had been a combination diplomat, soldier, investigator, and parent, and anything else that the job required.

She could do what Odgerel asked.

In fact, they both knew there was no one better, no one who would care as much.

Gomez already knew who her second in command could be. Wilma Goudkins had proven she cared in the exact same way that Gomez did. Goudkins hadn't just lost her naiveté during Anniversary Day; she had actually lost family. She would fight as passionately as Gomez would.

Gomez stood. It turned out that she hadn't needed hours after all.

Maybe Odgerel was as smart as everyone said she was.

Apparently, she had known exactly what Gomez needed.

Gomez smiled to herself. She was going to talk to Simiaar and the rest of her crew.

Deep down, she had no doubt they would join her.

But she would be fair, like Odgerel had been with her.

Gomez would give them a few hours to decide.

And she hoped they would all make the right choice.

78

After two very long days, Ó Brádaigh finally made it home. The little house he had bought with Laraba before the very first bombing over four years ago had never looked so welcoming.

He had spoken to his mother once every day, and to Fiona even more. She had begged him to come home, but he couldn't, not until he knew that Armstrong's dome was completely safe.

He had caught a few hours of sleep whenever he could, and he had eaten just as haphazardly. But he hadn't cared.

He had supervised every examination of the dome, and he had looked at each seam, each connection, personally. He had even peered at those explosives, so small and nearly clear. From a meter away, they had been invisible to the naked eye.

He knew how close the dome had come to complete disaster. He had been lucky.

Although Chief DeRicci hadn't called it luck when she had asked him what he had been doing in the substructure that day. She had said his vigilance had saved them all. She was talking about a promotion or a medal or something.

He had been so tired he couldn't track any more.

He staggered up the walk and let himself in the side door. His kitchen smelled of gingerbread, and his stomach growled.

He loved gingerbread. Trust his mother to remember that.

But after he pulled off his shoes in the tiny entry, he peered into the kitchen and frowned. Something was wrong.

Fiona stood on her stepstool, the one his mother always let her use when she helped with the cooking. Flour was everywhere, and it had the distinctive whiteness of Earth flour, not the yellow-tinge of Moon flour. Even Fiona's hair was coated in it.

The woman beside her was too small and trim to be his mother. And the woman's short hair curled slightly against the nape of her neck.

She looked like Berhane.

Only he had never invited Berhane to his house. He had worried about her getting too close to Fiona, an oversight he would rectify now. In fact, he was going to ask Berhane to marry him, and he was going to keep asking her until she said yes.

Only their engagement would be short—maybe a few days or a month, none of this years-long stuff that her ex-fiancé had subjected her to.

Ó Brádaigh blinked, wishing his imagination would settle down, and turn that woman back into his mother. He would contact Berhane once he had some sleep.

The woman turned and smiled at him.

"Welcome home," she said.

"Yeah, Daddy." Fiona climbed off her stool and ran toward him, hitting him with such force around his knees that he had to catch himself on the wall to keep from falling over. "Where've you been? Berhane's been cooking. We got tons of food, and we was going to wake up Gramma in a minute because it wouldn't keep."

Ó Brádaigh frowned. He was awake. He was wide awake, and that meant Berhane was in his kitchen.

"I hope you don't mind," Berhane said. "Your mother needed some-one to help her with Fiona, and I volunteered."

He wasn't sure when Berhane and his mother had had a chance to talk. He wasn't sure about anything, but he was glad for it.

"You can bake gingerbread?" he asked.

Berhane smiled. "I can do a lot of things."

There was something suggestive in that sentence.

Ó Brádaigh put his hand on his daughter's head, and then he bent over and picked her up. She had grown heavier in the past two days, or maybe he had just gotten so tired that holding her was an effort.

"We're going to give you food," Berhane said, "and then you're going to sleep."

"And then what?" he asked, his gaze on her. Flour touched the tip of her nose, and coated one arm.

"Then we're going to have a talk," Berhane said.

His breath stopped. "About what?"

"I can't say the word right now," Berhane said. "But it involves a future and a family."

He smiled. "Are you asking me for a commitment without using a word that starts with *m*?"

"Yes," she said.

"I was going to ask you for that same thing," he said.

"Do I get some?" Fiona asked, squirming in his arms until she could see Berhane.

"I think you will," Berhane said with a smile.

Ó Brádaigh smiled back. "I hope to God I'm not dreaming this."

"You want me to pinch you, Daddy?" Fiona asked.

Ó Brádaigh laughed. He was awake. And his future was staring him in the face.

His gaze was still locked with Berhane's. "No need to pinch me, baby," he said to Fiona. "That would hurt. Just give me a kiss."

So she did.

79

THE HOSPITAL ROOM LOOKED MORE LIKE A SUITE IN A HIGH-END SPA. Flint had never seen anything quite like it. At least, he knew his money was being put to good use.

He stood beside Zagrando's bed, arm around Talia. She leaned into him. Zagrando was propped up against a pile of pillows, his face pale. His eyes sparkled.

"So I get here in time for the crisis and sleep through it." He had spent the last few days in what the doctors called a healing sleep, so that the nanohealers could repair the extensive damage he had suffered in his fight with Ike Jarvis.

"You didn't sleep through all of it," Flint said. "You brought us some crucial information."

"Which, apparently, I gave to you in a completely garbled fashion. You could've used me." Zagrando looked disappointed in himself.

"You might've gotten in the way," Flint said, but he was lying. He probably could have used Zagrando. And Talia.

But she had guarded Zagrando and stayed calm during the crisis two days ago. She had closed the door to Zagrando's room during the chaos caused by the release of images, and she hadn't known anything about the potential destruction of the dome until the crisis was over.

Flint actually had the luxury of easing her into the news about Crater de Gerlache. Talia had mourned the loss of life, but she also understood how the loss of that city had led the rescue of the Moon.

"I'm glad you're here," Talia said to Zagrando. "You're someone I can talk to besides my dad about clones."

Zagrando gave her a penetrating look. "No one else knows?"

Flint felt her head shake, gently hitting his biceps as she did so.

Zagrando nodded a little, then his gaze met Flint's. In that gaze was an understanding for both of them. Being a clone had just become a lot harder than it had ever been before—and it hadn't been easy before.

"Probably best," Zagrando said.

"I know." Talia sounded miserable. "I don't know what to do about it."

"We'll talk," Zagrando said. "Because something happened to me after you left Valhalla Basin that helped me understand what you're going through even more."

"What?" Talia asked.

"Turns out someone made a clone out of me too." He leaned his head back against the pillows. He looked exhausted.

"I think that's enough for today," Flint said. "Let's let him rest."

"I've been sleeping since I got here," Zagrando said, his eyes closed.

"And you're going to sleep some more," Flint said. "Talia and I will be back tomorrow."

Flint tightened his arm around Talia and half pulled her away from the bed. They were almost out of the room when Zagrando said, "Hey, Flint."

Flint turned. "What?"

Zagrando's eyes were barely open. "I'm impressed as hell with what you did the last few days."

"Thank you," Flint said, a little surprised.

"I figured someone had to say it." Zagrando closed his eyes, and within seconds, his head slipped slightly. He was already asleep.

"He's right, Dad," Talia said. "You did it."

"No," Flint said. "It took hundreds of us, maybe thousands if you count everyone in all the domes."

"Based on information you put together," Talia said.

"That others provided," Flint said. "It took a community to save the Moon."

She wrapped her arm around him and squeezed. "I'm glad it did," she said. Then she added in a very small voice, "Are we going to be safe now?"

If the circumstances had been different, he would have given her an honest, adult answer, that no one was ever really safe, that life could change in an instant, and it would always surprise.

But she knew that. Her life had changed in an instant, and because of the man on that hospital bed, she had a new life with Flint on the Moon. She understood that.

And it hadn't been what she was asking. She was asking if this crisis was really over.

"We're safe, Talia," Flint said. "I promise."

"I thought so," she said, and then let him go. "I just wanted to hear you say it."

He smiled as he watched her step out the door ahead of him. He hadn't realized until that moment that he needed to say it out loud.

The crisis was over.

They were safe.

He pulled the door closed, and followed his daughter into their future, relieved that their lives were returning to normal—one step at a time.

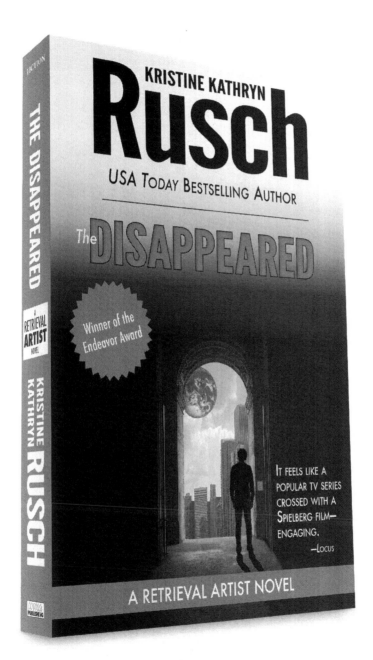

Can't get enough of the Retrieval Artist Universe?
Check out the Endeavor Award-winning novel that launched the
series, *The Disappeared*, available now from your favorite bookseller.

ABOUT THE AUTHOR

USA Today bestselling author Kristine Kathryn Rusch writes in almost every genre. Generally, she uses her real name (Rusch) for most of her writing. Under that name, she publishes bestselling science fiction and fantasy, award-winning mysteries, acclaimed mainstream fiction, controversial nonfiction, and the occasional romance. Her novels have made bestseller lists around the world and her short fiction has appeared in eighteen best of the year collections. She has won more than twenty-five awards for her fiction, including the Hugo, *Le Prix Imaginales,* the *Asimov's* Readers Choice award, and the *Ellery Queen Mystery Magazine* Readers Choice Award.

To keep up with everything she does, go to kriswrites.com. To track her many pen names and series, see their individual websites (krisnelscott.com, kristinegrayson.com, krisdelake.com, retrievalartist.com, divingintothewreck.com, fictionriver.com). She lives and occasionally sleeps in Oregon.

47840413R00242

Made in the USA
San Bernardino, CA
09 April 2017